THE DAREDEVILS

A NOVEL

GARY AMDAHL

SOFT SKULL PRESS
AN IMPRINT OF COUNTERPOINT

This book is a work of fiction. Names, characters, places, and incidents either are
products of the author's imagination or are used fictitiously. Any resemblance to
actual events or locales or persons, living or dead, is entirely coincidental.

Library of Congress Cataloging-in-Publication Data Is Available

Names: Amdahl, Gary, 1956-
Title: The daredevils : a novel / Gary Amdahl.
Description: Berkeley : Soft Skull Press, [2016]
Identifiers: LCCN 2015036912 | ISBN 9781593766290 (softcover)
Subjects: | BISAC: FICTION / Literary.
Classification: LCC PS3601.M38 D37 2016 | DDC 813/.6--dc23
LC record available at http://lccn.loc.gov/2015036912

Cover design by Kelly Winton
Interior design by Tabitha Lahr

ISBN 978-1-61902-618-6

Soft Skull Press
An Imprint of Counterpoint
2560 Ninth Street, Suite 318
Berkeley, CA 94710
www.softskull.com

Printed in the United States of America
Distributed by Publishers Group West

10 9 8 7 6 5 4 3 2 1

for Leslie Brody, who inspired this novel's first draft in 1984, and who refused to let me give up on it, even when I suggested I would burn it and myself up before I returned to it, even when there was an actual burning of one draft—even when I threw another draft out with the garbage, retrieving and saving that ream and actually hiding it from me, with the help of our late great friend, the poet, writer, and teacher Joan Joffe Hall, who sent it to me ten years later, and to whose memory I also dedicate this book.

"Hand this man over to Satan immediately,
so that we may save him later."
—The First Letter of Paul to the Corinthians

". . . and it turned out that not from cunning and not
from fear were they so hushed within themselves,
but from harkening."
—Rainer Maria Rilke, Sonnets to Orpheus, #1

"A life is manly, stoical, moral, or philosophical, we say, in proportion as it is less swayed by paltry personal considerations and more by objective ends that call for energy, even though that energy bring personal loss and pain. This is the good side of war, in so far as it calls for 'volunteers.' Even a sick man can willfully turn his attention away from his own future, whether in this world or the next. He can train himself to indifference to his present drawbacks and immerse himself in whatever objective interests still remain accessible. He can follow public news, and sympathize with other people's affairs. He can cultivate cheerful manners, and be silent about his miseries. And yet he lacks something which the Christian par excellence, the mystic and ascetic saint, for example, has in abundant measure, and which makes of him a human being of an altogether different denomination."
—William James, Varieties of Religious Experience

"Fear . . . invites the Devil to come to us."
—Robert Burton, The Anatomy of Melancholy

PART ONE:

THE TRUTH *A* AND THE FALSEHOOD *B*:

THE OLD STAGE SET
COMING APART AT THE SEAMS

Two boys squatted together on either side of an open limelight box. They were adjusting the mixture of gases entering it, with an intensity of care—both nodding silently as if at the idea of it—that was preternatural. The block of lime began to glow, and the light grew brighter and brighter until it seemed it could become no brighter, not in this world, and still it grew.

But then the older boy's sense of care appeared to slacken while the other boy's intensified—perhaps in compensation. Both boys felt this change with a shiver.

The older boy went down the main aisle and climbed up on the small stage, across which the curtain, depicting a tranquil northern lake, was drawn. He was wearing a false auburn beard that was much too big for his face, a monocle, a cream-colored suit that was his size and which in fact he owned, and a bowler hat that was also comically big, forcing him to tip it stylishly to one side to keep it from interfering with the all-important monocle. Because the side flaps of the limelight box had not been clapped in place, light was not focused on him but filled the entire theater. He saw the other boy, who was closest to the source, in a heavenly, deathly light that disturbed—even perhaps, in the strict medical sense of the term, shocked him: hellish and heavenly and dead and alive and perfect. It was one kind of light but another as well, a light that was even stronger, even stranger: he thought it must be a kind of hallucination or a kind of madness. He did not feel well. And yet he was able to make a bizarre distinction and say that neither did he feel unwell.

His friend, who was the son of the plumber who ran the gas for the theater, wore a greasy newsboy's cap that hung down over the sides of his face
like the floppy ears of a hound, and a pair of short pants that were comically
large: held up by braces, they were like a stiff gabardine barrel into which
he'd climbed to hide himself, the top crossing his bare suspendered chest,
the ragged hems brushing the floor and under which his toes peeked out.
He had a fat, wet toothpick in his tiny pursed mouth, so that from the stage,
in that incredible light—light the older boy perceived now as "sensitive," so
sensitive it picked up motes of dust and magnified them—he appeared to be
smoking a cigarette or small, fancy cigar.

The older boy watched the other as intently as the other watched the
flame. He positioned himself exactly center stage and let himself be hypnotized. The light was a host or vector of some kind of fever, a means of gen-
erating or regenerating through fever a superior or at least supernatural life.

Father had said: it was only acceptable temporarily, for a very brief time,
to be susceptible to that kind of day-dreamy indolence or outright weakness
of mind, if that was how you insisted on seeing it, if at the same time you
were reconciled to the unspoken but daily admonition that the only trans-
formative powers to which a man, Charles in this case, might aspire were
political, Christian, and expensive.

"I am wearing this disguise for no particular reason," he announced.

He was speaking loudly and clearly, but in a special way, as if performing. Was he performing? He mused in a satisfied way. He was sure he could
pass for twenty in the disguise, even though he was a little short yet—and,
most importantly for the immediate artistic concerns, his voice had not yet
broken. He tapped the jeweled end of a walking stick in the palm of his
hand, as if he was waiting impatiently for his friend to do something. And
there it was again: Performing? If so, for who, and why?

Toulouse-Lautrec, he wondered. Was that who he was thinking of? I
need a sketch pad. His voice was sure to break any minute. He did not know
if he wanted it to happen or not. If Mother intends to castrate me, she has got
to act now, he thought. I'm joking, he thought. Right? How good, really, is my

voice? Good enough for Mother to want to cut my balls off to save it? How many times had Mother said, "You can never find a castrato when you need one"? Many, many times. If Mother thought someone had failed to catch her witticisms, she would back her horse up and gallop over them again.

It was the finest treble San Franciscans had heard in a generation of boy choirs. How many times had Mother said so? How many times had people owing nothing to Mother, under her influence in no readily apparent way, said so?

Many, many times.

He could sing well.

He knew it was true, even if he refused comment. It was an accident of evolution. Not the right word, he knew, but that was how he saw it: it had come down through the ages, a million years of yodeling *homo* this and *homo* that and landed in his pristine voice box. He believed it—the essential, ideal Voice—had reached its zenith in Mother's contralto, but he was her baby. His brothers and sister could sing—as certainly could Father—but not like he could, not like Mother could.

An accident. Or gift from God, depending on whom he was talking to and what kind of mood he was in. And just as Plato said would happen to an ideal, it was degenerating—even as he spoke! He had to laugh at that one, and in the peal of that angelic laugh he thought he heard the first creak of a shiver of a crack beginning to form, his perfect little larynx beginning to bulge and thicken and coarsen.

Mother? Sharpen the knife.

He called out to Little Joe who was still muttering and tinkering with the limelight: he told him he thought it was funny. In a distracted stage whisper—incredibly enough, Little Joe seemed to be performing too—faintly annoyed perhaps, or even "faintly annoyed," the toothpick stretching the corner of his mouth, Joe asked Charles what it was he thought was funny, and did he mean *funny strange* or *funny ha-ha*.

Charles considered the remark. He felt an urge to get down off the stage, to tinker and advise and pester, as an adult might, not to "play" with his friend—the specter of that kind of performance rose and fell ominous-ly in Charles's soul before he had a chance to acknowledge it, as what, a loss?—but engage him as his brothers did their opponents in the debating club across the bay in Berkeley—*surely my young friend understands that his abridgment of my remarks constitutes a fraud*—but the remark stayed in his throat and unsettled him somewhat. He looked at Joe and could not help but wonder if he wasn't after all talking to a gnome or a dwarf or a wizard—or the ambulatory foetus of such fantastic creatures. Then he recalled the boy's father asking the same question, "Funny strange or funny ha-ha, Mr. Minot?" calling him "mister" instead of "young sir" as he usually did. And recalled too this colorful workingman's fondness for toothpicks, all fourteen members of his colorful working family seeming to chew them at once.

But it was as if he, Joe, were the one putting on the show. That was what was funny.

"What?" Joe whispered, preoccupied but not annoyed.

Charles could hardly hear him. "*I have often been struck,*" he howled in that chilling way that only a strong treble can, "*in my many days and nights in the theater, during rehearsals or between acts, at how much more interest-ing the stagehands moving the furniture and props about are than my fellow singers and actors.*"

He had made many sorties in this mode of the theatrical extempore, was constantly improvising, well, what would you call it, wit? Ready intel-ligence? Rhetorical exuberance?

But this: this was something different. He certainly had his rhetoric down and was more than facile in his manipulation of it, but had he not said something interesting as well? In a theatrical way? Falsely magnificent but with an aura of strange truth faintly glowing around it?

Joe made no reply; not, Charles thought, out of a lack of sophistication, but because he'd reached a critical point in his tuning of the gas.

The limelight now poured from the box so brilliantly it almost made its own sound. Joe himself was an incandescent ghost. The seats for many rows behind him stood out blood red, little rips in the fabric clearly visible, like gaping wounds, each snarl of thread or nubbin a blemish, or hairy mole. Most of the small theater was in fact illuminated, the carved demons and angels of the proscenium arch looking blinded as if by attempted entrance to the Eternal Paradise of the stage, just beyond the Earthly Paradise of the curtain.

Suddenly Joe flipped the lids of the box closed around the filament, focusing the light onstage and causing himself and most of the theater to vanish in the deep black spaceless space of the surprised optic nerve.

Charles let the walking stick swing to his side and raised his free hand to his face, shielding his eyes.

Certainly it is a kind of fever, he thought.

"Only it's in reverse," he said, continuing the earlier thought. "I am onstage, but watching you offstage."

Then Joe went too far and the limelight went out with a loud firecracker pop. "That's funny," he said as the darkness and silence overwhelmed them. His small, soft voice was musing and concerned. Charles could hear it perfectly now: it was genuine.

"Funny strange?" he asked, decreasing the volume but intoning grandly, "or funny ha-ha." His voice filled the theater in an imitation of the corrupt, jubilant oratory of his father and his father's friends. "I say to you, funny straaaaaaange? Or funny HA-HA? Ladies? Gentlemen? Which, I put it to you now, for the hour is upon us, will it be?" Charles brought the walking stick around to his front, folded his gloved hands around the fake jewel, and waited.

"You're strange," said the quiet voice barely making its way out of the darkness. "You can take it from me. Anybody says you're not, you tell 'em come see me. We'll set this person straight."

Charles nodded solemnly. It was true as true could be. It was 1906, and all bets were off. *La Belle Époque* was over. Everybody agreed the world had never been stranger. Europeans were expressing cheerful optimism in the so-called great alliances, but that didn't stop them from thinking there was something terribly strange in the air. A new world? Not the Americas, not the United States of America—something far more new? Was that possible? It was the American Century. Father's good friend President Roosevelt had said so. Charles was expressing neither idle nor psychotic conversational wonder. He wasn't good for much more than nodding and smiling and furrowing his shining young brow when the conversation was politics but that did not mean he was failing to take it in, somehow, on some level of concern, and Father made sure he got the basics, over breakfast, with the others, and had a first-rate opinion ready if called upon to amaze everybody with his firm but gentle Christian savoir faire. Father also urged Charles's older brothers to go to Japan, if they wanted to steal a march on the young men who were too focused on simply making a pile of money as fast as possible and spending it in Europe while there was still a Europe to be purchased.

"Go to Japan. You will not regret it."

"We're Californians, Father. We are Progressives."

"California is not what it once was, gentlemen. Neither is Progressivism. *Go to Japan.*"

A little light could be seen now way up high around the edges of the doors leading to the third-floor lobby, and though it was a weak and alien, an unpleasant light, he made his way off the stage and into the disorienting maze of voice-filled stairways. He did not emerge until he was on the third floor. As he opened the stairway door, he glanced at the row of little rectangular casement windows. They showed oddly vivid rectangles of a grassy square and the empty space that would soon be the foundation of the Silesian Brothers church. To the left of the little windows were big French windows, opening onto a small balcony. He meant to examine the strange images made by the little windows, but went to the big ones. It was a warm, still, sunlit afternoon. The park was divided by the setting sun into shadow so lustrous it was almost golden, the darkest amber maple syrup you could find, or molasses, and a solid, marble-hard and almost deathly white. Limelight white. There were paraders on the far side of the park, accompanied by a small brass band that he couldn't hear, going around the square, and they moved from golden darkness into blinding light and back into darkness. Charles tugged a key from his waistcoat pocket and opened the doors.

It took him a moment to sort out: the paraders were shouting something he could just barely hear in a military cadence in the absence of music from their band, while directly below him, just across the street, a small group on a bandstand was singing a folksong. The bandstand was draped with red, white, and blue bunting, and there were large flags hanging around their poles at the corners: the USA, the California, and two he couldn't make out, labor unions no doubt. The marching band began to play, but as they were on the far side of the square, Charles couldn't make out much beyond the unmistakable rhythm of the march.

This was one of the sensations that stayed with him: music, acting, performance was everywhere he looked. It wasn't an intellectual observation, it was a feeling. Nobody was not performing. That was to say, nobody was not holding their real selves back, in readiness for something else he and they could not imagine.

Nobody was not performing: it must be a consequence of the expulsion from the garden. A mass psychosis that nobody noticed anymore, or cared about.

There was a large crowd, he guessed, massing mostly out of sight toward the intersection of Stockton and Columbus.

The folksingers crooning on the bandstand with their backs to him, arms linked around waists, tightly swaying, were apparently a barbershop quartet, but a girl, or a small young woman, hopped up on the stage and stood in front of them. She was so small Charles couldn't see over the massed backs of the large men of the quartet, but he could hear her over their harmonizing quite clearly:

> *"They go wild, simply wild, over me*
> *I"m referring to the bedbug and the flea;*
> *they disturb my slumber deep, and I murmur in my sleep,*
> *they go wild, simply wild, over me.*

Oh the bull he went wild over me,
and he held his gun where everyone could see.
He was breathing rather hard when he saw my union card,
and he went wild, simply wild, over me."

Charles leaned over the balcony, counting: Hundreds of people? There were shouts, some booing. Popular tunes with seditious lyrics made many San Franciscans uneasy to the point of irritation—he had often heard the vogue for it derided—and diffuse applause muffled by something pointedly not the wind, as there was still not the hint of a breeze.

A sandy, treeless little park, on the edge of a sandy treeless peninsula where cold wind off the ocean was a constant—and it was hot! *Gosh*, it was hot! Charles plucked the handkerchief from its pocket and mopped his brow as if he were actually sweating, not to mention speaking aloud, and looked back through the doors for Joe, who was not there. He had never been so hot, he thought. April? Hot enough for ya? Astonishing!

Nerves, he thought. Flop sweat. Though I am not actually sweating, not actually performing.

He wanted to get back to the little windows, and started to when it came to him: they had seemed in that moment like paintings, not windows. Then something below had caught the sun and flashed, or he saw movement across the park . . . .

Two men brought a podium to the front of the little stage, and another man ascended the platform. He strode to the podium, took fierce hold of it, and began to speak in the loud but measured tones of the orator that Charles liked so well to study. First impression: somewhat less jubilant and corrupt than was the norm. The speaker apologized, because what he had to say was pretty dry stuff, and he wished he could rhyme and sing it, but alas, he could not. His job was to report on the progress of some twenty-odd trials of union organizers going on at that moment across the country, from sea to shining sea. He described the plaintiffs and the sort of municipalities in which they found themselves imprisoned in a few vivid words, the charges against them, and the nature and sufficiency of the evidence supporting those charges. He then ranked these trials on a scale of one to ten, according to the types and amounts and relative effectiveness of the perjury being committed in broad daylight by the various jubilant and corrupt prosecution teams. A score of one meant that there was no perjury involved in the trial, while a score of ten indicated plainly and simply a trial in which nothing but perjury was going on. Only one trial scored lower than a five, and a round dozen were rated at ten, and he shouted those "*TENS!*" with increasing volume, matching the rising noise of the crowd, but before he could gloss his findings, a wave of booing and catcalls overwhelmed him. He tried to speak over it, and there were apparently a large number of people trying to counter the catcallers with applause and whistling, shouting, "They will all be killed like the Haymarket Martyrs were if we don't do something right now," but he could not make himself heard. Someone directly below Charles in a pocket of resonant silence said, "Good, kill 'em then!" Then the speaker was hit squarely in the chest with a tomato. It looked, to Charles, as if he'd been shot with a twelve gauge. A great red stain appeared on his white shirt and he fell over backward, knocking over several chairs in two rows and toppling the men sitting on them. He came to rest against one of the poles holding the Stars and Stripes and knocked it half-over. Getting up and reaching for it, it fell completely. Miraculously, this resulted not in retaliatory violence escalating to general mayhem, or even in postures of indignation and barking, but in crowd-wide laughter, rippling, like the sound of vast flocks of settling birds, from all corners of the park. Even the men on the platform, the speaker included, could be seen with their mouths wide open, laughing heartily.

What kind of performance was this? Real or fake? Were they performing *in* reality but playing fast and loose with what they believed? *For* reality with some kind of fealty for the real, for the sake of reality with convictions that kept them on the straight and narrow? Were they performing in some way against reality? Did they want to change reality? Was it a fantasia on themes of reality? He was a musician first and foremost—but did this have anything to do with music? Did they mean what they were saying? If the crowd did try to string them up, would they plead that strength of characterization, along with native rhetorical talent and tricks of the trade, had overwhelmed them and consequently the mob? That it was what it all too often looked like: Just a show? Political vaudeville? Were they joking and were the jokes being taken seriously? Were they deadly serious but being taken as comedians?

Charles understood that perjury was commonly held to be antithetical to due process and the proper, effective functioning of the laws of the nation, that it was in fact a crime itself, and that to believe or even suggest otherwise—that it was in fact a way to function effectively—was to hold yourself open to scornful cries of *cynic* (from friends), *depraved cynic* or even *depraved adolescent knee-jerk cynic* (the adolescent being his older brother Andrew), and *anarchist* or worse from people wishing to defame you. "But perjury," Andrew said, "let me be frank, I don't care what names you call me, I am merely attempting to think clearly about what is real and what is not, about the way things really are, perjury is only perjury if someone makes it so. If no man of steadfast Christian honesty and sympathy makes it a crime, then it's as true as anything else the prosecution carts out. To merely say something is perjurious, to even think you can prove it in some legally binding way, is to whistle past the grave." So while Charles was inclined to like men like the speaker on the platform with the tomato stain on his shirt, as a man of principle and clear thought and articulate speech, his insistence—his genuine, not feigned (it seemed) insistence, because he was a warm and sincere person (it seemed)—insistence on truth and compassion were, just as Andrew's were, embarrassingly out of place in an empire. The insistence on *ideals* when things came and went so remorselessly, changed so mercilessly—it was a childish insistence, a childish violence, a temper tantrum, even if it became murderous. Charles liked, admired these men, he would never say otherwise, but knew, just as Father knew and had gently cooled and corrected Andrew, these men were clowns and headed for catastrophe.

He was not really confused at all about what kind of theater it was.

There was a way, Father had said, to live always in sight of Christian ideals and yet rule the world.

To live within Christian ideals and be buoyed up by them, said Andrew, as you rule the world.

Standing on the little half-circle balcony outside the French doors of the tall and narrow jewel-box theater where, in just a little more than a day—tonight, tomorrow, then tomorrow night—he would sing with Mother the *Stabat Mater* of Giovanni Battista Pergolesi before the most important men and women in the world-embracing world of San Francisco music, he thought: I am a clown and I am headed for catastrophe.

Because I want to be.

Because I am a daredevil!

If there was a chance for a man to be something other than a victim or a villain (he had heard this said in his own home, in the company not just of his illustrious family but a table brimming with important men and women, of somewhere, someplace where things were very bad, not the United States of America, someplace in old mad Europe, he could not have been more than seven), his only resort was to become an artist, or art itself if that was possible, or more like art than like life, away from the silly made-up conclusions that come, it was said, from close attention to, a thorough inspection of life, of reality, of truth. The trial is perjurious? *The sky is blue: make it rain. Be a rainmaker in a time of nothing but blue skies.* Charles came, young and innocent as he was, to these unpleasant opinions because Father was so adept in the law and politics, and because he insisted his skill was moral and that his morality was exclusive, and because he put a lot of pressure on his sons to attempt to become, one of them—*why not?*—the president of the United States, *experimenting on them*, sometimes overtly and explicitly, sometimes, he was sure, subconsciously, having Charles read a certain book that had been forbidden Alexander, Andrew, and of course Amelia, or meet a certain person—even going so far as to allow a life in the theater, a life, an apprenticeship to life of law and politics . . . singing and acting? It was hard to reconcile in a man who took the law and politics so seriously that he had not been deterred by being shot in the head. Charles, Father reasoned, needed to know how to improvise and project *character, and how to make that character work for you, make you entertain and persuade.* Or just exactly the opposite: forbidding him certain behaviors that got blinked at in his older brothers, so that he might know how to project no character whatsoever . . . *experimenting* on Charles, carefully, to be sure, with a sense that a great deal was at stake, but experimenting nevertheless. And that went for Mother too: rediscovery of lost Italian Baroque composers, commissioning a biography of Scarlatti *père*, authentic practices—and all of it coming down on Charles's head with her revolutionary idea to use a boy whose voice had not yet broken instead of the lyric coloratura everyone else was settling for as the piece made its bid to break into the world's repertory.

But here, here is what he honestly thought: people are not really all that interested in truth most of the time. They are interested in what makes them feel good, and this goes in high and mighty courts of law too. You *define* what makes you feel good as the truth, or as a truth, as something true, you *assert* it, you *defend* it, you try to *win people over* to your way of thinking, and finally you *impose* it. What the speaker on the platform was doing was bad theater—*common theater.*

And as if to confirm him in his magically superior thought, a man holding a placard identifying himself as a representative of the International Radical Club, stepped up to the podium. He was attended by another man holding the fallen flag, and they were gesturing comically to each other in the midst of the confusion, and generally people still seemed to be laughing. Everyone was laughing but Charles was uneasy: it was still just bad theater. This man he knew, a nutty professor in Berkeley who was possibly speaking in several different languages. And for it he was pelted with vegetables. Another man, holding a placard over his head that said LOCAL 151 OAKLAND, was big enough, and loud and angry enough, to make himself heard for a minute, but this clarity was met by the crowd with louder, articulate cries concerning the citizenship of the speaker. He said he was a citizen of the US of A, which meant, for starters, that he was free to stand up where he was and say what he'd come to say, admitting that his audience was free too, to heckle him. Then someone hidden from Charles's view, but unmistakably using a bullhorn, said, "Free to be a goddamn coward, I guess!" As he leaned out and scanned the square looking for the bullhorn somewhere, perhaps under one of the young, dark, flashing trees up toward Filbert Street, Charles saw, where before had been one or two cops, there were six or seven now, and where before had been a single mounted policeman, just in sight up Union, there were more than he could count. Yes, everyone was laughing but something bad was going to happen. The new speaker had his arms over his head and was apparently shouting, judging the by the way his body swayed and snapped, but Charles could make out very little over the roar.

Then the bullhorn: "ARE YOU A CITIZEN?"

Speaker: "OH, PLEASE, WILL YOU SHUT THE HELL UP WITH THE CITIZEN NONSENSE NOW? WE HAVE HAD QUITE ENOUGH OF THAT!"

Bullhorn: "DO YOU BELIEVE IN GOD?"

Speaker: "NO, I MOST CERTAINLY DO NOT!"

Bullhorn: "IF YOU DON'T BELIEVE IN GOD, HOW DO YOU EXPECT YOUR TESTIMONY IN A COURT OF LAW TO BE BELIEVED?"

Speaker: "I EXPECT NO SUCH THING YOU GODDAMNED IDIOT!" He tried to continue, and went on for some time as the crowd grew more and more restive, more and more loud, more and more, it seemed, unhappy, describing anarchism, with great difficulty, as admittedly a destructive force, but destructive only of ignorance with knowledge, fear with compassion, despair with ideas—but this made little sense to either Charles or the crowd: Leon Czolgosz, for instance, had not destroyed ignorance with knowledge or any of that, choosing instead to destroy the president of the United States with a gun. What kind of anarchist Czolgosz was was just another analysis of the fluctuation of the plot: *bad theater.* Then he said the magic words, the fighting words: that anarchists fought capitalist pigs by practicing birth control, and warmongers, when war came, as it surely would, by refusing to fight. It was on its face reasonable enough, but perceived to be otherwise because the crowd's list of anarchists who fought off despair, fear, and ignorance with murder was quite long: an anarchist—and this was true too—tried to poison three hundred people at a dinner honoring Archbishop Mundelein. An anarchist had stabbed King Umberto, ripped the eyes, ears, tongue, and fingers off the prime minister of Spain, and hung an empress of Austria by her female sexual part on a meat hook. So it was said. They cared not a jot for human life—not even their own! They would just as soon shoot you in the head as look at you, even if, *perhaps especially if*, you were a comrade. Read the right Russian and you would learn that they blew themselves up just to practice—or even for the fun of it. The speaker's truth was real but meaningless and he should have known better. Refusing to fight? *They were killing machines.* Henry Clay Frick was no Christian statesman—Father went so far as to say he was a nauseating halfwit, dressed up as the crucially clever and ruthlessly capable Captain of Coal—but Alexander Berkman had not argued with him, he had hacked at him with a knife. People were really mostly upset by the poisoned food at the dinner for the archbishop. The erratic Andrew had tried to make a joke about Catholics but Father had shut him down with unprecedented anger, or unprecedented feigned anger. That had just happened and three hundred innocent people looking only for a good meal and a holy celebration had gotten sick, had vomited themselves nearly to death. Charles had been reading a story about San Francisco's response to anarchism in one of the newspapers scattered on the table that morning. Both of his older brothers had been home, and the three young men had had a jolly breakfast:

"Authorities—" said Charles. He and Alexander were sitting together over the *Examiner* while Andrew stood bent over them. He had recently shaved off a thick dark-red moustache and looked now, Mother had said, like an egg. His naked upper lip seemed to reveal something unpleasant about his politically erratic personality.

"Who?" he asked, as if he had not heard well.

Father walked in.

"*Authorities*, Andrew," said Father. "And that is my point. *Authority*."

"It's a free country," said Andrew conversationally.

"Well, sir, may I suggest you don't know the meaning of the word."

"Certainly that is possible, sir."

"Authorities have identified ninety-eight persons in the Bay Area alone known to be dynamiters. They are going to come down hard on these ninety-eight persons. Whether, Andrew, they *do* anything or *not*."

"Whether, I suppose, they are actually even dynamiters or not," said Andrew, his conversational tone now pointed and irritating.

"That's *right*, you goddamned sarcastic know-it-all."

Alexander and Charles looked up from their newspaper, and Alexander coughed. Andrew laughed, and then Charles laughed too. Because he liked and admired his brother.

"Chick," said Alexander. "Look here. What Father really wants to say to you—at least what I want to tell you and what I think Father will tell you as well—"

Charles was trying for a deep man's voice: "'Top-secret and high-level actions on the part of government authorities—'"

"What?" giggled Andrew, helplessly. "Who? What?"

"'Authorities!'" hollered Charles. "Authorities! And private crime specialists are at work in the city disentangling the local strands of the gigantic web of anarchist plots to uh, to uh . . .'"

He was running out of steam over the grandiosity and the ridiculous words, and losing the sense of the article. Alexander peered closely, then yanked the paper from his brother's hands and assumed a high-pitched society lady's wail: "'Assassinate, to assassinate John Pierpont Morgan and other money and um, and um . . .'"

Andrew leaned over Charles's shoulder and pretended to sound out *munitions*.

"'Money and moo-nit-ions barons,'" Charles continued, "'of America. The heads of these plots are Germans. The German anarchist has the shrewd, ever-, um, ever-, uh . . .'" He moved his lips but said nothing, waiting for

Father to stop imploring the ceiling and come back over to them. "'Anticipating,'" he said. "'Shrewd and ever-anticipating.'"

"What does it mean, Al?" asked Charles.

"I don't know," said Alexander.

"Yes, you do," said Charles. "You're just being shrewd."

"I wonder," said Father, "if any of you have ever known what you're saying or if you're just freak-show chimpanzees dressed up like nigger minstrels."

He seemed appeased somehow. Amused again as was his wont.

Charles picked up the narration. "'Soooooo-preme delicacy,'" he orated in the mock-deep voice, "'is called for in the task of giving these anarchists all the rope they can use. They are not children, and dealing with them is not, therefore, child's play.'"

Andrew and Alexander adored their little brother. Their high regard for his gifts, his obvious intellectual and artistic capacities and talents, his precocious social charm, often caused them to overlook or ignore their sister, Amelia, who had nothing, it seemed, but nervous beauty. Mother was strange, sometimes amusing but more often obscurely pointed, and not a moment-to-moment force in any case, not in their neck of the public woods, as she was almost always, these days, dealing with scholar-gangsters in rough old Naples. It was Father who troubled them the most: he had been an austere and humorless man in their early experience—possibly as a result of having been shot in the head, it had to be admitted!—though gentle, who seemed only to notice them when he prayed with them, if that was not a paradox, if those were not mutually exclusive duties, as they had seemed so clearly to them to be, at night before they went to bed. They had developed impersonations of everyone in the family, and the primary device in Father's characterization was to never quite look you in the eyes, or only occasionally, with frightening intensity—a nervous habit nobody else in the world had been forced to consider and interpret in parley with that candid, clear, genial man. It also made the impersonation seem quite wide of the mark to everybody but themselves, certainly not as hilariously apt as the coquettish giggling and suddenly lunatic shrieking of their "Amelia" or their "Charles": several firm hand shakings and in a girlish voice, "Good of you to say so."

And they wished to speak to him, now, of Father, as they did with each other, because, they said, Charles appeared to have a sort of friendship with the man, a dangerous one, certainly, but of a strength they could only wonder at. They wanted Charles to advise them, to teach them how to talk to Father about baseball and football and hunting and fishing and the ranch up in Fall River Mills—all of which were central family enthusiasms either old or new, and which were regularly used as a means of not talking (or playing) law and politics but which seemed to have no life where Andrew and Alexander were concerned, at least not anymore. Alexander spoke of these subjects as what he believed to be the keys to an ominous but appealing new kind of relationship—ominous because something he couldn't understand or name depended on it; and Andrew in turn warned Charles that this forbidding but interesting man was nursing the pain of some terrible secret they could not even begin to guess at but which, if they were to look for precedent in their own lives, must revolve around . . . but Andrew faltered. He did not know what he meant. He could not say what it was that he did not know, other than that it was Father. As the beloved darling baby of the family, maybe Charles had some insight . . . ?

His brothers had been born to govern the nation. They were intelligent, sympathetic, ambitious, principled, firm in their exclusions, biting in their ideas for reform, but generous in their humanity. Father loved them more than he could say. But he did try, and Charles said so.

"He seems to care," Andrew tried again, "more for things that aren't political. For anything that isn't political. Now. Suddenly."

Charles said nothing because he had nothing to say, and Andrew shrugged.

Alexander motioned to one of the serving women and asked for a horse and buggy to be put in motion so that he and Andrew could get to the wharves, a boat, and Berkeley.

Charles left for the theater, not wanting to miss the speech-making in the square promised for that afternoon.

Another marching band assembled under Charles's balcony. As soon as he saw them, so did the band across the park. They were visibly bestirred and instantly began sounding their horns. From below came horns answering in clear if hysterical defiance, ripping scales, barking arpeggios, or simply blaring and shrieking. But if at first it might have been taken as something like the unlooked-for acoustic property of some strange concert hall—an orchestra tuning up and its echo seeming to come from the lobby—it became, for Charles, something else altogether. It was not two sets of cacophony, separated by shouts and murmurs. It was a complicated heterophony, a single melody being varied constantly and simultaneously by voice of instrument, rhythm, pitch—and only apparently randomly.

Yes: he could hear a design. Designs. An infinite number of designs within the one.

Then noise died down and all he could hear was a hum of voices, a steady monotone. Then a trumpet directly beneath his feet played five notes: B-flat for three beats, a low C-sharp for a beat, up to E for a beat then up an octave to E-flat for two, finishing with three beats again at B-flat.

He leaned out over the little balcony, swiveled left and right: no trumpet in sight. Leaned even farther, so that his legs were up in the air and he was in danger of falling.

Across the park: the answering notes in perfect imitation, but as if from the center of the galaxy . . . .

It was an incredibly odd collection of notes. It made him think of Little Joe in the heavenly and hellish light.

He went inside, closed the French windows as upon a dream, and headed for the stairway, noting again the picture-like windows—which had not lost that quality of vivid immobility as the angle of the light changed and the sun began to flare on the ocean, and which now joined the five notes and the brilliant white light—staring back at them as he took the first two steps down, misstepping and flailing out for the handrail, skidding two or three steps before he could catch himself in the deepening darkness of the well.

On the stage he found the members of Mother's "authentic" ensemble—a string quartet, a bass player, and a chamber organist—taking their instruments out of their cases. The organist was watching the stage manager and a few hands wrestle the ornate and unwieldy organ in place. Little Joe and Big Joe and a few of Joe's brothers watched the hands grunt and shuffle and count off to each other. One of them was staring at the organist in some kind of disbelief or incredulity. Charles watched everybody watching everybody else.

The first violinist, a rugged-looking man who would not have seemed out of place directing traffic in and out of a placer mine, though quite old, was at his side before he knew it. He asked if Charles was going to hear Caruso, who was singing Don José in the Metropolitan Opera Company's touring *Carmen* at the Mission Opera House that night.

"No excitement will be allowed," said Charles. "Mother says we rehearse and hit the hay."

"I wonder," said the old man, "if she means to apply the prohibition to us." Charles grinned at him in his superbly social way. "I'm not joking," said the man, rather crossly, looking around in annoyance. He focused on the organ. "It's beautiful, isn't it?"

Charles agreed. It had been modeled, it was said, on the water organ carved into the pedestal of Theodosius's Obelisk, built according to Mother's specifications—that was the official line at any rate—by Moody and Billings in Detroit, a maker better known for their barrel organs, on one of which the organist had been rehearsing.

Referring to this, the old violinist said, "Ernst is delirious."

No one on the bustling stage dared, it seemed, to enter the limelight, which was focused on two chalked X marks, where Charles and Mother were to stand when singing.

Mother walked into the light.

Was she beautiful, as people told him? Was she daunting, as people told him? Was she inexpressibly kind and sweet beneath the intricately worked armor of hyper-privileged can-do? When they sang the *Stabat Mater*, they were to seem a single voice, winding in and out of itself, moving away a note or two up or down the scale, or less, usually less, ceaselessly weaving sound, exchanging notes, while the quartet and continuo ticked away like a cosmic clock, or a pedal on a slowly spinning loom . . . his heavenly cherub-treble to "her darkly radiant, and yes, frankly imperial contralto"—the voice of not merely an ascendant United States of America but of a triumphant leader of the tired, old, confused or simply inferior nations of the world, a Statue of Liberty with a world-class voice, sixty years old, four children: Mother. In a way it was embarrassing to think of any part of one's self as being "sinuous" with one's mother's self, not to mention "hauntingly sensuous," but to hear it, to hear that single voice moving ineluctably toward two and back again to one, one note striving to become a different note, the second note striving to stay as it was—that was an altogether different matter. The voice had evolved and was part of a rising convergence that was very close to God.

Charles knew it and Mother knew it. And they both knew each other knew it.

"Ineluctable," from the Latin for the struggle to be free or clear of something.

He had looked it up. Everything about it made him uneasy—or frightened him outright. This was why you knew how to talk about baseball and football, and why you took the trouble to be a good shot when killing sickened you. It was perhaps why Father responded to you so warmly, when all the talk on the surface was of more rising convergences, of Christian evolution and fate.

The second violinist played the five notes and Charles shivered. Had the first violinist noticed the shiver? What if he had? The second violinist must have heard them as Charles had. But would it do to ask him? He had to admit it, shivering, that he was afraid to ask. Mother's intention in the early going was simply to do justice to Scarlatti *père*, to Alessandro (the father of the keyboard composer known and loved by generations of supple parlor virtuosi such as, for example, Father and Mother, Alexander, Andrew, and Amelia), a genius who had been made out by "the Victorians" to be some kind of villain who'd "nearly destroyed dramatic music." Mother had commissioned the biography, and one thing led to another . . . and here they were: scholars of music, specialists in the baroque, Mother's man in Napoli, leading figures in the "authentic practices" movement, seeking on behalf of and with the support of Mother—on her behalf because she was an incontestably great singer and with her support because she was incontestably wealthy—to recreate the way the music made by the Italians and their northern imitators sounded in 1650, in 1700, in 1750 . . . so it was easy, on one hand, to say that the five melancholy notes that had apparently lodged in so many minds were, for Charles, merely pegs to hang his own anxiety on . . . but on the other hand, where had they come from and how had they come by their power?

Mother, in the limelight, sang the five notes, and Charles's knees wobbled. He felt his rectal muscles loosen and he thought he might piss his pants as well. It was absurd, it was humiliating, and he did not understand it.

Mother was looking directly and intently at him as she spoke: ". . . a trumpeter in the band representing the Building Trades Council—" (described for her friends who were unfamiliar with San Francisco labor politics as a group of unions that passed knowledge and membership along only to the sons of union members with a guild-like sense of mastery and exclusion), "—played them in a lull, and a trumpeter in the band representing the San Francisco Labor Council—" (who sneered at such feudalism and were drawing dangerously near the controversial if not outright suicidal acceptance of negroes, the Chinese, the what-have-you, Indians from the Stone Age!), "—picked it up. It was so forlorn and lovely, but it seemed to be a battle cry, because the bands began to move in opposite directions, so as to meet somewhere on Union and do this tiresome thing which is all the rage now, march into each other's ranks and fight out it, note for note, "A Mighty Fortress Is Our God" versus "La

Marseillaise." Whose tune will prevail and why? What a question! But those five calling notes—so strange! So enchanting!"

The house lights had gone down without Charles noticing. Mother spoke to him as if in a play in a dream. Plays within plays within plays—there was no end to it. No beginning. And that was the question: the question that could not be answered. One recognizes oneself, and in that recognition, listen closely, Charles, my poor darling boy, in that recognition one is spontaneously able to recognize all the other selves in the universe. One sees them, literally, as one encounters them, and extrapolates the infinite rest. Those which seem "rare and strange" are no different than those which seem ordinary: they are all complete and particularly themselves. And there, dear Charles, is where we come to ruin and sorrow as human beings. We see the particular and cannot conceive the whole, or sense the whole and cannot remember the particular. We cannot hold them both in our minds at once. It is impossible. Think of the rhomboid your mathematics tutor drew for you: the crystallographer Herr Necker's cube. The soul tears itself to pieces knowing that it cannot know.

But she was not speaking. He was not hearing. He was not even thinking. She was gesturing impatiently for him to join her. Tonight was a run-through. The second movement was all his: if he was bad tonight, he would be good tomorrow. God help him if he was good tonight. But good or bad, it would be over. Then it was either to bed or to Caruso.

When the strange noises began . . . early in the morning, Charles snug, cozy, dreaming deep meaningful dreams, meaningfully complex psychological dreams, not the insipid nightmares of a little boy . . . and the house to shake, and things to fall, with the discrete recognizable sounds of falling *now* and smashing to pieces *later*—he thought he could hear the falling of the object through the air, or its creaking away from its place, and only after some time the shattering, breaking noise, but it is certainly possible that he was still in some way dreaming—and finally the house to seem to jump down on its foundation and collapse, Father had them (Mother, Amelia, Charles, the servants) out on the streets immediately, and it was easy, too easy, to see how you got things done. In the early going it was "frightening," of course it was, but it was the consequent sadness that Father urged Charles to repel, brutally if he had to. He quoted Montaigne at him, which was something he did under ordinary circumstances too: "I neither like nor respect it, although everyone has decided to honor it. They clothe wisdom, virtue, conscience with it! But the Italians have baptized malignancy with its name. It is always a harmful quality, always insane, always cowardly and base, and the Stoics forbade their sages to feel it." And while the thought would ring quite resoundingly in his memory a hundred years later or however long it had been (he didn't know and didn't care—though his secretary informed him it had been less than twenty): Sadness? The brutal, if necessary, repulsion of sadness? He wondered: Have I got that right? He wanted to laugh in Father's face. Where does sadness come into it? He was only twelve years old but had to say it was ludicrous: The great magical city, isolated by the blue blue ocean on its chilly yellow hills and impregnable in its glorious golden, silver, railroaded Wild Western American queenliness, had crashed to the ground in less than a minute and broken apart and burned to ash so easily that he could not think of it except as something of no or little consequence. It had disappeared. The entire vast intricacy, the little cosmos. What had it been that it could disappear like that? Whatever it was, it had been swept up and away in poisonous black whirlwinds. The dome of City Hall looked like the burned-out and still smoking cage of a monstrous bird against the red sky and the bellies of buildings seemed to have been ripped open, spilling iron intestines and organs composed of brick and wood. Faces of buildings had been stripped, revealing tiny stage piled upon tiny stage, floors and floors and rows and rows of secret rooms thrown open and lit as if to prove there were no other kind of drama than pitiless silence and nakedness. The dead men and women on the sidewalk, shrunken and blackened and charred. The first time they'd encountered such a corpse, his first thought was that it was some kind of objet d'art, and he'd turned away. Amelia said, "Oh my God, it's a man." They'd drawn nearer and suddenly ice was running up and down Charles's spine, his head was spinning and his knees gave way. "No," he said, getting up quickly but with help, "it's a woman." There was no sign of gender on the corpse, almost no sign of species, but something in the black hard lava of the head seemed . . . feminine. It made no sense at all that it should matter, even when it had mattered so much just a few hours earlier, but it harrowed him. And the horses, those poor magnificent horses, swollen and deformed, turned to grotesque marble statues, the hideous chess pieces of a gigantic blazing weeping demon who was sweeping the piles of junk along the streets with the skirts of his robe as he staggered and flew in little hops in search of something they could not guess at. At some point—it must have been the second or third day—he found himself standing with his older brothers, Andrew and Alexander, and Father in front of the theater. They were banishing sadness. The building had not been altogether destroyed in the earthquake—it was in fact in relatively good shape, but was going to be dynamited along with hundreds of other structures as breaks against the fires. They were using black powder, which created a hundred little fires for every break it might or might not reduce a structure to. Who had told them to use black powder? Who had authorized the use of black powder? Father had angrily asked these questions. But black powder was all they had. The texture of the sky was of dense roiling low clouds, but its color was luminous orange and they were not clouds. Shadows as stark as any cast on the sunniest of sunny days attached themselves strangely to people standing or lying on the street, but they were dark red instead of black. They lit the fuse and waited. No explosion was forthcoming, though many could be heard elsewhere in the city, single tolls of immense bells. Father and a man he knew, an engineer from the Spring Park Water Company, a private holding and distribution system in which Father held a significant number of shares and which seemed, secretly, to be, somehow, at issue, as there wasn't a whole lot of water to be had, waited incredulously a minute or two more, then walked up the steps to the front door of the building. The other man picked up the dead fuse and examined it just as Father's hand reached for the doorknob and the powder exploded. The engineer was killed; Father took many shards of glass and splinters of wood in his face and neck and chest, and one big piece nearly eviscerated him and broke his hip, making him fall backward down the steps, taking Charles with him, who passed out and broke an arm in the fall but who was otherwise unhurt.

When he returned to consciousness, he realized he had been elsewhere. And realized as well that he had not returned to the place he had retreated from. He was lying next to Father in the street and people were shouting in the distance and hovering above him. Father liked to say, quoting someone else, that a man could believe boldly in truth A—that Jesus, for example, had suffered and died for your sins, or that the things around you constituted a reality, a real world—and escape thereby a belief in falsehood B—that Satan owned your fallen soul, or that the things around did not constitute a real world, were not real—but simply disbelieving B did not mean you believed A. In fact, by simply disbelieving B, you could fall into other falsehoods, C or D, that were just as bad as B. Or you might escape B by not believing anything at all, not even the Truth.

"Nothing has been lost here," Father whispered to him, "that cannot be replaced. Easily and swiftly replaced. Not this building, not this city. Not me. Not you."

So, Charles thought: nothing had been lost because nothing had been there in the first place. Father continued to croak and bubble and spit: "Virgil confirms this for me: '*nothing unreal is allowed to survive.*'"

"Yes, Father," Charles whispered, trying to sop of some of Father's blood with his own shirt, not really knowing what he intended to do with the blood once he'd collected it: wring it out over Father's intestines and hope it seeped back to places where it would do some good? Wring it out somewhere else, in an effort to tidy up? Point was, he was trying! He was banishing sadness, as far as anyone else could tell. He was clean and cool and clear. And these qualities would surely not be lost on Father, for whom Charles wanted to appear fearless. He was utterly afraid and not at all confused about it, but for Father's sake, he wanted to appear as something he was not.

PART TWO:

"THE AMERICAN"

"The thing is consistently, consummately—and I would fain really make bold to say charmingly—romantic; and all without intention, presumption, hesitation, contrition. The effect is equally undesigned and unabashed, and I lose myself, at this late hour, I am bound to add, in a certain sad envy of the free play of so much unchallenged instinct."

—Henry James, Preface to *The American*

"In the theater as in the plague there is a kind of strange sun, a light of abnormal intensity by which it seems that the difficult and even the impossible become our normal element."

—Antonin Artaud, "The Theater and the Plague"

Auditions—the third round of auditions—for his production of Henry James's *The American* included a Polite Parlor Questionnaire. He did not know what else he might do and was afraid his theater would be stillborn. He had seen more than a hundred persons in three days and could not remember a single distinguishing feature: the faces were all round white balloons, all but featureless, atop stick figures, which were tap-dancing with canes and bowler hats, singing "Row, Row, Row Your Boat" in four parts all by themselves, and concluding, as if delivering a punch line, "Our revels are now ENDED! This actor, as I foretold you—" while waving little American flags. He believed he would have laughed had he possessed a sense of humor, something he believed he neither possessed nor wished to possess, believing himself to be essentially and perfectly humorless. He sat in a composed way and neither smiled nor frowned when he thanked them. He was acting for them. He was a Mystery. He was the Ghost of a Secret Theater and he would populate his theater with these shrieking stick figures, if that was the only way open to him.

The idea of an ensemble of local actors, highly trained in ancient and exotic techniques was, of course, ludicrous.

Some of them were friends, if he could in fact be said to have friends, and they could not fail to find his vision laughable. It was not even, technically speaking, his vision: it was the legendarily ludicrous but defiantly potent Sir Edwin Carmichael's vision, which he was purchasing, owning, operating, with sir Edwin's guidance.

He would move to Paris, tomorrow, if something galvanic failed to happen—if he failed to make these frogs hop.

But what could happen in a Polite Parlor Questionnaire?

"What is for you the greatest unhappiness?

In what place would you like to live?

What is your ideal of earthly happiness?

For what faults do you have the greatest indulgence?

What is your principal fault?

What would you like to be?

What is your favorite quality in a man?

What is your favorite quality in a woman?

What is your favorite occupation?

What is your present state of mind?"

I might be thinking of a way of life that includes everything. A way of theatrical life that shows real life up for the sham and horror it is.

After the earthquake and the fires, his voice had broken. Mother had not made good on her threat to castrate him, and he decided in the hideous croaking aftermath of the break that he would never sing again, except as his explorations of the theater might call for it. His mind had not broken, had it? What did the voice have to do with it? The voice was what he had charmed and disarmed the pretty ladies with.

Oh yes, he had seen them thinking, as if they were characters in a comic strip with thought balloons puffing from their temples, that after all this was San Francisco and they might very well get away with it.

But Voice was now Mind.

And Mind required Stage.

Breakfast had always been a good time for miniature debates, such as might ensue once polite parlor questions had been asked and answered. But once he'd dressed and made his way to the dining room, he found only the twins—brothers who had been born the year after the earthquake in a fishing village in the south of France, Cassis, in a house once used by Napoleon as headquarters—and Father working their way rather desultorily but with good humor through a hypothetical labor problem.

"The painters' union," Father declared, "wants to limit the size of brushes. Are you for it or against it?"

August (Gus) replied that it seemed clear that if they had bigger brushes they could get the job done more quickly.

"I can confirm, then, that you are against any legislation that would restrict the size of a paintbrush?"

Anthony (Tony) suggested that the painters would want above all to get the job the hell over with and go have a beer. If they had, say, two- or three-man brushes that were ten feet wide, they could be out of there in no time. They wouldn't have to spend twelve hours a day, six days a week, slopping paint up and down a wall. They could listen to music, read a book—or even go to the theater! He flashed a grin at Charles. "I would advocate," Tony went on, "discounted tickets for workingmen in those circumstances."

The twins were fair-skinned and freckled, with red-gold hair and handsome, ordinary features. Both of them knew how to beam, and would do so after an exchange like that. And while Father was still understood to be a rough and candid outdoorsman who had gambled on riverboats and been gunned down in a court in Arizona and who could beam with the best of California's grinning Western swindlers, and who was in fact one of a handful of men who had been nicknamed "The Regenerators," who had battled graft in the courts and rebuilt San Francisco with their own hands, he also still believed that Jesus Christ was his personal savior and insisted on rather passionately Puritan manners: Gus would sober up at that point but Tony continue to grin, even as he apologized.

"I'm sorry, Father."

Mother, Amelia, and Amelia's husband, the Reverend Doctor Thomas Ruggles, entered the dining room. Charles pulled his watch from its pocket and saw that it must have stopped sometime the night before. He was disoriented by the idea more than he thought he should be. It in fact troubled him, and he looked around the room, wondering if he was being seen being troubled, itself an act of discomposure and even guilt that troubled him even more. He felt sweat forming on his face. Why did he care what time it was? If he was sweating, why not act it out? See it through and *be sweaty*.

"Mother? Amelia?" asked Tony. "I hope you'll forgive my rude remarks." Trying to make the grin rueful. "Reverend Ruggles?"

"We don't know what you're talking about, Tony," said Reverend Ruggles, "but that is no bar to forgiveness." Ruggles was small but agile and strong, built like a gymnast, and he put a headlock on Tony. He often came at you as if he wanted to wrestle or box, or walking on his hands. It was one thing to speak of a muscular Christianity, but who dared speak of a fun Christianity? If the clownishness, however, had not been in the immediate company of a deep, almost disturbing seriousness, it would have been a different matter. He was a Baptist but the family could not help but like him.

Amelia, a year older than Charles, had been, before the earthquake, incredibly high-strung and unhappy, but brilliant: like Henry Adams's wife Marian and Henry James's sister Alice, Charles sometimes said. He had grown up thinking she was going to die any second, that he would find her collapsed with a stroke or hanging by the neck, but had found wells of compassion rising up in her, where everyone had expected hysteria even in the very best, in ideal circumstances, and humility descending like a blessing, a consolation from a gentle, just, clear, and sweet heaven. She was an all but entirely different woman, and people did not shrink from speaking of her transformation as miraculous. She would only say that she had been saved, and that she wanted to bring the power and glory of the gospels, as she was only just beginning to see them, in their rags, speaking quietly, to bear on the social crisis that was threatening to destroy the greatest nation on earth. She had read Walter Rauschenbusch's *Christianity and the Social Crisis* when it was published in 1907, coinciding perfectly with the throes of her own rebirth—and possibly San Francisco's as well—in Christ, and when Rauschenbusch's disciple at Rochester Theological Seminary, Thomas Ruggles, had come west, she had married him.

"If they finish a job in one hour rather than ten, they get paid a dime rather than a dollar," Amelia said.

"Don't get hysterical, sister," Tony suggested in his precociously vaude-villian way, having heard Andrew kid Amelia in this way more than once.

"If a dime," Amelia said mock-tersely, "bought a dollar's worth of groceries—"

At which point Mother, out of hard-earned habit that would likely never fade, gently spoke her daughter's name.

"—then certainly they could take advantage of your fabulous discount, my *dear* little brother, but it doesn't, it's more like a nickel, so either they take longer to do the job and get paid a living wage or they hop to and starve to death."

Father thanked Amelia with jovial conclusivity: yes, her brothers, both the younger and the older, were dolts but they would run the country.

Amelia smiled and said they ought to consider ten-man brushes that could be controlled by a lone halfwit and so expensive that no single painter could afford it, leaving the purchase as usual to Big Business.

In the old days, she would have then nodded at Father in a final attempt to be courteous—not to mention knowledgeable about the imperatives and requisites of actual large businesses—before dashing at the dining-room door, struggling as if drunk to open it, slamming painfully into the frame, and staggering into the hall. Mother would have offered the rest of the family a tastefully understated look of comic surprise, and they would have resumed their meal.

Now, however, the Reverend Ruggles, who had relaxed his grip on Tony's head but not released him, put a head-lock on Gus, and the three of them began to laugh and struggle.

It had happened so often that it was referred to as a Ruggle-struggle.

The boys flailed and grunted and Thomas shifted his weight about.

When the boys gave up and went limp in his embrace, he said, "Your sister has learned to talk rough with her brothers, but don't take lightly what she says. It will be very easy for you to say to her, and to all women, 'And what in the world does a woman know about it?' So I want to urge you to think very seriously about what women may know about things. All right?"

The boys cheerfully agreed that they would do so.

Charles said, "I'm asking whoever wishes to answer: 'What is for you the greatest unhappiness?'"

Father was smiling vacantly, eyes angled to the side of his plate of bacon and eggs. He looked as if he had not heard a word anybody had said for some time. Mother was staring at Father. She turned to Charles, puzzled at first, then annoyed.

"What kind of question," she asked, "is that?"

"In what place would you like to live? What is your ideal of earthly happiness? For what faults do you have the greatest indulgence? What is your principal fault?"

"In Anatarctica!" shouted Tony, "where I would never have to hear questions like those at breakfast."

Charles half-smiled at him.

"I'm kidding you, Chick!"

"The ranch," said Father. "It is my ideal of earthy happiness."

"Simply existing there?" probed Charles, with faint but apparent testiness. "Standing in a meadow? Rocking on the porch? Soaping the saddles? Those are all fantasies that depend on a state of mind, a condition of soul. Continued indefinitely without change. Which is impossible."

"You asked me what my ideal of earthly happiness was and I—"

"I too," said Amelia, "would like to live at the ranch, breeding Appaloosas, but my ideal of earthly happiness is working in a hospital twelve or eighteen hours a day. I think particularly a hospital for the insane."

"Yes," said Pastor Tom, "you see, that has been my point all along, that living an ideal of earthly happiness is not only possible, it is preeminently so, supremely and excellently possible. It is simple to do and it is easy to do. The spirit is reticent. The ego is aggressive. Surrender is the antidote."

"Surrender to what, the ego?" asked Charles, laughing lightly and mirthlessly.

"When you surrender, when you let your ego collapse, you achieve union with God. In that union, a life of humbly helping other people seems . . . ideal. Happiness follows, as our Oriental friends like to say, like the wheel of the cart follows the hoof of the ox. The line is from their *Dhammapada* and refers to suffering rather than happiness, but the implication is that if you want nothing and accept the world as it is, you will cease, at least, to suffer. One substitutes love for selfishness. It is revolutionary but can be accomplished in the wink of an eye. 'Whoever uncouples the religious and the social life has not understood Jesus. Whoever sets any bounds for the reconstructive power of the religious life over the social relations and institutions of men, to that extent denies the faith of the Master.'"

"Thank you, Pastor Tom. For what faults do you have the greatest indulgence? What is your principal fault?"

"I have the greatest possible indulgence for all faults. My own principal fault? I think the best illustration is to be found in the proud ease with which I answered your question."

Instead of politely acknowledging his brother-in-law's wisdom and humility, he turned to his little brothers.

"I sure shut you two up, didn't I."

They had long since ceased to smile and were now silently gauging Charles and Mother.

"Yes, Charles," said Mother, "you certainly did. Was that your goal? To cause your brothers to stop laughing and begin to worry about you? Or were you playing to Amelia, hoping she would say something careless about your own mental health that would confirm you delightfully in your new role of theater visionary. Your board wants you to produce a play by Henry James, a play by Shakespeare, and a play by August Strindberg. They would like to see you do it with a small ensemble and the plays in constantly rotating repertory. They would like you to bring to bear current ideas in design. They would like to see charming, interesting shows, and they would like to see the house at capacity every night, as they rightly are concerned about viability in the long term. I would never have even so much as spoken Sir Edwin's name much less invited him here had I known how vulnerable you were to spiritual imbalance."

"Mother's answer stands like a druidess invisibly behind her actual speech, as per usual. 'Spiritual imbalance'?"

"Sadness," said Father, "is the fault for which I have the least indulgence. The Stoics forebade it and I—well, you know this already. You'll have to pardon an old man who has used up all the brains he had and is limping along as best he can without any."

Charles gave nobody the chance to laugh. Father was playing at seeming as weak and old as he actually was. As far as Charles was concerned, he was demonstrating how he could not be replaced: not swiftly, not easily, not at all.

"Father, what is your principal fault?"

"That I think I have none!" Father laughed loudly and longly, allowing everybody but Charles and Mother to join in. "No, no, my greatest fault is that I am old. I gave my life to San Francisco and have nothing left."

"Excepting San Francisco herself, of course," said Pastor Tom.

Father smiled but shook his head. He still looked like a gunfighter losing at cards.

"I put one Jew behind bars," he said. "Other men rebuilt the city."

"One Jew, perhaps," said Mother. "But you must admit an important Jew."

"Boss Ruef was not important. He was a sitting duck. He was a bagman."

"Sitting duck," said Gus.

"Bagman," said Tony.

"For your father, boys," said Father, "and your father's friends."

"Oh, Father, please," Mother moaned deeply, gorgeously, "*shut up*."

"The Regenerators," said Tony.

"That's right," said Father. "And remember, when you ask a Jew how things are going, across the street or around the world, and no matter what may in fact be going on, he will say, 'For the Jews, not so good.' My point being that anybody could have done what I did, and that I don't really deserve the name 'Regenerator.' I speak in all humility and bearing foremost in mind what Pastor Tom said earlier."

"But Father!" shouted Gus.

"You took a bullet!" Tony continued his brother's complaint.

"In a court of law!" finished Gus.

"Twice," said Amelia. "Don't forget Arizona just because you hadn't yet been born, my lads!"

And Charles said: "What would you like to be? What is your favorite quality in a man? What is your favorite quality in a woman? What is your favorite occupation? What is your present state of mind?"

Nobody replied. Everybody looked at their plates. Someone sighed. The twins began to eat again. Soon everybody had taken at least a forkful and appeared to be musing rather than resentful.

"*Your* present state of mind," said Mother. "What about that? I would say it's horribly and gratuitously antagonistic. Why is that?"

"Not antagonistic. Humorless. These are important questions. You see there is nothing 'polite' about them. I intend to ask the actors who have survived the second round of auditions these very questions. Those brave enough to answer thoughtfully and honestly I will invite to be part of my ensemble. And for every show we do, there will be a second unspoken and invisible performance going on at the same time. The audience will see and applaud the unreal play, completely innocent of the knowledge that the real play cannot be seen without destruction of the unreal."

"STOP TALKING LIKE THAT!" sang Mother radiantly.

Pastor Tom nodded.

Amelia had tears in her eyes.

"The population, the audience, without question wants to hear its own story. They want to tell it and they want to hear it. They want us to know what it is without them telling us, assuming we have the same story they do, and will tell it. We are all San Franciscans, we are all Americans, and so on. There is great trust in these names. But they have in truth failed to remember accurately what has happened. They have lost the power of accurate memory. We all have. If in fact we ever had it. But particularly within the confines of this ruined city we are merely branded automatons."

"But the city is no longer ruined, Charles," said Amelia, walking her tone perfectly along the line between perplexity and helpfulness.

"Have it your way," said Charles. "I would think, though, that you of all people, you and Tom, would know that all the cities of the pleasure planet are ruined, that there are many who actually like wholesale destruction for its own sake, that is to say, someone honestly if hideously committed to, how shall I say . . . to change. 'Thou (the human being) are that which is not. I am that I am. If thou perceivest this truth in any soul, never shall the enemy deceive thee; thou shall escape all his snares.' Can anybody tell me who said that? No? Saint Catherine of Siena. My theater will be a rough and immediate theater, but it will above all be a holy theater. A holy theater in an empty space."

"Empty space: of that there can be no doubt!" said Mother. As for holiness, I think rather 'spitefulness' or 'mean-spiritedness' is the word you are looking for."

"No, 'holiness' is the word."

"Boring," said Mother. "Boring, mean-spirited theater in an empty space."

"Well," said Charles mock-amiably, "I sure hope not. But people will be bored no matter what you do."

"Wrong side of bed, Chick?" asked Father.

"No," said Charles. "I levitated."

"You know I don't care for sarcasm," said Father, smiling, "especially from my sons."

"You have been taking jabs at everybody here," said Mother. "You have hurt everybody here with your nonsense. Can you please tell us why you have embarked on such a course? I want to blame Sir Edwin because I am surprised and disappointed at what a stinking drunkard and fraud he is, but you cannot be so easily—"

"—and swiftly replaced?"

"—excused."

"I am rehearsing my life."

"I asked you once before," said Mother quietly. Then she really let go with everything her extraordinary voice had to give: "*STOP TALKING LIKE THAT!*"

Because she had sung it, Charles applauded, briefly, politely. And said, "Father, if I hurt your feelings with what I said about destruction and change, please forgive me. It wasn't meant to hurt you or even refer to you. Everything I know about the world I've learned from you and I am grateful for every last bit of it."

"Of course I forgive you," said Father.

"The sarcasm is a weakness I hope I can learn to do without."

"I'd rather you were sarcastic," said Mother, "than humorless."

Amelia wiped her eyes and smiled. Tom nodded. The twins veiled their interest somewhat successfully. Mother glared and trembled, so finely that it could not be seen by the others save the strange rigidity. Socially Darwinian Christians, thought Charles, laboring for the glory of a Socially Darwinian Jesus Christ and the Socially Darwinian Regeneration of Socially Darwinian San Francisco when—and this was the kicker—they didn't know the first thing about Darwin! Everything was an accident. Father paid lip service to the idea when he said everything that was lost could easily and swiftly replaced, but he didn't understand what he was saying. If he did, he would save his numerous foes the trouble and shoot himself in the head.

Though Germany had declared the North Atlantic a war zone, Father and Mother left the next week for New York, where they boarded a ship that took them to Iceland. For the fly-fishing, Father had said, in no mood to talk to Charles about anything serious, or anything at all, really, even though he said he had forgiven him. *For the salmon.* Indeed it was possible they were going for the salmon and the sea trout. There was a joke in there somewhere about brown trout and German submarines, but no one felt like making the effort. Charles had fished with flies a great deal when they had lived in Paris but summered in Scotland—not to mention golden days camping with Andrew and Alexander and even Father on the rivers of northern California—and if he could not help but continue to remember it as a pleasant pastime, indeed as golden, he could no longer find the time or rather the inclination to find the time to go fishing. Strangely, he could no longer even imagine himself standing in a river making a cast. He could see such a picture—could not help but do so, but it wasn't himself he was seeing: it was a kind of photograph of Charles Minot, someone he had once known but lost touch with. *An old friend*, if he could be said, as the quaint old saying had it, *to have had any friends*. A character he had played, more likely, the idea of which still made him nervous, alert, ready for performance. He knew he ought to examine that inability to truly imagine himself fishing, but chose not to—or rather, he could admit it, was afraid of it—as it appeared to have something to do with wishing to fish in the dark. The dazzling dark of the Sufis, the dark light of the Gnostics, he thought. Was that a good, true image, from Zoroaster's Good Mind? Or was it a bad image, from the Destructive Mind of a Person of the Lie? What he believed, secretly and more deeply than he thought possible, was that in the pitiful understanding of men, *universal darkness* was called *celestial light*.

Because they were afraid of the dark.

Because they were Bronze Age bullies and nitwits who worshipped the sun.

The Devil lives in darkness because he hates the light? Demons crouch in dark corners? He begged to differ: the Devil lived in merciless light, light that showed through bodies, that exposed everything to everybody, that extended into space, a line, a bit of geometry that winked out once it left a man's weak and suffering mind and entered the super-abundant emptiness of the heaven he could not imagine, could not perceive, but which he would come into, be born into, just as he had been born into life and light.

He had seen this light at work: it had destroyed Little Joe. He was crouching in the dark and he was not a demon and the light had destroyed him.

He could quote Tennyson, if anybody wanted to get tough with him:

> "Yet all experience is an arch wherethro'
> Gleams that untravelled world, whose margin fades
> Forever and ever when I move."

Heaven was dark.

Heaven was a dark theater.

A dark theater, the lights of which picked out Evil.

The mounted policemen began cantering toward the little platform stage that the antiwar people had erected. The crowd, entirely pro-war as far as Charles could tell, was either unwilling or unable to disperse. People, mostly young men and boys, ran here and there and shouted. Charles thought he heard screaming as well. Distant screaming, which was hard to be sure of. In all likelihood it was feigned screaming, coming from behind and below him in the brand-new theater that Mother and Father had built for him—it was nearly impossible for them not to, if you understood that it was simply a consequence of rebuilding the city—exactly where the old theater had stood. He stayed with his arms spread and his hands on the handles of the French windows as if he had just flung them open and was going address the nation, until the crowds, dispersing and gathering and dispersing, were gone. Everybody seemed to be laughing, no matter what they were doing: getting smacked with a baton across the back of the head, watching someone else get smacked with a baton across the back of the head, *smacking someone with a baton across the back of the head*. It made no sense. Mounted policemen had made their way through group after group, but it had seemed like a carnival. He had heard screaming, he was sure of it, but had seen no one lying in a pool of blood, within a circle of strangers. The sun was setting, and in the deep clear twilight some fireworks were being discharged somewhere near; they rose and shone as if they were not only on fire but gave off a kind of glossy, lacquered light—everything looked that way, buildings, people, earth, sky—but he could not tell if they were the fireworks of patriots or of radicals. It was a carnival, and its theme had been the war in Europe. No. It made no sense. People would not be celebrating carnage and horror. Perhaps it was not supposed to make sense . . . ? Why did he wish anything to make sense? He of all people! He went back down the stairs and into the theater and stood at the railing of the little balcony. The stage was now full of people. His people. "Friends." They were arranged in small groups and engaged in discussions. Some of these conversations were calculated, their subjects free of apparent context or even forthrightly nonsensical, their objectives contrived and variable, delivered with courtly animation from angelically bright faces—this was a vision of hell. The other conversations were conducted in dusty darkness, or at least away from the pools of light, by nearly immobile and featureless figures, and this was heaven.

Charles breathed evenly and slowly though he could feel his heart pounding in his fingertips and teeth, and he smiled faintly as these visions appeared and disappeared before and below him. The feverish light did indeed seem to determine the quality of life, as he had always suspected. He had read, in an account of the Indian wars, that one great and defeated chief had weighed his options and declared that heaven was no place for a man and he wanted nothing to do with it—and yet his place, Charles thought, was so clearly here on the border of heaven and hell that he could not help but feel some relief at the sight of it.

An actress he hoped might prove suitable for the big roles sat wrapped in mummy-like winding sheets approximately in the center of the little theater, under its chandelier, which hung from the underside of a shallow dome painted with peacocks, owls, a buck deer and doe, vines with berries and flowers, and a wizard with a flask out of which streamed a banner with the words *eamus quesitum quattuor elementorum naturas.*

Her name was Vera.

Vera K., born of Russian parents in Muscatine, Iowa, where she had worked in a button factory.

Muscatine was the Button Capital of the World.

He picked up a sheaf of papers from the seat next to him, riffled through them until he found the page he was looking for, then read it aloud but not loudly, looking down at her. She probably couldn't hear him, but would she turn round, look up?

"What is for you the greatest unhappiness?"

"I sometimes, too often, think I am no longer competent to live in the world."

"In what place would you like to live?"

"The world."

"What is your ideal of earthly happiness?"

"Forgoing happiness."

"For what faults do you have the greatest indulgence?"

"I'm not sure what you mean by 'fault.'"

"What is your principal fault?"

"Ah: my recurring inability to believe I can live in the world."

"What would you like to be?"

"Oh! What all the young women have said to you goes double for me: the star of your shows!"

"What is your favorite quality in a man?"

"A fine critical apparatus focused on whether or not I am kidding."

"What is your favorite quality in a woman?"

"A fine critical appartus focused on whether or not I am kidding."

"What is your favorite occupation?"

"Acting truly."

"What is your present state of mind?"

"A nearly overwhelming feeling of joy that I can live in the world after all."

Vera, alone in all of histrionic San Francisco, had been worthy of the Polite Parlor Questionnaire. In her presence, as she answered the questions slowly and eloquently, he had not been able to feel like anything but a prince in a fairy tale.

He stared down at her intensely, imagining taking her sheet off and finding her naked beneath it, moving his hands over her neck and shoulders and breasts, kissing her deeply but languidly—and falling again under the spell of imagination, believing for a moment that he could cause the seduction to happen simply by staring down at the woman with his remorseless will.

It had happened before, and more than once.

Of course he would hold and kiss her in coming rehearsal many times, but the emptiness of those experiences would confound her completely—he would see it in her big glistening brown eyes—and throw so profoundly the question of the nature of pleasure into terrible doubt, that he would be forced to refuse to acknowledge those embraces as in any way representative of what he hoped to accomplish. He supposed that he was compensatorily cold to her. And the nature of what he "hoped to accomplish" was decaying swiftly too, anyway, after some ridiculous failures in New York that winter— from what had seemed at first simply a case of ceasing to neglect the pursuit and seduction of women, as he certainly had, in favor of the cultivation of artistic vision, to a struggle with physical impotence, the staving off of something pathological.

He was quite sure she could not act, and had cast her—the others as well—precisely because he was sure she could not act. The skills usually acknowledged as essential to or at least encouraging of dramatic presence, when they had been displayed for him, to him, for his approval and plea-sure, only made him uneasy. It was like he had said to Little Joe ten years earlier: he would rather watch the stagehands. If such displays went on too long, they began to fray his nerves. That she made him feel like a prince had nothing to do with anything.

Because one of the plays they were rehearsing was *Romeo and Juliet* (the other two were August Strindberg's *The Spook Sonata* and Henry James's *The American*), swordplay had broken out on the stage and in the auditorium. Swordplay often broke out if Charles was even momentarily absent, because actors were like children and directors were like forbidding fathers. Most of the group of fifteen were the legendary friends or friends of friends from Berkeley, if he could be said to have friends, but there was no mistaking it: a father and his children.

With the probable exception of Vera in her grave shroud.

Two duels were taking place, one in exaggeratedly slow motion that seemed Oriental in its precision, the other fast and awkward and accompanied by a great deal of laughter, yelps of pain, and shouted apologies. Five other young men were trying to sort out the fundamental moves of a brawl, made uneasy by Charles's suggestion via Sir Edwin Carmichael that choreography was the antithesis of violence, that a fight was ugly and embarrassing, and that all attempts to make it a pleasing dance must be in vain. The different son of a different plumber and one of his older brothers were clacking lengths of doweling with each other. Charles, to no one's surprise, had been schooled in fencing since he was old enough to wave a small toy sword, and was in fact the ensemble's Romeo, but was concerned that hour with *The American* and so was armed only with monocle and walking stick. As he watched and breathed and was content—for a moment—to feel the blood pulsing in his extremities, over the din of mock-fighting and outside the theater, he thought he heard more firecrackers going off.

There was a release of light somewhere over his shoulder and a withdrawal of it and a faint clap, followed by the shushing of heavy fabric over the carpeting of the balcony's center aisle; he could just barely hear it over the voices below. Then came the cloud of smell: stale tobacco and fresh burning leaf, alcohol on the breath and in the cloth, some kind of ammoniac solution, and an alarmingly bracing body odor. This was the theater's artist in residence, Sir Edwin Carmichael. He was visiting from Verona, where he had his own theater and school of design, named after its principal funder, Lord Howard de Walden. He had acted with Henry Irving and designed sets for Konstantin Stanislavski. He had designed and directed a production of *Dido and Aeneas* that had almost single-handedly revived interest in the English Baroque composer Henry Purcell—which was where Mother had come in. The man wrapped his cloak more tightly around his frail and trembling body, trapping the stench of himself but allowing the fabric to send eddies and gusts from its folds. He was an artist's artist and his black, bloodshot eyes were in no way diminished by the shadow of his great slouch hat. He was shivering in the wretched cold of the peninsula's

summer, but all he could think to say to his young hero was that his dinner disagreed with him; he was digesting it poorly—belly inflated like a
medicine ball and shooting fireworks at the back of his throat—and could
not think straight. His breath was unbearably laden with garlic and deeper
evidence of the indigestion, and Charles leaned away. That Sir Edwin could
not think straight, and yet was up to admitting it, this was a confusing sign
in his experience: too much steam building up in a kind of self-conscious
engine already starting to shake and rattle its bolts. Sir Edwin claimed to be
a futurist, but Charles was hard pressed to understand what such an identity
entailed. More specifically, but even less clearly, he was a vorticist—that was
to say, not Italian, but something "like a futurist" from "the vortex of London." He preferred "found sound" to composed and performed music—but
was an acknowledged influence of the Second Viennese School—and was
very much in favor of the war: war was "the one great art," and the only way
civilization had to remove the more "festering and stinking of humankind's
many gangrenous limbs."

Charles and Sir Edwin watched the rehearsal, its director absent but
lurking, disintegrate: acrobatic silliness, exaggerated, mask-like mimicry
of primary emotional states in ridiculous contexts, and the kind of minc-
ing mock-violence that had actors chasing each other around tables with
very small steps, furiously waving their arms and puffing their cheeks out,
not knowing what to do once, for instance, one character succeeded in getting his hands around the neck of another character, whom he ostensibly
wished to throttle to death. The plumber's sons broke off their swordplay,
and Sir Edwin suggested to Charles that even the children found it all unbearably childish.

"I would rather you tried, all of you, really tried to hurt each other. This
waggling of fingers and chasing someone whom you clearly do not want to
catch—it's appalling! Don't you think so, Charles? I mean, really. It's insult-
ing unless your audience are children eating birthday cake. You know how
to use a sword." It was true that he was able to fence dramatically well; and
while fencers perforce show each other the slenderest profile, Charles often

found it possible to drop the point of his foil to the floor and advance, spine straight and shoulders square, one, two, even three long arrogant strides directly into his opponent's range. "Go down there," commanded Sir Edwin, "and shove it up someone's arse, why don't you."

"My position, Sir Edwin, is that somersaults and comic faces are delightful."

"They make me want to vomit."

"The thought of attempting to wound someone—"

"Yes, but that's just it! The thought of the attempt—precisely!"

"—to wound a brother or a sister is abominable, maestro."

"Stop and think a moment while your fluttering little heart becomes a piece of pumping meat again."

"I find it directly opposed to the nature of the theatrical enterprise."

"That is not only sentimental horseshit but the foundation of everything that is infantile in the arts."

"Maestro, this may in fact not be a heaven fit for heroes, but I find I do not much care. I wish only to examine the nature of the real via actions of obscure delight." Charles had done a great deal of debating in the course of his superb education—and was uncomfortably aware that he did not actually know how he felt. He was uncomfortable as well with his facility in the face of such an absence or ignorance.

"You're simply naïve," said Sir Edwin, apparently able to read minds.

"Maybe I am," Charles admitted.

"You are wrong."

"Maybe I am."

"You could not be more wrong. That actors should feel delight at behavior so remote from actuality, from consequentiality, from truth, is almost unforgivably wrong. The urge to wound, to really and truly wound, is the only force that can actually animate lifeless words and weary gestures—the only force, at least, that an audience will sit still for."

"They seem to be willing to sit through just about anything." Charles surprised himself with this remark: Was it a truer self at last beginning to emerge?

"Do not confuse desire with pleasure." Edwin spoke with muted passion.

"I must beg your pardon, maestro. Your meaning is obscure."

Both of them were acting, not altogether happily, but evidently unwilling or unable to leave off, to break into sincerity and earnestness.

"Do not confuse *desire*, I tell you, with *pleasure*." It was possible Sir Edwin was frustrated, annoyed. His vehemence was pitched uncertainly. He was either in the grip of something, or pretending to be. As he was a drunkard, it would never be certain.

"Having still no actionable clue as to what you are talking about, I will nevertheless promise you that if it is ever within the scope of my immature intellect to distinguish the two, I will do so. I will attempt to do so, at any rate—for no other reason than that you have said so with such clear strength of feeling."

"*Goddamn you*." Suddenly Sir Edwin was no longer acting. It was a gift.

"Goddamn me."

"Goddamn you."

"All right then," Charles said, still game, but inwardly beginning to shy. "Goddamn me."

Sir Edwin turned away in disgust and Charles saw that though he had not exactly missed the man's inscrutable and alcoholic signs and crucial but murky inflections, he had, once again, ignored them, and was now, consequently, imperiled. Sir Edwin was panting with stifled rage.

"I tell you to go down there and act like a man, to grab those infants by the scruffs of their necks and shake them until it's clear they are no longer in their playpens—and you simper like the rich parlor fucking smart ass that you incontrovertibly are and will always be. I tell you it's nauseating and you become a pale imitation of Oscar Wilde. I CAN'T STAND IT ANYMORE!" The last was a shriek and he was now very nearly in tears. "Over and over and over again—do you not, do you *really not*, are you *incapable*, completely FUCKING INCAPABLE of understanding what we are struggling against? Conformation to the etiquette of the stage, to its infantile rules and bourgeois complacencies—it's like fucking a corpse. It's loathsome. Or it would be if it were real. It is merely ridiculous, merely embarrassing."

Sir Edwin sat down and pulled his cloak around him so that not even his eyes could be seen. He hunched forward and appeared to be weeping, but made no sound. After a short while, he seemed to relax. He sat back and the cloak fell away from his face. He breathed deeply and evenly.

"And so," Charles said, "just to make sure I understand you, I am to not confuse desire with pleasure. Was that it?"

Sir Edwin refused to look at him.

"Was that fucking *it*?" Charles demanded.

Sir Edwin was weary now, and wise. "I meant only to suggest that there are layers and layers of desire for pleasure. We actors revel quite rightly in these superficial desires, in the gratification of these superficial desires—that is what we are paid to do. Still, the corpse is a corpse and her cunt is full of maggots. I'm not trying to be outrageous—you know this as well as I do. We all know. What you may not know is that beneath all those layers of pleasures is a primary desire. We may think of it as an original desire. We may think of it as a primal desire. You must show us, if you can, what it is to want food, to want sex, to want to brain another man so you can have his food and his women—but you are exhibiting the superfice. You may bring something to life if you are successful. And that is the great desire you must not confuse with pleasure: simply to be alive."

He began weeping again, loudly, with a kind of abandoned happiness, and Charles descended to the stage.

The stage was high enough so that when Charles came to the leading edge of it he was looking at his actors' shoes as they shuffled and swept left and right, forward and back. He tipped his head back and called out for everyone to mark out a playing space and begin to go through the motions and whisper the lines of whatever scene marked their entrance into *The American*. After they'd done so for a few minutes, over the gentle, strange murmuring punctuated by the creak and clap of the boards, he told them to speak up and to slow down.

From the balcony Sir Edwin shouted. "NOTICE HOW THE NATURE—"

And Charles took it up, almost as if he were echoing Sir Edwin: "Notice how the nature of what you are doing changes along with the speed, your apprehension and judgment of what you are doing."

A few more minutes passed and he climbed up on the stage, moving around an imaginary painting on an easel, speaking Christopher Newman's first lines of the play—"That's just what I wanted to see!"—while the young woman who was the imaginary painting's painter, Noémie, fell in with him.

"Now half again as slow and notice—"

"NOTICE HOW YOUR THOUGHTS STILL LAG BEHIND YOUR ACTIONS, EVEN WHEN YOU HAVE COME NEARLY TO A STAND-STILL!"

"Move as slowly as you can move and still maintain a sense of one single continuous movement and notice how your thoughts still lag behind your actions, which indeed are reactions themselves to something we cannot see, name, understand."

"ASK YOURSELF WHY YOU DO NOT FEEL WHOLE WHEN YOU ARE A CHARACTER!" shouted Sir Edwin, who then began again to sob, loudly—and, it had to be said, histrionically.

"Pick a new scene," said Charles. "Move normally, speak softly."

Vera—Claire de Cintré—joined him for their first scene together. Charles spoke his lines with her for a while—"It's as if there had been a conspiracy to baffle me tonight: we have been kept asunder from the moment I arrived"—then said, "Indeed, as Sir Edwin suggests, you know who you are at the expense of being happy. Ask yourself why that is. Know that you will never be happy until there is no division between you and the other characters. Know that you are sinning when you are isolated and alone on the stage. Know that sin means only that you have missed the point and that repentance means only to change your perspective. You in your isolation have created the other characters and now you are afraid of them, of what they will do, of how you will act in consequence. You created them but you are afraid of being dragged into their lives. Do not be afraid, my actors. You are living in a constant state of anxiety and anticipation. Change your sinning way: everything is waiting for you, here on the stage, in the character of the other."

Again he gave them just a few minutes, two or three, then asked them to slowly and gently cease to speak and move. He asked them to savor the silence and stillness and yet remember where they were and what they were doing. When they were ready, calm and alert, they were to return to the scenes they had just been acting but include the other characters in the scene, two or three others, reform, as it were, and choose a property that was important to the scene, a chair or an easel.

"You will never be convincing on a stage, my friends, if you cannot treat your props properly. You must see and use them—and allow them to use you—in exactly the same way you see and use and are used by the other human beings onstage with you. A chair is every bit as miraculous as a human being is. Look at the chair, feel it. It is floating there in space just as you are. Just as the planet does. Its constituent parts are your constituent parts. You may wish to think of yourself as related to your property interdependently. This in truth is how we live. Distinctions between consciousness and self-consciousness, between organic and inorganic are only superficially true and useful. Consider the story the chair will tell: as we are flesh, it is wood, fashioned by a maker in a shop, who got the wood from a timber merchant, who got the wood, with subtle but overwhelming violence, from a tree in the forest. Of course you tell yourself you know where the tree came from: it grew from a seed. Break open the seed: Is it empty or merely invisible? Without water, and soil, and sunlight, what will come of it? What is water? The wave recognizes itself only when it is washed upon a shore. Instantly it vanishes, is withdrawn from the shore into the singularity of the ocean. What is soil? Light? Where does light come from and where does it go to? Does it come from darkness and go to darkness? Does it need darkness in order to claim its singularity? Does darkness need light to claim its singularity? Does darkness come from light and go to light? 'Brief as the lightning in the collied night that, in a spleen unfolds both heaven and earth, and ere a man hath power to say, behold, the jaws of darkness do devour it up. So quick bright things come to confusion.' All this coming and going implies time and space, a clock and a grid. Who built this clock? Who drew and laid down the grid? Who declared five senses and no more? What is a senseless man? What is a dreaming man? What is man dreamlessly sleeping? What is prior to logic, to reason? Is character, your own and your character's character, a matter of outward performance and social polish, as La Rochefoucauld would have it, or of inward essence? Where is the Christ who promised to show us what could not be seen? Why was this gnosis banned from our Bible? Where is the Christ of the Upanishads? Why must we hear only Jeremiah when our cities are destroyed? 'Behold, that which I have built up, will I break down. That which I have planted will I pluck up.' The worker is hidden in his shop. The work has drawn a veil over the worker. Only on the stage of simultaneous being and not being can we see the work and the worker together."

Charles ceases to speak. Slowly the ensemble follows him into silence—and it is only then that they realize the cellist of the continuo group Charles has engaged has slipped in sometime during the weaving and fallen immediately under the spell, providing a single unceasing ground note, moving imperceptibly up to the sharp, then back down to natural, further still to the flat, then up again. No one moves, everyone listens. There are more persons in the theater than he had thought. Children, mostly. Children of the crew, he supposes.

Vera tries to catch Charles's eye, but he refuses—or is intent on something else. She wants to see how seriously he has taken himself—taken himself as opposed to what he has spoken of with such bafflingly strange eloquence. She wants him to remember that it is a game. Rather: she wants that belief confirmed in herself. He has either over-rehearsed or, how shall she put it . . . lost his balance. He is, she thinks, using one of his pet phrases, "out of joint," and she wants to know which of these metaphors he prefers. She sees how liable he is to become an icy clown or an ironic lout if he is not understood and applauded. That a spell was woven she cannot deny, but now wants out.

A little boy, no more than five, who has been standing very near them, only half-there, like a sprite, or a cupid, he is so chubby and pretty, like a cupid carved in the corner of a great ceiling now mysteriously between herself and Charles, says—no, sings, chants—very clearly and sweetly in the silence, "When I put a chair in my head, it's so I can sit in my head. I take my body apart and put the pieces in my head. And then I sit in my head."

He is the plumber's son. Again and again and again, he is the plumber's son.

Cheerful laughter chitters and laps around them.

Charles claps his hands. She sees he is not laughing, but, to her great relief, would like to.

"And what's yer name, young feller?" Charles asks him.

Suddenly shy, he looks down, then, spinning, runs stage left and disappears in the shadows of the wing, shouting for his father, who is standing and chuckling in the middle aisle of the steeply raked orchestra seats, under the chandelier, where Vera had been sitting in her winding sheet. Laughing loudly, father calls out to son.

Allowing himself to smile, Charles addresses his actors. "I know you don't all have all of your lines yet, but find a script and, quick as you can, let's run through the whole play, shouting your lines as fast as you can say them and running around the theater until you run out of breath! That includes the balcony, the wings, the stairways! Run until your heart is pounding! Noémie! Lord Deepmere! Start us off, please!"

Thus was the story told of the wealthy Californian who goes to Europe in search of art, of beauty, who falls in love with the widow of an impoverished aristocrat, and who encounters simultaneously a deep disdain for his lack of family and a deep lust for his surplus of money—in about a quarter of an hour of helter-skelter hilarity . . . while outside, a tiny, celebratory, nominally pro-war rocket rose up on a thin line of fizzing and sparking red flame, broke the window next to the one Charles had left open (there was, in the immediate aftermath and first stages of investigation, some suspicion, for a moment or two, that someone had secretly entered the theater and opened a window on purpose). It exploded loudly but without much force, and began to burn itself out smokily in the carpeting. Which in turn caught fire, spreading quickly over the floor and consuming the false dome, under which hung the chandelier that was the main source of general lighting in the theater. When they smelled smoke and looked up and saw the paint begin to bubble, the ensemble, already darting and jogging, moved in confused anticipation toward the center of the theater, their lines trailing off and the speed of their movements slowing. When it became clear that the ceiling was burning, they scrambled left and right past the velvet seats, then up or down the aisles toward the stage or the exits, from which vantage points they watched the chandelier go dark. Shouting *run run run*, they all ran. Some of the last, Charles included, heard the heavy, slow crash in the darkness.

He held a novelty handkerchief—red, white, and blue, stars and stripes, mandated by his board for publicity purposes—to his nose and mouth, and bent low as he could, bringing his knees nearly to his still falsely bearded chin, and walked up the front stairway to the second-floor lobby. The haze either stung and filmed his eyes and distorted his perception of the red-carpeted, red-wallpapered stairway, making it look narrower and steeper and higher than it was; or was he perhaps simply light-headed from the smoke . . . ? This may be the beginning of my death, he thought. Will I know? Each second growing more and more certain until the final moment when the smoke is gone and my head is cool and there is a flash of clear light and I know that the sham is over and that I am, how do we say, dead? The lobby was like a mountaintop cave, a small dark mouth opening in the swirling mist. There was no trace of a wise man—he was all alone and could hear the building whispering, moaning, shouting restlessly to itself. It did not wish to die, and yet was willing to burn. Sir Edwin's aesthetic love of destruction, of collapse and immolation, did not extend, it appeared, to those things of his own which he wished to preserve. He had begun to ask Charles in a normal tone of voice, manly but urgent, one understood, one knew, brooking no bullshit, straight to the point, if Charles might consider dashing in and retrieving a few valuable bits and pieces of theatrical memorabilia—but he hadn't been able to maintain the tone. He lost control of his voice and his face and his hands at the same moment: he squeaked and shrieked and shook like a leaf. Charles couldn't look at him and turned away in disgust. His prize possessions amounted to museum pieces indicating the aesthetic ancestors of what Sir Edwin called "The Free Theater" but which everyone else referred to now as "the Minot": a portrait in oil of the Duke of Saxe-Meiningen; a spotted and torn photograph of the Meininger Players assembled on a tiny picture-frame stage somewhere in the heart of Thuringia or Saxony; another, blurry and desiccated, of those same players either lying facedown on a mattress or huddled over it as if about to pounce on it, grinning melodramatically (the use of the mattress to muffle offstage "crowd noise" was legendary in the birth of "stage realism"); more photographs of Andre Antoine and his Théâtre Libre, and the famous "missing fourth wall" stage set put together with junk lumber and cast-off furniture; wood-cut prints of Sir Edwin's fantastic, eerie set design for the Moscow Art Theater's *Hamlet*. Charles yanked paintings and photographs down from the walls, wrapped them in a tablecloth, then smartly rapped a display case, breaking its glass. He thought he could stay in the burning room forever: *this was how things were.* Nothing could have made him happier, more deeply content. But he balanced two miniature stage sets on top of the bundle of pictures and autograph letters, stuffed two small sculptures under his arms, and made his way back down the stairs. They had become something like the face of a cliff, and he walked perpendicularly to it, defying gravity. Then he was in the main lobby and he could hear crackling and crashing and the firemen shouting inside the theater. Then different shouts and cannonading bursts of water. Outside on the street, Sir Edwin had gotten hold of himself and lit a cigar. Drawing voluptuously on it, he stared at Charles with a strange, almost mocking, superior gratitude. Both men were slick with soot-black sweat, sticky with blood from small wounds. Edwin seemed satisfied with the show of destruction and manly staving off of destruction, now that it was all over—even pleased. He spoke with fatuously coy irony of a dream to use the sounds of the firefight, from gush of water to shriek of fear, from splatter of horse dung to clatter of shoes on cobblestones, in place of the small orchestra: "That," he insisted, "was the music of the future." Firemen trudged past alternately muttering and braying with victorious exhaustion. Charles and Sir Edwin could hear hot wood sizzling and steaming above them in the black building, and smell the wet ash, the burnt spores and flowers of mold. Charles was nauseated by the ridiculously sweet smoke of Sir Edwin's cigar, and disgusted with his reinvigorated incoherence and perversity, but they were walking now and had passed into a livelier block, full of restaurants and saloons, people with stuffed bellies and laughing mouths, and Charles surrendered to a fleeting vision of his master's alcoholically perceived but immutable truth. Something "great" might be revealed if he did something "real" on the stage. Let it happen to me, he thought, seeing in his mind the crackling flames in the lobby, as you say it will. Then someone came running after them to tell them that a little boy, one of the plumber's sons, no doubt, had been found under the chandelier.

Father and Mother returned safely from Iceland, revealing that there had been as well a detour to the Svalbard Archipelago, on Norway's arctic coast, with a Boston coal baron named Longyear. Andrew and Alexander came from Sacramento for a short visit to welcome them home, and they were joined a day later by Amelia and the Reverend Ruggles, who had been attending a meeting of President Wilson's Ecumenical Council. Because Charles no longer lived at the family home, and had not seen anybody in his family for quite some time, he wore the false auburn beard when he came for dinner. Neither Father nor older brothers nor Tom Ruggles, seemed to notice. Amelia pretended not to, and Mother merely watched him, as was now her wont, closely but neutrally. Only the younger brothers, Gus and Tony, saw it for what it was. They laughed hysterically but quietly between themselves, and would not reveal the source of their amusement. The men discussed the trip to Iceland, and Charles pretended to be surprised, even a little ashamed of himself, when he appeared finally to understand that the purpose of the trip had not been sport fishing, that the reference to the tying of flies had been ironic, and that the facilitation and encouragement of negotiations for control of Iceland's commercial fisheries had been the real activity, along with the study of general opportunities for people with ships, which were carrying mutton and stockfish to Belgium and France, where normal husbandry had been interrupted by the sudden deaths of millions of young men. Iceland was Danish, Father said—as Danish as Mother, whose great-grandparents on her mother's side had been born, lived, and died in that country—but was seeking its independence. Denmark had, during various decades of the last few centuries, been desirous of, even desperate for, buyers of Iceland, but independence had never entered into it. Now it appeared that the United States might one day not too far in the future consider purchasing the country. That was the kind of place America was now. Just as a rich man might buy himself an island and declare himself king of it, a rich country could buy a poor one and run it like any other business. And while the Icelanders, Father admitted, were experiencing a desire for nationalism that was moving and gratifying to witness, and while they were justly proud of operating the world's oldest parliamentary republic and causing a society to subsist in which neither a ruling clergy nor aristocracy could find handholds—he wanted very much, and he said this twice, wanted very much for Iceland to understand, yes, first and foremost to understand and then naturally to accept, America's influence, and, not coincidentally, to prosper as they had never done before. Not ever, he repeated coolly. They had demonstrated perfectly well that the end of communal anarchism—and Charles particularly should understand the term was being used advisedly but pointedly—was poverty. Grinding, centuries-long famine and misery. They take their fish from open rowboats, he said, and so can spend no more than a day at a time on the water, and shallow water at that. Which does not prevent them from drowning at an appalling, not to say incredibly unprofitable, rate.

One hundred sixty-five men had been drowned in a single day—which was not only a terrible tragedy but a significant percentage of the country's male population. Decked ships from England had been fishing Iceland's waters for centuries, literally centuries, but the new steam-driven trawlers were simply sweeping up everything in their wake. Not because, Father went on with a more pronounced gravity, their captains were heartless sons of bitches or blind idiots, or because their owners were evil villains working hand in hand with corrupt tyrants, but because the world was changing and the English could no more *not fish* from their overwhelming trawlers than Charles could not *not enjoy*, for example, his motorcycle rides now that he had acquired the capability for that powerful—make no mistake about it—thrill.

"So fishing was good," Charles said.

"You know I don't care for sarcasm from anybody—"

"Yes, you have said so."

"—much less my sons—"

"Yes, I understand."

"—so don't let me hear it from you again."

"It was *a joke*, Father."

"It could indeed have been one, but was not," said Father with mild authority. "The mean look in your eye gives you away. I don't like to hear what comes out of your mouth when you look like that and I don't like to see you look like that."

"All right," Charles said, reddening over the auburn beard, which now felt ridiculous. "You put me off-balance with the motorcycle reference. I sold or am selling them all. I am no longer interested in thrills."

"Are beards back in fashion?" he asked.

"*No*," giggled Amelia, "they most certainly are *not*."

"You look like your grandfather," said Father. "Quite remarkably."

"Yes," said Mother. "He does." The father-in-law was clearly present, while the son clearly was not.

Mother and Father both murmured with bemused approval, and it was hard to say if they suspected the beard's falseness.

"I was wearing it when the theater caught fire. I can't bring myself, for some odd reason, to take it off."

No one knew what to say. One of the girls appeared in the doorway and indicated that the chauffeur was idling in the eastern portico. The family collected themselves and went out to inspect Father's latest purchase, a new automobile, a Mountain Wagon, manufactured by the Stanley firm and powered by steam. There were four rows of bench seats and no roof. If it proved a reasonable conveyance, they would take it to the ranch. The controls of the steamer, however, baffled the chauffeur, Albert, a tiny man who'd once been a jockey, causing some embarrassment and minor delay. After a few anxious minutes, they set off for the Presidio, and a picnic. Mother became convinced as the journey wore on that the boiler would blow and kill them all, and swore that her first ride in the Mountain Wagon would be her last. Everyone began the ride wearing goggles and dusters, but shucked everything when it became clear they weren't going to reach any terrific velocity. Father in fact felt it safe enough to put his big-brimmed Western hat on. With his long coat and knee-length boots and immense drooping moustache, he once again looked like the rancher he sometimes thought he would liked to have been, or the cavalry officer he had been in his youth, once in a while even perhaps a gunfighter, a righteous gunfighter, of course—certainly a San Franciscan from the old days. When these characteristics came to the fore, there was almost no hint of the refined and sophisticated man of law, the prosecutor of graft in the city's Golden Age of Graft, "The Regenerator," one of those men who are seen behind the man at the podium, the westernmost confidant of Colonel Roosevelt, a potential purchaser of Iceland.

Charles moved his goggles carefully to his forehead and made sure his beard was still securely fastened to his face. Then he moved the goggles from his forehead back over his eyes with a snap that he hadn't intended and which caused some pain to his blush-sensitized face.

"Mockery is for weaklings," Father said, returning to his earlier remonstrance, but drawling noticeably this time.

"'I am a weakling,' he said mockingly," Charles said. His beard lifted up and flew away without a sound.

He could feel Father staring at him with dark gunfighter impassivity for some time. It was certainly not a mean look, but for all its immobility of feature it was a violent one. The wind ruffled their heads of luxurious Minot hair. The picnic was being hosted by the detested but important San Francisco businessman and socialite, Durwood Keogh. Keogh was a director of United Railroad, and was widely considered to be both audaciously younger and more winningly handsome than could rightly be expected of one of the ultimate authorities of so deeply entrenched and spectacularly powerful a presence in the daily life of the nation as a railroad. Some frankly dismissed him as a figurehead, a playboy, and a dolt. Others thought he was secretly accomplished, and, ominously, "more than able." A few political philosophers of influence, however, holding leisurely conferences at both, interestingly, the Bohemian and the Pacific clubs, presented him as neither dolt nor efficient executive disguised as dolt, but as purely ruthless, or ruthlessly pure, in the service of convictions that were not his own, which could not be his own as he was unable to think on that moral level, but which he held, as a mean-spirited child holds candy. With a delight, that is to say, that obscures the poisoned ferocity of the need. Father believed he was dangerous in just this way: purity was ruthless, he said, again disregarding his own purity, his own ruthlessness, because they were products of deep belief, not superficial greed and power: Keogh had no staying power, while Father had Jesus Christ. But his neighbor be damned, he loathed Keogh personally as well. He had done his best to put him and all his associates, avowed and otherwise, behind bars, and it was none other than Keogh's uncle, the *ur* robber baron, whom he'd caused to flee the country. The Jew in jail, and the spectacularly corrupt robber baron fled: Father's legacy, in case anyone cared to remember the horrible failure of the Spring Park Water Company when the quake and fires had destroyed the city. And of course they'd found a way to shoot at him. He was always getting shot at—it only strengthened his disdain for shooters. But nothing had ever come of it, and here they were, nine years later, their mutual hatred softened with a kind of nostalgia for the shooting, and the volcanic hatred that could bring things to a shooting pass, and even the kind of respect that comes when two men find themselves not only still standing but thriving, in Golden Old California, when so many others were dead and gone.

Keogh had just returned from a trip to Mexico with General "Black Jack" Pershing. They'd been sent to apprehend or kill the internationally infamous political celebrity and terrorist Pancho Villa, who had crossed, a couple of months earlier, the international border into the little adobe village of Columbus, New Mexico. There he had murdered a dozen and a half of the tiny town's citizens, pillaged it, and burned it to the ground. Pershing and Keogh had failed in their mission and seemed almost forlornly stupid as they wandered about northern Mexico—at least from the vantage point of the northern capitals of the United States—but nobody blamed them, as that vast and primitive country seemed to have been expressly designed as a haven for barbarian villains.

So said Durwood Keogh anyway, leaning against his automobile in his jodhpurs and tapping one long strong flank with a crop. He made it look like the Minots had gathered around him, but it was he in fact who had approached them, affably, sportingly, generously. They all had bigger fish to fry, did they not?

It was preparedness for war in France that Keogh had taken up as his cause and duty upon his return to San Francisco. He had been named grand marshal of the Preparedness Day Parade, three months off yet, scheduled for mid-July to dovetail with Independence Day, but already a major and popular theme of civic discourse. German spies (a term synonymous with anarchists for more than a decade now) were said to be preparing too: to bomb the parade, kill paraders, and make a mockery of freedom and democracy. The attack on the Minot Theater—so went one highly controversial strand of public discourse—had merely been an exploratory jab.

Charles had never heard such an idea, but remained impassive and silent, as did Father. Were they suddenly playing some kind of poker? Mother, nearly under her breath, begged Keogh's pardon, but Keogh ignored her.

They were going to blow the city to pieces.

Charles remained as he was, resisting the urge to say that cities were made to be blown to pieces, that in reality they were in a constant state of being blown to pieces and rebuilt, so what was Keogh's beef?

Keogh had organized a volunteer cavalry troop—businessmen with time on their hands, fellow socialites, most of the polo team from the Burlingame Country Club—and got them immediately front and center in the public eye. There, it was stated proudly and unconditionally in all the best and most trusted newspapers that they would function as a deterrent to the mad, the craven, and the un-free. They might lunch at the Fairmont one day, conversing by way of exaggerated anecdotes about tactics, then be off to the beach or the Presidio. For security reasons, times and places were never officially announced, and Keogh often took his boys to a place other than the one to which he'd said they be going, sometimes in the company of a professional cavalry officer for drills, sometimes not. Spectators in the know (Amelia Minot Ruggles, for instance, who did in fact work twelve hours a day in various hospitals but managed to remain informed, discreet, sophisticated, and sympathetic) arrived punctually at even the most secret exercises, accompanied by reporters from William Randolph Hearst's *Examiner*.

"Sanguinary feeling for an all-out war with Mexico is building, wouldn't you agree, Minot?"

"Not at all."

"No, of course not." Why he had opened with reference to his failure, rather than the triumph to come, was mystifying—unless you understood he wanted a fight.

"How much money did you and Black Jack spend on your vacation down there? 130 million dollars is what we all heard."

"You've got to spend money to make money. You know that very well, Bill! You know that better than most of us, I dare say! 'The Regenerator!' Why, your office supplies bill alone . . . ! Genuine expense, Bill, don't get me wrong! I'm not complaining even if some of that ink went on my indictment, which I have hanging in my office, did you know that? I say your office supplies bill alone could have bought you, where was it, Iceland? Lucky for you, you had that vacuum tube to the White House and a Moral President who didn't think twice about using federal money to help his old friend buy, what was it you used to say, good dogs who do what they're told? But listen, that's all water under the bridge, forgiven and almost forgotten. We're talking about *now* and we're talking about *Mexico*: these people are the enemies of our country. You're going to count beans in the face of racial degeneracy and unrepentant hatred?"

"The enemy is in the main amorphous, and where it has recognizable form—say a *bandito generale*, for example—the checklists for confirmation that he is indeed foe and not friend never quite tally up convincingly. Wilson can't tell, and none of his men can, either. Some honest men think Villa should have, *could have been*, our friend. But we're too busy tinkering with what we think are the mechanisms of the oldest civilization in this hemisphere, mechanisms so complicated they are useless to the Indians or whatever you call them when they've sold their white blood for a mess of potage."

"I am impervious to your speeches, as you well know, Mr. Minot!"

"You can't tinker with another country."

This struck Charles as a rather flat contradiction of Father's recently stated principles, but he said nothing, suspecting there was an important distinction to be made somewhere between the tinker and the purchase.

"Destroy it, then. Occupy it and do your ciphering afterward. Pick your man and tell him to duck. It can't be Villa because Villa is an unstable warlord. Pick one of the others. Carranza. Who cares. Huerta would have sufficed, even when you accepted the idea that he was a mean drunk with more Indian blood in him than white. And don't talk to me about Wilson. He's a fool and a coward."

"Come now," said Reverend Doctor Thomas Ruggles with stern serenity. "Come now."

"Zapata," said Charles in an even but loud tone of voice.

"Zapata!" cried Keogh. "Go down to Los Angeles and make a movie about him! He's so romantic with his big dark eyes under that fabulous sombrero. I want one just like it. In fact, I have one just like it. Have him walk quietly into a saloon and run the camera in close to his face. Make the shot all mustachios and burning commitment. Make no genuine alliances with him, however. Spend nothing of value on him. He'll go to pieces in no time. He's a sensitive warlord. He will cry when things turn out badly. Interesting that you should find him compelling."

"This is stimulating, Captain Keogh, Colonel Keogh—" Charles admitted and paused "—or whatever the fuck you think you are, *Generale Keogh*, but the war in Europe, you must admit, you of all people, certainly now has priority. I mean, haven't you got enough to do?"

Everybody but Father looked away.

"Two birds with one stone," said Keogh. "Just have to figger mah tra-*jec*-toe-reez."

They were then joined by Sir Edwin. He appeared to have been sleeping in his clothes, possibly for weeks now, on the floor of theater's green room, and was quick to tell people how stupid and heartless he thought they would be when they criticized and mocked him for it, or even questioned him on the subject. It was a living thing, the theater, and he would no more leave it in its wounded condition than he would the bedside of a sick child. He spoke at first in French, for no good reason, soliciting views about the Stanley Steamer.

"It looks like one of those magnificent things one threshes wheat with and which one day reveals its true, dark, and misunderstood nature and kills all the unsuspecting farmers having lunch in its shade," said Sir Edwin.

"It is not nearly so large as a threshing machine," said Father reprovingly. "It is a toy compared to a threshing machine."

"And yet how many times more powerful than a horse!" shouted Sir Edwin.

"It is," Charles said, "slower than a horse, and ungainly. You might get around town just as easily in a threshing machine."

Sir Edwin began to speak English and turned to the weather, which, though of course mild, was nearly unbearable for one as unwell and raggedly worn as himself, who frankly admitted he had sacrificed his manly vitality for his art.

"Don't think I don't regret it," said Sir Edwin.

"You regret it, do you?" asked Father.

"I do."

"I don't believe you."

"Lucky for me, I don't give a damn what you believe!" shouted Sir Edwin, loudly, more loudly, perhaps, than he'd thought he would. He was so tired he thought he might become delirious.

"You can't have it both ways," said Father. He was amused by his wife's artist, his *son's* artist, for God's sake, but this amusement was mitigated by a general distaste for people who boiled over too easily, like spoiled horses, and who thought it was all right because they were thoroughbreds. He felt as well the strong man's increased desire to defeat a weaker man once that weaker man has displayed the weakness and its probable trajectory toward greater weakness—if he could use such a term, he did not like it at all, but how else might he put it—decreased vigor? Increased vulnerability? Fever? Nausea? Infantile impotence? Terror?

"Both ways? Describe, please, these two ways which are no longer mine."

"Soulful visionary and virile man of consequential action."

"I was encouraged in my youth, it is true, to think that the artist was like no man so much as a religious martyr, the practical consequence of which was the subtle but steady wasting of my resources and the silent but insidious ravaging of my health. But I am making up for it now with the *vivid, vital violence* . . . that only the mortally wounded . . . *apostate anchorite* is capable of."

Sir Edwin was very pleased with his speech, but was not quite finished. Trembling with vengeful glee, he thrust his ace in Father's face: "And besides, I have your son to do my living for me."

Father smiled patronizingly and shook his head. "You have no such thing," he said in seemingly gentle reproof. "Charles is enrolled in your little kindergarten here of public performance, but will soon be moving on. He has real work in Minnesota in the fall. The Commission of Public Safety."

"You won't," asked Keogh, "be going 'over there'?"

"He will be going over there by staying here. There is a formidable enemy here as well. I'm sure I don't have to tell you so."

"Terrible news, however the situation stands, about your theater," murmured Keogh. Something in his tone of voice, however muted and drawling it was, alarmed Charles and caused him to look directly into Keogh's eyes. The penetration was allowed for a moment. Keogh then smiled and turned to Amelia.

"We want," he said, "to help in any way we can. Of course with money, but publically, morally, we want to do everything that can be done to help bring a patriotic show like *The American* to its rightful audience.

"They are saying now—" Amelia began.

"*Who* is saying now?" interrupted Mother. "Who is saying *what* now?"

"It was a small fire, I am told," said Father. "Easily contained and causing little damage. Everything can be quickly and easily replaced."

"That is excellent news," said Keogh, smiling at one and all.

"A boy was killed," said Charles.

"—that it was deliberately set," Amelia continued, picking up the controversy of the earlier strand in the conversation left dangling. "The fire marshal believes a small explosive device was launched by a cadre of anarchists under cover of the fireworks display—that is to say, by one of them, a crack archer who used a window purposefully left open as his target. And yes, that a child was killed makes the investigation far more important than it might have been, Father."

"I left the window open," Charles said. "And the arrow came through a window that *wasn't* open."

Father nodded, but nobody really cared very much about that sort of detail.

And so Charles sat on the blanket feeling weak and stupid and cold, shivering in the ridiculous details of a political melodrama he could only just barely stand imagining, while some of Captain Keogh's horsemen twits dug small holes out in the field and Amelia—to his great surprise on her favorite horse, Jolly—barrel-raced around them. Drinking wine one glass after another, he dozed off, and woke to cheering. A horse and rider went thundering past, the rider hanging off one side of his mount and snatching something from the ground and hauling himself back upright in the saddle. There had been a strange sound and a spray of dirt. Another horse and rider appeared at the far end of the field. They galloped past and again the rider hung off low to the ground like an Indian, snatched something that made a small explosion, and rode off shaking his prize. "What are they doing?" he mumbled. Father shaded his eyes and looked down at him. He was insubstantial in the overpowering light. Charles repeated the question, sitting up dizzily and shading his eyes too.

"You know very well what they're doing," said Father. "It's traditional amongst cavaliers," he said. "An exercise in . . . in . . ."

"What is?" Charles asked, standing unsteadily. "What is an exercise in what?"

Charles looked over at Sir Edwin and told him that chickens had been buried up to their necks. Horsemen rode by and snapped their heads off.

"Ah," said Sir Edwin.

"This isn't a war they're preparing for," Charles went on equably, "it's a joke. It's pitiful, really."

"If you can't enjoy the day, why don't you go home," suggested Father. "And shave. You look like a bum. A drunken bum."

Cheers from the far end of the field made their way down the field as another rider charged toward another chicken. People were shouting now and laughing. Charles could see heads turning up and down the field. He lay back down and closed his eyes to the sun, lids burning blood-red and luminous, brain hot in a cold head and reeling. He put his hands over his eyes just as Mother softly exclaimed that, oh, it was Amelia. And there she was, Charles's mad saint sister like an Amazon Godiva, long chestnut hair in streamers behind her, hanging low and bounding off Jolly's flank, his spotted coat brilliant in the intense sunlight, his great crazy head nodding rhythmically as he charged. Knowing it was a chicken buried there, he now saw it, its ridiculous startled head straining upward, jerking left and right as it fought off both sleepiness and fear, and then gone, appearing before Charles and Sir Edwin dripping in Amelia's glove in much less time than Charles thought possible, Jolly reined up in front of the family, Amelia laughing hysterically, laughing and laughing and laughing, infectious but frightening, Mother and Reverend Ruggles both rising to steady her, laughing a little themselves too, helplessly, but wanting to calm her before something happened. But it was too late and Charles knew it. She flung the bloody scrap of chicken head at Sir Edwin. It landed on Charles's stomach. After a moment, he daintily plucked it up and laid it aside. Then he stood and removed his vest and listened to Amelia sputter and whinny, his little brothers shriek with pleasure, and Mother say to Father that that was it, that was enough, it was too much, we've got to get everybody out of here.

Later, at the house, Charles found himself standing rather forlornly with Mother and Father.

"Amelia wants to hurt me too," said Father. "I don't understand why."

"You've got no business lecturing Charles, then, William, now do you?"

"Charles and Amelia are two quite distinct matters," said Father.

Mother spoke as soothingly as she always did, but took Father very much by surprise. The Spring Park Water Company scandal came and went, and for the moment, was among them. Father's eyes grew quite large and moist and he looked away from her. All around them, in other rooms, the family were hooting. Charles could hardly hear them, but he could see them, as plainly as if the house lights had gone up in the middle of a scene.

Early in the morning a few days later, because Father had made a strange, unlooked-for point of it, Charles decided to get rid of the last of his motorcycles: a Belgian Minerva and a big orange Flying Merkel out of Pottstown, a V-twin displacing sixty-one cubic inches. He entered a shop not far from the theater that appeared to be closed: no one was about and he could hear no sound coming from the back rooms, the mechanics' bays, nor the offices along the little mezzanine gallery. Sunlight was slanting in through the three big but fly-specked and cobwebbed windows and the manufacturers' logos painted on them—the Indian, the Cyclone, the Thor—which in turn burned like brands on the oil-stained wood planks of the floor. At the far end of the display case, which glowed in the rare sunlight as if stuffed with diamonds and silver and gold, a grimy and tattered piece of red cloth hung over the narrow doorway that led to the parts bins. The sunlight struck it as a spotlight would a stage curtain, and he found himself staring expectantly at it. It was easy to imagine a kind of comical-nightmare auditorium behind the red curtain, a long and narrow corridor of a stage, an auditorium for puppets compared to the vast stage and wings and unknown world at his back, people perched high above him on the shelves, cackling and buzzing—poor people, because it was "the anarchy of poverty that delighted" him—waiting, waiting for the swollen, thunderous music of the final scene, waiting for the death of the beautiful young tragedienne, waiting for something they could not name, or perhaps only for Charles Minot, a person simply standing there, no particular lines to speak or props to hold, no marks on a carefully measured floor to hit with the grace and precision of a dancer. He edged his way around the display case and stood before the curtain. Something in the distant reaches of the cloudy sky happened and the light faded slightly, drawing swiftly back toward and then into the windows, then brightened again, flowing back across the room to the curtain, red to gray to red. He reached out and touched it, patted it, looked for the fold that might part it just a little, and the musicians in his mind uneasily awaited their cue. Then he clutched the soiled, limp fabric and threw it open.

Walking toward him, at the far end of an astonishingly long and narrow aisle of beetling shelves, was none other than his actress, Vera.

His first impulse was to shout her name and run down the long aisle, take her in his arms and kiss her, but she seemed to be going away from him rather quickly—not running, but going further and further as if by rents of unconsciousness in his perception, and then suddenly she was gone. He let the curtain fall in alarm, strode backward into the display case and banged it loudly, rattling the chromed fittings, the sparkling jets and needles, the red, white, and blue handlebar streamers, the glinting opaque glass and glistening black rubber of the goggles. He set his hands upon it and leaned over, as if to settle and dampen the jingling things and suggest a casual interest in the concentric piles of gears next to a typed and folded card listing ratios and prices. He assumed Vera would reappear, in the shop proper, shortly, and prepared a smile for the young woman's arrival, conscious that his instinct had failed him, that he had, no other way to put it, fled in the face of her appearance and disappearance. But she did not reappear. And what, after all, had she been doing there in the first place? After quite a long time, he moved stealthily back to the curtain and pulled it slowly away: Vera had her back to him, about halfway down the aisle. Still he could not call out to her: Was she really there? He let the curtain swing stiffly back in place.

Above and behind him, a door in one of the mezzanine cubbyholes was opened with a bang on its hinges and closed with an even louder bang. He craned about and looked up but no one appeared.

Vera was now standing in the doorway, holding the red curtain aside with one finger. She and Charles regarded each other in what seemed like a long silence. Then he greeted her brightly, pretending that if they did not exactly know each other very well, they had seen each other around, were a part of the big happy family that the shop really was, fancy meeting you here and so on. She raised her head slightly, narrowed her eyes, and smiled faintly. Sandy hair, a face somehow smooth and clear and weathered at the same time, and smooth, deep, clear black eyes, sculptured lips. She seemed neither to know Charles nor to care that she did not. And yet there was something of remembrance or premonition in her mild, indifferent scrutiny. Charles was more fascinated than confused. Fascination precluded confusion. She nodded almost imperceptibly—or was he merely imagining such a validation of his wounded, vaunted instinct—then suddenly brightened, laughed, and said that she worked there. She said "Just a sec," and turned back into the narrow aisle and let the curtain once again fall. Had she been lost in thought? Or had she been appraising Charles privately, or remembering their professional embraces and finding some genuine erotic content, and was just as startled to see him as he was to see her? Perhaps she was shy and manifested it with a kind of mystical hauteur. Perhaps she was drugged. Perhaps he was drugged. Indeed he felt somewhat high. Perhaps she had not been there at all. It was just barely possible, but possible nevertheless. Believing her to be, in that instant of embarrassment and redoubled desire, *the most beautiful woman he had ever seen*, he struggled to hold her image in his mind, but could not recall, a second later, a single feature. Sandy hair? Dark eyebrows? Flashing teeth? He moved like a puppet to the curtain and drew it back but she was nowhere to be seen.

He moved silently, with a kind of dreamlike dread and volition, down the aisle, calling out a greeting every few paces, until he reached the end, and retraced, silently, fully awake now for just that moment, his steps, parted the curtain yet again, and found the room noisily full of people, bustling about as if, yes, as if they were on a stage set: three colorfully distinct pairs of men coming one after another in a train through the big double doors with crated motorcycles, another man, a Mexican probably, a gentleman at a small table cluttered with newspapers against the far wall and the last window, which appeared to be pulsing now, faintly, with ore-bearing light, and four men again leaning over the gallery railing but not in shadow—at least three of them—this time, and laughing as if at a baseball game or in a saloon of the Gold Rush years. These four looked like rough and tough men—certainly not the hard but jolly mechanics— if not altogether desperados, and their laughter was clearly not the kind inspired by mirth or light-heartedness, but rather of defeat, despair, mockery, defiance. Still they appeared to have popped out of stage doors and were about to sing. One was a sleek and pink-faced gorilla with a luxurious head of hair, another had sunken cheeks and a monocle, the third had a round and close-shaven skull and a week's growth of beard, and the fourth hung back in the shadow of a pillar. There were a couple of young men too, boys, who were trying to look and act like customers standing on either side of a yellow Beveridge Cyclone. They were younger than Charles, but not much, dirty and unnecessarily loud, boasting in an Italian dialect he could not make out. Beyond Rome, beyond Naples. Eboli perhaps. Sicilian. A lot of shu-shu-shushing. Sicilian. The truth was they offended him in some way he could not articulate. They looked like gang boys hoping for a chance to do something outrageously violent and useful. One of the men looking down at the shop from the mezzanine half-turned and let another man cross the trembling resounding gallery behind him. The man descended the stairs against the far wall of the shop, banging loudly on each step. He was owlish-looking, with large eyes that seemed nearly yellow behind his thick spectacles, and great shaggy brows shooting like black-veined bolts of lightning from the bridge of his equally remarkable nose to his bulging temples. He smelled strongly of whiskey and Charles faltered a bit before this predatory but teetering ferocity. He carried his hands before him, not quite balled in fists, as if wishing to grasp some invisible thing and tear it to shreds. Not appearing to notice Charles, the man left the shop, negotiated his way through a particularly dense crowd on the sidewalk, waited for a cable car, several Fords, and a horse-drawn wagon to pass, then crossed the street and entered, with exaggerated gestures of formality, into conversation with a jitney driver who was smoking a cigarette outside his little bus. The driver took an envelope from the owlish man and the two shook hands. Another man, wearing a bright red driving cap and a big black moustache, who Charles thought owned the shop joined the owlish man and the jitney driver, and after a moment they all crossed the street and entered the shop. The Owl stood center stage and announced that he had "spoken to the president," and that said president had agreed to give him, Owl, it seemed, but possibly the others were included, sixty thousand dollars.

"You spoke to Mahon," said Owner. There was no incredulity, feigned or unfeigned, in his voice.

"Yes?" confirmed Owl querulously.

"Sixty," repeated Jitney, not with incredulity or sarcasm but awed unbelief.

"That is," said Owner, now with admiration but still cool, "an awfully fucking immense deal of change."

"I TOLD YOU, YOU COCKSUCKERS!" shouted Owl in a friendly but nevertheless alarming way.

"Mahon is a decent chap," said Owner. "He's in town?"

"He is not," said Owl. "He is in Washington conferring with the heads of a few other important unions."

"And where is the money?"

"Pinkerton," murmured Jitney, his gaze serenely focused outside the shop, on a trolley car on the far side of the intersection. "On the back step. I don't know if he's getting on or off. On. No. He's getting off, he's getting off and—"

"Quickly, then," said Owner, moving slowly away and turning his back.

"It's coming in an unusually circuitous fashion, and we need Farnsworth to receive it here in an unusually quiet corner," said Jitney.

"No one knows where he is," said Owl conversationally. "Is he in prison?" He laughed bitterly, and both Owner and Jitney let smiles pass over their faces.

"I'll find him," said Owner. "I'll find Vera and Vera will find Little Billy Farnsworth, the only man among us who isn't afraid to get his hands dirty."

Owl softened and saddened perceptibly. "It's true. And I love Billy, I truly do. He's good and he likes getting dirty. I rode with Eugene Debs," he went on.

"Yes, yes," said Owner, moving another step away and lighting a cigarette to cover his unacceptable nervousness.

Owl turned to Charles as if he'd been part of the conversation all along. "On the Red Special in 1908 and we got a solid million votes. *One million American socialists.* Debs and I will both be in prisons before the end of the war—but I intend to bring down United Railroad before they nail me."

Father's well-known hatred of URR may have had a great deal to do with the apparent ease in which Charles had become part of the general group—along with the nasty Sicilian boys—if not in the know. Or it may have had very little to do with it. No one seemed terribly interested in oaths and the cover of darkness. He had been in the shop two or three times, getting rid of his motorcycles . . . but had Vera been there all along, watching him, wondering if she might audition . . . ?

Owner was counting money in the till but could not help turning and shouting with a great flashing smile, "*SIXTY!*"

"Mr. Minot!" Owner slammed the register shut and turned his attention to Charles, who bowed perceptibly but not dramatically.

"Are you here to give me the Merkel?"

"Yes, I am. And the Minerva."

"Pardon me, Mr. Minot. Would you repeat what you just said, sir? Days and nights of internal combustion have weakened my ears as well as my eyes. My nerves are shot and I can hardly walk a straight line. Everything tastes of oil and my fingers are numb from the vibrations."

"I say I am here to sell you the Merkel and the Minerva."

"Ah, that's what Oi t'ought you said."

The men at the railing regarded Charles impassively, the Italian boys fell silent as if embarrassed. The men carrying crates stood outside smoking, and Mexican murmured to himself, apparently translating a story in the newspaper.

Charles had never looked at the photographs and advertisements papering the walls, but did so now. One caught his eye. Five men with their arms slung around each other, hanging on and sagging against each other, clowning and making faces. Rising massively behind them was the heavy lumber of the armature of a great bowl-shaped track in—he leaned closer—in Detroit. In huge white letters, ten feet high and nailed to the outermost studs, the sport's chief attraction was spelled out: NECK AND NECK WITH DEATH. The man in the middle, upright, grinning, had either told a terrific joke or was the only sober member of the group. The other men were convulsed in hilarity, faces as blackened as if they were pretending to be a nigger minstrel banjo band, with wide, white, clean rings around their eyes where the goggles had been. Beneath the clean and sober man in the middle were the words "Daredevil Derkum and his friends are neck and neck with death—AND THEY USE OILZUM!" Derkum was a man well known in California racing, who was also a fireman on the lead engine of the Owl train that ran every night from Los Angeles to San Francisco.

"How's your old man?" asked Owner.

"He's fine, he's fine, he . . ." Charles said, faltering a little in the face of all the apparent knowledge of his family strangers were ready to draw on—strangers and Vera. "He's just back from Iceland."

"Iceland!"

"Yes, as strange as that may sound: Iceland."

"Business or pleasure?"

"Fishing."

"Fishing! Fishing—for what sort of fish might one angle in Iceland? Let me guess, let me . . . grayling?"

"Umm, no, you'd think so, wouldn't you, but interestingly enough, no, no grayling."

"Trout, of course."

"Browns, yes."

"Nasty fish, the brown. Cannibal fish. That's what I hear."

"I think they prefer baitfish to their own, but sure, I guess that's true to some extent," he said with the return of his casual authority.

"*German fish*," continued Owner. He winked.

"Oh yes, of course. German fish."

"It's in all the newspapers. A German fish and they are eating up all the good American brook trout. *And* they're supposed to be inferior on the table."

"Au bleu, with the right wine, they taste all right to me."

There was a brief silence and then the place was roaring with laughter. When it subsided, Owner gave Charles a wry but gently consoling look. "Char," he said. "That's what I was thinking of earlier. The rare and mysterious arctic char."

"Sure, lots of nice species of char. But it's the salmon they went for."

"Of course. Salmon. How could I forget? Salmon! So the fishing was good?"

"I couldn't say."

"No?"

"I mean, I haven't heard."

"But generally, the reputation of Iceland is . . . ?"

"Good, yes, very good."

"Why else go to Iceland, right?

"My father says it's the most beautiful country in the world. Volcanoes with glaciers creaking around them. Fifty-mile-an-hour winds straight from the North Pole and you can stick your hand in a creek of nearly boiling water. They're only just emerging from the Middle Ages, thanks ironically to the war in Europe."

"But ironically too the war in Europe makes it a risky business to go steaming about in the northern Atlantic, does it not?"

Charles shrugged. "He likes to fish."

"But you do not?" asked Owner. "Like to fish."

"Oh no, I do, I do, I do very much, but I'm, uh, I'm, uh . . ." Charles faltered again, inexplicably. "I'm in a play and . . . you know. Vera too—"

"You're an *actor*," said Owner, a bit like a lawyer.

"*Yes*," Charles admitted emphatically, maybe a bit testily. "Yes, I am. Several plays, actually. A season of them. In repertory."

"And the shows must go on."

"That's what they tell me. Even if the theater is burned to the ground."

"The Savoy is a beautiful building. We were relieved to hear the damage was not great and that repair will go quickly."

"Yes. We found the money pretty easily too. Mother finds the money. She used to sing, but she prefers now just to find the money. The insurers feel now that the fire was not caused by a firework launched by, they think, some trolley drivers who were celebrating something about San Francisco's role in the war that one of the city commissioners said, or promised, or promised to say at some point in the near future. Or didn't say. Promised not to say."

"*Not* caused," Owner repeated.

"That's right: not caused. I'm not sure about any of the details. I should be, but I'm not. But it was late at night, after that . . . anarchist picnic . . . ."

Everyone in the room was suddenly uneasy. The results of the investigation had not yet been made public. Charles had forgotten that. This would be news to them: that they, or their friends, had done it. If in fact these men were actually anarchists. It was a leap, but they had the look and feel and sound of, well . . . anarchists, did they not? Which meant that it was to be understood as a blow against, Charles supposed, the aristocracy, or perhaps the aristocracy specifically involved in what was perceived as a patriotic theatrical production of a play called *The American*. The aristocracy specifically known as "the Minots." Known more specifically in that room as "Charles Minot." Father's adventures in the punishment of graft and his hatred of URR were, the thinking was evidently to go, not good enough for the anarchists. Whatever Father may think, may wish and yearn to believe about his progressive Christian politics, it was too little too late: you get your ass ripped apart like all the rest of the rich people.

It was as preposterous a lie as they'd heard yet in the city, but still it gave them pause and made the room, the shop, the big happy family with its radical character actors ranged up along the mezzanine rail and its colorful young Italian criminals, all terribly quiet.

Charles thought what silenced them was the shadow of lies to come falling over their stage. His stage, their stage, everybody's stage. The little old stage set about to come apart, once again, at the seams.

"And what is the name of the first show that must go on?" It was Owner's shop and he would conduct them through a reasonable conversation that eased their vague fears.

"*The American*," said Charles.

"Sounds patriotic!"

"Well, yes, it is and it isn't. You see . . . Vera, I think, could tell you—"

"Fits the mood of the city, certainly."

"Yes, that is certainly so."

"Henry James's *The American*? Or some other sort of American."

"Henry James, right. Adapted it himself, I understand, from his novel."

"He's dead, you know."

"No, I did not know that."

"Couple of months ago."

"I see, I see. That's, well, that's . . . too bad. I'm sorry to hear it. Did you, do you, like his novels . . . ?" Charles couldn't believe he was discussing literature with a daredevil, but pressed on, making a note to ask Sir Edwin if he knew about "his friend" James's death. He was sure he did not, and would extol it as the man's supreme fiction.

"Yes, I do," said Owner judiciously. "And I don't care who knows it. Once I learned to read I didn't care how complicated things got. I think I've gotten to where I prefer them complicated. Simplicity is some kind of snake oil. Simplicity is, you know, like the story of the little theater that wasn't damaged in a fire set off by an errant firework but by evil men who are not like us and who hate us and who hold human life in utter contempt. You?"

Somehow he knew he was back to the novels and stories of Henry James. "Yes. I think I've read most if not all of the New York edition."

"And your theater is physically viable, is that right? Structurally sound?"

"Yes, that's right, and we hope to open very nearly on schedule," said Charles with once-again-regained composure and authority. "*The American* is in terrific shape, August Strindberg's *Spook Sonata* is very difficult—do you know Strindberg? He was given an anti-Nobel a few years ago, just before he died."

There was some clapping, whether in honor of the inventor of dynamite or of Strindberg it was hard to say.

"Difficult—" Charles began to say but could not repress the laughter that was going around the room, a strong suggestion that it was the inventor of dynamite who had been applauded, "—difficult I say to work on but very exciting, and *Romeo and Juliet*, well . . . *there are a lot of lines to be memorized there*, of course, but we think we'll be ready with what our artist in residence calls a dream of the future."

"*Romeo and Juliet* as a dream . . . ?"

"Yes, sir."

"Of the future."

"Yes, sir. That's the phrase that keeps coming up in our . . . our talks. The deaths of Romeo and Juliet, and Tybalt and Mercutio and the rest of them, are not causes for sadness and grief and weeping."

"No?" Owner was amused but deferential.

"They are sacrifices in a glorious cause."

"Ah."

"Yes. They are . . . *hastening* the downfall of the corrupt . . . *forms* . . . of their fathers. Their poisonous ways and decadent tyrannies. When they are together and in love, they are actually . . . in the, uh . . . in the future. You can tell it's the future because the lighting is different and we speak differently. The violence all takes place in the present. We use it as a kind of way to rend the fabric . . ." and here Charles faltered. He was tired of this faltering and could not understand it. *Sooner walk into a burning room than subject oneself to the judgment of strangers who act like they know you.*

The hidden Vera once again saw the icy clown just beneath his handsome features, the ironic lout just beneath his goodwill.

"Yes?"

"Of time."

"Probably a little too sophisticated for me."

Charles took a good breath and recovered himself. "I'm not sure that that is the word for it. Sir Edwin is a visionary and freely accepts ridicule on that count. There's a good deal of entertaining sword fighting, in any case, and poetry."

"'Sir' Edwin?" asked Owner.

"Yes. An English knight." Charles chuckled falsely, grinning, to make up for it, with even greater falsity around the room. Because it sounded like an exit line in a scene that left the audience roaring with laughter, Charles decided to make for the big open doorway, at that moment a great archway of light.

"You'll leave the Merkel with us, then?"

"Yes, and the Minerva!" Charles shouted, stunned that he'd forgotten why he'd come. He took a few uncertain steps back into the gloom. "Tell Vera I—"

"MINERVA?" shouted Owl. "WHAT THE FUCK IS A MINERVA?"

"Belgian make. Minerva. 1902."

"What's the kid talkin' about?" Jitney asked Owl.

"HE WANTS TO SELL US A BELGIAN WAFFLE! YOU HUNGRY?"

"No interest in the Minerva, Mr. Minot," said Owner. "You have to shut the engine off to change gears."

Charles stopped then and turned and held up his hand as if he were departing a group of able and courageous men with whom he had accomplished something of sentimental as well as practical value. "THOUGHT IT MIGHT BE OF VALUE TO A COLLECTOR," he fairly bellowed.

"NO COLLECTORS HERE, KID! ONLY DAREDEVILS!" Owl bellowed back.

"THANK YOU! THANK YOU ALL! YOU'VE BEEN A TERRIFIC AUDIENCE! PLEASE BE SO GOOD AS TO CONVEY MY GREETINGS TO VERA!"

"VERA WHO?" Owl redoubled his bellow.

The laughter in the shop continued until Charles was quite a long way down the sidewalk and out of earshot.

Vera watched all this from the other side of the curtain, holding it closed and revealing only the unnaturally white oval of her face, wanting only to play a game, hoping Charles would overcome his politeness and a profound and certain confusion and come running down the aisle again to find her. Yes: she wished it was a game. But if it was a game, what kind of game was it? Who would win and who would lose and, in the end, would they know why they had played? Her salon—at what passed for one without the structure and animation of money, at her *salon des pauvres*, somebody had nicknamed it and which had stuck, *le Salon Romantique et Revolutionnaire*, she preferred to call it, with pride that was maybe a little defensive, a little guilt-ridden as she had always wanted to be part of a smart set and had just begun to learn French—there, yes, they knew all about it: Henry James would be taken at his word and escorted quite a bit further down the road, where his American would become not the fresh air in the moldy museum of Old World aristocratic privilege, bright and kind, resourceful and determined, but a ruthless destroyer of the weak, the sick, the ridiculous. *Romeo and Juliet* would be a savage and bloody fairy tale about utopia. Watching *The Spook Sonata* would be like taking a powerful narcotic that would set free the enslaved minds of its audience. They had heard these ideas proposed and articulated, and debated them with learned pleasure, like doctors in the amphitheater of a surgery. They were anarchists, so of course they were interested in all new theories of disease and cure, in plans for the real abolition of slavery, an understanding of true weakness, for the demolition of palaces and the deaths of tyrants. Still, she was uneasy. There was so much *authority* and *obedience to authority* in even the most charming and reckless of these speeches, so much *discipline* and *sacrifice* in even the daffiest of these aesthetics, that unspeakable atrocity seemed right around the corner. Petty despots would race up and down the high roads and the low roads like insane tinkers who'd wrested magical weapons from stupid sorcerers, or mountebanks playing the shell game and killing everybody who happened to win. Killing and killing and killing because even the rigged game could not be counted on, you had to kill them all, winners and losers alike, until you finally were killed yourself. No, she did not subscribe to endless killing. Therefore (she had to admit, because the continuity was as clear as day) she could not subscribe to the beginning of killing, either. She said as much to herself—later, of course, but not much later, to Charles—with a kind of gentle but false patience, knowing that she could scream and slap and break things that need not have been broken, and was, in her dreams, too often violent—even with loved ones, it troubled her to note morning after morning—hysterically and remorselessly merciless in her sleeping hatreds and vengeance.

As Charles made his ridiculous departure that day, he saw, thought he saw, Vera push her face through the greasy red drapery and then withdraw it. Perhaps he had seen it in the corner of his eye—the sudden absence. He could feel her every moment across all time and space, no? He was in love with her, no? Love was not thinking about love, it was not about lolling about in feelings of love, it was apprehending the movements of the loved one across all time and space.

She knew more than a little about Charles, and about his family—not simply because she was the hostess of a salon and a terminal of radical gossip but because they were a family about whom things necessarily were known. The desire of the people of San Francisco to have knowledge of the Minots was somehow virtuous—because they were in so many easily demonstrable ways so admirable and so detestable. And the release of knowledge from the family, too, seemed virtuous: We belong to our city, they seemed to admit and proclaim at the same time, to our state, to our country, our God. Playing dumb, sometimes just for the derisive fun of it, sometimes to draw out an unsuspecting and perhaps valuable speaker, was something she did frequently and too easily; she disliked the occasional arrogant nastiness and fundamental lawyer-like deception of it but also could not help but be fascinated by the newly visible person she saw, or thought she saw, blinking uncertainly but hopefully, where the opaque and therefore hostile stranger had been standing. This was especially the case, it turned out, with Charles, whom she was afraid she was prepared to like, despite his wealth, because he was admirable—and because, she was also afraid, he had a target painted on his back.

Taking his feelings as genuine, primary, and direct responses to recent, incontrovertible acts, and noting that all action was incontrovertible and therefore worthy of the most intensely rigorous scrutiny, Charles decided to invite Vera out for an afternoon at the Sutro Baths, on the ocean side of the peninsula. This was an extravagance of engineering in which seven tanks were flushed and filled daily by the tide, several of them heated for the purposes of relaxation, one filled with fresh water: two acres of swimming, diving, and bathing pools within a luminous structure—even on the bleakest and grayest of days—of glass and black iron that could accommodate fifty thousand swimming, eating, drinking, smoking, waltzing, and promenading people.

Vera said that she was familiar with the place: her friends had taken her there after a particular grim and grimy year.

They had taken the lift down from the sidewalk and were staring into the gloom of the basement beneath the motorcycle shop. After a moment Vera stepped across the threshold of metal and cement and motioned for Charles to follow as she opened a door and made her way through a damp dripping space redolent of burnt oil and mildew and gasoline, navigating almost purely by memory between piles of junk and frames of motorcycles like skeletons and disassembled engines with parts spread around them on greasy cloths, all shapeless masses shifting in the dark, until she came to a second door, on which she used a key, selected in darkness and fitted to its lock as surely as if it had been broad daylight. She entered the room and with a long, measured sigh, lit an oil lamp.

A printing press took up most of the room. She took a sheet from the press tray and brought it near the lamp. A cartoonist using pen and ink had drawn a doctor handing a rich woman with a single child a packet of birth control information with one hand, while waving away, with the other hand, behind his back, a poor woman with six or seven children. The caption read: THE BOSS'S WIFE CAN BUY INFORMATION TO LIMIT HER FAMILY AND THE BOSS CAN BUY YOUR CHILDREN TO FILL HIS FACTORIES WITH CHEAP LABOR. She moved to the washstand, glanced at herself in a tiny oval mirror with an ornate grillwork of vines and leaves framing it; then at the old printed slogan:

NO GODS TO FEAR
NO MASTERS TO APPEASE
NO DOGMAS TO RECITE

She stood for a moment staring blankly at it, then back at herself in the little mirror. Some breathlessly unmeasured time later, Charles watched Vera and Vera's reflection as she poured water from the jug into the bowl. She splashed her face and neck and arms and dried herself with a snow-gray towel. With the raspy cloth still to her face, she appeared to remember that she'd not locked the doors behind her. She hung the towel on its hook and turned to the door, where a man strange to Charles now stood.

He looked shy and arrogant on the shadowy threshold, a tender bully. Looking over Vera's shoulder at Charles he said, "I'm sure not that sleek asshole they call 'the American.' In fact, I look like a rat. But I'm not. And I do have whiskey and cigarettes." It took Vera only seconds to recover herself. "I like to drink," she said. "And I like to fuck."

His name was Warren Farnsworth and they had been lovers for some time, but it was understood that the room in the basement was a private, nearly secret place, where he was not, where no one, was welcome. "That's terrific," he said, stepping from the murky shadow into the yellow light. She saw where his dirty suit had been ripped, and fingered it. "Knifework," he said. "Fraction of an inch." He took hold of her fingers and held them for a moment. Then it became clear that he was struggling not to sob, and failing. He made several noises that were more like barks than anything else and his face was wet with tears. "I wouldn't have come down here if I wasn't at the end of my fucking rope," he whimpered. "Get him the fuck out of here, please." She held his head to her breast and then it was over. Warren was embarrassed and turned away. Charles excused himself and made his way back to the lift.

Vera saw Warren was very tired. It took him a long time to slip the coat off. By the time he'd hung it on the nail in the wall, she was naked and under the covers of the little bed. She was looking at the coat, glancing at him, and returning her gaze to the coat.

She thought its folds were as rich with texture and shadow as any Renaissance drapery or cloak, and that he was in every way a superior man—a storm of disgust for the wealth and privilege she normally held in prodigious equanimity had blown up out of a clear sky—to Charles Minot.

But in the wake of the storm: greasy gray pity. She did not enjoy the sex. It was in fact, she realized, the last time she would sleep with him.

Rehearsals the next day were devoted to blocking, to choreography, to the apparently essential movements of persons and things around the stage by means of a timing that was a subset of real time but which required its own very specific measurement, and the marking with chalk of certain apparently important spots on the boards where whatever might be said or done *must* be said and done. It was a different but equally real space and time. But because he mistrusted plans so fundamentally, preferring and hoping—Sir Edwin whispering narcotically into his ear and in his dreams—for a kind of improvised dance instead, he introduced a set of exercises that Sir Edwin had grouped under the heading, THE SHOWING OF HEAVENLY EFFECTS IN EARTHLY ACTORS. He also sometimes referred to them as "Colombian Hypnosis," as he had first seen it practiced at the opera house in Bogota. The purpose of the exercises was to prepare them for what would happen in performance, night after night: they would arrive at the proper place at the proper time, but it would be unfamiliar. Everything would seem to have changed, irrevocably and without a trace of the old and familiar, the chalked X marking the spot of the remembered thing. And so they worked muscles that would relieve them of the pain caused by the tension of being a stranger in a strange land, of living with what Sir Edwin rather awkwardly, in a very brief and incoherent pre-rehearsal speech—the offering of notes—called "the mental illusion of things that aren't really there."

They described circles in the air before them with their left hands, stopped, described crosses with their right hands, stopped, then attempted both at once.

They described circles with their left feet in the chalky dust of the boards and wrote their names in the air with their right.

It was difficult, Charles admitted over the murmuring and sputtered laughter, but not impossible. There was nothing in the body that forbade or prevented these movements. One of his university friends, a chubby red-faced young man who liked to wear short, wide colorful ties, Ted Blair, who could just barely resist Charles's authority—as most of the others could

not—cried out, imitating a Shakespearean declaimer, wanting to know what
was it, then, for God's sake?

The theater smelled strongly of sawn lumber and hot metal and everyone smelled and liked it. There was a haze of sawdust and perhaps the
memory of smoke in the air, faint, but thick enough to soften the surfaces
of things. They were at once omnipotent and unable to act. And knew it.
Hated it, the bizarre license and even more bizarre freedom, and did not understand it, their incapacity in the face of it all, but knew it, and continued
to mutter and chuckle. The echo of Teddy's voice faded into the darkness of
the balcony.

"What is it indeed?" stage-whispered Sir Edwin from the darkness.

Charles and Vera faced each other, not quite close enough for an embrace, but close enough for shapes and features to sharpen and brighten.
Then they became isolated and vivid. He held up his left hand, she, at nearly
the same moment, her right. They began, gently and tentatively, staring into
each other's eyes, to follow the movement of their hands.

The rest of the company paired off and did the same, some only just then
realizing how thick the haze was, and how terrifying the memory. Someone
said there would always be a fire burning in this theater. No one replied.
Vera pressed her hand forward, and Charles pulled his back. He lifted his
left knee, she her right. They continued these simple discrete movements for
a while, then began to combine them, lifting an arm and drawing back and
lifting a foot, as if cocking it to kick, balancing on the planted foot, drawing
the arm down sinuously, as if wiping steam slowly from a mirror.

Vera slowly stretched her neck and moved her face toward Charles's. He
drew his head back, doubling his chin. When she curved her spine toward
him, he arched his backward.

The movements of limbs and torsos and heads and even features
of faces became stranger and more difficult to follow. Vera and Charles
dropped to the floor on hands and knees, maintaining, trying to maintain, the exact relation of face to face, trying to match nearly indiscernible
twitches, flares, curls of eyebrow, nostril, lip.

They rose into a bobbing crouch, and their movements became grotesque. At first the grotesquerie was merely odd, but quickly became stylized, as if that had been the purpose—which, Charles noted with dismay, it had most emphatically not been.

Breathing became an essential part of what was now an amusement.

The respiration of the whole company became pronounced, then exaggerated, filling the theater with roaring and hissing. The acts became ridiculously theatrical: crucifixion, ravishment, courtship, buying, selling, courtship, submission, grandeur.

It was as if the company had stumbled on Delsarte.

Charles suddenly, without the least somatic warning or hinting glint in his eye to Vera, stopped and stood and clapped his hands once, sharply, loud as he could.

CRACK!

Vera scrambled to her feet and visibly, comically, refrained from clapping. Up in the balcony, though, a faint clapping was heard, as if in fading echo.

"Let this always be your relation to each other and your properties—at least while you are on my stage. You are at once omnipotent and unable to move. That is because you will always be caught up, trapped, in the rigid and therefore false drama of character-making—or perhaps I should call it 'me-making,' which happens off the stage as well as on the stage, in exactly the same way—"

"ME-MAKING INDEED!" shouted Sir Edwin from the gloomy balcony. "O ROMEO, ROMEO, WHO THE BLOODY HELL DO YOU THINK YOU ARE?"

As Charles was his company's Romeo, he winced inwardly, thinking Sir Edwin was speaking directly to him. He half-smiled, sourly, rolled his eyes.

In this momentary vacuum, Teddy spoke: "Rennie DAY-cart walks into a bar. Bartender asks him if he'd like a beer. Descartes says, 'I think not.' And disappears." Nobody laughed. Charles began to speak but was interrupted by wheezing from the balcony. When it lapsed into silence, he continued.

"You have no past but whatever you and I make up for you via a pseudo-Stanislavskian method. You have no future but a hope of applause in your own personal limelight. Your present is dictated to you by a script that seems to be autonomous but that is generated every second of every day via an iron-clad will that confirms you in your increasingly rigid beliefs about who you are and how you act. We're all having a great deal of fun with our misunderstanding of Monsieur Delsarte: we raise our arms quickly overhead then just as quickly throw our hands to our thighs, and *voilà*, we have induced laughter in ourselves and if we are lucky in our audience or at least somehow given an impression of it! HOWEVER: I want you to ask yourself what you might be forgetting. I want you to allow me to answer that question for you: you are forgetting that you are nothing without gesture. Try to speak without gesturing. Wrap yourselves in the winding sheets we have been using as we study Strindberg. Lie down in those sheets. Speak your lines. What happens? Meaningful sounds become less meaningful somehow. In certain circumstances they will veer dangerously toward annoying and incomprehensible noise. And unless you have been trained as Mother and I have been trained, you will not even be able to make your noise hearable. Certainly we can be noisy old interfering clowns if we choose to be, but even then, what kind of clown fails to make himself, to make his clowning, clear? What kind of clowns are we on this pathetic little stage?"

"PURVEYORS OF BOMBASTIC NONSENSE!" shouted Sir Edwin who was apparently on his knees in the first row of the balcony, for only his head could be seen, catching a little light from below, over the parapet.

The company looked up at him as one. He waved, waggling his fingers next to his monstrous head.

"We are nothing," Charles said, stifling incipient laughter, fearing Sir Edwin might think he was being made a fool of and hurl himself into the orchestra pit. The theater was so small and so steeply raked that he could conceivably land onstage and perhaps kill one of his actors along with himself. "Nothing without gesture and without an authentic *desire, need, love* for our properties. Have you not noticed how compelling a scene it is when two of our stagehands carry lumber across the stage, bang with their hammers, rip back and forth with their saws? When the plumber lights his oxyacetylene torch? When our stage manager confers with me about a problem in our schedule? These are 'real actions,' you will say, and must therefore have a kind of ordinary gravitas we perforce cannot have, because we are only pretending to act. But you will also say that we usually take no notice of these actions. We do here only because they move in such stark contrast to what we do. We who mince and blubber and wail and gesticulate, or stand helpless and stiff as ramrods, in the belief that our ridiculous fakery is exactly what the customer has bargained for and indeed delights in. Further, it seems apparent that the more ridiculously we behave, the greater their delight. But that is not so. Instantly—*instantly*—as soon as you step out onstage like some mechanical contraption, flapping your arms, grimacing with childish drollery because, oh, oh, the theater brings out the child in everyone, running on a teaspoon of steam that's hissing out your asshole, barking your tragic or witty lines or striking a pose like you're trying to plug your asshole, they will know that they have been had. When they throw rotten fruit and vegetables at us? Know why they do that? Not because they see how fraudulent we have been, but when they see how bad we are at being fraudulent! *Le geste est tout*! Everything in the world of the act, all communication is sung, or perhaps hummed is the better word, the humming accompanied by helpful gestures that people see instinctively and immediately as dance. Or if not immediately and as dance, then without much delay or doubt as something the woefully misunderstood and discredited Delsarte believed was 'the direct agent of the heart . . . the revealer of thought and the commentator upon speech.' The artist, and make no mistake, we are artists, should have three objects: to *move*, to *interest*, to *persuade*. We interest by *language*; we move by *thought*; we move, interest, and persuade by *gesture*. Speech is an act posterior to will, itself posterior to love; this again posterior to judgment, posterior in its turn to memory, which, finally, is posterior to the impression. HAVE I GOT THAT RIGHT, SIR EDWIN?"

"Yes," he said, barely audible from the balcony. "Do carry on."

"Which is to say, everything lies static and helpless in the brain until we can figure out how best to present our show to everything that we perceive to be outside our brains. Our audience."

Vera began to clap, but nobody picked it up, and she stopped.

Three days later, Charles arrived at the motorcycle shop, devoted still to the idea of taking her to Sutro Baths, to, generally speaking, picking up where they'd left off with the appearance of Warren Farnsworth.

"You said something about a bad year?" asked Charles.

They were standing on the sidewalk, waiting for a jitney driven by a friend of Vera's.

"Yes," she said. "Last year."

"What was it," Charles asked, "if you don't mind my asking, made last year so bad?"

"The free press became markedly less free."

"Did it indeed?"

"Indeed it did!"

"Beg your pardon if that sounded—"

"Not at all."

"—ironic. Life is ironic and I make it a principle to be simple and straightforward whenever possible to maintain a clear and useful distinction."

"Not at all, not at all! Clearly and usefully distinct!"

"Even more simply and straightforwardly I must admit I hadn't noticed—"

"No, of course not, you were looking at the surface of the newspaper. The repression was—*is*—being worked below the surface."

"Of course. I have no difficulty believing you. That is in fact why I am apologizing: that I should have been caught out staring at the surface. Me! It's absurd. I feel like an—"

"Well, you mustn't!"

"Very well. Thank you. Now please allow me to ask you how you yourself were able to see below the surface . . . ?"

"I defended the press in the basement. I gave over a good deal of myself to it, in a fanatical, Russian-style defense of the secrecy of the location of this press. For the sake of its freedom. A great deal. And I lost that great deal. I wasted it. Only three people knew the press was here, and because I was its minder, its drone, because I volunteered, I felt very deeply responsible for it, and I stayed there, in that room, for a year. I'm not kidding. A year. Never went out. They brought my meals into me, and yes, some books. What was I so afraid of? In the land of the free and the home of the brave? Isn't the freedom of the press secured in the Constitution? Who cared that we were printing what we were printing? You may ask all those things and be only reasonable. Maybe my fear was unreasonable! But let me tell you, this was a question—the location, the existence, of a certain kind of press, an uncontrolled press, *one that was in truth free*—that had *already had*, believe it or not, grave consequences attending its answer! Your father will never see a speck of evidence to back up my claim, but let me assure you, Mr. American, *it is true*."

Vera stopped, removed her glasses, and cleaned them. Holding them in her hand, she resumed her speech in a quieter voice. "Then I had a little bit of a collapse, my consciousness collapsed into a pool of tears, and you know, they got me out of here, *took me to Sutro Baths* and so on, but I didn't like being outside. I felt I was transparent. Almost."

Wildly in love with her, thinking just that, Charles said nothing.

"There's no way that can make sense. You give your life over to spreading the news, you know, letting people hear what's really going on, but at the same time you are yourself some kind of terrible secret that must never get out. Like I say, I was already pretty Russian around the edges, and I was reading Nechayev's *Revolutionary Catechism*. You know what I mean, I think . . . ."

She looked up and mistook Charles's expression of overwhelming desire for evidence that he did not in fact know what she meant, that he was disdainful almost to the point of anger.

And yet she drew much closer.

"The revolutionary can have no love, no friendship, no joy, no life, no self. All is required by the revolution. Everything is sacrificed for the sake of others. You starve for the starving, suffer oppression for the oppressed, terrorize for the terrorized, murder and destroy for the murdered and destroyed. But now I don't give a shit. I mean that in a positive way. The press is beautiful. It's just like William Morris's and he was a beautiful man: fine, okay, good. But its days are numbered. They're going to get it sooner or later and they're going to smash it to pieces, so why make myself crazy watching over it, like some daffy shepherdess. I'll use it while I can. When they take it, I'll use something else. See? I'm all better!"

Better or not, she appeared to have exhausted herself, for she sat down on a bench in front of one of the shop windows, this one displaying the painted symbol of the Flying Merkel brand, and held her head in her hands.

As they drove across the dunes of the Western Addition, Charles recounted his days as a competitive swimmer. "With my long arms and legs and broad shoulders, I was a natural swimmer and as helplessly gifted physically as I was mentally and socially. I quickly became captain of the team. Then a gentleman from Hawaii arrived on the scene. He was an ambassador of an ancient Polynesian pastime called "wave sliding," and was reputed to be an excellent swimmer as well. An exhibition race was arranged between the Sutro Baths Club and the Hawaiian, and while everyone understood that the Hawaiian was possibly the best swimmer in the world, it was also widely believed that old Charlie Minot could upset him, given the home water and proper circumstances. Some would have inserted weights in the Hawaiian's trunks but couldn't figure out how to do it without being noticed. In fact, we were neck and neck for the first fifty yards, the Wave Slider and the Boy Wonder. Quite a large crowd was in the grandstand, and they made quite a lot of noise in that echo chamber until the turn, when the Hawaiian pulled away as if he'd had a Swedish outboard motor attached to his feet. He finished the second fifty so swiftly he seemed to have been pretending during the first. That, Vera my dear, was in fact how I saw it, and I was humiliated."

Vera laughed at the idea of such trivial humiliation.

They arrived and walked into the large entrance hall. A photograph of the competitors was framed and hung in the gallery that marked a diversion to the Sutro Baths' Museum of California. The photograph was signed by the Hawaiian, who went on to win a gold medal at the Olympics in Stockholm and become the sheriff of Hawaii, and everyone is smiling good-naturedly in his dark and charismatic presence—"Save me," said Charles as he and Vera stood leaning toward it in serious examination, "over whom you surely see a cloud of truth passing. I was not only imperfect, I was cold. The women were all over the Hawaiian. Oh, I suppose they were in some sense all over me as well, given that I was wealthy and good-looking, and this was 1913 when all was well in our once-more-fair city—but a powerful force repelled them. I found them daffy, trivial. When pressured to treat some matter or thought with serious attention they became mean or defiantly stupid. Of course I was afraid I was taking my own—my own *what*, deficiencies of spirit?—out on them, didn't want them to feel repelled, and eyed them all as if I were simply a particularly choosy Don Juan. But something else, much deeper, much stranger, was wrong with me. I thought, yes, there is one reality that is immutable, and that is where my spirit resides, but there is another reality, one that changes constantly and which can be, which ought to be, somehow, enjoyed. But I could not."

Oh yes, he was a man, a holy Romantic man, and women still loved him, would still love him, after his voice changed, after he was no longer an angel. They would love him no matter what his voice sounded like. Love him because he was rough and immediate at the same time he was holy and remote. He was, on the stage of the theater of the universe, a great player, a great and holy player, capable of anything and everything. He would be loved immoderately and never forgotten. He would compose as Pergolesi had composed, if only for himself—the Voice was in the Mind—and live on brightly lit stages, exposing the real for what it was: a sham. And when he died, he would be remembered by everybody but mourned only by a handful, who knew who he really was, what he had really done, and the women who had shamefully, secretly loved him as a boy, who had petted and kissed him to the point where he'd had to take a firm step back and give them a look: a cock of the head, eyebrow charmingly raised, a half-smile. *You have enlightened me. Now, darling, go away.* Enlightenment, endarkenment—he had to fiddle constantly with his terms and in the end was not all that interested in consistency and cogency. If, in the back of his mind, there was tacit admission that once or twice perhaps it was *at* him the looks had been given, coming from the shadow faces above the long, slender, gloved arms that had removed the delicious cheeks and swelling bosoms . . . that hardly mattered, either. What mattered was the smell of the perfume. The taste of the skin. The faint rushing sound of the fabrics of their dresses. The looks in their eyes as they lied to themselves and saw him refusing to lie to himself, were frightened or in a sexually muddled awe of him—or, yes, appraised him from a new vantage point which they refused to let startle them: *The little angel wants me! This is San Francisco—might I . . . get away with it?* If they wanted it, they would have to come and get it, because he knew he did not know how to get it for himself. Or rather, he knew but felt a constraint he was not yet willing to loosen. But oh, he would give it to them and take it from them because he wanted it and wanted to give it away—but he knew. He was not a fool. The constraint was there for a good reason. He was a sound and balanced young man in a state of permanent temptation by Lust for the Unreal. Even if he went blind! Feeling alone would be enough, because the whole of his body could see: the palms of his hands following the curve of their shoulders, his fingers lightly tracing their lips—because, of course, out of tender pity, they would allow him to explore their bodies with his hands: *it was the least they could do for the little angel singing in the heavenly darkness.* Women would want to make love to his portrait centuries after he'd become rags and bones. He let himself think these thoughts. He could use them when he performed. He allowed himself to revel in it, but then, quickly, quickly, but not hastily, not insincerely or conveniently, the revelry would turn resolutely to revilement. He was not a rake. He would make no progress. After a while, he would step off the stage and never return. He would not, could not, hate his body. He would simply put it off. Yes, another controversial thought: sex was a childish thing. He would put it off, shake it off like a coat, fold it over the back of a chair, give it to the Salvation Army. San Franciscans who, let our wise little angel speak candidly for a moment, who more often than not were *not* the masters of the Deadly Sins they entertained, who were caught up in the whirlwind of politics and business of Regeneration, who said, who orated it, that they worked for the miserable poor, for the welfare of every citizen of—let us say it again, humbly, the greatest nation the world has ever known, but who, in the end, couldn't quite be parted from one penny of their profits or one wan meaningless exercise of power? Oh, it was not only the bedrock of the American way of life—whether they conquered their sins or their sin conquered them, or if it was a draw, an inconclusive negotiation, it was as important to Charles, the young man who had waited out his time as an adorable angel and was now ready for Regeneration of his own making, as anything could possibly have been. Charles aimed to be a Christian *artist*. A *humble* artist, not a crazed zealot. His heart was wholly engaged, as was his mind. If he was not a zealot he nevertheless saw no room for the compromise of his belief. The fevers came and went. That was life. He lived. As an eleven-year-old boy he had read, on his surprised and pleased sister's advice—she had been learning to calm her nerves not with the power and glory but with the solace and wonder, the serenity of Christ—Rauschenbusch's *Christianity and the Social Crisis* and then, in the wake of the disaster, the horror, he had seen the actual nature of the Universe. If the connection was obscure to his friends and family, obscure to the point of irrelevancy, that only confirmed him. You helped the poor with food and shelter and clothing and a love that was just like the love you had for yourself, and when that was not enough—as surely it could never be—you demonstrated the unreality of everything around them, thereby helping them by preparing them to die—not just die, but die with joy and relief and expectation of eternal bliss. Everything could disappear in an instant and be replaced in an instant. Everything in fact was destroyed and remade every instant. There was nothing more dependably solidly real than the imagination, and the best place to demonstrate the incontrovertible reality of the imagination was on a stage.

If you could not afford a ticket, space would be made for you anyway. He did not want to work it out systematically, philosophically. He wanted to make it. He wanted to make it appear on a stage, like a magic trick that suddenly made everything around it the illusion. There was your salvation, wretched of the earth: the only life is in Jesus Christ, and you have to be destroyed to know it. Watch the brightly colored mannequins on the stage and you will see The Way.

"Christopher Newman is the name of the character you are playing in *The American*." Sir Edwin spoke calmly but firmly to Charles, who had suddenly realized what an abyss lay between rehearsal and performance, and who was consequently experiencing the last condition he thought he would ever feel, that of "stage fright." He had somehow convinced or duped himself, via his own obscure speeches to the company, into thinking something was at stake that had never been at stake before, and was going to pieces. "You are like him in many ways, perhaps too many ways: Newman could have been your grandfather—"

"The chronology isn't quite right—more like a much older brother of Father's, or a half-brother from an earlier marriage."

"And while your diligence in constructing a biography of Newman that would have pleased Stanislavsky in the early years of the Moscow Art Theater is remarkable and laudable, it would not have much impressed the Stanislavsky of today, now that the idea that it can all be worked out in advance of the actor appearing on the stage and moving about has been repudiated as being of little avail when the actor does in fact appear on the stage and move about—repudiated as being an actual and frustratingly burdensome hindrance. The tone and volume of your voice, the manner of your accommodation of the other actors onstage with him, the nature and timing of your gestures and the effect the properties you handle has on you—this is as you have tirelessly and perhaps tiresomely noted is what matters, and is the means by which Christopher Newman might be located and animated. You are to spend no more time on thought, but quickly and quietly enter into what is to be done, whether you are James's Newman, Shakespeare's Romeo, or Strindberg's Arkenholz. If you insist in your panic on illustrating your speeches to make sure everyone understands, you will, I assure you, vanish from the stage. It is a magic trick, from which anti-magic will spring. You are a big, tough Christian." Sir Edwin was now, inexplicably, speaking with a Russian accent. Charles supposed it was because they had been talking about Stanislavsky. "You are at home in world."

"Do you mean me or Newman?"

Sir Edwin waved his hands in disgust. "I dun't care vhich one. You must be at home in vorld or we will bore audience to greatest disgust they can endure without throwing rotten wegetables at you. You must be, can only be, who you are. What does Polonius say to you, whoever you are, you ridiculous boy. 'To thine own self be true. And it must follow as the night the day, *thou canst not then be false.*'" He had reverted to stage English for this quotation and waved off Charles's certain question as to why he was talking about *Hamlet* all of a sudden.

"I understand that," Charles said, "but I can only play such a man as a cartoon."

"You can only be self as if you are cartoon."

"Yes."

Sir Edwin produced a notebook and asked Charles to read out a marked passage.

"'He was not given, as a general thing, to anticipating danger, or forecasting disaster, and he had no social tremors. He was not timid and he was not impudent. He felt too kindly toward himself to be the one, and too good-naturedly toward the rest of the world to be the other. But his native shrewdness sometimes placed his ease of temper at its mercy; with every disposition to take things simply, it was obliged to perceive that some things were not so simple as others. He felt as one does in missing a step, in an ascent, where one expected to find it.'"

Sir Edwin clapped his hands and stood up from his favorite seat in the balcony. He suggested loudly that if Charles moved about the stage as if both timid and impudent, such behavior would be tiresome for an audience and finally unendurable. It would be his own fault because he could not or would not get over himself and simply be himself.

"You are actor," said Sir Edwin. "Act."

"I do not have this character within me. I would be perpetrating a ridiculous fraud upon our audience if I pretended I did. And whether or not they find my honesty tiresome, as you say, I do not care."

"Stop whining and fretting and complenning and do what you must do."

"I am not whining and fretting and—"

Sir Edwin shot an arm out from beneath his cloak and silenced Charles: If he was this certain kind of very particular fraud, why then not simply admit it? Why not accept himself for what he was and have the courage of his convictions? If he was a fraud then why could he not say so to the people who mattered, the ones who were paying good money to hear what he had to say? If he was a fraud he should stand there and defraud them all, not whimper to his fellow infants.

"I am not whimpering."

"You are whimpering coward, Charles!"

"Do not call me a coward."

"Why! Iz not truth?"

"Is not hull truth," Charles mimicked faintly.

"You are coward. You say it many times yourself!"

"When I say that I mean something else entirely."

Sir Edwin swirled his cloak around himself as if he were waltzing with it. He made a grand gesture suggesting tragedy, then asked Charles if he did not know, could not tell, the difference between someone standing before him and earnestly trying to pass himself off as something he clearly was not, and an actor doing the very same thing.

"If you cannot, you are hupliss."

Somewhere in the deep backstage, the carpenter who'd been battening a piece of twenty-four-gauge sheet iron to make a thunder sheet, dropped it; the ensuing crash of thunder caused the troupe—most of whom appeared to have been chatting but who were actually practicing the ancient *commedia* skill of *grammelot*, or nonsensical speech—to fall silent, just as they would have for the real thing.

"Very WELL!" shouted Charles. "I am HUPLISS!"

Because his Russian accent was funny, and because he had been experimenting with makeup techniques that were supposed to make him look twenty years older but which actually made him look like something halfway between a Minoan god-king and Rigoletto, a court jester with painted wrinkles and a square, curly beard pasted on his jaw, and finally because the conversations that had been interrupted had been intense but meaningless, his temper tantrum triggered a hilarity that was almost unnatural in its duration. But at its close he too was wiping tears of joy from his eyes. He felt he had learned something of great value. He was at least at home in this world, and it was possible that he "loved" it, loved everything about it, including the crazy, stinking Sir Edwin, making believe, and his own stage fright.

They would open in three hours.

He sat slumped and ill in a low broken chair in the green room. His knees rose up before him, so low and broken was this chair, and because they were so prominent, he tapped first one and then the other and then the first again with his diamond-studded walking stick. After a few minutes of this, he rearranged himself, the stick now between his legs, bearded chin and dove-gray gloved hands resting on the pearly knob. He appeared to be listening to something or someone, but no one in the cramped little room was speaking.

His knees had brushed his chin when he walked up the smoky staircase the night of the fire—why had he felt so calm then, and so sick now?

There were six others: Teddy Blair, whose demeanor was unassuming but whose voice was both explosively large and exquisitely controlled, got up to look like a portly older man, perched on one arm of my chair, smoking pensively a cigarette in a very long holder; two young women, Vera dressed to suggest a princess of the Second Empire, the other, the shockingly pretty Mary Girdle, a social-climbing bohemian trollop, both staring at, alternately, themselves and each other in a big but cracked mirror framed with electric light bulbs which gave them looks of stark madness; another young man, a dandy from the Philosophy Club, Eugene Woodcock, playing a charming ne'er-do-well, who appeared to be praying, his eyes closed tightly, his hands clasped, and his mouth trembling with the shapes of words; also from Berkeley and the P. Club, a much older man not associated with the university, Leonardo Garagiola, playing a very old man; and a plain, athletic middle-aged woman only recently arrived from Michigan, Margaret Stensrud, playing an ancient dowager, who, with Leonardo, was peering intently at her game of solitaire.

There were others but he had lost track of them. He had never known them and he did not want to know them now.

Suddenly the old man broke away and walked briskly to the doorway of an adjoining room—one of the spaces of the theater that had been burned and only hastily repaired—where the others had silently chosen to sequester themselves. He looked in at them and rubbed his hands together as if in eager glee. Small, distracted chuckles could be heard for a moment from within. Then Vera, very much the princess, Claire de Cintré, suddenly shouted, "No, no, no, you look just right! You look perfect, you really do! It's the stupid play that looks wrong! You look *alluring*. You look *wonderful*." And the other threw herself into her friend's arms. They hugged and kissed and withheld makeup-smearing tears with desperate care.

Beyond the little rooms somewhere, the continuo group, augmented for opening night with a wind band, began to play "The Star-Spangled Banner." Charles laid his cane across his lap and bent forward, pale and sweating now, until his head was between his legs. They could hear the audience now too, singing along lustily. One of the plumber's surviving little sons stuck his head in the room and called out that the house lights were going to half. Charles dropped his cane with a clatter and vomited.

Little notice was taken. He himself was too exhausted to care. The Marquis de Bellegarde lifted his foot away from the splatter and said, "They start singing the national anthem and Chuckles throws up!" He stood and adjusted his false belly. "I'll get you a glass of water, bud."

"Here's a rag!" whinnied the dowager in her stage voice. "Poor dear!" She hadn't looked up from her game, however.

"How very ironic," the old man concluded, shooting his eyes comically left and right.

"Ironic?" murmured the dowager.

"That Chucky should vomit at the sound of the anthem when he's—"

"Mmm . . . ? Oh yes. Yes, I see what you are—MY GOD I WISH THEY'D STOP THEIR CATERWAULING!" She wiped her eyes. "It's like a church service."

Charles stood uncertainly, then drew himself up with a deep breath. To polite applause, he announced that he was all right and that he felt better, none of the diamonds had been dislodged from his incredibly expensive prop cane, everything, he was sure, was going to be okay. The dandy and the trollop left the room. The marquis said that it sounded as if half of San Francisco were out there.

"How many seats have we?" he asked.

The princess replied that he knew perfectly well how many.

Everyone was now on edge and eager to show it with any kind of clamped-down hysteria they could find.

The dowager swept the cards from her little table with a cry of outrage. "But I *don't*, dear!"

"One hundred and thirty-seven," Charles said, accepting the glass of water.

The plumber's son poked his head around the door again and said they'd sold fifty standing-room-only tickets as well.

"*No!*" cried the very old man.

"Yes they *did*," insisted the little boy.

Charles let the rag drop to my feet. The vomitus was actually little more than bile and saliva, and he toed the rag back and forth in it, soaking it up. When he stopped, he looked up to find everyone in the room watching him.

"*Where*," inquired the marquis, "is one's valet when one has *need* of him?"

"Fuck you," said Charles, without real conviction, rehearsing.

"Fuck me?" asked the marquis, equally wanly. He stood and adjusted his sash. "Fuck *you*."

Charles stooped and quickly brought the smelly, dripping rag to the marquis's nose, who scrambled out of the way, bumping into the very old man, who in turn sat down in the lap of the dowager, who had picked up her cards and dealt herself a new game. They all laughed.

"I'll beat you all with my diamond-studded cane," offered Charles.

"Oh yes, please!" they all moaned and jiggled.

"*Places*," hissed the stage manager, who appeared out of nowhere. "What on *earth* is the *matter* with you people?"

"You have upset my game," said the dowager coolly. "God*damn* you to hell."

She and the princess crossed themselves, the princess suddenly pale and crazy-looking, her deep voice even deeper now with dread. "Here we go," she said, as if from the tomb.

The dowager went to pieces again. "We are just not ready!" she shrieked. "I can't believe you're going to force us *out there* like this! To just . . . *throw us out there*! To the, to the . . . to the *dogs*!"

Charles sidled quietly over to the princess and told her that he was in love with her. He had clearly said it as Christopher Newman, but he had said it in a place where Christopher Newman did not exist. And saying so gave him an erection—he couldn't understand it: it was not something that would happen to Christopher Newman. Refusing to turn her face to Charles, Vera glanced at him with a kind of calm but insane expectancy.

"Do you love me?" he asked, not knowing what else to say, and having no time to think about it.

"No," she said, swiveling her eyes back at him. "No, Charles, I do not. But I will suck your cock after our first scene."

"You will?" he asked.

"Yes. I will."

"All right."

"Why *shouldn't* I?" she wailed in sudden terror. "Give me a thousand dollars and I'll do it."

Theater was happening and nobody could stop it.

Charles felt suddenly defeated. "It won't work. Never mind. If you need some money I'll give you some."

Sir Edwin stood in the doorway, rubbing his hands just as the very old man had done. Never before had he seemed so completely depraved a monk as he did then. Charles saw now only looks of panic and frank hatred on those faces that had beamed only the day before, the hour before, with childlike devotion and the most intimate trust in his mystic vision, and so was not surprised to see their Mad Englishman gone from the doorway when he looked back.

He walked from the green room to the nearest wing, still sipping his glass of water, and examined the scenery-flat flying ropes knotted to the pin rail. The knots, he believed, looked secure and well tied. He climbed up to the fly gallery: shipshape here as well. He was no longer ill, no longer afraid; he was in fact utterly oblivious to his surroundings. As if he were a casual bystander, he looked out onstage, at the "shabby sitting room on a small Parisian *quatrième*," sparely suggested by odds and ends of furniture collected from the theater's patrons—from people, he marveled, like Durwood Keogh. He loathed Keogh, of course, but could not say why, not precisely, in that moment anyway, and was stricken with gratitude at the gifts of furniture. The curtain was still down, but he could feel the force, the weight of nearly two hundred expectant people just beyond it. He felt curious and intrigued: it trembled, whatever it was out there, a faint wave that rippled from one end of the curtain to the other, as if the breathing of the audience had taken on the properties of a breeze. The idea that they were not individuals, but rather one great thing, was not new to him, or theater folk in general, but he felt it now—not in his guts, where it had just finished making him nauseous, but in his heart, where it made him not brave but fearless: he didn't care. He didn't think he cared, anyway, didn't feel that he cared. And wasn't that how daredevils felt? It was only *one thing* and he didn't care what *one thing* might think or say about him, or even directly to him. It knew nothing of him, after all, if it thought he was not part of its own "one-thingness" and its judgment would perforce be poorly constituted, superficial, beside the point if not altogether contemptibly mean-spirited. He was now a little angry, and when he realized it, was surprised at himself. He wanted to be calm again. Not caring was not an acceptable alternative. He wanted to be serene and helpful. But that was not how he had been trained to enter the scene.

"They will get the show they deserve, eh?" whispered the marquis, plumping his belly.

"We had better be good," Charles whispered, his heart suddenly pounding.

"Yes," agreed the marquis. "They will tar and feather us if we aren't."

The curtain rose in voluminous, screeching jerks, and what had only seemed a polite silence was now terrifying condemnation. A man in the balcony cleared his throat.

Would the balcony collapse?

The footlights, which still ran on gas, snapped and quivered behind their mesh grating. The dandy chased the trollop, Noémie, around the stage. They scampered and minced in a way that made his heart sink. Noémie then stopped in her tracks and the dandy nearly collided with her: it was slapstick. It would be all right because slapstick was foolproof. She held up an imperious finger and said, "I declare that if you touch me, I'll paint you all over!"

And the audience, unaccountably, roared with laughter.

"What do you know," whispered the marquis. He and Charles exchanged an incredulous but pleased look; the laughter was infectious.

He couldn't wait now to get onstage. The first scene was interminable and then there he was, striding languidly, confidently, handsomely, richly, "the American," into the limelight. He approached a painting around which Noémie coyly fluttered. He stared and stared for what in a theater seemed a very long time, a dangerously long time—but it was working, he could feel it and he liked it—and then he judged it. He pointed with his fabulous walking stick.

"That's just what I want to see!" he said with clear, carrying warmth.

The audience knew he was a man for whom people would wait, for whom *they* would wait. They wanted to wait for Christopher the American. They wanted to know what he thought and why he liked the painting so much. They wanted, in that strange and almost perverse turning of the table that sometimes happens in show business, his approval.

Charles's approval.

Noémie contrived to appear indifferent. "I think I've improved it," she said of the painting, looking not at it, but at Charles. She could feel the audience's wish to participate in his world, and saw that she could bask in their love if she played her cards properly. She quietly let her admiration become apparent as he let a good deal more of his character appear.

"Well," he said, "yes, I suppose you've improved it; but I don't know, I liked it better before it was quite so *good*! However, I guess I'll take it."

He was neither, strictly speaking, himself nor Christopher Newman, and his agonized, neurotically observant introspection seemed vain and peculiar to him now, in that moment. He was acutely aware of employing himself to create the illusion of Christopher Newman, and confident that nothing could be more natural than to do so. "He" was a decent and amiable but shrewd and relentless man who'd made a fortune after the Civil War and who had come to Europe to spend some of it, a lot of it, "learning about beauty." When the beauty turned out to be visible to him solely in the face of a young French widow, and he was confronted with the absurd strictures of the ancient families of the aristocracy—who were eager to bathe in the rivers of his cash but who could never allow him to marry one of their own—his quiet outrage and candid determination to have his reasonable but passionate way filled the theater. He loved the sad and lonely Claire with all his great and open heart, and he would be damned if he could not make the world work the way he wanted it to work.

The one great thing took him in, amplified him a thousandfold, and sent him back to himself in wave after wave until at the end it all seemed to be crashing on the stage. They were already cheering and whistling and stamping before he could say his last lines: "Ah, my beloved!" and kiss Claire's hand, causing her to cry—she who had been so remote and resigned to despair for three solid hours—"You've done it, you've brought me back, you've vanquished me!"

Just before the curtain-closing kiss, he shouted, bellowed really, in his superb opera-quality tenor, as it was now quite hard to hear, "THAT'S JUST WHAT I WANTED TO SEE!"

The orchestra played a Sousa march throughout the rainstorm of applause, while the cast, bowing repeatedly and smiling broadly, waved little American flags. The only cloud of truth that passed between himself and the audience was his glimpse of Sir Edwin in the wings. Neither smiling nor frowning, seeming neither pleased nor relieved, he watched Charles demonstrate his gracious ease, his graceful courage, in Neverland—and of course Charles watched him. He had not the faintest throb of an erection: *dead dead dead.* An erection was, he had decided, the only sure indication he was alive. Millions of souls, swiftly and easily replaced, every time he came. So yes, he was troubled even as the packed house cheered and cheered and cheered him.

Around a lighted doorway on Filbert, halfway between Stockton and Grant, next to the motorcycle shop, he could make out ten or fifteen figures, people, no doubt, conversing unintelligibly and waiting for their turn to ascend a narrow flight of stairs. Those in the yellow light gestured to those in the shapeless dark. When he appeared, way was made for him, as it always was, and he climbed the stairs slowly. He reached the yellow lamp itself and perceived it as some kind of lamp in a fairy tale, with a life of its own and a secret, or as a beacon very far away that only seemed near because of a trick of sorcery or atmospheric anomaly. A small group had formed around this light and in the open doorway. Talkers gestured carelessly with drinks as they worked elaborate rhetorical figures. He entered an apartment in which a common party or reception appeared to be taking place. Noisy and crowded, the room looked as if it had been shaken in the earthquake and neglected since. It appeared to tilt: the lines of the walls, floor, and ceiling seeming neither parallel nor perpendicular. Wallpaper, depicting various scenes from *The Odyssey*, hung in peeling strips from the walls, and the floorboards were warped and discolored. The place was less sturdy than a stage set, and less convincing. There were newspapers everywhere, scattered as if they'd been caught by a wind, stacked in sloping piles next to anything that might support them, rolled up in people's fists, spread open on tables.

Turning from the crowd to the wall and the bookshelves against it, he saw many volumes of Balzac, in French, bound in blue. He selected his favorite, *Le Père Goriot*, opened it, or rather let it fall open to a page upon which it had, clearly, many times before been opened, to where the cynical, worldly wise lodger Vautrin is exposed as a criminal mastermind. He read to himself, translating the French and remembering the English: "Vautrin was at last revealed complete: his past, his present, his future, his ruthless doctrines, his religion of hedonism . . . his Devil-may-care strength of character. The blood mounted in his cheeks and his eyes gleamed like a wildcat's. He sprang back with savage energy and let out a roar that drew shrieks of terror from the boarders." Is Monsieur Vautrin here tonight? he wondered. Is the owner of this building some kind of Vautrin? Is there perhaps not a flaw of Vautrinism in all of our characters?

He picked up a newspaper to cover the swell of this attractive thought: *The Tremor*, one he'd never seen before. The masthead lettering was drawn as if it stood on shaky ground, little shivering lines suggesting vulnerability, uncertainty, and the front page featured a cartoon of a Pinkerton detective, a tiny but slope-browed and lantern-jawed head atop a huge, grossly muscled body spilling from a shapeless coat, drawn with a heavy but expert hand in dark smears of charcoal. The caption read, "IF YOU CAN'T BEAT 'EM, FRAME 'EM." He studied the monstrous detective and saw now a little round bomb, spitting sparks, tiny as the fellow's head, concealed in a meaty fist. Opening the paper, he glanced at one column, "The Fine Print," and another, "A Fair Shake," then shuffled and squared the pages, folded the paper neatly, and set it on the shelf next to the Balzac. A pleasant sense of peril overcame him, and he looked around the room with a mixture of furtiveness and mock-furtiveness: Were there in fact bombers here? Real bombers, dressed and speaking like ordinary citizens concerned about culture and the public weal? He remembered a breakfast table talk from a decade earlier: Father's insistence that ninety-eight known dynamiters in the Bay Area were going to be rounded up, whether they'd done anything or not, whether, he had asked with the sarcasm his father detested, they were dynamiters or not. Might the place be raided by "authorities"? Might there not be people here wearing serious disguises—that is to say, real disguises as opposed to the fake ones they used on the stage? Might not the ratio of disguised to undisguised people be excitingly large?

He thought for a moment of a painting Mother had bought when they were in Paris, an Ensor, a crowd scene in which the difference between a mask and a face was hard to see, as all seem caught up in some kind of knowledge giving way to terror.

The man nearest him, as tall but lighter both in weight and color, whom he thought he might have seen that strange day in the motorcycle shop below, when he'd come to unload his Merkel and the laughable Minerva, began to speak more loudly than he had been, to the man he was not quite hiding. "Dickens," the man said, "and Dostoyevsky did not write books, they wrote newspapers! Why, a list of passengers sailing on the *Kronprinz Wilhelm* is more nearly a work of art than a novel by Thomas Hardy!"

He liked all three of the novelists named, and couldn't begin to understand the speaker's complaint. Neither could he begin to feel a duty to inquire and comprehend. He had no wish to be caught up in popular criticism, and looked away at a large poster just on the other side of the bookshelves. "The I. W. W. is COMING!" it proclaimed across the top, while at the bottom demanding or suggesting that the observer "Join the ONE BIG UNION!" A handsome, young Wobbly, bare-chested and muscular, appeared to be climbing right up out of the picture and the smoking mills in its background, over a barricade and preparing to hurl himself into the room.

"No, give me Henry James when I want a novel." The tall, fair man who disliked Hardy and Dostoevsky and Dickens had shifted his stance and was now openly looking at him. He glanced at the poster and again at Charles. "Looks like you!" he shouted with theatrical bonhomie, then resumed his jolly and opinionated conversation with the hidden man, who peered around his friend and smiled at Charles. "We also spoke of the meanings of strange words: *flic, gigolette, maquereau, tapette,* and *rigolo.* I bought a naughty silk scarf and a pair of Louis XV candlesticks. I had an omelet at the Café de la Regence, where the actors from the *Comedie Francaise* have lunch in their makeup!" The hidden man shifted his position and both men now looked at Charles, as if, it seemed, he were an actress in her makeup. He had surely seen the hidden man in the shop that day as well. The tall, fair man then shook his head at the hidden man, who said, "I am preoccupied with thoughts and images of death, most certainly. Let us find actresses."

Another man, much shorter and skinnier, with fierce, sharp, tiny features, including a moustache of very few but longish hairs, and a shock of blond hair angling off his small head, had drawn up in their lee. A kindly looking, older woman held his arm. Charles recognized him after a hazy swarming pause in which his knowledge overwhelmed his ability to know he knew: Warren Farnsworth.

"Does look like you," said Farnsworth. "But you're somebody else entirely, isn't *that* so?"

"It's true, yes, I'm afraid you're right," Charles confessed suavely. "I am someone else entirely."

"Do you," Farnsworth asked suddenly, without preamble, but slowly and quietly, "think they will bomb the parade?"

"Parade?" asked Charles. "Pardon?"

"The Preparedness Day Parade?" Farnsworth seemed incredulous now, instantly annoyed.

"Oh yes," Charles said, quickly and reassuringly, "Durwood Keogh's project."

Farnsworth flared his nostrils at the mention of the playboy railroader, and breathed with difficulty for a moment. Then he worked out a way to smile at Charles again.

"Do you think they will?"

"Do I . . . ?"

"Think they will bomb the fucking parade." Farnsworth's smile had become exaggerated, his eyebrows wagging as if to say, you're very bright, but see if you can follow me now. He spoke in a quiet and friendly way. The woman, without weakening or exaggerating her features, shushed him.

"No, no, I—"

"You think they *won't*, is that right? That they *will not*?" Farnsworth probed with great care.

"No. I mean I don't know," Charles said. "I mean I sure hope not."

Farnsworth sighed. "I've been taking bets all month." Suddenly but tenderly he had Charles's lapel between finger and thumb. "'I hope not' doesn't qualify. Those days are gone. I was certainly a man who lived in hope! Do you read the papers? Because they're making threats. 'We will bomb you warmongering bloodsuckers back to the Stone Age.' Is this the work of some inept or cowardly crackpot? Or one of us here tonight? Which is not to say there are no cowardly or inept crackpots here! But you see, you have all the elements in place now."

Farnsworth waited for an answer.

"Yes," Charles said. "I do?"

"Place your bet!"

"I'm sorry," Charles pled. "Sounds like a great deal of fun but I'm afraid I can't."

"STOP LOOKING AT ME LIKE THAT!"

Startled, Charles nevertheless understood the command to be not directed at him, and he looked over his shoulder as—deciding at the last moment—
a vaudevillian might.

"Come, come, Mr. Farnsworth, leave the gentleman alone now," said the
man, whom Charles recognized as "Owner."

"If he's everything they say he is," said Farnsworth reasonably and calmly, "then the last thing I should do is leave him alone." He refocused on
Charles. "Are you everything they say you are?"

"I don't know," Charles said. "I'm afraid that's just another question I
can't answer, much as I'd like to." Succumbing to the guilty pleasure of sarcasm, he added that he'd thought it was understood that he was someone
else entirely. Farnsworth ignored him—he was already too goddamned
oblique—but the woman fixed him momentarily. Her gaze was like a vise.

She said, in a sweet and gentle voice: "If you are everything they say
you are, if you're William Minot's son, if you're 'the American' everybody's
talking about, then I think you would be concerned very deeply indeed with
the Preparedness Day Parade and what may or may not happen on that day
and to whom."

"Well!" Charles exclaimed, "for starters, excuse me, ma'am, I guess I'll
have to say I'm not everything they say I am. It's true I am William Minot's
son, but it's also true that if he learned I was talking to a socialist he'd send
me to my room without supper."

Surprisingly, Farnsworth laughed heartily at the notion, as did Owner
and the tall, fair man.

"And 'the American' is a role I play onstage. I don't know what the hell
it has to do with anything you're talking about. Unless it's money you want."

"Fuck your money," said Farnsworth with a frightening turn of humor.

"Look here, old man," said Charles with an all-purpose British accent.

"No, *you* look, sonny boy."

"I'm here to see my friends and you are not one of them and that's it."

Owner inserted himself between Charles and Farnsworth, actually put
his arm around Charles's shoulder, and steered him a step or two toward

another room. "Vera is here," he said. He was gesturing around like he was a pimp. In apology or at least recognition that his sudden, if masked, truculence might have been inappropriate, Charles nodded at the woman who still held Farnsworth's arm. She begged his pardon and introduced herself as Minnie, Minnie Moody. She said she gave piano lessons, and that no working life ought to be without music. Surely as gifted a singer as Charles Minot would agree.

"Oh yes!" she cried, "I remember!"

Charles nodded respectfully at her and said he was pleased to meet her and that he couldn't agree more with the idea that music should be a part of every person's life. She said she had had a ticket to hear him and Mrs. Minot sing Pergolesi the night before the earthquake.

Charles stared at her, genuinely amazed.

Farnsworth looked like he might boil over again, and she moved him away. Charles eased his way through another thick crowd, making for the center of the room. A dozen chairs were arranged in a circle and he could see the faces of perhaps nine of the people sitting in those chairs, as well as the faces of the people standing behind the chairs, hanging over them like drooping flowers. The chair nearest had a very high back and concealed whoever was sitting in it completely.

The discussion was of the war and fears not just of the entry of the United States into it, which was assured now, but of conscription. Charles had a very simple belief about wars, about fighting: every culture he knew of venerated its warriors and applauded the skill and bravery of those warriors in battle. They accorded them great respect and furnished them with medals or other insignia to distinguish them from those who had not fought. He wanted to believe that he was intelligent and strong and brave, that he was, despite his metaphysics, the leader of men Father insisted he was or could be—or could have been—something along the lines of Prince Hal—that when the skies trembled and the caves were not safe and people could see and hear and feel unmediated the wrath of God, he would stand firm because the wrath of God was *so amusing* to him, and consequently was determined to go to war—he really couldn't imagine the alternative (though one indeed had been bandied about to the point where it seemed a certainty, one that would keep him stateside) war was every bit the natural disaster that an earthquake was, the force of evil in human nature just another kind of trade wind or ocean current—so he listened to this discussion with something like aggrieved confusion. Because he had been taught to keep an open mind and nurture a reflexive sympathy for Christian Americans, he was able to listen through the murmur of his misunderstanding, and came to think toward the close of it that he could certainly forgive a poor man for not wanting to fight and likely die for the welfare of rich men, and could understand as well the general argument of the radicals—that the working people of the world had no quarrel with each other—but felt even more strongly that he himself was of a class, or a caste within a class, of honest, principled, capable men who were utterly depended upon by their fellow citizens to fight the dishonest and unprincipled tyrant when that tyrant moved to subjugate his neighbors. Stirred by the conversation with Warren Farnsworth and Minnie Moody, his blood not boiling but as nearly so as he ever allowed it, he would have spoken had not the woman sitting concealed in the chair stood and revealed herself.

It was Vera. She came around her chair and people in the way moved obligingly. Standing in front of Charles, revealing a possibly true self at last, she extended her hand, and he took it. Her face, in repose, in that moment of repose, was half-mad, one of those faces that when split down the middle and the halves viewed separately, suggests two different people. How had he not seen it before, in all his deep probings in rehearsal? But she had only to smile, brightening the dark features of her face and the whole room with it, to banish this superimposition of schizophrenia and confirm that he really did know her, and she him.

"First, allow me to congratulate you on behalf of everybody here," said Vera K., in a perfect imitation of a fashionable society hostess, warm but even, "on the splendid job you are doing in *The American*."

"Thank you," responded Charles, naturally picking up the same tone. "I don't know how I could be doing it without you!"

Everybody laughed heartily.

"No one is clear on what makes a good job a good job when it's that kind of work you're doing—all right, that *we* are doing—but we all agree you do well."

"Thank you," Charles repeated, this time with more feeling, but with a great deal of doubt as well, centering mainly on who "we" was.

"Nor do we understand what we're supposed *to do about it*."

"I'm sorry," Charles said, doubt metastasizing, "I'm afraid I don't understand what you don't understand. Given that you are so intimately involved. Is this some kind of inquisition? Have I been set up?"

"Some of us—if you will allow me to be frank and revealing and come swiftly to my point? Thank you. Some of us feel we ought to tar and feather you."

"I see!" Charles said. "Yes. Now I understand you."

"Maybe that strikes you as simpleminded of us."

"Not at all. I'm glad you could tell me so straightforwardly. I would never have come had I known, but having come, I am very grateful that you could tell me as quickly and succinctly as you have. Really, I am. Very grateful indeed."

"How very charming of you to be so sympathetic to our really helpless reactions to your play. Because we were helpless. We were just like children. It wasn't until the illusion had faded that we were able to realize just how much we hated you."

"Ah, but if it's hate you feel, then you really *must* excuse me."

"If we could excuse you, we wouldn't hate you!" This was said clearly in an attempt to delay his departure, and Vera continued in different vein. "There's been a great deal of talk about you. Speculation is running high. Our expectations are consequently exaggerated, and our eloquence fails us just when we would like most to compose a little sinfonietta of clever conversation for you."

This was such a polite and formal speech that he had to bow. When he straightened he said that he was sure he wasn't worth all the trouble.

"Whether you're worth it or not, or whether you think you're worth it or not, the trouble is being taken." Vera returned to her seat but did not sit down. "Do you see? What you think of yourself doesn't matter. Nor do polite demurrals." She seemed to be trying to be helpful rather than hurtful. Her dark eyes were impossibly large as she studied him, goofily big, and one of them seemed to be canted slightly away, so that the most imperceptible movement, the most minute readjustment of focus, seemed loaded with danger and meaning.

"Jules insists you're not at all like 'the American.'"

"Whoever Jules is, I'm flattered that he paid enough attention to me to gather the raw materials necessary to form even a superficial opinion."

Owner identified himself as Jules, and extended his hand. Charles took it and shook it and smiled at him in just the way his brothers had parodied him years before, confirming whomever in the continuing belief that they were friends putting on not only a polite show but an important one of formal salon manners. And of course they were, but that was not all that they were doing.

"Now you're flattered! What next, Mr. Minot! Raw materials . . . !"

"I admit I overextended myself there. That kind of talk might pass in the debating hall, but has a hollow ring, I hear it quite distinctly, here with the radical set." Charles was angry now, and had become so without actually knowing that it was happening. Vera and he were at the very least friends. There was no call to play him publicly like she was. Or was there? What was the point? Why was she working so hard to appear to hold me in contempt? "You are more amenable to fire-breathing and the violent homilies of failed tradesmen."

"Let me just ask you this: what is it that you were doing up there on the stage that makes you 'the American,' and why was everybody going nuts as they watched you do it?"

"First off, I am not 'the American.'"

"You're not?"

"You're being ridiculously disingenuous, Vera."

"Well, who the hell are you then?"

"Charles Minot."

"Who becomes somebody or something eight times a week called 'the American,' but who cannot or will not, for undisclosed reasons that nevertheless make him look like either a stooge or chicken, own up to it and tell us what we're supposed to make of all the whistling and cheering and boot-stomping and flower-throwing he so easily and naturally elicits when he *is* 'the American' he insists he is *not!*"

"You are pretending to be a simpleton, Vera, just to get my goat and perhaps the applause of this audience here around us. Now are you or are you not a simpleton?"

"What are the consequences of my deceit, Mr. Minot?"

Charles laughed, hoping that Vera might too, but she did not.

"I suppose," he said, "you get my goat and the applause of your friends!"

"And the consequences of your deceit, Mr. Minot?"

"It's not deceit, Vera."

"It looks very much like deceit!"

"Yes, but there's a long history of people of goodwill, like us, all over the world agreeing that it's not."

"Excellent: What is the consequence of this deceit that the world has decided is not deceit? Surely it has a consequence no matter what we call it . . . ?"

"Surely." Charles smiled.

While he was smiling, Vera told him that the consequence of his deceitful display of American character would be to help spur the country into the war, that he was part of a propaganda machine, a mouthpiece, a puppet, and when everybody was done cheering, a million Americans would have joined the ten million dead Englishmen and Germans and Frenchmen.

Charles, strangely, continued to smile. He said he was doing no such thing, and that the only person he was encouraging to go to war was himself. Even more strangely, Vera broke into a grin. She demanded to know who was being disingenuous now. She seemed on the verge of flirtatiousness.

"I'm not responsible for the fucking crowd," Charles said, taking himself completely by surprise with the vulgarity. Had her sudden and shocking smile elicited this roguishness? Had he only just remembered that he was amongst safecrackers? He continued with an air of having learned something the hard way. "The audience gets the show they want. And if they don't get it, they get what they deserve. What I want and what I deserve just don't figure. What *you* want and what *you* deserve are different concerns, you incredibly deceitful and hypocritical woman!"

The dense formation of the people in the room shifted in some small way, and Charles, feeling the movement, looked away from Vera to see Sir Edwin standing next to Jules the Owner. They were standing side by side, two dark men with flamboyant moustaches and luminous eyes, who could have been taken for brothers. Sir Edwin made a face of great disdain and said that the actor was a lightning rod and nothing more. If he was a good one, he might conduct violent force from the heavens for many years, but if a bad one, if there was some small fault in him, he would be burned to death at the first strike.

And Jules said, "He's an ordinary kid. He's one of us, or he could pass, even if he is filthy stinking rich. That's what I told you, Vera, from the very first, and I know you know it's true."

Charles affirmed that it was true: he was an ordinary kid. He believed nothing of the kind, but this seemed an appropriate falsehood.

"Just stupefyingly rich," Vera reminded him.

"Yes," he said evenly, "that's right. Here we are back at money! How surprising! How refreshing!"

"Whose daddy thinks he will be *pwezzydent* some day!"

"I'm sorry: thinks I will be what?"

"You know what's worse than an actor whipping up the patriots?"

"Yes, I'm afraid I do."

"A stupefyingly rich actor whipping up the patriots."

"Do you people really not get it? I am not Christopher Newman and I did not whip up any patriots."

"Oh, but see now," said Vera, going to him and caressing him, soothing him, as well as giving him an instantaneous erection, which dizzied and thrilled him even more than he had been, so much so that he felt light-headed, drunken, "there's where you are wrong, dear. You are Christopher Newman and you did whip up the patriots, but it's all right, it's all right, shush now. I was a French princess and I helped you."

"There is no connection between Christopher Newman and myself."

"No connection? Shush now. Of course there is."

"No *real* connection."

"No *real* connection, all right, shush now, can you?"

"Did you just say you *helped* me?'"

"To be fair," said Sir Edwin mildly, even disinterestedly, "the better job he does, the more tenuous is the connection." He slipped into his Russian accent. "All this talk of *rill* is mislidding."

"An ordinary kid," said Jules, "one of us, rich, sure, but here's the difference: he can stand there alone on that stage, naked for all the costumes and disguises, in a pool of light, and know that we are all out there looking at him and judging him. And not be afraid to stand there. Doesn't have to say a word. Doesn't have to light a cigarette or look out a window that's got a piece of tar paper where the glass should be. Just stand there and not be afraid of us. That's *some* kind of American, at least. I mean here tonight, Charles, not on *your* stage."

Vera was positively hugging him now and suddenly he could not have been happier. "I know," she said, cooing. "I know, it's the other Americans, the ones who are watching and judging. They're stampeding their little selves."

"There's all kinds of Americans, surely," somebody in the crowd observed with a kind of sententious quiet.

"What kind of American are you, Shirley?" asked Warren Farnsworth.

There was a brief silence, as Farnsworth's tone had not been altogether "in the spirit" of the conversation.

"My name's not Shirley. It's Vera and Vera's not my real name, either, because I wanted to have a revolutionary name, the name of a brave woman who had sacrificed everything for the cause. The name of a Russian. That's the kind of American I am. I was born and raised in Muscatine, Iowa, and worked from the time I was born until just, I don't know, a few months ago, a year or two, in a button factory. My task was the most tedious task in the factory but it was critical as the factory could not sell mixed buttons. I and my friends graded the buttons according to manufacturing defects, natural stains, color, luster, and iridescence. I also sewed buttons to decorative cards, for a while. I tried to drown the owner in a big tub of buttons but even though I failed I had to leave town. Now I print revolutionary materials on a secret press. NO GODS TO APPEASE, NO MASTER TO BOW DOWN TO, NO DOGMA TO RECITE! That's what I say, and that's the kind of American I am!"

Sandy, golden hair, dark eyebrows, tall and slightly stoop-shouldered, with very thin and long arms and legs, but very pretty; she had the kind of red-cheeked and golden-curled glow one saw in advertisements, and she beamed modestly as the *salonnières* cheered and whistled their approval of her speech. Farnsworth was so much shorter than she was, and uglier, that Charles could not veil the derision in the look of superiority he shot at him. He looked like a rat at this distance. And yet his eyes had been far more intelligent than those one saw in rat faces. And they were kind—or if not exactly kind, understanding of something not usually or easily understood. When the applause died down for Vera, Farnsworth—being, everyone assumed, her lover—was persuaded to describe the kind of American he was.

"I am a good citizen and I proved it by learning a trade. I was born and raised on a farm but my daddy beat me so I left and learned how to cut leather for the soles of shoes. No, I'm sorry, wait, my daddy died and left my mother and my nine brothers and sisters and me with his brother-in-law, who had a cow way out somewhere around the far side of Jamaica Bay. Had one cow and I milked it until I was twelve and then my mind turned to other philosophies. That was when I learned how to cut linings. Satisfied with my progress toward heaven, I became a streetcar conductor for the fun of it, the sheer daredeviling hell of it, don't you know? It's true I was guilty of nickel-ing now and then and it's also true I came into possession of a set of burglar's tools. Don't ask me how. They were there in the morning on the doorstep and that's all I know. I took them in and cared for them like they were my own. But that wasn't any kind of life so I decided I would go to Mexico to help Pancho Villa with his revolution. I made it as far as Los Angeles, where this strike was going on. The Wobblies were striking . . . a shoe factory! I made a deal with the Wobblies I was playing pool with that I would get a job as a lining cutter—because it was as a lining cutter that I had made my stand as a citizen!—and report back to the Wobblies on the activities of the scabs and their leaders. The Wobblies said okay, that sounded like good fun and off I went. Only they forgot to tell everybody that I was only *posing* as a scab—and here I think I can speak with some authority about what our young thespian has been up against—and I got the fucking shit kicked out of me. Once we got that straightened out, I went back to spying, and I framed some scabs. Then I decided I would find out where these strikebreakers were coming from. I borrowed one of Julie's motorcycles and I tailed one of the owners of the factory for a few days. Then he got wise to me and led me back to the factory, where he ran me over and a bunch of scabs who'd been hanging out at the paymaster's window jumped me. I would have been killed, stomped to death, if it hadn't been for somebody in this room whose name I won't say in case there's somebody else in this room who wants to put him in prison. He was unbeknownst to me playing craps with the guard and getting him drunk, after which point he undressed him, dressed himself up as the guard, took his keys, and went into the factory where he smashed up some equipment. When he was about to make his getaway, he saw them picking me up and throwing me down and he rides up on his motorcycle in his guard's uniform, blowing his whistle and firing his gun! That stops everybody cold and he says, 'Warren Farnsworth, I believe?' I still don't know if he's a real cop or who he is, but at least I'm no longer being thrown up in the air and landing on my head, so I jump on the back of the motorcycle. That's the just the beginning of my story, but that's the kind of American I am."

When Charles tried to leave a few minutes later, Vera stopped him.

"I wonder if I might have a private word, Mr. Minot?"

"Oh, do please call me Charles. And please speak freely."

"I want you to know that despite all this business, we, most of us, thought that whatever it is you did up there, you did it well. You did it astonishingly well. And whether most of us can admit it or not, we derived a definite benefit from your performance."

This rather awkwardly delivered, terse, formal speech that in no way addressed her current concerns was nevertheless stunning and magical in its effect. It suggested very strongly that a woman could after all assuage hurt feelings, shore up a shaken foundation, smooth ruffled feathers, provide shelter, refuge, and that part of what he felt—he no longer had to feel ashamed about it—when he felt desire for women was a desire for consolation, and warmth, and peace. Finishing with her smile a gesture that Mother may have begun once when he was a little boy but left undone, or never made in the first place, Vera opened herself to him, and utterly transformed herself.

"That's very kind of you," he said, still guarded. "Thank you for taking the trouble to say so."

"We were rough with you," she apologized.

He contrived to be gallant. "Not at all. I deserved it. If I can't take responsibility for my actions on the stage, then I *should not mount it.*"

"Oh, Charles, you are not responsible for what we make of your actions."

She seemed to be speaking very softly but he heard her quite clearly. The noise around them rose and fell simultaneously as the crowd gathered and dispersed and gathered and dispersed.

"No," he said, "I suppose not. But part of my responsibility is to expect . . . I mean to say, if I clamber up on the stage and make a speech, make a big fuss over myself, I can't expect people to listen to me only as I wish to be heard. I can't expect them to listen to me when I want them to listen, understand what I want them to understand, and treat me as I wish to be treated!"

"That's right," said Vera. "You can only treat them as you wish to be treated. And that is what I'm trying to say to you: you treated us to the best you could do, and I for one am grateful."

"Again I must insist: you are too kind."

"Tell that to the man I tried to drown in buttons!"

"Ha ha, yes, yes indeed," he said. Then: "Did you really try to drown him?"

"*Oh, Charles.*"

"In buttons?"

"Why not in buttons?" Then, much closer: "It was an *act.*"

"Yes, of course," he agreed, but not really understanding in what sense she meant what she said.

"This is what I wanted to talk to you about!" she whispered with lovely ferocity in his ear.

She stepped back and stared at him. It was a haughty, lascivious stare that still somehow promised a warm oven of sympathy and relief.

"Follow me," she both suggested and commanded. She took his hand and drew him through the kitchen and a bedroom to a door that opened on a steep and dark staircase. The light from the bedroom failed to penetrate its depths, but Vera began her descent with an alacrity and agility that he found inexplicably exciting: it was almost as if she'd leapt into a well. He followed as quickly as he could and when he reached the bottom step he could see Vera's face glowing in the darkness. She now wore a serious look that thrilled him to his marrow. There was heartache and loneliness in it, but it was perfectly calm and its desire was incontrovertible. He took that face in his hands and kissed it. There was a great deal of strength flowing through her hands and lips, but they remained exquisitely soft. Excluding the stage embraces and adolescent silliness, it was possible that this was really and truly his first kiss. It seemed the first time a kiss had been mutual, had been expressive of something other than a reflex. He now felt as if he'd been born to it. He wanted to kiss Vera for the rest of his life. He clapped a hand around the back of her skull and one around a buttock, but just as it had begun it was over and Vera was laughing. She led him through a darkness of crates and he thought perhaps the frames and disassembled engines of motorcycles until they came to another door. He tried to recommence the kissing—he had found his métier, he was a natural—but Vera pushed him away and took off a bracelet, from which evidently a key jingled, because a lock was clicking and the door was now open. He stood in the doorway of the room that held the press as Vera once again disappeared in darkness. He realized he was panting and tried to calm himself. He had lost his virginity years earlier; he had never kissed a woman as he'd just kissed Vera. The light from an oil lamp appeared, not too far away but far enough for the hiss and sputter to be nearly inaudible, and slowly, as if it were filling the room with water, began to illuminate its shapes and limits. Taking up most of the room was the printing press, which seemed for a moment to have gargoyles attached to its outermost parts; in a corner was a simple wooden washstand on which were placed a pitcher and a bowl and a small towel, all of which appeared snow-gray in color but which slowly became yellow as he looked at them. A tiny oval mirror with an ornate grillwork of vines and leaves framing it was hung on the wall. Next to it was a piece of paper, old newsprint, yellow, tattered, smeared, on which he, drawing nearer, read the slogan Vera had proclaimed only minutes earlier, in another world:

NO GODS TO APPEASE
NO MASTERS TO BOW DOWN TO
NO DOGMAS TO RECITE

In this dark and strange cave-like place, it was incantatory, *incantesimo*, not defiant, a relic from an ancient rite and not a political battle cry. Altogether there was a faint sense of hallucination gathering, and while it didn't dampen his ardor, he felt a certain elevation and refinement of what, until that expanding, nebulous moment, had seemed almost brutal in its perfectly ungovernable simplicity.

An unmitigated or unadulterated seriousness had overtaken Vera as well. He moved around the press and found her sitting on the edge of a small, tidily made bed. She patted a spot beside her and he sat down. A natural shyness had caught up with them.

"Here is what I wanted to say," said Vera tentatively. "I don't think we should go to the theater to see plays about politics or our lives. I mean, they are wrong to make you stand for something and say you're good only if they agree with you. The reason I think that is because the theater is a dreamy place, it's not a real place. I mean, everything in it seems like it's happening in a dream. And when you're good, as you were good, Charles," and here she paused to kiss him warmly and lingeringly on the cheek, "you do things you would never do in real life, but exactly the things you would do in a dream. As *we* were good. I'm sorry I've been baiting you like that all evening."

"Well, yes, it's—"

"Let me finish. Everyone knows we're not saying what you think, we're just repeating the lines you memorized, and we're doing something we prac-ticed over and over again. And everybody knows that we do and say the same things night after night, but *they don't care because it's a dream.* At least it is if we're good. If we're bad, it isn't anything at all like a dream. It's ridiculous and pointless. As you said so many times in your impassioned provocations to the company. It makes a person feel *bad* to watch it, rather than strangely *happy.* I'm not very smart, certainly not in your league, anyway—"

"I'm not smart," he said urgently. "Please don't think I'm smart. They teach you how to make speeches after dinner and I can fake everything, even being smart, I spent four years studying the classics, but I'm really just a fool."

Vera paused to consider her new lover in the lamplight and ended by smiling at him mysteriously. She then continued her thought.

"I'm not thinking this stuff up originally," she said. "This all comes from a friend of mine, Jules's wife, who died three years ago, Rosemary—"

"I don't believe you. I'm sorry your friend died, but I don't believe you're simply parroting—"

"—and she said it much better than I do. I'm just agreeing with her because I think it's true and important. I think that all good actions have a dreaminess to them that you can't describe or deny. If you do something and it doesn't feel right, you know it's the wrong thing to do. And the harder you push it, the more wrong it feels. When you do something and it feels right, you know it too. And the more right it is, the more like a dream it is. The more you look like you rehearsed your lines, the more like you practiced your movements. It's like nothing happened before you started to set you up, or cause it, and the future doesn't matter, either. The effect is for someone else to think about. And when you're done, you can almost hear the applause. Even though you know there's no one out there. That's why I came to you. I have always wanted to act, and then I came up with these other ideas that . . . I don't know . . . made it imperative."

"I often dream," Charles said after a brief but thoughtful, and somewhat tense, silence, "that I am about to go onstage, and not only can I not remember my lines, I know I never learned them in the first place."

It was as if the ground had now been carefully prepared: Vera pushed him backward on the bed, unbelted and unbuttoned him, and commenced the kissing of his swollen cock. He could not have been more astounded by this abrupt and unprecedented action. He was, in a sense, dismayed. The idea, he thought, was merely fashionably dissolute in his leading lady, a venting of sexual energy that was common in the theater; but with Vera it was work of another order, and he felt, despite the incredible pleasure of it, faint at heart and unequal to the challenge. He thought how terrible it would now be if he lost her. Now that he loved her. Needless to say, he felt fraudulent because he did not understand what love was and when the body followed the mind in a perversion of the proper method of the sane and effective actor, when he lost his focus and became impotent, he could only sigh and say, "Now you know the real me."

"Nonsense. But you've got to go. Warren has promised to kill you. He won't, of course, but we can all save ourselves so much trouble if you just quickly go *now*."

Attendance numbers remained high and the crowds wildly enthusiastic as July 4th approached. Charles continued to be nauseous before every performance and to wave a little flag during curtain calls. Amelia fell from her horse while chasing Durwood Keogh on the beach but was lucky enough to have broken no bones on the soft sand. Laughing and crying at the same time, she allowed herself to be carried by Keogh to her limousine. The Reverend Thomas Ruggles was in Washington, DC, and so was unable to do the carrying. As he was leaving, Keogh said, "Your brother is becoming pretty well-known, isn't he. And well-liked." But as she wasn't sure what he meant by the remark, she merely looked at him in frank but patient disdain, which seemed to please or at least amuse him. She told her brother about it, wanting to warn him that if she was allowing Durwood Keogh to pick her up and carry her about and coo over her tenderly, then scandal, ruin, and catastrophe would follow as surely as the oxcart follows the ox or however it was he liked to put it . . . but no, no, no, it was worse, it was that if she was allowing Durwood Keogh to seduce her, the poison was very deep and it was far too late to do anything about it, the whole family would die or was already dead and just didn't know it, that was the way Amelia saw things and if Charles had once been willing and able to discount it, he surely and sorrowfully could do so no longer. She tried to tell him traps were being laid and if he thought he could merely continue his policy of being blithe about it in public, ecstatic for his theater-folk, and contemptuous in his soul, he was wrong wrong wrong. He was a fool and she had never before thought that of him. She wanted desperately to return to selfless toil in miserable hospitals but could not. She did not know why. She tried to tell him, to ask him, but he was feeling too charismatic and powerful to even listen, much less reply. She feared he would shake her hand and murmur, "Good of you to say so." She wanted to make fun of him and for the two of them to laugh, but she could not, they could not. Something was over and while many things remained possible, many things had become impossible as well. He found it hard to think of anything but sexual relations with Vera—even to the point of hardly recalling his bizarre impotence. He wanted desperately to love, to be in love and to love, and if the shadow of death hung over the stage, well, he did not understand death very well, either. Father certainly had tried to see to that, but Charles had been neither bright nor willing about Stoic sensibility.

After inquiring politely in Jules's office, he made his way across the gallery and down the stairs into the shop, then across that room, passing men he now knew by and large to be other than what and whom they appeared to be, walking swiftly but awkwardly with a self-consciousness that was like a great weight on his shoulders, his legs strangely stiff, his face suggesting an errand the goal of which he could not keep straight from the one thing he must avoid at all costs. He made his way around the glass display case and walked past the cash register to the dirty red curtain, which he parted clumsily and carried with him one or two steps down the aisle of spare parts. He walked with an air of complete freedom that was thoroughly but incompetently, amateurishly feigned through the back rooms until he found a way, a way different than the one Vera had used the first time, down into the cellar and through its milky, oily darknesses to the door of the room that held the press.

This door hung slightly but heavily ajar, the seam a less oily, more milky light than that in which he stood. He pressed against the door carefully but firmly and heard the sound of weights being transferred by gears and pulleys, and, not incongruously, that of water being poured from one container to another.

And there they were, the snow-gray jug and basin, Vera with her back to him but her face visible in the tiny cloud of the mirror. On the washstand stood a large full bottle of whiskey. Its cork lay on the floor and the burned smell of the whiskey made its own invisible little fountain over the bottle. The smell of ink and naphtha and damp paper was otherwise so strong in the milk and oil glowing around the lamp that he thought he could see particles of ink and paper floating as if in solution, microscopic bubbles of ink and motes of paper debris.

It was all a little too vivid. They began to make small talk.

"High grade of white," said Charles, fingering a sheet of paper in the press tray.

"Cost a fortune," said Vera.

"Smooth finish."

"It's lovely paper."

"What made you choose Vera as a pseudonym?"

"Vera," said Vera, "was chosen in honor of two Russian women."

He smiled in friendly anticipation of an anecdote, but felt a sensation something like that of hearing a drip from a leaking roof strike the pot set below it faster and faster.

"One Vera killed the governor of Petersburg. A General Trepov, I was told. A terrible tyrant, had a man flogged for failing to remove his cap. You know the kind of asshole. Vera sat in his waiting room with, I don't know, a hundred other petitioners, half of them dying, the other half wishing they were dead, and when he came up to her and asked her what her complaint was, she said, 'You are, General Trepov,' withdrew a pistol from her cloak, and shot him dead. Then she sat back down. That's the part I like best. Sitting back down. Twenty-four January, 1878, seventeen years to the day, as it happens, believe it or not, of my birth, in Muscatine, the Button Capital of Iowa. The other Vera was a leader of The People's Will. She participated in some of the various attempts made on the life of Alexander II, you know, rolling a bomb under his carriage and having it roll out the other side before it exploded, stuff like that. But they got him in the end, never fear."

"You really know your business," said Charles. Vera looked at him skeptically, and he said, "I mean your history."

Vera burst out laughing. "My business, yes indeed!" She stopped laughing rather suddenly. "Rosemary taught me everything I know. Via Jules, who had all the books in the first place. I would be a frustrated dolt without them."

He nodded as if he knew this to be so, strangely, because it was not flattering to Vera and he had not meant to do it. Then he turned to the press. "It's beautiful." He glanced at Vera in a way that suggested he was talking about her and not the press. "It's like William Morris's."

"Yes. Didn't I say so . . . ?"

"Oh yes, you, it's—yes. Have you read *News from Nowhere*?"

"No."

"Well it's a good novel if you ever have some time on your hands," he said, a little combatively. Did he want to replace Rosemary and Jules as her tutor? He seemed so absurd to himself that for a second he thought he might jump up and run away.

Then she was hanging in his arms and crying and they were kissing ferociously; she smelled of tobacco and tasted of salt and as they moved around the press to the bed he saw a white ashtray full of crushed and burned butts, black sprinkles of tobacco, blacker smears of tar. He became ravenous, ravening, for other deeper riper smells and slicker textures.

Afterward he accepted a drink of whiskey. He had drunk before, but not much, had never been drunk, a little wine at table that he had to admit enlivened him rather ominously—but never drunk. Drunkards were unknown in the family and avoided publicly. It went down hard but flowed smoothly into every vein and artery of his body and at once both warmed and cooled him so that he felt satisfied and lustful, depraved and magnificent, languorous and on fire, all at once. He fumbled wanly with a cigarette and came to think that he had been wrong about alcohol and tobacco. All he needed now was a firearm—which of course were not proscribed but only easy to lay his hands on up at the ranch. Vera gave him another drink and then put the bottle out of his comically flailing reach, telling him sternly that further drinks would place his erection in jeopardy. He laughed with derisive abandon at the thought of impotence.

Everything that had happened to him had happened long ago and far away.

There was in fact a revolver beneath the bed but Vera kept this information to herself. In the exhausted peace that followed what seemed like a never-ending cycle of dazed orgasm and reawakened lust, in stinking darkness of the little room, in the quiet glugging of whiskey from the bottle and smacking of lips, he felt he had come to an earthy and practical under-standing of everything he hadn't been taught in school, in books, sermons, talks with Father, Mother, Alexander, Andrew. Plato and his *Statesman* were particularly, grievously, wrong. A hero was born to ascend the heights of human courage and ecstatic selflessness but just as surely to descend to the hell of vice, sin, squalor, and barbarism. Not to dwell there, nor strictly speaking to enjoy it, but to save good people and punish bad people. No, not even that: simply to know. It was so simple, and he glowed with gold and iron certainty of it. The lamp hissed and sputtered, the light evened and faded and died, and at some point he understood Vera had risen to shut and lock the door. Then she was beside him again and he slept for what seemed like years, dreaming of many small groups of people, all of whom seemed to know and respect him, even to look to him for guidance, as they made a serious but pleasant journey, on foot, through a hilly forest. The sound of their footsteps was somehow the most remarkable feature of the dream. Then an electric light was turned on and blinded him. He had not known there was an electric light in the room, and he was unable to think beyond the strangeness of it, certain only that he was no longer dreaming.

It was a light for corpses, not living people.

In the dream he felt blind and possibly dead. He became frightened. He turned his head and saw Warren Farnsworth staring at him from the door-way. The look on Farnsworth's face was one of inscrutable grievance and Charles's immediate reaction was to be annoyed. That was when he knew he was awake. It was, however annoying on the surface, a look he would never forget. When had he stood up? Was he naked? Farnsworth swung a black-jack high and hard into his temple, and he went down.

If he thought that Jules would be a source of support as well as enlightenment in this new situation, he was made immediately to understand otherwise. He sat on the edge of the little bed and Jules stood over him, his finger leveled angrily at Charles's face. This finger hovered just this side of focus and it irritated him a great deal. Jules meanwhile was trying not to shout, trying not to sputter. He had no trouble with what Farnsworth had done! He would have done the same thing in his place! A woman Charles did not know, who was wiping the blood from Vera's face with a rag and hot water, looked up at this. She looked angry or disgusted or defiant, and yet said nothing, returning carefully to Vera's brow, which was split open. It was Charles, Jules said, still not quite shouting, thrusting the finger even nearer, that he had all the trouble with. He did not know what the fuck Charles was doing there. Vera, with difficulty around the rag, said that he was there because she had invited him. Jules had to wonder then what the fuck she was doing there as well. Vera stared at him, aghast, around the woman's hands and the bloody cloth.

"Awful lot of poor decisions made here tonight," she sputtered furiously, "and you are going to choose *mine* to condemn?"

Charles said he was there because he loved Vera. The woman shushed him, speaking clearly to him but not looking up from Vera's wound, waiting for Jules's hypocrisy to catch up with his anger, which it finally did. He deflated visibly and hung his head. He was ashamed of himself, he apologized, but managed to leave the room nevertheless with an air of unappeased anger. The women smoldered with scorn while the bandaging and smaller, murmuring ministrations went their full course and were, at long last, complete.

A little while later, Jules, the woman, and Charles escorted Vera to the office of a nearby dentist who was competent to stitch flesh, and this man, though sleepy or drugged, put twelve perfect stitches over Vera's right eye. It was then decided that drinks were in order, so they went to the Fior d'Italia and sat outside. Vera insisted on whiskey, so a bottle and a pitcher of water were brought to the little table. A glass was prepared for Charles and he drank it in a manner and at a speed that seemed commensurate with the tempo of the table, but it went with incredible speed straight to his head. He had not realized how earnestly in composure he'd been holding himself. Not one

breath or flicker of muscle had been expended that was not strictly necessary. With the coursing of the whiskey, however, he began to feel as if composure were a gift of the gods, and he glowed with easy gratitude. Anxiety
and tension and pain he hadn't let himself recognize began to flow out of
him, like blood from a mortal wound, and he laughed warmly and generously but quietly at whatever was being said.

"He had no business being down there," Vera said flatly but with conviction.

"No business?" Jules wondered. "*No* business?"

"Shut up, Jules," suggested the woman quite pleasantly, whose name
Charles still had neither caught nor sought.

"We had an agreement," said Vera, less flatly and with less conviction.

"What sort of agreement?" asked the woman.

"No doubt," said Jules breezily, "an unspoken one."

"Shut up, Jules," said Vera.

"That room," the woman reminded Jules, "was until very recently a room
about which there was an unspoken agreement on which lives depended."

"Until very recently. More recently it's become a room about which
agreements can be negotiated. Pretty much on the spot. If need be."

The women reserved their answers and the table was quiet for a moment.
Conversations from other tables washed in as if the table were a container being filled. Then Charles told Jules to shut up, even though he hadn't actually
said anything. The table became so quiet that it seemed it had in fact been
filled with a viscous liquid. Lacking the bearings his ears might have provided, he lost himself and had difficulty focusing on his companions. Once he
thought he'd looked them all in the eye, he shrugged in a kind of apology and
said it was a matter of comic timing. One feels a rhythm that one cannot resist.

"*That is my room,*" said Vera, her teeth angrily clenched.

"It is," said the woman. "He's got no business appearing there, as it were,
on your doorstep assuming rights and privileges he does not have."

"Never has had and never will have," said Vera. "Whatever *the fuck* he
may think about it."

"You're his girl, Vera. You can't pretend—"

"I am not his girl!"

"Vera, look, no, of course you're not 'his,' but he thought so, and you know he thought so. You let him think so, isn't that right?"

"No, that is *not* right."

"I think that's right," said Jules.

"Shut up, Jules," Charles said again.

Jules turned on him instantly and had his nose almost touching Charles's nose. "Tell me to shut up one more time and I'll make you suck your own cock, you understand me?" He was speaking softly, but visibly trembling.

Charles looked away with a sneer, but felt the woman touch his arm, and looked back.

"Tell me you understand me."

"It was a joke."

"Do you understand me?"

"Yes," Charles said, not sobering up exactly but gaining some purchase he hadn't realized he'd lost. "I, um, yes, I understand you. I apologize. I am sorry and I understand you, loud and clear. I—"

"Thank you. Where was I?"

"It's all timing," said Charles. "My timing's off. That's all. Don't get so—"

"Vera is not Warren's girl, no matter what Warren thinks," the woman reminded everybody.

"Underwear in a fucking *bundle* over some piddly little thing like timing—"

"He doesn't own me. Where does he get off thinking he owns me? Where *the fuck* does he get off thinking *that*?"

"*The Revolutionary Catechism*, maybe," the woman couldn't resist saying.

"I thought we were done with that horseshit," said Vera.

"Oh, we are," said the woman.

Suddenly Vera was shouting and crying. "I CAN TELL YOU I AM DONE WITH THAT HORSESHIT!"

"We are all equal and we are all free," said the woman very quietly, more or less into Vera's ear, and Vera quieted down. Jules took a drink and then Vera took one. After a moment, in which he was obsessed with notions of timing, Charles took one.

"I've got to read this *Revolutionary Catechism*," he said. No one said anything, either in reproach or agreement or even indifference, and he pulled the bottle over again. It was a prop. He poured himself, ever so carefully, a drink, and ever so carefully slid the bottle back to the center of the table. He drank the drink with careful *savoir faire* and sat back judiciously.

"It's got absolutely fucking *nothing* to do with the fucking *Revolutionary Catechism*," said Jules. "He's a man and he thought you were his girl. He's a lonely guy and he leads a pretty rugged life. He does all the shit work and he thought you respected that more than the rest of us do."

"I did," said Vera. "I do."

"He probably thought you were not only his girl but a refuge."

"All that is true but I AM NOT HIS FUCKING GIRL!" Vera was shouting again. "I'VE GOT TWELVE FUCKING STITCHES IN MY HEAD! IS THAT WHAT A GUY DOES TO HIS FUCKING REFUGE?"

"YES!" shouted Jules.

"HE PRACTICALLY BASHED MY SKULL OPEN! I SUPPOSE HE CAN FUCKING KILL HIS FUCKING GIRL AND YOU WILL BUY HIM WHISKEY AND CIGARS TO CHEER HIM UP!"

"I'm not here to defend him," said Jules, shutting down abruptly.

"No?" asked the still nameless woman.

"I am here to say he is thinking certain thoughts and will continue thinking certain thoughts and we all had best take those thoughts and beliefs into account in order that they not have permanent consequences."

"If I see him again, I'll fucking kill him," said Charles.

"He's probably saying the same thing. Where does *that* leave us?"

"All right now," said the woman. "You're drunk. Shut up."

"I'm drunk?" Charles asked. "Because my *timing* is off you think—"

"*You're drunk*, Chuckles," said Jules. "And if I'm not mistaken, it's the first time. You got fucked and you got drunk and now it's beddy-bye time. Back up to your palace on the heights, looking out over your glittering little city by the sea."

White-hot anger flared up in Charles. It was so sudden and so strong that it took him by surprise and he could not properly direct it. But his face became a neutral mask of its own accord and he said he did not have any trouble sorting out the ethics of their little situation. He said he would fuck up the little prick if he saw him again. He said he would kick the little bully's ass until his spine snapped and then he would roll him in a ball, stuff him through the hole in an outhouse, and piss on him. He admitted he was drunk and that his timing was off but asked his friends to fully describe what aspect particularly of that condition troubled them so. He was able for the first time in his *fucking life* to say what was on his mind, do what he felt like doing, and if that offended their dainty anarchism, well, he could live with *that*. He launched himself into a dramatic lecture on the classics because it struck him as a spectacularly appropriate thing to do. That was to say: *spectacular* and *appropriate* at the same time. He was a Platonic Republican Gone Mad. Did that make any sense to them? No? Jules said he knew Plato as a fellow who kept the cards pretty close to his vest, oftentimes said what he meant but said he didn't really mean it, and vice versa. Sometimes he's talking about the state, sometimes he's talking about the soul, liked to talk about Ideal Forms but was seriously involved in smoky backroom politics in Syracuse.

Charles waved his hands to dispel Jules. "*Flux*, he shouted. *Flux*. First you have Heraclitus, who says everything is constantly changing and then you have Parmenides who says nothing ever changes. Plato—who, you're right, Jules, had to keep them close to his vest because he was born and raised amongst tyrants at war—Plato says there is one world of unchanging perfect forms and ideas, and another one, the one we live in, that knows only corruption and degradation. That is to say, this world isn't the real one and all changes occurring in it are for the worse. But here we are. How can we make most of the people happy most of the time? Communism. The leaders live like the slaves, which is to say, *not badly*. Wealth and poverty are both corruptions of the Original Happiness. But because I'm educated, I get to be a leader. I get to be a leader because my father was a leader. My son will be a leader because I was a leader. But if my son doesn't measure up, boom, he's not a leader anymore. He's a soldier or a worker. Vera grows up as a button worker but shows such incredible intellectual vibrancy everybody agrees: *she should be a leader*! Voilà. Vera's a leader. Vera and I are trained to think it virtuous to die in battle. We are trained to be clever and savage. We can't listen to sad music or imitate inferior people, like in a play, or listen to poetry in which the gods are mocked. The gods are corrupt to be sure, but they come from God. We ought not raise our voices. We cannot indulge in unchecked laughter." Here he laughed in an unchecked way, somewhat comically, somewhat hysterically. "No sorrowful Lydian tunes, no relaxing Ionian tunes: only Dorian and Phrygian for, respectively, courage and temperance. Can't eat fish. Meat must be roasted. No sauces. No confectionery. We will never need doctors. We must experience enchantments, e.g., terrors that do not truly terrify, bad pleasures that do seduce the will. 'Worlds on worlds are rolling ever, from creation to decay, like the bubbles on a river, sparkling, bursting, borne away.' All of our efforts must go toward keeping ourselves still and quiet and sparkling until we burst or are borne away. And I'm saying, yes, Plato's got it right, this is not the real world, everything's changing, and all change is for the worse. But I am exempt because I have been inspired by a god. I am bidden to cause change. Eros and Dionysus will see me through. You anarchists are merely confused—at *best* confused, at worst *hypocritical*—eccentrics."

He felt no remorse the following morning. His head ached, and he was embarrassed by some of the things he had said, but on the whole he believed he had released something in himself that had been imprisoned. But when he arrived—riding a horse—at the shop to pick up Vera for their date, he found the unnamed woman standing in the shade under the awning. She started to say something, but stopped when Vera tapped on the glass behind her and waved at them. Charles waved and smiled at Vera, then returned his gaze to the woman, not so much encouraging her to say what she had to say, as daring her. But the woman said nothing. She refused to look away, but would say nothing.

The Minot party was once again parked at the end of a long line of limousines on a dirt road that led to a clearing deep in the Presidio. Charles arrived with a woman nobody knew and whom nobody sought to know—apparently one of his actresses. Even if she hadn't had stitches and bruises on her face and been the subject of rumors relating her to terrorist factions within San Francisco's radical labor organizations she would have been ignored. His family had attended opening night and been wholly caught up, they said, in the enthusiasm—and Mother had been quoted in the *Chronicle* saying she was "delighted but not at all surprised" at her son's accomplishment. Amelia had been quoted in the *Examiner*, where she insisted that he could not be more proud of her brother, while her husband laughed off suggestions that theater had no place in a social gospel. Alexander and Andrew assured the critics from the *Call* and the *Bee* that everyone in the capital knew about what a treat the production was, and how there was serious talk of bringing it to Sacramento. Al, who was Governor Hiram Johnson's Chief of Staff (they had come together in '08, when Father took a bullet in the Ruef and Schmitz graft prosecutions and Johnson took over the lead, and stayed together when Al helped run the VP side of the 1912 Bull Moose run—and he had Huguenot blood as well, endearing him to Mother), Al went so far, with enthusiasm he admitted was somewhat calculated, as to say that "The American" exemplified everything progressive politics in California stood for. And Charles's younger brothers had been at nearly every show the first two weeks of the run, putting their arms around the shoulders of all the actresses, hanging on them, resting their heads against their necks while they applied their makeup, staring raptly into the mirrored eyes and quickly becoming part of pre-show superstition. Little charming rich boys: How long would they last in this pristine state? But it was pointedly not spoken of during either breakfast or dinner. Mother had made it clear that she had neither the time nor the inclination for any conversation along those lines, she hadn't the strength, and that had been that.

Meanwhile an incommunicado, possibly sequestered Vera had broken cover and asked to be taken to a Preparedness Day cavalry drill. Charles dismissed out of hand a feeling on his part that he deserved to know where she had been and simply stared at her with baffled longing. If he had understood her in the least way, he would have pressed her, but he did not. He believed he loved her.

"Why in the world would you want to see a Preparedness Day cavalry drill?"

"I want to actually see this man Keogh. The man who represents United Railroad. I've hated him blindly for so long. I want to make a man out of him."

Vera smiled.

"You won't roll a bomb under his carriage, will you . . . ?"

"I am not a violent person. Surely you have understood that much."

She let her fingers play lightly, as they might have when they were exploring the pseudo-Delsarte, over her wounds.

"If I recall correctly, you took the name 'Vera' in honor of—"

"I was foolishly attracted to the idea of frail little women murdering tyrants when I was younger. I have changed my mind. And look, if you want to the know the truth—"

"Why in the world would you think I wanted anything but to know the—"

"—Vera is my real name, my given name."

"Well that is just very strange that you should tell me it was assumed, then."

Vera sighed and smiled. Hadn't the strangeness of things been apparent from the very beginning? And who, after all, was Charles to speak disparagingly of such a condition?

Charles felt like Hardy's obscure Jude, confronting the nervously enigmatic Sue Bridehead, and was reminded of the literary opinions of the tall, fair man at Vera's salon.

"Who was the tall, fair man attending your evening? Hates Hardy."

"I don't know. A visitor from New York. He's come to help with . . . with something I don't know enough about to speak of. I didn't meet him. I don't know what he does."

Charles felt even more like Jude, and it surprised him: to think of himself as one who did not, could not understand, who was obscure for all his charm and wealth.

Charles had promised her a show and said that his family pretending to not see her was just the beginning. They watched Amelia as she went into the trailer they'd towed behind the Mountain Wagon, and backed her horse out, taking no nonsense from him though he was clearly in a mood for much nonsense, hopping about like a big cat and chuckling and bumping people around. She saddled him and said his name softly and sweetly over and over again, just for the pleasure it gave them both, then mounted him, and trotted off. The drills were again taking place at the far end of the clearing; occasionally a band of cavaliers would thunder toward them, turn as if barrel racing, and thunder back.

The drills looked, at that distance, formless, an amateur polo match, and Charles tried to interest himself and Vera in the picnic food, opening several bottles of wine and wondering if he might drink a little, or a lot, of it. He could clearly feel that within himself some kind of wall had been breached. Because Vera was nervous and increasingly awkward in her gestures and speech, he poured them each a big glass. They walked a few steps away to the shade of a big spreading tree and drank the wine slowly, Charles saying a few inane things about its character, Vera agog then outraged at its price, drinking it defiantly as if it were water. When they were done, he returned to the basket, refilled the glasses, and walked back to the tree. They clinked glasses and smiled at each other. His brother-in-law, the robust, handsome Thomas, man of God but manly man as well, a man for genial living as well as serene acknowledgement of the life to come, was back in town for a brief stay, and was quick to demonstrate that his calling in no way prevented his being judicious about the quality of wine his family and friends might moderately, or even a little immoderately, indulge in. Had not Jesus spent a good deal of miraculous force in changing water to wine at the wedding feast in Cana? If some now wanted a savior who would change wine to water, he, the Reverend Thomas Grant Ruggles, was not among them. Many friends streamed past, enjoyed a glass of wine, and complimented both Thomas and Charles—pointedly or casually ignoring Vera according to their social skills—on their accomplishments, so different in nature and practice but so similar in purpose, as the nation moved toward war.

Amelia cantered back and forth across the clearing, getting Jolly to rear up once or twice when people she despised came too close—friends who, she suspected, frowned not only on her husband's carefree indulgence of wine, on her brother's theater—on her and Mother's theater, as they had each contributed significant sums during the fund drive—no matter the beneficial effect it was clearly having on the spirit of the city, but who she suspected thought terrible things about her after she had fallen from Jolly and been seen in the arms of Durwood Keogh. Keogh was one of her great and dear father's most certain enemies! No one need to be told that again! And while she supported Father's wish to put all that behind them and unite as the country joined the European war, she had made her feelings plain to the gallant captain, and extricated herself from his ministrations as soon as he had been able. If she had been seen laughing, that was because her nerves were bad—had always been bad and were getting worse, after what seemed like decided improvement when she had been working so hard in the city's hospitals.

Some of her closer, truer friends who were also horseback joined her and they sat their mounts while Thomas with studied meekness handed up glasses of wine and little sandwiches, describing the wine as he did so perhaps too lengthily and fulsomely, as her friends pursed their mouths and raised their eyebrows in suppressed fits of giggling. Then quite suddenly, for many of them had become lost in the wine, Durwood Keogh was upon them. He dismounted and smiled boyishly as he made his way to the picnic basket. Thomas, smiling broadly and shrugging off some of the meekness in favor of hale heartiness, poured the playboy a glass of wine, and watched with mock incredulity as Keogh downed it in two or three gulps. Everyone laughed. It was impossible to dislike Keogh on that level. He was sweaty and dirty and tanned and robust and impeccably dressed. He smacked his lips and indicated he wouldn't mind another.

Glass in hand, he came and stood over to where Charles and Vera were stretched out in seeming indolence. Charles lay with a blade of grass in his mouth and an empty glass balanced on his breastbone, head propped on two thick pillows, embroidered pillows, the design spreading out from his head like a kind of intricate halo, dense with signs and codes. Vera reclined next to him, impulsively, for show, running her fingers through his hair.

"I enjoyed your show," said Keogh. "Really did. I don't see enough theater but I know what I like and I thought your show was first-rate."

Wondering where Father was and hoping Keogh might go on a little too long and seem foolish, Charles said nothing until a silence had grown all around them.

"Well, thank you," he said at last, dismissively. "Did you really think so?"

Keogh now paused. "Yes," he said. "I did indeed."

"Thank you for saying so."

Gus and Tony, who were trying to climb the tree, collapsed snickering.

"We ought to talk sometime," said Keogh.

Charles, surprised, smiled defensively and shook his head. Vera sat up.

"I know you think—everybody here thinks—that that would be tantamount to treason, but it isn't."

"What ought we talk about?" Charles spread his hands to suggest he had no idea.

Keogh spoke calmly. "Your brothers are in Sacramento, and no doubt they will get to Washington soon enough. But there are hopes building around you that are of another order. Is that not so? Come now. You shake your head and I think your modesty is genuine but that doesn't change a thing. Your father is able and strong and resourceful and—"

"Captain Keogh, please don't tell me what my father is."

"Very well. I will tell you what I am, and that is, if not your friend, at least not your enemy. You must think I hate your family and dream only of revenge, but that is not so. We want to see you do well, just as your father and his friends do. That is all I wanted to say to you, but you see of course that it's quite a lot. Too much, perhaps, eh? Enough said, then. We've got a war to prepare for! Are you going to wait for the declaration? I hear rumors that you may have some interesting work to do in where was it? Minnesota? The Dakotas?"

Given the first part of Keogh's speech (which Charles flat did not believe, political plans for him having been abandoned years ago) the second seemed—to him, at least, if not to anyone else in the group—so loaded with venom he could hear a ghostly Amelia warning him about it in a whisper, a whisper he thought he could hear so clearly he looked over at her, seeing her look back at him with intense meaning. It occurred to him, in the shape of an inarguably attractive idea, if not necessarily a good one, that he might knock Keogh down, right then and there, that he might advance fearlessly into the man's range and knock the sonofabitch down, and stand for a moment over him in contempt. And because he was learning to be an actor in the most dangerous sense, he felt his body preparing itself. But this was, fortunately or unfortunately, only one sequence of thought and action at work in him, and he could not help but admit, conversationally and politely, as was his usual wont, that he saw it was his duty to fight, that the only way he could reconcile a life of wealth and privilege was to sacrifice it for those who had neither, at which point Vera interrupted with an air of frank wisdom, saying it was the duty of the poor to have their vitality sucked out of them as a class with their personal blood as it sprayed out on battlefields, she would say it if nobody else there had the nerve. She was ignored, of course, and Charles continued, saying that if war was not declared soon, he would indeed go to Minnesota. It appeared to be his duty.

"A duty," said Keogh, "and maybe something of a pleasure. A serious pleasure, to be sure, and possibly dangerous, but a pleasure just the same for a young man. No, no, I understand. But don't get tied down by anything that might happen in Minnesota. We'll be in it. Less than a year. We'll all go together, give the Kaiser a good old-fashioned American kick in the ass. What do you say, Charles old man?"

Inexplicably, he grinned. He hadn't wanted to give anybody the impression that he liked the idea of sanctioned violence any more than he did unsanctioned violence, but he did not want to go on talking to Durwood Keogh, and a grin seemed the way to end it. He grinned and shook his head.

Pastor Tom and Amelia and their friends had helplessly formed a circle and were watching Charles, Vera, and Keogh rather breathlessly, while behind them horses raised and lowered their great heads, their eyes black and their gazes miles away. Only Amelia's bristle-maned Appaloosa showed crazed rims of white.

News that he had escorted a woman nobody knew to one of Captain Keogh's cavalry drill picnics was quickly united to gossip that he had been seen at a gathering of anarchists in the Latin Quarter. More unfortunately, it coincided as well with the shooting death of a policeman, by "an anarchist, a Russian anarchist," no less, with ties to forgers and, even more sensationally, white slavers. Permutations of the gossip and newspaper accounts occurred rapidly and unpredictably. They ranged from the patently ridiculous—Charles Minot was the white slaver and cop-killer—to the undeniably true: Charles Minot had attended Vera Kolessina's self-styled "romantic and revolutionary" salon. But when he arrived at the shop the next day to take Vera once more to the Sutro Baths—just an ordinary fun-loving, life-loving young couple—and see, more professionally now, the line clear but porous, if she was ready to return to her role (which had been taken on admirably, as if almost always the case, by an understudy) she could not be found. Cool but imperious, he demanded news of her whereabouts from everybody he saw, but nobody he knew was to be found, either. He went without asking leave of the boy at the cash register—one of the Italians he had seen that first day?—who opened his mouth and raised his hand but said nothing and did not move, through the greasy red curtain, down the aisle of parts, and down the stairs into the basement. No one was there, either. He came back up and apologized to the boy for his rudeness. Then he stood outside, back against the window, scanning the street. After a few minutes, someone tapped the glass behind his head, and he turned, thinking it would be Vera's face in the gloom he saw, as it had been the day before, but it was the Italian boy's. He came outside and told Charles that he should not seek to find Vera. Warren Farnsworth had heard about the cavalry picnic and threatened to kill both of them if he found them together. The boy was quick to assure Charles that Warren would do no such thing, that he was a sad and passionate alcoholic but no killer, that he had had many opportunities for what everybody seemed to agree would be good murders, but had eschewed them all, flatly, without second thoughts. He would gladly break the kneecap of a scab, and facilitate acts of sabotage, but drew a very clear and porous line. Nevertheless, Vera was hiding. She did not want to see him, and had explicitly asked him to convey that wish with whatever emphasis it might require to penetrate his arrogant skull. His words, *signore*, his words! She was nobody's girl and was sick to death of men in any case. What astonished Charles, when he went over it later, was how little he was moved by Vera's rejection, how little he feared Farnsworth's wrath. The boy asked him if he liked morphine and Charles said that he did not especially, but would get back to him.

Later he was standing next to the jitney bus of her friend Izzy Minkowski. It was empty and driverless, and he was waiting for that man to emerge from the throng. A blocky, dusty-looking man in a light suit and white fedora walked past several times. Charles tried not to notice him, but saw him often and clearly enough to think he must have suffered some kind of curse and was slowly turning to marble; the man's eyes, not quite fully closed, gave the impression of the blindness of statues. He walked stiffly but surely, moving out of people's ways, looking up and down the street they were on, and the one intersecting it.

Suddenly Vera was at his side, touching his arm.

"Oh, what *shall* we do," she mock-wailed.

"Go back to the Presidio and bury Durwood Keogh up to his neck. Ride by and let the horse shit on him, I don't know."

"Bury Durwood Keogh and yes, sorry . . . ?"

The street was loud.

"Never mind. Cavalry drill."

"Yes, of course I know what you're talking about, I just didn't catch the end. Snap off his head like one of those poor chickens?"

Vera came around, faced him, looked at him with pointed noncommittality. The glance lingered and became a searching stare. Charles stared back at her as if his life depended on it, but Vera severed the connection after only a moment or two. Smoothing her hair, she spotted Minkowski muscling his way across the street. He was short and dark, square-headed with a pronounced five o'clock shadow and brilliantly oiled hair. They embraced soundlessly, pecking on both cheeks. Charles meanwhile was fighting off, or rather pretending to fight off while succumbing and finding incredible pleasure in, a plan to offer Vera huge sums of money, everything he could lay his hands on, to literally cross oceans and climb mountains for her, to even—he could not stop himself in time from this darker desire, this outright evil—kidnap her, take her to Kathmandu . . . or Iceland, yes Iceland, and make her a baroness of volcanoes and glaciers, because he could do that, or nearly so, he could do whatever he wanted in this ridiculous illusion of a world and what he wanted, what he wanted more than anything else he could imagine, wanted so badly he felt he was going to explode, was to be with Vera. After perhaps a minute of this mania, he began to calm down, but could not take his eyes off her lips.

"Let me ask you a question," said Minkowski. "Are you leaving town before or after some sonofabitch gets shot in the head."

Charles stiffened and Vera exclaimed that she was not leaving. Minkowski narrowed his eyes and nodded.

"This," she said, "is the American you've heard so much about. Charles Minot, Iz Minkowski."

Charles reached his fine aristocratic hand out a great distance to shake Minkowski's huge dirty paw.

"Related to the grafter?" asked Minkowski. He held and shook hard and did not smile.

"Graft prosecutor," Charles said, retrieving his hand with some effort.

"Wha'd I say?" Minkowski demanded.

"You said grafter," explained Vera, as if her friend were about to fly off the handle.

"I did?" He seemed contrite but still would not smile.

Vera nodded and Charles smiled.

"I guess there's no love lost between your old man and Keogh either, huh?" asked Minkowski.

"Not a great deal, no," Charles admitted gravely, dropping the smile, at which Minkowski finally smiled and Charles sneezed, suddenly and without the faintest tickle of warning. He made a big show of it, happy to have some stage business, staggering a little with the force of it, wiping his nose with a flourish and inserting the handkerchief with exaggerated care back into his breast pocket. They walked the few steps to the little bus and Charles shook his pockets for nickels.

"Vera always rides free with me," said Minkowski. He put his heavy hand on Charles's arm. And squeezed. "And that goes for Vera's friends too, see?" He looked back and forth between them, as if to ascertain what kind of friends they were—if in fact friends at all, despite everything he had heard. "Speaking of friends, how is Julie?"

"High as a kite."

"I would be too. I would indeed be too."

"How are things with you?" Vera asked Minkowski.

"Oh, fine, fine. Some dick tried to sign up for music lessons with Minnie Moody, you know, and another lunkhead has been trying to get a date with his sister. Moody's sister, I mean," laughed Minkowski. "You never know about these shitsuckers. Brother, they are comical. Can you see it? This thug trying to come off like a handsome rake, when it's clear as the busted veins in his great fucking honker of a nose and the stinking derby on his tiny head that he's a drunken bully, ignorant and mean like they all are." Minkowski now sneezed but appeared not to notice. "And how about his pal the gorilla at the keyboard. Can't you see it? 'Chopsticks'? 'Mary Had a Little Lamb'?"

Charles laughed, but neither Vera nor Minkowski joined him. He said that Minnie Moody had actually purchased a ticket to come and see him sing Pergolesi the night after the earthquake.

"Goddamn them all to hell anyway," said Minkowski vaguely, meaning not Minnie Moody, or Charles, but some others.

"Anybody been round to see you?" asked Vera.

"I guess they have!" Minkowski shouted with sudden fury. "Him and his pals in various combinations."

Vera turned to Charles, but kept Minkowski in view, giving him significant looks as she spoke. "He refers to a man we believe to be more or less running San Francisco's secret police."

"*Secret police*," Charles murmured appreciatively.

Minkowski stared with unblinking neutrality at him, then glanced at Vera, who went on. "His name is Rudy Swanson and he used to work, we believe, for the Pinkerton Agency, but now heads something called the Public Utilities Protection Bureau, an organization formed by Pacific Gas and Electric, the Sierra and San Francisco Power Company, and who else . . . ?"

"PTT," holding up three fingers. "And, ummm—"

"Right, Pacific Telephone and Telegraph," said Vera, holding up four fingers, "and Western States Gas and Electric." Up came her thumb. "The Northern Electric Railroad. I think that's it, isn't it?" Minkowski nodded, then shrugged. "If we have the right fellow, he was the one sitting next to the public prosecutor at Tom Moody's three Martinez trials."

"You know Tom Moody, do you?" Minkowski asked Charles.

"We met, yes, coupla times, upstairs, downstairs." Charles gestured over his shoulder. "We spoke very briefly."

"They've been trying to frame dear Tom for several years now," said Vera wistfully. "And this *person* Swanson, who has absolutely no business being in a courtroom, was there helping pick the goddamn jury, whispering advice—but failing, here's my main point about Swanson, failing three times to get a conviction."

"He has been all over Farnsworth," said Minkowski, "for three weeks now."

An awkward silence ensued. Finally Vera looked expectantly at Charles, who said nothing, waiting.

"He offered Warren some money," said Minkowski.

"Don't tell me how much," pleaded Vera.

"Five grand."

"Oh my God."

"Five *thousand* dollars."

"That's too much for Warren to bear!"

"Then he waltzed over here and offered me the same."

"He did not!" shouted Vera incredulously.

"I told him he should keep his money as he was going to need it when the subornation market heated up. Then I told him to get the hell off my bus. And he says, with a grin that looks like he should be pie-eyed but he's not, those pale baby blues burning away in their sockets, he says he guessed he could have my jitney license just like that, and he snaps his fingers, if he wanted it, and rip it to shreds right under my big fucking Jew nose. Which he then pretends to do, like a mime, you know, very detailed and precise, ripping it eight times and then brushing his hands off. You're doomed, he tells me, why don't you wise up, URR's gonna have you off the heavy traffic streets within a matter of weeks, and then out of business altogether, so wise up, wise up, wise up, it's like a little refrain he singing to me now, *wise up* and I said I guessed I could make a living some other way than a nickel at a time driving a goddamn bus and he sings some more at me, wise up wise up wise up, only this time he's friendly as can be, almost sweet, you know. 'Won't take much,' he says, 'to convict the sonofabitch, just a little circumstantial what-have-you, and, by the way, what *do* you have, a detail or two or some general notion we can cook up for show-and-tell later on?'"

Minkowski's eyes widened startlingly, and Charles prepared himself to laugh at the joke he thought was surely coming, but Minkowski merely whispered, "Here comes the sonofabitch now."

It was the man Charles had noticed earlier, the man of marble. He was now entering the bus, which dipped, as if with great statuary weight, toward the curb. The man, Swanson, smiled hugely, with his mouth open and red, and raised the narrow slits through which he gazed back out the door at them so wide it became comical and then unsettling. They entered the bus. Swanson appeared to relax: it was as if a statue were coming to life. He held out a nickel to Minkowski, who took it with a show of distaste.

"Remind me," said Swanson with a rough, deep voice, "to buy you a decent cigar one of these days." He sniffed the stale air of the bus's interior and shot a reproving glance at its driver.

"Don't smoke," said Minkowski.

"Hell you don't. Seen you do it." He touched the wide brim of his marble hat and said to Vera: "Seen you too. Daring for a dame."

"No, sir," said Vera, "I do not believe that you have." She beamed.

"What's your name again . . . ?" asked Swanson amiably.

"Pardon me," said Vera, still smiling prettily. "I do not hand my name out to just any old clown who happens along with a wish to know it."

"*Warum nicht*? Got something to hide?" Swanson's round face got rounder and redder. "I'm only kidding you, miss!"

"What is your name, sir?" asked Vera. It was unlikely but possible that Swanson did not in truth know who she was, merely of her and not by sight, as Vera had been peripheral to his and his employer's concerns for several years, and figuring hardly at all on the West Coast. So she pretended not to know his name or face, either.

"Swanson," said Swanson, "Rudolph Swanson," leaning toward Vera over the back of a seat and holding out his hand, but looking Charles up and down. "I'm with the public utilities. What do you do, miss? If you don't mind my asking like you did your name, which I respect but do not understand. Still in school? This must be your boyfriend! Say, don't look like that! I'm a friend of your owner/operator here, and I guess you are too, by the way you've been chatting here so earnestly. So that makes us friends or at least I hope so. That's how I like to approach folks. Don't mean to pry, I most sincerely do not."

Within the narrow confines of the space left in the air by the detective's bullying garrulousness, Charles thought he ought to say something, felt something like a manly duty to speak up firmly but diplomatically, but was confused and could think of nothing to say. He felt naked and afraid of what would happen next—not an actor at all. If the man was a big-time Pinkerton or ex-Pinkerton, why did he not know who Vera was? And himself too: How could he not know he was talking to William Minot's son? Was he pretending not to know? If he was in deep with the URR people, he was capable of any grotesquerie Charles could imagine. He decided, in that moment of equal and opposing forces—youthful bravado working on youthful fear with traces of erotic mania still filtering out of his blood—to act as if he knew the answers to these and other questions. It was a kind of dramatic irony, not as he and Sir Edwin theorized and practiced it, where the real and the faked real were both unreliable, but as he'd understood the idea from lecturers at college: he would know something his audience, the marble detective, did not, thus giving himself the upper hand and perhaps causing the man to see the episode as a *show*, and be amused, entertained by it, rather than as a *part of life* and therefore requiring action, a judgment and an action, such as: they are a threat to the public welfare and I must crush them. Yes, that was it. The idea blazed past his eyes, streaked through his mind like comets crashing into planets that awoke and trembled with lust—who would be the actor on this stage? Who would get to act, and in the service of what would that action occur? He raised his head imperiously, and stared with rich-boy hauteur into Swanson's pale eyes. Swanson closed his mouth and blinked. Charles felt unimaginably powerful. He relaxed.

"Wait, sure," said Vera. "I know you." She freshened her smile, making it friendly again. In that instant he felt he could never act again unless she was acting with him. "Don't I? Weren't you in the papers a while back?"

Swanson snorted. "Nope. Not that type."

Charles remembered several articles in the *Bulletin* that Father had put under his nose over a hundred breakfasts, having to do with abuses committed by private detectives. He continued to stare with a thrillingly detached, level cool—encouraged wildly by his perception of Vera's similar condition—at Swanson.

"What type are you?" asked Vera.

"Say, you some kind of detective, little girl?" Swanson winked at Minkowski, who was black in the face with rage.

"Who," asked Vera, "did you say you worked for?"

"I insist you tell me who you are before I start repeating myself!" chuckled Swanson.

"Aren't you that famous detective? The one that beat up that fellow in the hotel room in where was it?"

"Oh my goodness!" shouted Swanson. "Certainly not!"

"It must have been that business in Stockton, then, the uh . . . oh, let me see, let me see now, the ummm—"

"Merchants and Manufacturers' Association," Charles said, drawing on resources he'd not had to measure or verify before speaking as casually as if the subject were baseball and the consequences for error nothing more serious than a corrective wisecrack—or lines in a play. "You played for them couple years ago," he went on, as everybody ceased what they'd been doing in the scene to stare at him in astonishment. "The, uh, the sheriff there arrested a fellow who'd been, what, attempting to plant dynamite, wasn't it? In the Sperry Flour Mill? If I'm remembering this right, and I sure could be wrong, don't quote me—and in the lobby of the Stockton Hotel . . . ?"

"Yes!" said Vera, "that's right, and the Stockton Iron Mill and a couple other places but the sheriff—" she paused to feign a giggle behind her hand, "—*the sheriff* figures he's got some kind of anarchist for sure, couldn't be happier, couldn't be more proud, you know, and then he finds out to his *horror* that the man is in fact a detective's assistant in the employ of the Merchants and Manufacturers' Association! That wasn't you? I mean the detective, of course, not the knucklehead assistant." Vera smiled coyly.

"I'll tell you what," grinned Swanson, "you're one well-informed god-damn little schoolgirl."

"I'll tell you what, Mr. Swanson, I'm not a goddamn little schoolgirl. I'm a citizen of the United States of America and I like to read the newspapers, I like to read them all, you know, and the *fine print* too, just to make sure everybody's getting *a fair shake*."

"Fair shake! Hear that?" Swanson addressed his question to Minkowski. "Fair shake? I don't—a fair shake, you say. I don't think so. Not in this world. I mean, really, come now. If you aren't a little schoolgirl, you're sure acting like one!" He laughed good-naturedly. "The last thing this world is is fair. You just have to get over that! Find out how things go in a general sort of way, and then do like most everybody else does. But a *fair shake* now, isn't that a newspaper itself? Kind our friend the driver here likes to peruse? Get all squinty-eyed and black-furrowed over? I read those rags too. Don't I?" he asked Minkows-ki, who turned away, started his motor and revved it angrily—probably doing it some damage, Charles thought: settle down, don't let him get to you.

"How 'bout you, Mr. Minot?"

Minkowski let his motor fall to idle and Charles took a slow, deep breath. He was known, after all, to this disgusting and dangerous man, and was now not at all sure what that knowledge meant. He glanced at Vera, who glanced back as if she thought he was forgetting his lines, and smiled discreet encouragement.

"Mr. Swanson?" Charles began.

Swanson interrupted him. "*The Alarm* and *Forward* and on and on—what else? *Backward*? I read this guy Berkman's paper. Tries to assassinate Frick back in Homestead, goes to jail, gets out, comes here, an *anarchist*, mind you, a murdering godless fucking anarchist—excuse me, miss—and he starts a paper called the *Blast*. Hard to take a guy like that seriously, you know what I mean? But what are some other newspapers? This is fun, help me out. You must get around, Mr. Minot. *Cronaca Sovversiva* and *Broyt un Frayhayt*, there's two more." His pronunciation of the Italian and the Yiddish was faultless. Then he mispronounced them, as if having fun.

"I'm afraid I can't help you," Charles said. "Those are all foreign-language newspapers, aren't they? I was brought up to read the newspapers of Christian white men."

"Now there you go, that's it, exactly!" Swanson's slitted eyes grew horribly wide again, and his wide red mouth opened with amused pleasure. "Foreign nationals behind every one of 'em! It's not American radicalism at all!" He suddenly pulled a wad of bills from an inside coat pocket. "Here's the five thousand I promised you," he stage-whispered, holding the money out to Minkowski, who reached for it. Swanson withdrew it slightly, waving it back and forth. "Just promise me again you'll do what I asked you."

"Give me the money you fucking asshole and we'll see what happens," said Minkowski genially.

Swanson laughed, stopped, then laughed again, and it seemed like the thing to do. It was infectious and effectively handed, Charles saw, the stage back to the strange detective, who was getting something like applause somewhere in his perception of the interior of the bus. He laughed a little longer, enjoying it clearly, then waved good-bye as he stepped from the bus and almost instantly disappeared into the crowd. Just as they were exhaling, he scared them all by appearing at Vera's open window.

"I know what *you'd* do, miss," he said, "with five grand."

"You *do*?" she giggled.

"Climb up the tallest building in the city and put one of those electric signs up, like your friend did in New York a few years back, way up there on the top of that tower over, uh, over the uh . . . Madison Square Garden, jeepers, how I lose a name like that beats me! At the feet of lovely Diana, that big old naked lady who spins around like a weather vane."

Minkowski engaged first gear and jumped away from the curb.

Charles saw it: the faint red letters, hundreds of feet up in the murky night, coming down Lexington from the Armory Show and all its insane new art, hoping to catch the first performance of the pageant of the striking Paterson Silk Workers at the Garden, turning on Twenty-Sixth, and seeing it over the treetops of Madison Square Park, floating in complete cloudy darkness above the feeble gaslight of the streets, as if written in fire that had burned itself down to embers—this was the work of someone Vera knew? He had been there—of course he'd been there! And had Vera not seen them? He thought she had.

He could not get the picture out of his mind. 1913. Alexander was already the governor's chief of staff in Sacramento, and Andrew was figuring out what do in the wake of the humiliating Bull Moose defeat—not to mention the attempt by Schrank on the former president's life: had the attempt been made in California, it might have occurred to Andrew to protect "Uncle Ted," and gunshots had always sobered the family in ways gunshots did not ordinarily sober people—e.g., by seeking cover, either physical or psychological, panting, giving thanks to God Almighty that they were still alive, committing themselves to kindness and gentleness for the rest of their days, or casting about hysterically for a weapon to call their own. No, the Minots had, rather like T. R. himself, received gunshots and other potentially mortal wounds as signs from God that they had been chosen for great work. Charles had several semesters at Cal under his belt, was restless, and of course, while they were ascertaining the nature of the next bit of great work, they had come across the country to see the Armory Show!

A small crowd of ticket buyers had gathered around the box office window. Charles parked his Studebaker at the far end of the block and removed his goggles. He was much too preoccupied with Vera's sudden transformation in his mind—from what to what, it was hard to say, beautiful young woman to daredevil, dangling herself high above the city to declare an era in which no one need be afraid? From somebody he wanted to fuck to somebody he wanted to worship? Much too amazed to care about the crowd, and they appeared to be cheering anyway, more cheering knuckleheads waving signs—but it was hard in the deepening twilight to tell. He moved unsteadily down the alley toward the stage door, his stomach rising and falling and percolating its acids. He put his hand on the railing that led to the door and prepared himself to see his nausea through, to, as it were, stick a finger down his throat and be done with it, bear the grave responsibility before him, do the ridiculous and false thing they expected him to do, or brave and true, depending on your mood and point of view, enter into the nightmare time and space of the stage and humiliate himself in an ill-conceived and awkwardly played-out bit of fraudulence, then emerge from it, miraculously relieved to find it had been worthy and real, bursting finally with gratitude and love of life, wryly amused at his earlier childish torments and wading into the riotous esteem of his fellow San Franciscans. Yes, that was how it was—or could easily be seen to be.

He went down a dark corridor that still smelled of sawn wood and fresh cement and hot metal, crammed with old clothes from centuries, even millennia, past, odd props the use of which could not be guessed at, and junk, plain junk, that had been accumulated in the drive for funding, seeing no one, hearing no one and nothing, and entered into the dressing room where the other actors sat slumped and stinking of paints and creams and anxiety and indigestion before streaked and spotted mirrors throwing back hideous made-up masks. The princess's understudy looked up at him. "Aren't you the daredevil," she enunciated.

They were all, he realized in a surge of bile, looking at him through the predatory safety of their mirrors, two banks of them on either side, three apiece, six faces, a gauntlet . . . but rather than plunging him into a deeper vomitous misery, it, to his great surprise, emboldened him.

"What," he demanded, "is the matter with you children now?"

They looked away, six different moues of sarcasm, bored, it now seemed to him, with their anxiety and his late arrival. Then the old man, Garagiola, stood up and told him to go soak his head. He used his old Brooklyn voice, a sign that all was not well, and that he was feeling peevish. "Aw, go soak yuh head," he said with a small dismissive flip of his liver-spotted and veinous old claw of a hand.

"*Relax*," said Teddy Blair, rubbing his false belly. "For Christ's sake."

The electric lights went off and on, and the old man squeaked with annoyance. "Now what the hell was *that*?" shouted Blair.

"That's just what I wanted to see!" Charles said, striding confidently on-stage, but it was clear that something had happened and whatever he was pretending to see was not what the audience or his fellow actors were see-ing. He felt quite alone. The city was ruined. The vast schematic in his mind diagramming all the points of warmth and assurance and connection seemed no longer to apply, though he moved from one to the next and the next as if they still did, feeling perhaps a faint tingle or echo at the climax of each moment. He seemed somehow onstage and yet not in the play. He was neither Christopher Newman nor Charles Minot—which, after all, was part of what he'd been playing at all through rehearsals. The context, though: it had changed. He did not know in what way it was changed, nor exactly how the change had come about, but it was no longer, in any way, a positive environment. He was in some way he suddenly understood very well, *nobody*. But nobody where and in the service of what? Whenever the audience laughed or drew in their breath, or when he touched another ac-tor, when he, for instance, embraced the false princess, the non-Vera, and kissed her with the by-now-lifeless facsimile of passion, he felt as if he were watching someone else. He no longer felt safe. He knew in the back of his mind that this was no way properly to act, and he consequently became frightened. It was not the simple if nauseating and paralyzing anxiety of stage fright, but a kind of pathological anomie—if in fact it was pathologi-cal to see things as they were, to feel isolated and disoriented and friend-less. But he broke off the kiss at just the moment he always had done, the audience began to applaud as they always had done, the curtain surged across the stage and swept back and the audience continued to applaud, though not quite thunderously now, he noted, and saw as well that the house was not quite full.

"That wasn't so bad," murmured Teddy, holding his false stomach before him as if it were disgusting. No one replied, cleansing themselves as quick-ly as they could and dressing for home or for nightlife—which was not,

Charles mused from his terrible distance, out of the ordinary at all. And then they were gone. The hands and the manager made noise for a while and then they too were gone. He went back onstage. Where was Sir Edwin? He called out, softly. A single limelight blasted out of its box, illuminating like desert sunlight a section of the balcony, and he looked to see if one of the plumber's sons was again experimenting with the gas, but he was nowhere in sight. Again the light, in the absence of any other, struck him as if possessed of sound, and in the slowly drifting dust of the audience's departure, it appeared to billow. He had once, not long ago, dreamed he was sailing alone through the Golden Gate, and felt the wind, the famous wind, almost imperceptibly slacken. His telltales fluttered. When they fell limp against the sail, he perceived the event as ominous. He was as usual not overly concerned, certainly not frightened—he never was in life, he reminded himself, much less in dreams, no matter how dreadful or sorrowing—but remembered that the wind was something emphatically not under his power of control. It had nothing to do with his family's wealth, but rather with the turning of the planet in space, and he could call as loudly as he liked for a certain level of performance in that strait, but the answer would always be the same: here is how the world works. He called out his first line to the empty theater: "That's just what I wanted to see!" but the world had changed in some subtle way, the world was working itself without him, and he imagined Vera sitting at the back of the main floor, in the darkness under the balcony. "The telltales are fluttering! They're drooping!" he called out, thinking that one consequence of this change—whatever else was happening, had happened, or would happen— was that he was completely in her power, as hypnotized as if she were a mad-bombing Svengali. If he had always seen himself in the world as somehow *playing*, he now saw himself in a dream that was darkening even as he watched it unfold around him, deepening in tone at the same time it became more vivid and fantastic: the little house orchestra executing a precisely controlled *allargando*, something out of Wagner, *Das Rheingold*, as the characters, people near and dear to him as well as strange and new, took on the costumes and gestures of the fairy tale, and as the footlights snickered and fizzed and went out one by one across the stage, became the unstrung puppets of their own fantastic shadows.

The theater's marquis was dark but he could still see quite plainly CHARLES MINOT AS THE AMERICAN. He looked up and down the street: it was not a lively street and was deserted now, and dark. The wind was cold and he put on his leather jacket and began to walk to his automobile, the only vehicle left on the whole somber street. Turning to get one arm in, he saw a large white shape against the brick of the building. He stopped and looked at it: it almost seemed a basement window filled with light, a scrim, or some kind of magical portal. Then he saw it was a sign and had a long wooden stake attached to it. He went over to it and turned it over: CHARLES MINOT IS NO AMERICAN!!! Another behind it cried, SHAME ON YOU CHARLES MINOT!!!

The house declined steadily and visibly each night, which turned out, of course, to be a good thing. Father brushed it aside as a knee-jerk popular response against which there was no, never had been a, remedy. It was a little wave. Charles was not fooled: Father was visibly relieved, almost cheerful. The only question was, what kind of relief, what kind of good cheer was it? There were two distinct modes: either he felt he had gotten his way, or he knew something, something that only the rulers of the city could know, and was pleased that he did not have to be, as it were, patriarchal, judgmental, and dismissive about something he had always had little sympathy for in his son's life—but what could the nature of such knowledge be? How could a play, that Father found trivial, matter politically, even when it was, if it was, the politics that happened around the Tree at the Center of the Universe, with its roots in corruption and decay and its flowers in heaven?

Before *The American* was canceled, and the openings of the theater's other two shows indefinitely postponed, a bomb, contained in a small suitcase, was hurled, or more properly, dropped, from the balcony. It wasn't clear if the bomber was trying for the stage or the audience, but the bomb killed actors and wounded musicians: Grandpa Garagiola, portly Teddy Blair, pretty Mary Girdle, Vera's blossoming understudy Catherine White, community-minded newcomer Margaret Stensrud—who came off the stage into the wing with such force that she knocked Charles unconscious—and his friend Gene Woodcock were all blown to bits. Charles was broadly believed to be the bomber's probable target. But he had been offstage—so briefly, an exit, a breath, an entrance—at the moment of the explosion. Had it been just bad timing? And if he was he the target, why was he the target? Because he was "the American"? An oligarch? An oligarch in the making? Was it simply a blow at the aristocracy as made manifest by the Minots and their theater and their disgusting play? Or was he the target because he had been associating, as the protest signs made clear, with anarchists. Was he perhaps not the target at all? Had an anarchist meant to scare the war-mongering general public? Or were the railroaders, working on a decade-old grievance with William Minot, simply doing what they did best: destroy—either good or evil, depending on your point of view. These possibilities, along with the indispensable frame-ups—railroad barons framing anarchists, anarchists framing railroad barons—merged and then, in an orgasmic release of spermy public rumor-mongering, was made manifest in what the Buddhists call "the ten thousand things," an effectively infinite process of variations of the species *conspiraciensus*.

He was summoned to Fall River Mills, to the ranch, where everybody, including Amelia and Pastor Tom, his two older brothers and the women they were engaged to, his younger brothers and a platoon of their friends, were spending the summer. He had not wanted to seem to be fleeing the city, the horror, as his family had, and decided to stay for as long as he could stand it. He felt he could stand it forever with Vera, but her whereabouts, he was once again told, were unknown, and he saw he could not press his concern, not an inch. Two weeks later, on the day of the Preparedness Parade, dispirited and restless and confused, he went to the shop and found it full of new faces. Nobody could tell him where even someone as integral to the shop as Jules was, either. A mechanic who claimed to have done some work for him told him he thought they were going to watch the parade from a rooftop of a building on Market. He gave Charles the number, then asked him if he knew of anybody who wanted to buy rare old motorcycles.

"Like what, for instance?" asked Charles, sensing a joke in the offing.

The mechanic, pink lips reaching out from an oily face to close around the mouth of a bottle of beer: "Like an '02 Triumph with a Belgian Minerva motor?"

Someone standing near said, "What's that?"

The mechanic said, "This is the kid had a Belgian waffle he wanted to unload."

"Minerva," Charles said. "And my name is Minot."

"A Belgian Minot and his name is Minerva."

"Other way around," Charles said.

"Whatever," said the mechanic.

"I'd take the waffle," said the other man, "but who needs a Minerva? You gotta shut the engine off every time you come to a stop, don't you?"

The mechanic nodded and belched. Charles thanked him for his help, left the shop, and made his way as near to Market Street as he could get. Walking through dense and happy crowds waving flags, he heard a marching band. Climbing five flights of stairs, he came to the last door and stood before it. He knocked and waited. Knocked a second time and continued to wait. Then opened the door and stepped into the sunlight. There were enough people on the roof to make it impossible to see everyone at once, and he paused on the threshold. There, he saw that everyone he could see was looking at him.

He knew they were looking at nothing, at an actor, and was untroubled.

He saw Vera, deep in conversation with the woman he had met the night Farnsworth had beaten her up. Talking to the woman but looking at him.

She saw Charles see her and looked away.

His heart began to thump—insisting he was something—as he searched the crowd for Warren Farnsworth and his sworn agency of death. How Farnsworth's jealous wrath could prevail, even survive, in the face of a mass murder only days old, Charles did not know. Appraised calmly, from a crucial but not necessarily great distance, it was impossible to countenance. No sane man would kill another who had just survived a bomb blast over a sexual matter. Remove that distance, though, and place your mind back onstage with the carnage, with the severed limbs, the rolling, rocking heads coming to a stop in the limelighted pools of brilliant, smoking, crimson, still-spreading blood, the heaps of intestine and organ meat that had been actors draped like bunting on the furniture or fallen like confetti on paraders . . . and whether or not you thought they could be replaced and that the show would go on, as everything was replaced and every show went on, and that terror was ordinary and that there were no sane men, not in the moment of the act as every moment was a moment of an act, there, on the stage, you saw that everything was possible and that the only way to go on was to see that you were some kind of nexus of nothing, or nexus of everything, if you preferred, and therefore immortal. In other words, Warren Farnsworth could very easily step up and stab him in the heart, or—how had Father's Montaigne put it?—make a person repent by killing them?

He saw "Owl," Tom Moody, who was wearing a large sombrero, talking to a Mexican gentleman he had seen before, and Moody's wife, Minnie, but no sign of Farnsworth. He moved to the edge of the roof, where people were lining up and leaning over the wide stone parapet, watching the miniature paraders below draw slowly nearer and nearer. Then the entire street was alive, as with a single undulating thing. As far as he could see in either direction, the street was filled with tight formations of marchers, throbbing with manifestations here and there of the great power of crowds and parades, colors flickering and changing, the formations seeming to move without moving, little flutterings on the edges and deeper within the only evidence of propulsion. The noise was now steady and loud enough to cause the people nearest him to speak up and lean together, nodding emphatically at everything they heard and said to each other. Distant whistles and cheers and rolling hurrahs rose and fell in the flux of sound churning below them. The first band disappeared in the southwest and a second appeared in the northeast. Slowly it made itself heard. Banners swayed with the labored gaits of their holders and with the wind, which came and went pleasantly. Keogh and his cavaliers had been at the head of the parade, and Charles had not seen them. Someone he didn't recognize was taking pictures, endowing himself with what would later be a priceless collection of photographs: influential and sometimes infamous San Francisco radicals laughing and goofing around and looking, if you didn't know who they were, like picnickers. Walking among the crowd—everyone nodding politely and sometimes smiling gently—he saw the tall fair man who had so disliked Dickens and Dostoyevsky—and Hardy, he sputtered to himself with faint but real hysteria in his inner voice, how could ANYONE NOT LIKE THOMAS HARDY?—and listened to him tell a story about himself and, if Charles understood correctly, Jules, kidnapping the obnoxious son of the headmaster of their private school, binding and gagging the boy and locking him in the basement of a summer home in Watch Hill, Rhode Island, leaving him there and being delayed in their return by a hurricane. The Mexican gentleman, he learned, was preparing to leave San Francisco, to meet his brother in St. Louis, where together they would raise funds for the defense of a third brother, who was still in prison in Mexico. These were men, he was told by the woman whom he'd seen huddled with the now-vanished Vera, the likes of which you could not find outside of Mexico and Russia, men who gave up wealth and power and privilege to help the downtrodden.

"You won't find them in America," said the woman, "that's for sure."

"No," said Charles, edging away, "you sure won't."

"No indeed," she confirmed, following him. "In America, you find 'the American,' don't you?"

"Yes," he said. "I think that's safe to say. I'm not sure why you think you have to say that to me now, but—"

"Look," said the woman, "I'm not going to *bite* you. I'm as horrified as I can be."

"I'm sure everybody is horrified. Perhaps only the bomber himself is not."

The woman's lip, her whole lower jaw, began to tremble. Her eyes without warning clouded with tears and reddened.

"I happen to think the bomber is not excluded from horror."

The woman sniffed and choked when she tried to speak. "I am so sorry. We, I, none of us, we never never hated you."

"I can assure you that I do not feel hated, and never have done."

"No, no, no," sobbed the woman without moving her face. "Hate is so, so, so wrong."

Impassively, slowly, carefully, Charles reached into the pocket of his jacket and gave the woman a handkerchief. She dabbed at her eyes and blew her nose, handed it back, smiled.

"We love 'the American.'"

"I am sorry to say I never learned your name, after all we've been through."

"Lucy."

"Where," asked Charles, "did Vera get off to?"

"I don't know. She saw you."

"Neither she nor I were blown to pieces the other day so I am thinking she has *got* to be on the planet somewhere!"

Lucy stared at him, frightened.

"Is Jules here?"

Still frightened but speaking blankly. "Yes."

Minnie Moody was telling someone that she had for a fact given piano lessons to a Pinkerton detective. "He was Polish and liked the Chopin mazurkas I played for him."

Turning away with a half-smile, Charles heard the end of another story. "The defendant jumped to his feet and shouted, 'Gentlemen, let me ask you, do you believe a man such as this one we have before us?' He was sobbing with incredulity, let me tell you, as we all would have been, knowing the asshole he was talking about. 'You wouldn't whip your dog on the testimony of such a creature!' he plead. 'No honest man would! Any man who would believe such a man would not deserve to have a dog!'"

And Charles laughed knowingly with the rest of the crowd, seeing that they were watching him and hoping—he judged—that he would laugh. He turned, the wind catching his hair, and saw Vera leave, the Mexican gentleman holding the door for her. He thought of following her, but did not. He watched the photographer take a few more pictures, then asked if he could look through the viewfinder. The photographer gestured toward the camera, and Charles bent toward it. Just as he was about to straighten up and step back, he was astounded to see Vera and Jules step into the frame. They smiled broadly, waved. He straightened up and stepped back.

They were already at the door.

Another wave from Vera and they were gone.

On Steuart Street, across from the Ferry Building, where the paraders had gathered to begin their march, the last of them were heading out: some very old men, Grand Army of the Republic veterans, some Sons of the American Revolution, and a group of Spanish-American War heroes, displaying the battle flag of the First California Volunteers. None of these men were hurt by the blast of the copycat suitcase bomb, which exploded just after the Volunteers had begun to march, but forty others were, and ten of them were killed. A policeman caught a little girl by the ankle, but had only her leg to show for it. The rest of her was some ways down Steuart. Three deaths elsewhere in the city were almost instantly connected to the bombing of the parade. The bomber, it was conjectured rather swiftly and easily, either just before or just after he'd activated his bomb and left it in its suitcase at the corner of Steuart and Market, had stabbed to death three people with whom he was associated in some way: Jules Beveridge, Lucille Olivet Brown, and Amado Joaquin Fernández de Lizardi (an erstwhile minister in the Juarez cabinet in Mexico City, exiled and in hiding with his brother). Brown and Fernández de Lizardi were found together, naked, in a bed in the basement of the motorcycle shop owned by Beveridge. The room housed a printing press, and the shop was frequented by radicals of every type—including anarchists. Warren Farnsworth was arrested in a doctor's office where he was trying to get ointment for his eczema; and while claiming innocence, did not explicitly repudiate the idea (instantly current in the papers) that once he'd begun murdering—or had committed his soul to the unforgivable horror of it—he found he could not stop himself. Arrested also, on the Russian River while claiming to be fishing, was Thomas Moody, allegedly the mastermind of the plot, and Israel Minkowski. A dozen other men and women, including the infamous anarchist, Alexander Berkman, were arrested but released soon afterward.

PART THREE:

"THE WATCHDOGS OF LOYALTY"

"'He will repent it,' we say.
And because we have given him a pistol shot to the head,
do we think he repents it?"

—Montaigne, "Cowardice, Mother of Cruelty," *Essays*

"A man whose brain does not work at all times, but only at pain-
ful moments, is often haunted by thoughts of madness."

—Anton Chekhov, *Lights*

Charles crossed from Saint Paul, where he lived, to Minneapolis on the Marshall Street Bridge. It was an unseasonably warm day in mid-November. The sky was low and shifting: gray-minded, he thought, irresolute. Was he? No. Susceptible to it? Yes. Perhaps. Spatters of rain the size of silver dollars appeared with loud cracks on the sidewalk, as if in prelude to a summer thunderstorm. He boarded a streetcar with a sense of portentous displacement in space and time—but of course he was among strangers in a strange place, about to commit strange acts—or rather, to commit himself to one single act of strangeness. That was to say—finally, he hoped—to act wholly outside himself. He wanted to appear as if he conformed to the idea everyone who saw him might have of him, and then . . . and then, well, yes, he hesitated even then, he didn't know what he meant, he didn't know what he meant.

He wanted somehow to act outside the natural corruption and degradation of his time. He was still Platonic enough to think one man's actions could momentarily halt the flow of perfection to chaos, could in some small momentary way harken back to the perfect forms, the perfect ideas, to God. *It would still be an act, I would still be an actor, Plato, if he knew I still saw myself as upon a stage, would condemn me, or at least insist I remain in my makeup, singing, imitating, ridiculous—to stay away at all costs from the world of the simple, the clear, the austere, the virtuous.*

But he thought he had learned something from his friends, the so-called anarchists, and he wanted to know what it was like, what it might be like, to feel the faintest tremor or breeze or falling of the shadow of what it might be like to live that way, with no dogma, no gods, no fear.

It was all he had ever professed, but now saw so clearly, so painfully, how his profession had been vitiated by dogma, by a god, by fear.

The car's driver wore a button he'd not seen before. It was yellow, had a number and a date on it, and a picture of a streetcar with the letters "AA of S" and "ERE of A." He sat down behind the driver, leaned forward and asked what it all meant. Without turning his head, the driver replied, "Amalgamated Association of Street and Electric Railways Employees of America. Don't confuse this here yellow button with the blue one now. Them blue buttons are company buttons. They say 'Trainmen's Cooperative Association' on 'em, but it's a darn lie. I'll tell you what some citizens do and you can do what you like. They see a blue button and they spit on the nickel before they hand it over."

"I've got a red button myself," Charles said.

The driver slowly turned around and gave him a look. "You what?"

Charles didn't think it was exactly with brotherhood that he spoke, but couldn't say for sure that it wasn't, either.

"Red button?" asked the driver.

"Card to tell the truth. You want to see it? IWW?"

The driver only continued to stare.

"Keep your eye on the road, friend."

"Last man called me 'friend,' friend, had his tongue ripped out."

"What a strange world you live in, friend."

It was a lie: he was no more a Wobbly than Mother was. He was closer at that moment, if such a thing could be measured with any accuracy, to wanting to be the president of the United States than a Wobbly, which was to say, not at all. But he wanted to appear for a moment as a Wobbly, and so he did. The driver turned away, and he spoke no further to him.

He got off at Nicollet, near the ballpark, and stood for a moment listening for the sounds of a game he realized only after a few long seconds he couldn't hear because a game could not be in progress so late in the year, however wonderfully warm and ideal for baseball the weather might be. The rain came forth suddenly, in blowing sheets, with lightning in the now suddenly black western sky. He got a car north and noted the yellow button. Downtown he walked east, getting soaked but not minding it, to the Milwaukee Road depot and the Chamber of Commerce building, home of the globe-encircling Grain Exchange. He pushed through the doors and immediately got a good looking-over by people in the foyer. The roar of speculation broke and crashed, subsided in a kind of ominous hissing, gathered again, broke and crashed, broke and crashed, then built steadily into a roar that did not break. His thick hair was slicked in broad daggers about his skull, his shirt was plastered to his back, his trousers dark and heavy with rainwater, his feet squirming in clammy beds of stained leather. *Who's this?* everybody passing seemed to want to know. He ignored them and looked over a railed balustrade down into the big octagonal trading pit; then up at the huge French murals celebrating grain and its harvesters—so great on these vast paintings, he thought, and so obscure off them. He looked with some knowledge but not much interest at the giant quotation chalkboards and the tiny women on thin ladders and quaking scaffolds, covered like spinsters in dust, erasing figures and chalking new ones without surcease or visible complaint or difficulty or even, given that he couldn't make out their faces and made his judgments based on posture, care. They had a mark to make and could not know or care what marks were being made at that moment by others of their kind. That was how he imagined their lives anyhow. A group passed near him, a murmur against the roar. A man with a small megaphone walked at its head. "Designed by Misters Kees and Colburn, it is the largest primary wheat market, and the biggest cash grain market, in the world. It is the only commodities exchange offering futures in dark spring northern wheat and sunflower seeds. It is the . . ." and they were swallowed up, bullhorn and all. He mounted a broad marble stairway that led to the mezzanine, where the oceanic sound was much reduced. Halfway up the narrower stairs to the second floor, it was lost entirely. His legs felt heavy, bound by the damp cloth and leaden with anxiety, and where only minutes earlier he'd found the rain almost exhilarating he was now nearly miserable, as miserable as he ever allowed himself to be, as unsure of himself as he had ever been, as nervous as if he were suffering Chinese water torture. By the ninth floor, the floor to which he'd been directed by Father's cousin's secretary, the blood was banging and clicking in his head and he was breathing in gasps. It was an eerie floor, where nothing seemed to have moved for years, and it amplified what he recognized as akin to stage fright. He found a men's room and retched in a stall. Once his wind and false but necessary sense of self was restored, he stared at himself in the mirror for a long while. No one came in while he conducted that silent, secret interrogation. He splashed cold water on his face, toweled off, ran a hand through his drying, thickening hair.

There was no glass in the door that bore the number he'd been given, and no one appeared in answer to his knock. He paused for a moment, put his hand carefully on the knob, turned it, pulled the door open, and entered the room.

Three men were arranged at the far end of a leather-topped table with green lamps on it. One man was at its head, the other two pushed away from the table in their leather chairs, fanned out and not quite facing him in perfect symmetry, as if they were posing for a photograph. Which of course they were: a photographer banged his tripod exiting another door to Charles's left, next to which he saw, as the door closed, a fifth man sitting on a plain wooden chair with a notebook on his lap, his lips pursed, looking back at Charles over the top of a pince-nez.

"Here's our young daredevil," said one of the men at the table, a balding man with burning eyes. He stood up: his body was a large soft triangle. "You know he is because he just walked right in when nobody came to the door! Have a seat, Slick." He smiled ambiguously, a vigorous, good-looking, intelligent-seeming man, Charles thought, but there was something in the way he held his head, thrust it, or in the way he pulled his lips back, widened his eyes . . .

The man at the head of the table, balding too but with larger features and a more expansive, athletic, unruffled, and almost kindly demeanor, looked

Charles frankly up and down. The third man, gray-haired and wearing luxuriant silver moustaches, did not look up from his neat stack of documents.

He thought of all the successful men he had known in his life, all the company men, the men of business and empire, of politics and religion—sound men, powerful men, strong men, overlords and overseers, aides, secretaries, footmen with enough influence to put a thousand men out of work with a wink, men who dressed the king and drank deep choking drafts of humiliation so that they might wear nice suits of clothes and eat real turtle soup. And he thought of the men who had no power and never would but who dressed and acted as if they did: there, certainly, was another kind of false acting, acting that revealed nothing but sordid pathetic fear, pitiful men lashing out with tiny scratching hands, making squeaky threats and running away, hunched over . . . surviving. And he thought of his brothers and their friends from Harvard, the neo-Benthamites, Utilitarians, the "new men" who saw politics as a science, business as a science, not as a means of managing the welfare of the country or distributing its wealth, as Father and his friends saw it or pretended to see it, but as a means of establishing and securing power, demonstrating over and over again their superiority with displays of dismissive affability, bored ignorance of everything but the spectacular wisdom that had landed them so much *loot*. And then there were the men in this room. Instantly he smelled their nauseating corrupt power and waited with dreamlike confidence that was not his own as one by one their hands rose from their laps to find a glass of water or a pen, and he could see and confirm his hallucinatory foreknowledge that, a la Strindberg, they were blackened with use, crusty with blood. These were operational men, men who liked, or perhaps even needed, craved, to go down to the pen to slaughter hogs. They were field generals, crazy men, he figured, and almost admirable for it, men who got up on horses if they were drunk or mad enough, and either dodged bullets and reaped the rewards of notoriety and a grateful country, or were shot down to die in the mud and shit like common slaves. This was a frontier state, he reminded himself. They were all barbarians. Subjugate, wander, forget. That was why Father had currency, why he had respect and even in some quarters admiration: he lived in the Old West and the New West with equal conviction and consequentiality. Oh, he had all the power Father and Alexander and Andrew had, and more besides, at least potentially, because he saw what might be a way around dogma and God and fear, but he was not sound, not sound. Never really had been. Not in the way a pseudo-democratic oligarchic capitalist had to be.

Charles returned the careful, neutral regard of these three men, these three of the eight commissioners of Minnesota Public Safety, lawyers all, hard, practical, profoundly but carefully unprincipled men.

"A good deal of authority has been invested in us," said the vain and stately man, still not looking up from his papers. "Mr. Minot, your . . . uncle? Cousin?"

"My father's cousin."

"Whoever he is has no doubt alluded to our sanction."

"Oh, surely you know who—they named a town after him in North Dakota!"

"You—what? Yes, oh yes, of course, just a—never mind that. You will need to know a little more about us. That is all I meant to say."

"But not much more!" the triangular man shouted, laughing in apparent good humor.

"Mr. Minot is my father's cousin," Charles repeated, hoping to draw the vain but shy man's gaze from his papers. "Not my uncle. He has a town named after him in western North Dakota."

And that man did so. He was not shy, but so apparently full of undirected hate that it was distracting him entirely. "Is that so?" he said. "Yes, yes, of course, didn't I just say . . . ?"

The affable-seeming man said, "We have prepared a report for the edification of our agents, and herewith present it to you."

Charles was quite sure this man was the governor of the state. He knew the governor sat on the MCPS board but was surprised to see him here, now.

"Do you know," said the triangular man, "we never thought to ask if you can read and write, Slick!"

"Yes, sir," Charles said, "I can do all that."

"Ladies and gentlemen!" he chuckled. "The next president of the United States!"

"I can do all that and more besides," he said, staring first at the triangular man, then at the hateful, vain man, then at the affable-seeming man, the governor.

"'Do you know,'" mimicked that man, raising his eyebrows in reproach. "I don't see where the profit is, John, in making fun of our agents. Particularly—"

"Well," said the triangular man, "I do, and that's enough, isn't it? Isn't that what we've been saying here, and agreeing to so tiresomely? My guess is Slick understands me. Slick? What say?"

He had been gesturing at Charles with his head and let one of those nods bring his face fully around to him. Charles took a moment, a stage moment, to smile, feeling it to be a great but necessary expense. "Sure I do," he said brightly.

"See?" asked the triangular man mock-plaintively.

"His father," said the affable man, "Theodore Roosevelt himself—"

"Yes, yes, yes," said the triangular man. "Begging your pardon, Governor, begging your pardon, Mr. Minot, sir."

"Not at all," Charles said. He and the triangular man shared what seemed to be a sincere smile.

The first man resumed his briefing, regaining his athletic kindness. "Three laws, as you know, were passed in reply to President Wilson's call for preparedness. The first outlaws syndicalism in all its forms, and in all kinds and degrees of participation. For example, 'interest in a subversive organization' is now against the law. So we have a question or two about . . . about your associations in San Francisco."

Charles was deep in his character and did not blush. "Which associations particularly? I really have no idea what you think you know about me. Apart, of course, from nearly having been blown to pieces."

"The associations that result in the signs being waved about on the street in front of your theater—"

"Before it was blown up."

"—insisting you weren't an American," said the triangular man. "Associations with people who threw the bomb at you in the theater. People who threw the bomb at the parade."

Charles held up his hand. The triangular man noted the raised hand and waved his own in response. "These may be people you are or were associated with in a friendly, an unfriendly way, a friendly but peripheral way, an unfriendly but peripheral way, people to whom you are antagonistic in one way or another and who find you an antagonist as well, people with whom for all intents and purposes you have no relations whatsoever but who can *be associated with you in certain analyses*, people with whom you are associated only because you have tried wittingly or unwittingly to destroy each other."

Charles kept his hand raised throughout the speech but at its close gently replaced it on the table. "That covers the waterfront," he said. "A waterfront in which I have absolutely nothing to hide or be in any way ashamed of."

"I know that!" chortled the triangular man. "Jeez! You think that means we're not supposed to ask the questions, for Pete's sake?"

The third man, the vain and hateful man with big silver moustaches, cleared his throat. "We can, for another instance, shut a newspaper down."

Charles appeared to lose his patience: "Yes, yes, yes, you could do that several years ago. A fellow can wonder if the chief of police is a blustering pomaded halfwit—and be packed off to prison for it. What are you crowing about now, you blustering pomaded halfwit?"

Triangle laughed. Vain blustered. Governor smiled.

"The second law," said Governor while Vain dabbed at his lips with a handkerchief, "requires aliens to register with us. This is due, as I am sure you suspect, to the high percentage of aliens in the ranks of the subversive. The third law creates us."

"Though of course we were already here," said Triangle.

Charles nodded at him and Triangle winked.

"The whole time," said Charles in the spirit of the wink. "All along."

"It gives us," continued Vain with forced and comical austerity, "a budget, sole discretion over that budget, and dominion over the first two laws. We can require people to appear before us, as in a court, and, well, just generally, in layman's terms, do all the kinds of things a court would do to them. We are a public safety commission, and that says it all. We have counterparts in every state of the union. Though it must be said, nowhere with quite the, uh, quite the . . ."

"Say it!" said Triangle. "Power! I can't stand this coyness about our authority. We have got what we need and that's all that need be said about it. To blanch at a word with all we've got to accomplish . . . !"

"He is not blanching at words, John!" shouted Governor. "Look how red and wet his mouth is!"

"All right now," said Vain, suddenly tranquil. "I'm sure I do not much care when playboys shout abuse at me. This particular playboy was the target of anarchist bombers so I am willing to ignore most of what he feels compelled to say, for the sake of bringing him on board as we have already decided to do, for many good reasons that have nothing to do with his reckless manner. The main point here and now is that there's a lot of flexibility in these laws. There's a lot of vagueness in them, frankly, and that means flexibility for our agents and the administrators who direct them or who report the actions of agents to us—to the commission's secretaries, rather. Which is where we see you working, Charles."

All three men looked at him, and he nodded with a show of interest in his eyes.

"Theoretically, we can get tripped up any number of ways if something serious comes howling out of the, uh, the *traitorous hinterlands*, if you will, into the courts, but we are *not*, Charles, thinking in the long term, if you follow."

They all looked at him again. This time he remained impassive. No eye work.

"We've got room for fancy footwork here and there, and by fancy footwork I mean big boots coming down hard. We can take care of business now, and when the war is over, we will have done our best, done our part. The courts can then strike down this, strike down that, water down this provision, reduce the scope of that—be as liberal and half-hearted as they like, but it won't matter. We will have done the hard part. It's what we've been asked to do, and I am confident we will succeed. I'm sure you understand, Charles."

All three regarded him a third time, and he remained, to his own surprised dismay, impassive. Why not pretend to share the enthusiasm? He could not help but stare at hateful silvery Vain, but did not reflect his hatred back at him.

"You're a fart smeller," said Triangle. "Isn't that right? I mean, smart feller, sorry."

"I'd rather not say," Charles said, taking recourse in breezy irony.

Triangle laughed. "So there's really only one thing I need to know before we stamp this application A-OK. And that is, can a smartass like you mix with stupid people?" He smiled at Vain: "A smartass playboy?"

"I may," Charles said warmly but firmly, "have bantered amusingly with the president when I was barely old enough to speak—the colonel loved that kind of repartee especially, as his youngest son Quentin was gifted in that way too—and my father may once upon a time have had very great ambitions for me, and I may be here because influential people think this is an important step for me whatever and wherever the end may be, but I am, honestly, a playboy. I'm a spoiled rich kid and my desire is to produce avant-garde theater and musical compositions. I'd also like to race motorcycles—which should go a long way toward explaining my presence in that shop, you have surely remarked already—maybe invest in a banked board track and fix races for the benefit of myself and select friends. That's a popular sport, motorcycle racing. Stupid people love it. Dirty and dangerous. And what's more, to answer your question directly and candidly, *I like stupid people.*"

"Ah, I like this guy," said Triangle with a broad beaming smile and cheerful light in his eyes.

"We are unclear about proceedings against the bombers, and we are told you may enlighten us," said Vain.

Charles reached into his coat pocket. "Assuming it didn't get too wet to read . . . I, yes, here, let me see if any of this is news to you. One year ago, Mr. Thomas Moody, aka Owl, a known motorcyclist and frequenter of the Beveridge shop in San Francisco's North Beach or Latin Quarter neighborhood—where I too, as you have noted, was seen and heard to engage in spirited discussions—as well as an openly declared Wobbly, cleared the last of three trials revolving around the bombing of a Pacific Gas and Electric tower in the San Bruno hills outside the city. That is to say, briefly, that he was found not guilty due to a lack of evidence. Citing 'triple jeopardy,' Moody went to ground. He assumed disguises, gentlemen, and laid low. In the spring of last year, he was arrested in Martinez, California. A skiff he had been sailing inexpertly in the Carquinez Strait had run aground. He said he had been fishing but the skiff was found to hold the following articles: a .30-30 Winchester rifle with a Maxim silencer and one box of cartridges, a .38-caliber automatic Colt revolver and ammunition, a twelve-gauge shotgun with its barrels painted aluminum and a box of shells loaded with buckshot, thirteen dry-cell batteries connected in series and soldered to an alarm clock, a five-hundred-foot spool of wire, fourteen electric exploders or caps, containing fulminate of mercury and attached at regular intervals to the wire, assorted tools, and a pair of gloves. There was, however, no dynamite in the skiff. Neither was there guncotton or nitroglycerin. Without the last three ingredients, if you will, there was no bomb and no case. However! After the bombing of my theater, an investigation commenced that paid most of its attention to those people who frequented the motorcycle shop. My father had been informed of my proximity to that place and these investigations, but chose not to inform me. His motives are frankly unclear to me, but I am always grateful when my father forbears. Two of the people who received special scrutiny in the shop were Warren Farnsworth, a known collaborator of Moody's, and Vera Kolessina, who operated a press located in the basement of the shop that printed several radical newspapers, including the infamous *Blast,* edited by the even more infamous Alexander Berkman. Miss Kolessina, for reasons that are as unclear to me as the motives were of my father, was a member of my acting company. It was believed that she was 'having an affair' with me. This is not true. It is, however, quite true that *I wished* to 'have an affair' with her. I like Miss Kolessina. I admire in her many qualities that I choose not to elaborate here. I find it hard to believe that she is in truth involved in these bombings in which she is implicated. That she has not been charged, or even arrested, I should point out, attests to her genuine and impregnable innocence. The glaring light of the investigation would surely have revealed a telling detail by now. However! Because I am a true believer, along with my father and my older brothers—not to mention my sister and her husband, who, as you know, advises President Wilson—in progressive reforms, and, most emphatically, a citizen who loathes with every fiber of his being that Russian and German sort of radical militancy, that terrorism that finds its expression in murder, in mass murder, in the violent hatred of violent hatred, in the taking up as a cause the killing of those who have been chosen as the ones who must be hated and killed, who have come to think of the cause as killing rather than any improvement of conditions that provoke hatred and the desire to kill—which is specious at the outset: *a desire to kill?*—because I am a true believer in American democracy as a philosophical ideal and its institutions as practical realizations of same, and because I hope to continue to play some role in that practice, I have tried and am happy to say succeeded in persuading Miss Kolessina to help me help you to help the president here in Minnesota, to root out disloyalty and sedition and the sources of corruption and terror, by doing what we have learned, in our little histrionic way, to do best: assume disguises and infiltrate the realities of people who do not suspect us for what we are. Specifically the Equity Cooperative Exchange and the Nonpartisan League, and by extension, the Socialists."

Vera and Charles sat in a windowless room about as big as a sleeping berth in a railcar, stood on its end (for the ceiling was very high); what little space there was to move around in was taken up by filing cabinets and boxes, from which paper spilled like water. If you bumped into something, paper sloshed about you. A stack of newspapers had risen perilously close to the gas lamp on the wall. Charles guessed it was mildew that he smelled. The man on the other side of the tiny desk—on which he had cleared something like a tunnel through which he might address them—was a representative of the Nonpartisan League, an organization founded in North Dakota, where they'd had spectacular success, winning control of the state legislature, but were now running afoul of businessmen seizing the opportunity of the war to assert "preparedness" and holler "sedition." He was outlining their grievances, which Vera jotted down on an IWW notepad.

Charles brought her wherever he went as a supervisor for the Minnesota Commission of Public Safety, claiming she was his secretary, for no other reason than he wanted to see what would happen if anybody someday happened to identify her as the Vera Kolessina who had been implicated in the Preparedness Day bombing in San Francisco and other assorted murders. He was ready to say he had "turned" her, that she was no longer "an anarchist" and wanted only to help the state save the lives of innocent people. She was in fact "known," by persons such as this man from the NPL, to be representing the Chicago Wobblies, and this made some interviewees uneasy: he, for instance, had been dealing with Detroit Wobblies, but Detroit Wobblies, Vera assured him, had sticks up their asses. "They say you Chicago people are grandstanders," said the NPL man. "The Detroit people say that," said Vera, "precisely because they have those sticks up their asses. If you want to play chess, go to Detroit. If you want to get out of the mess you're in, talk to me."

The man looked nervously at Charles. He was there, they told him— and "believed it" themselves as well—as a secret agent. He wasn't really there. He was really and truly working for the Minnesota Commission of Public Safety *and* the Chicago IWW, who really and truly had no quarrel with each other, at least while the war was on. He would be inside, privy to any plans regarding the NPL—which was just more evidence that Chicago wasn't fooling around while Detroit was complaining that their coffee was always served lukewarm. He was an extraordinarily influential person, despite his youth. There was a town named after him in North Dakota, and he knew Teddy Roosevelt. He might someday be president of the United States! Crazier things had happened. And his sympathies were with working people. He was doing real work, field work, because it was believed it was time, just as it had been time for Henry V, to be awakened and despise his former dreams. There was hope in certain quarters that the United States might be presided over by—he mock-stumbled here, over how to characterize his sham self—by someone like, like, say, Marcus Aurelius.

The NPL man sat back in his chair and blew his cheeks out. He looked back and forth at Vera and Charles for a while—not with incredulity or suspicion or irritation, but as if it were all just then becoming too much to bear. Then he seemed to give up, or to come to terms with it.

"Why is it," he asked, drawing his great thick eyebrows together, "that a single company can control line elevators, terminal elevators, commission houses and mills, have tidy arrangements with the railroads *and* tell a farmer how much he will get for his produce?"

He was the kind of salesman who seemed to want answers to rhetorical questions, so Charles said he didn't know, at least in specific terms, and neither did Vera, who nodded.

"Tell me," he continued, "where else a consumer tells a producer what the price of the product will be! Tell me why a farmer can't tell the railroads how much he'll pay to get his wheat to Minneapolis. Tell me why there are no terminal elevators in the entire state of North Dakota. Tell me why it is—" he waved off Charles's reply, "—why it is that of all the farms in North Dakota in the year 1890—" he consulted his figures, "—6.9 percent of them were operated by tenant farmers, in 1900 8.5 percent, and in 1910 nearly *double* that. Tell me why every newspaper in the country will run stories with huge headlines of how 'European' orders for two million bushels of wheat have suddenly and mysteriously been cancelled, driving the market into a crash, and not a one of them will run the story that states unequivocally that the first story was a goddamn hoax! Tell me why the price of a bushel of wheat always drops at harvest time and rises once the millers own it. Tell me why we are supposed to believe that 'our leading citizens' would never 'stoop so low as to use false weights' at their elevators, while farmers will lie, slander, cheat, steal—even murder, I suppose!—to continue their profligate lifestyles, anything to continue to live like the corrupt prairie barons they are denounced as. Can you? Tell me?"

"Darkness," said Charles, "is on the face of the waters."

The NPL agent narrowed his eyes.

"I'm not sure that the farmer you idealize is anything but another kind of businessman," suggested Charles.

The NPL man said, "Let us talk for a moment about wheat grades."

"All right," said Vera, licking the point of her pencil. "The less talk of murder the better, you ask me."

Again the man gave her the same dark look he'd just given Charles. He was confused, and angry because he didn't think he was there to be confused. "There's #1 Hard, #1 Northern, #2, #3, and #4. There's also No Grade and Rejected. Have you got that? It's pretty confusing. You've got to have a good hand with grain, a good eye, and a telephone number of another fellow with similar attributes and a like mind who will back you up when you are accused of downgrading at the elevator, he can confirm your grade instead of upgrading like he would normally. Everybody in the NPL has had that happen to them: you sell and it's #2 or #3, but when it gets to Minneapolis, the train ride has miraculously transformed it into #1. Well, that's just what a broker does, that's what they tell me anyway, and we ought to keep our heads down and our mouths closed and let the man do his fucking *job*, but first tell me how it is we get docked for 'impurities, dirt, and other seed' in our wheat, have to pay the freight on this exceedingly heavy pile of impurity, only to learn later that these impurities have been screened out and sold as stock feed for twenty dollars a ton by the very folks who said it was worthless, and an inconvenience to them for which *we* should have to pay?"

Vera and Charles smiled and shook their heads.

"'Darkness on the face of the waters'?" The man's eyes were small and black beneath shaggy graying brows. "Kinda crack is that?"

"Means the same thing as a smile and a nod," Charles said evenly. "Don't get your underwear in a bundle. It's a good story and you tell it well, but it's not like I haven't heard it before. VERA HERE GREW UP IN A BUTTON FACTORY, YOU GODDAMN BONEHEAD!"

The man merely glowered and sunk deeper in his chair. Vera apologized for Charles's rude behavior. She felt sorry for the man, in truth, because it was believed he was playing fast and loose with NPL funds, and things were only getting faster and looser; he was an ideal target for Justice agents, easily turned when things finally got out of hand, and Vera had been asked to establish a relationship with him of simple goodwill and trust in the hope that he would not turn when the opportunity to do so came around. Some of the men she knew thought it was women's work, and some thought it was shit work, but Vera liked it, and everybody recognized it was something she did naturally well. She said, somewhat deprecatingly, that she thought it "suited her personality," and it reminded her of her duties at the *Passaic Weekly*, the job she'd found when they left Lawrence after the fiasco of the Children's Crusade, and moved down to the even bigger strike in Paterson in 1912. That paper's editor was now doing time in prison, and Vera believed she might lend some kind of attenuated moral support by practicing reportorial skills, talking to people, and taking notes on a little pad.

She wanted only to leave San Francisco and never return, because to either stay or return would be to confront how little she mattered in the big fraudulent scheme of things as they were apparently playing out. She knew everybody from one end of the investigation to the other, but her associations were not deemed criminal or even of interest, and neither the team of prosecutors nor the team of defense lawyers had required her testimony. The only way such exclusion made sense was to see that the trials had their own special trajectories already plotted out, as if by artillery engineers, and these flights were taking place in their own special place, in their own special space and time, ironically free of the laws of space and time, in a kind of air-that-was-not-air, air so rarefied it was often—in effect, in a subtly theatrical effect that only occurred to the players and the observers deep in the backs of their minds and only when they were thinking unguardedly—nearly impossible to breathe.

She could not keep her mind, her "mind" as she increasingly thought of it, a thing that could not be explained with words—or did she mean to put quote marks around "her," as if that were the thing that could not be explained, owner and proprietor of an organ of meat, of pudding, designed to carry traces of suffering and horror balanced by traces of peace and pleasure, simply so that *it could go on* even if she could not—she could not keep away from vivid recreations in her brain of the theater bombing, the understudy who had died in her place—someone who had died for her because she was not available—the parade bombing and the murder of three of her friends and the framing of at least three others, and so she had decided she wanted to die. Understudy be damned: it was her job to die.

But in the end she had been persuaded to go to the Wobblies in Chicago, hearing the repeated advice from friends who seemed so far away, and then so near, and then so far again, and coming to think that she ought to work again, slowly and steadily at something deemed to be of use by somebody who claimed to know, willing to do anything, but making clear a preference, without resort to emotional violence, for activity that would not result in bloodshed. The unhappiness of railroad people, short of bloodshed, would be an ideal goal, she said—any railroad and any people associated with any railroad—as they were convinced beyond a shadow of a doubt that URR, that thugs in the employ of Durwood Keogh or Keogh's security chief, the marble-like mercenary Rudy Swanson, had not only helped frame Warren Farnsworth and Tom Moody for the murders and the bombings, but actually killed Jules Beveridge, Amado Fernández, and Lucille Brown, for no readily recognizable reason. It was possible too that they had organized and staged the bombing, rather than simply availing themselves of it. The Chicago Wobblies believed that worse things were happening, or were about to happen, in Minnesota, the flour capital of the universe, than anyplace else that came readily to mind, but Jules Beveridge, no more than a month before he was murdered, had met his old friend from Philadelphia days and the Point Breeze board track, a Swedish engineer, Stringberry, who was developing a new motorcycle with a Chicago businessman named Tom Peacock, and these men had unqualifiedly endorsed her. Why? Charles wanted simultaneously to know and not know. The possibility of decisive, consequential action seemed greater the greater the knowledge the actor possessed—until the actor thought about it a little longer and came to the conclusion that less knowledge made for purer acts. Greater knowledge could easily become a burden, an increasing weight that would slow and eventually stop an actor in his tracks. But purity . . . ! Ruthlessness and horror surely rose up in the shadow of purity, did they not? Charles could see Father so clearly, eating breakfast, saying just that.

But there was a kind of purity in Vera, something like purity, that partook nothing at all of ruthlessness, of certainty, hatred, violence. There was in fact something in Vera's character as Charles had observed it—and that was an extremely rigorous distinction he was well aware of—that dismissed those elements entirely from sullied political ideas of purity—in fact purified it. He could, alas, only see its shape. Its nature was obscure.

From Saint Paul, Charles had written to her in Chicago at least once a week. They were not exactly love letters, but contained evidence of what she was prepared to accept as a kind of energetic devotion to her well-being. It was foolish, she told herself, to pretend she didn't care for this devotion. And she wondered too where the harm was, given that her days and the days of everybody she cared about were numbered, if she were not at least a little in love with Charles Minot, the millionaire playboy? She had wanted to kill herself in San Francisco, and what she was doing in Chicago did seem very much to be only the work the men didn't want to do, work the men thought women therefore ought to do.

The next week it began to snow. Vera, who was living in a room in a house, at 130 Virginia street, that Charles had found for her near the Saint Paul Cathedral and Father's cousin's castle-like structure on Summit Avenue, cried out with delight and fond memories, while he, though he had seen snow, a good deal of it, in the mountains, was fascinated as only a boy from San Francisco could be. But it didn't stop snowing until the new year had come. The average was nearly a foot a week. On a Thursday or a Friday or a Saturday—always, it seemed, at the end of a week—a blizzard would come howling down from Alberta, they were told, Alberta clippers, drop a foot of powdery dry snow, and depart for Chicago. The winds piled up immense drifts, and the below-zero air that followed like a swelling sea the crashing waves of the storm, froze the drifts solid as iron. People walked on them to the tops of their houses. To the west, on the Dakota borders, herds of cattle, sheltering in coulees, were buried alive. A train, too, was buried, near Minot, though no one died. Warren Farnsworth was tried and found guilty of the murders of Lucille Olivet Brown, Jules Beveridge, and Amado Joaquin Fernández de Lizardi—these in addition to the ten people killed in the Preparedness Day Parade bombing and the six in the theater bombing. He was sentenced to hang for the former, and life imprisonment for the latter—the idea being that he was a pipsqueak of a boy (he was twenty-two but looked sixteen) and a natural rat (he only, unfortunately, looked like one) who would likely tell investigators a great deal more about his anarchist and labor radical masters once he was in prison with certain death approaching. Tom Moody was found guilty, largely on the strength of the ball bearings and .31- and .32-caliber bullets found in his apartment—items similar but not identical to the shrapnel in both suitcase bombs—of masterminding the bombing and was sentenced to hang. His wife, Minnie, and Israel Minkowski were acquitted—largely, it was believed, because the public's distaste for what was increasingly seen as shoddy prosecution was rising like bile in the back of the throat. A threatened indictment of Alexander Berkman, the most well known of the more than twenty suspects in the theater bombing, never materialized, never for any of them, for possibly the same reason. A great deal of perjury was reported in the newspapers, but nothing came of it. Meanwhile, in Saint Louis, Missouri, in the thriving Mexican expatriate community there, Amado's brother, Julio, was found bound and gagged with a bullet hole drilled through his brain, and Vera began to wonder if it was the Fernández de Lizardi brothers who had been the killer's targets; that Lucy had been killed out of obvious necessity, being in bed with Amado, Beveridge surprising the killer as the killer made his way up from the basement and Beveridge down to find his lover with his friend; and that the killer was not in any way connected with PG&E or URR detectives, but was a mercenary, perhaps associated with the Pinkertons—who certainly, according to the Chicago Wobblies, felt they had carte blanche from the Mexican-hating Wilson administration to act covertly, preemptively, and outside the law— in the employ of the psychotically unstable Mexican government of Huerta. And indeed, once the two brothers in exile had been assassinated, the third, in a Mexico City prison, was promptly executed. Then there was another big bombing, on Wall Street in New York. Italian anarchists were blamed, thirty people died, and it was only a prelude.

Vera sobbed, mostly for Warren, whom she had loved, for what seemed like days and nights, then laughed for days and nights, and finally settled into a routine of sudden laughter and sudden weeping. To live was to suffer, she would say earnestly in between these fits: there was no getting around it, and she had always known it. Now perhaps she could articulate it for herself and stop worrying about it. Suffering was not merely central to life, it was essential. Suffering did not *happen to* life, it *was* life. She did not like to equate evil with suffering, or suffering with darkness, because evil was an effect of suffering, not a cause and because darkness was often a great solace—it was one of the reasons why she had always cherished a secret love of the theater—but the idea of a life as a point of light falling into darkness was the easiest way to put it. Life was a kind of ignorance of something real but insensible and unreachable—and how could one fail to be ignorant of that sort of reality! Well, however one managed it, one was not ignorant. One saw life for what it was, a kind of sleep, a drunkenness, an entanglement in the senses and emotions and consciousness, an entanglement in limbs that secreted a poison or a drug that numbed and addled and made one homesick . . . for the place or the condition or whatever you wanted to call it where people did not go to the theater to throw bombs on the stage, where the guilty did not put the innocent in prisons to rot or be hung, where children . . . oh, she could not bear to think of it. But it was where the moth would go to the light and not be destroyed, but rather become the fire.

Charles traveled often that winter and was often delayed by snowfall, but never buried alive. Vera often traveled with him, sometimes on business of her own—she met regularly and frequently a speaker from the NPL named Daisy Gluek—sometimes not, and they went at each other vigorously on these trips, because sex was one of the only activities available to persons bound in suffering and drugged with visions of home, performing "the act" here, there, and everywhere, sometimes with mouths locked together, swallowing all sounds but a muffled hooting, other times crying out as if for salvation from a god neither believed in, Charles duck-walking with pants and long johns around his ankles, Vera climbing aboard as she might a train whistling its departure. They went for long, numbingly cold walks between blizzards that only seemed to refresh and invigorate them. They kissed each other's cold red cheeks and panted hot moist air into each other's mouth. Charles begged her to marry him, and she begged him to stop asking her.

He went mainly to bakeries and the offices of commercial fishing operations, some dairies and bars, as well, as the state had put several food programs in motion that were perceived to be vulnerable to abuse by one radical group or another. One called for licensed agents of the state to catch rough fish—carp, dogfish, redhorse, mooneye, suckers, sheepshead, etc.— that would be marketed at state stores with a profit margin of no more than 3 percent, which meant both a steady supply of fish for strapped consumers at about half the usual market price, and a steady profit for the state— plowed, he believed and had tacitly confirmed, into the purchase of rifles and ammunition for a new "Home Guard." Commercial fishermen felt pinched, however, and Charles's job was to interview them, to measure their level of hostility, and listen carefully for tips about what that hostility might drive them to do. Milk producers were presented with a fixed price per quart that they could charge Twin Cities wholesalers, and told they must lay open their books.

In the far north, where the temperature regularly dropped to thirty and even forty and once fifty below—"It's no colder tonight," he was told in the town of Tower, "at the Arctic Circle than it is right here!"—he interviewed saloonkeepers: though the region, due to "county option" and various Indian treaties, was virtually saloon-free, enormous amounts of liquor were nevertheless being shipped in—ostensibly to individual consumers— via a loophole.

Vis-à-vis bread, the big millers were judged to be reasonable in their pricing, while small bakers were making out like Mexican banditos. These bakers protested while the millers clucked in feigned dismay. Charles interviewed bakers by the dozen. Many insisted the war effort was a hoax, but he winked and lifted the pen ostentatiously from his notebook for the length of these remarks.

And it was, in those moments, that he began to understand what he was doing.

He was heeding a secret, nascent impulse. He saw that he could act *cleanly*, without recourse to questions of personal prosperity. He saw that he could in effect trust himself, and that he should trust himself. He was not insane. He was not the aristocratic man of privilege gone nihilistic, not the practical Platonic republican driven into psychic exile by catastrophe and the emptiness of philosophy. Nor was he a man of peace, a soulful man: he was at war with the vastness of petty falsehood and needless suffering. He was no longer divided in himself, self against self, by fear and contempt of fear. He did not know how he had come to it, but come to it he had. He was not a radical, certainly not an anarchist, at least as its advocates described

it. He had no genuine interest in the rights of the workingman, in labor reform, in racial equality, in progressive politics.

Or did he? He took it back: he had an interest, but not a personal interest
in those things. He had no agenda to advance, put it that way, no cause to espouse, no principle to maintain, no belief to kill or die for. He had no wish to
make people repent and therefore had no desire to put bullets in their heads.
He was perhaps an anarchist in the way that Vera possibly was an anarchist:
that is to say, *she was not*. Not really. If she had ever called herself one he had
not heard it. They were not divided in their selves: that he could say. They were
not afraid: that too he could say. *No one is ruling? Then all are ruling.* And if
all are ruling—if all are letting all rule—then that rule "speaks the truth" because there's no call for a deception; that rule is "just, generous, hospitable,
temperate, scornful of petty calculations, scornful of being scorned." Oh yes,
he had read Emerson, to be sure, but he had not come near an understanding
of him: he seemed to think himself an idealist and immediately admit that
idealists were especially subject to cant and pretension and lofty ineffectuality,
that rather than having Truth, Goodness, and Beauty inhering in each other,
Beauty was supreme. Charles had no interest in Beauty because, before Vera,
it had seemed false. Father despised Emerson—despised New England, really,
and everything it stood for—and so, he supposed, had he despised him as
part of his intellectual inheritance. "Our virtue trips and totters!" He had said
so himself! "It does not yet walk firmly. Its representatives are austere; they
preach and denounce; their rectitude is not yet a grace. They are still liable
to that slight taint of burlesque which, in our strange world, attaches to the
zealot." Like Plato it was always correct to praise or despise him, but something of a sin to understand him. Charles had come to want to understand
these great men. And he came to understandings so quickly and surely that he
was almost ashamed of his body, that thing that could be so quickly and easily
replaced, so quickly and surely that he had to have been helped, by his strange
friends, the daredevils. *I learned how to do a thing without a wish for reward
or a fear of consequences.* It gave him enormous energy. He felt whole and
uncomplicated. He felt he was part of an uncomplicated whole. He felt that

when conditions were sufficient for manifestation, he would manifest, and when they were not, he would not. *The universe had come together to make me.* It expected nothing of him but to be. He was free. And it was precisely when he found himself lifting the pen from his notebook and in effect winking at the baker who declared the war effort to be a hoax—a declaration that *I now knew was against the law, was seditious, and punishable by imprisonment if he was lucky and lynching if he was not*—that he knew he was free. He smiled inwardly to think that he was a hero. That he had found a way to become a hero. He could do whatever small task presented itself to be done: instead of calculating reward and consequence, he could lift his pen from his notebook. He cared one day, one hour, about nothing beyond seeing to it that the baker not be harassed and tortured. The next minute, hour, day, he would perform another brief act that might forestall cowardice and cruelty. That was all. It was so simple, so clear, so fine.

And he was able "to be in love" with Vera.

Which was not to say that he was free of his creamy blue-veined marble character, his personality of privilege and its habitual weaknesses, its routines of intellectual passion—the nearly impervious Charles Minot-ness that was inseparable from the dictates of his ceaselessly and excellently-trained brain and the receipt of constant confirmation from all those other brains around it—of the reality he had counter-trained himself to disavow for a decade. He was not free of the necessary falseness of reality, not free of the stage, but wished to be. He embodied this wish as "Vera."

He found as well that he was becoming altogether welcoming of alcohol and narcotics and firearms—things that had never had lives of their own, things that had been present, certainly, but only unremarkably so, in a family whose patriarch was not only a Westerner, but one who had been shot twice representing law and order and nearly been blown to pieces in a natural disaster. He was susceptible to "thrills," to "somnolence" or at least to the ideas of same, to inner thrills, if he could put it that way, and superhuman manifestations of same—thanks to Vera, who had her own frank but mysterious need of them in her drugged entanglements, and thanks to the fact that someone had tried and nearly succeeded in blowing him, Father's boy, after all, to pieces in a political disaster—shredding, if truth be told, his nerves once and for all. Vera knew, had known for some time, long before she met Charles, how perilously close to sudden death she—everybody—was living. But that was remedial, not mysterious, a superficial explanation, not a need. When she talked about it, when she felt she could and wanted to talk about it, she could only speak of home and exile. The world is the dark and our home is the light. Evil wants to return to its home in the light just as much as good does. Good and evil was useless distinction, if not an altogether maliciously false one. Charles said she was a gnostic and that he wanted to learn the gnosis from her. Which of course made her laugh and cry and laugh and cry, and drink and fuck and take on a reckless attitude to work that could, at some point in one of a hundred projected futures, become dangerous. That *would*.

But if there was nothing you could do about it, did you want to talk about it? Or not.

Vera struggled with what she quickly chose to call her "addiction"—though to what, precisely, could not be ascertained—far more desperately than Charles did—she had been at it longer, he supposed, but he was better at it because his nerves, he now saw so clearly, had been ruined when he was a child, and it made him weak and sick. Vera was not sick and weak or fragile, but she spoke more and more of a friend who had died in New York three years earlier, Rosemary, who was simply a fragile person, talking as if Rosemary had been a part of her that had suffered and died to allow Vera to suffer and live. It was a variation not at all lost on Charles of the understudy who had been onstage where Vera had been meant to be. Rosemary had a story about her father, who worked on a match factory, toiling over phosphorus fumes that had made his bones brittle: Rosemary said she saw her father step awkwardly from a curb, saw the twisted ankle break, saw her father falling and cracking to pieces, and it seemed to Vera more and more likely every time she told the story. She had left Muscatine and buttons for Willimantic and thread, and a strike that was getting national attention. Body and soul were strung together with Willimantic thread and wrapped in smoke. It was possible Rosemary was some kind of otherworldly creature, a goddess, even, Vera didn't know. But she clung to her as the world wove the fabric of affliction ever more densely.

"We lived," she told Charles, "in a worker's paradise. That was how I liked to put it, it made Rosemary laugh, and that was all there was to it. We were just teenaged girls, and we liked to laugh. We called ourselves 'The Champions of Work' and we whistled a great deal. The owners were in fact kind and generous people, decent, intelligent people, and were famous for those qualities in all the mill towns of southern New England. They built an opera house in which works by all the greatest composers were performed: Verdi, Rossini, Bellini, Donizetti, Ponchielli, Puccini, Giordano, Cilea, Catalani, Leoncavallo, Mascagni—oh, I could go on and on!"

"You will forgive me if I don't quite believe you."

"I remember German and French names as well—tip of my tongue, can't quite get to them, though I am sure I will remember before I get to the end of this story. We never saw a performance, of course, but the owners made sure that singers with incredibly loud voices and insanely gorgeous clothing provided free concerts in the parts of the mill that weren't so noisy you couldn't hear even the loudest tenor wailing directly into your ear. Once there was a free concert by the lake in Coventry, on a Sunday. There were many, many people of Italian ancestry working in the mill (myself included) who could appreciate the lyrics just as they were sung, but we were proud of the diversity of our workforce: it's not much of an exaggeration to say that we came from the four corners of the earth. The owners, I know for a fact, subsidized the emigration of peoples from fourteen nations, including Syria, Borneo, and Patagonia. We enjoyed exotic foods, vibrant festivals celebrating ancient and obscure rites, and the glorious singing I have already mentioned, the singing of songs that made the whistling we engaged in while working something entirely out of the ordinary. We sang, too, once I'd taught the words to her, seeing who could sing the loudest. She fancied herself Italian, and could have passed for Italian in all but the most rigorous of audits. Rosemary said she knew nothing of the circumstances of her birth. I could not imagine such a life. I could not believe it was true—but of course she was right: none of us can know. I was not at all sure but I think I envied her: all that trackless solitude where there was nothing for me but immensities of architecture. She did believe that the man and the woman with whom she lived in the earliest years in Willimantic were in fact her mother and father. The father had been employed for several years as a matchmaker, which meant that he worked unshielded over great tubs of white phosphorus, the fumes of which in that cramped and dirty, unventilated shop rose up and hung in the air like the ghosts of all the tyrants of history and prehistory, or like fallen angels from which even evil had been wasted, leaving only a radiant, naturally occurring poison. With his head in these clouds twelve hours a day and his hands in the tubs dipping and plucking thousands of little sticks, he began to come apart. At first made only nervous and irritable, he suffered headaches and losses of memory that he knew were so near and yet gone, she said, that they reduced him to weeping. Then he became simple and docile and yet somehow witty, full all of a sudden and for no reason with gems of wisdom. He spoke in a kind of singsong that often rhymed. As his brain became desiccated, so did his bones become brittle. His jaw rotted and his teeth fell out, and one day, waiting for the Sunday excursion train to Coventry where we planned to sit by the lake and listen to the lapping water and hopefully the opera stars too, holding Rosemary's little hand in his frail yet still warm and big own, he stepped off the curb, found the street further below than he'd imagined, and broke his ankle when he touched down. In a kind of chain reaction, the bones of his left leg broke, and when he swung himself wildly to the right, the bones of that foot and leg snapped also. He collapsed in a bloody, powdery heap, pelvis, backbone, and neck cracking in swift succession. Finally his poor skull shivered like an egg-shell, leaving smiling face and cooling brain to rest softly on the cobbles of the street. Thus, at any rate, did my Rosemary narrate the tragedy, the tale of the matchmaker sick with phossy jaw who broke his leg stepping off the curb: many times and in many places, for many different reasons. She did not understand what had happened. Neither did I. She did not understand where her father had gone, nor why. Neither did I."

"Nor I. Even though he is still here."

"She blamed herself and yet could not understand where she had sinned or erred. And in what way, exactly, was she being held responsible? She had been a very small child and the truth, she suspected, was that she remembered nothing, that some other kind of activity was taking place in her mind, that, perhaps, an agency representing some other kind of reality, dreams, for example, that wasn't so difficult a concept, that an agent of dreams was operating while she was awake. It was dismissed in all but the most credulous quarters—even by sympathetic listeners—as apocryphal, as propaganda, propaganda of a different sort of deed, a story of a life, understood and made to function as a folk legend to comfort and amuse the weaker and more poor, who cannot understand the actual workings of alchemy, the medical arts, and the large-scale drift of money, the things you were born knowing, my darling Chuckie!—but believed devoutly by a few, myself included, who claimed to have seen it happen. I will swear to it if need be. And when, some time later, perhaps as short a time as a few days, perhaps as long a time as a year—Rosemary could not say and neither can I—her stricken, suffering, perhaps overly sensitive mother in turn died—whether of causes natural or unnatural, by her own hand or the hand of God, her story too is ambiguous—all that Rosemary could find in their meager belongings to tell her who they were, now that the testimony of their presence no longer sufficed, was a last will. It was written in a shockingly violent, nearly indecipherable scrawl and blot, and we treated it, in yet another of our games, as a treasure map. Places of birth were stated— Lower East Side and Canarsie—but believed to be false. More suitable nativities were imagined. Ages could be puzzled out with arithmetic. Her father, Rosemary calculated, was twenty, her mother nineteen. Lines at the bottom of the document, where their names would likely have been entered in less violent circumstances, were left blank. Rosemary thought she sewed it into her skirt. Wandering about the town, she found herself at the well. That was how she put it: 'Mother died and I wandered off to a public space where I might be afforded some amusement.' After drinking, looking around, drinking again, daydreaming out loud and drinking finally to soothe a throat now quite raw from talking to herself as she wandered, and from crying, she began to muse with the complicated fancy and helpless rigor that is the hallmark of the philosophy of children. She considered her condition—its causes, effects both immediate and clear and as yet unknown, and her prospects—then came out of what can only be described as a delightfully enchanted fugue, marked equally by a sorrow that was not indulged in and practical resolve that had little relation to reality, and saw three persons approaching. Used to the hustle and bustle of her small city, to herds of people being driven here and there with an urgency just shy of stampede, the sight of a small and isolated group, in the middle, as it were, of a nowhere we had conjured around ourselves, made her uneasy. They appeared to be dressed alike, too, in heavy black robes or cloaks or skirts and shawls, and this kind of uniformity of course makes ordinary people uneasy. Then she saw that they were old women and that their faces bore the look of kindness that only tremendous age and silent suffering can account for. They bid her a good afternoon, addressing Rosemary as "Little Girl," which she did not mind the least little bit. Her name, and the strikingly pronounced emphasis on the "Little" of Rosemary's, gave her the strange impression that it was an Indian name but the old women resembled in no other way Indian squaws as she had seen them, in illustrations. She had no idea, either, what time of day it was, but saw suddenly, as if invited by the immediate presence of the three women, how sharp and long the shadows were around her. She was surprised by the pale and empty sky, believing that it had been cloudy, turbulently and loweringly so. She then wondered if she hadn't simply imagined the clouds—or, it occurred to her, strangely, for a reason she could not quite come to, but which she felt came from her father's ghost—had they not gathered in response to her histrionic sulking? The season, too, was middling and mysterious: Were there buds on the trees, as she remembered it, or were they bare; and if bare, had the leaves just fallen or were they about to appear? The air was warm but the wind was cold—or was it the other way around? Warmly reposing in a cleft of rock, or cooling pleasantly in its shade? She did not know, she did not know, she did not know. Clambering down from the rocks, she debated naming herself to these strangers, and decided not to, asking the women instead if they were Sisters of Mercy. It was a phrase she had heard and liked, one that she associated with the Maker of Heaven and Earth, and that seemed to describe them in the same way Little Girl did herself. 'Little Girl and the Sisters of Mercy!' chuckled one old woman. 'We have a fairy tale on our hands!' said the second, smiling but with an air of prudence regarding a serious if not grim responsibility. 'Sisters of Mercy,' murmured the third. 'I should say not.' 'Are you,' asked Rosemary, 'servants of the Devil?' 'No!' laughed the first woman. 'No, no,' said the second, shaking her head judiciously. 'Yes,' said the third in her odd but clear murmur."

"This happened in a theater, did it not?"

"Rosemary laughed as her father had often laughed, calling a bluff, and demanded to know which one of them was telling the truth. Or which two.

'The first to speak told the truth,' giggled the first woman, 'and so did the last. The second was a liar.' 'Now, now,' remonstrated the second. 'Let's have no paradox here.'

'Certainly we are sisters,' said the third. 'But we serve no one and do not know the meaning of mercy. Finally, Little Girl, if you must ask us which of us is telling the truth, then I simply do not understand what we are doing here talking to you, when there is a world full of people just as confused as you are but who frankly have their wits about them.' 'I AM NOT AT ALL CONFUSED!' Rosemary shouted. The old women flinched, ducked, cowered, stepped back, and drew closer together. When they had finished doing all this, Rosemary understood that they were only feigning alarm, and were in fact having some fun at her expense. When they saw that she saw, they left off pantomiming and came boldly around her. 'You are very bright, Little Girl,' said the first. 'It does my heart good to see such warmth of brain in one so young. I believe you will become wise as the years go by.' A gust of wind blew the hood of her cloak from her head. Her blue eyes twinkled in her wrinkled, grizzled face. 'You are very brave, Little Girl,' said the second. 'It does my mind good to see such warmth of heart in one so young. I believe you will turn away from no fear in the war to come.' Another gust blew the hood of her cloak back as well. Her eyes were green as emeralds. 'You are very dark and frightened, Little Girl,' said the third. She was barely audible in the rising wind. 'I have never seen such anger, confusion, and recklessness in one so young, and it quite undoes me to imagine how you will make your way in the years left to you. I believe you will find little peace in them.' The wind was very strong now, and loud, and gusts of it smote the three as if with fists. Their garments fluttered around their trembling limbs, flapped and snapped until finally the hood of the third lifted away from her head, billowing and falling away. Her eyes were black but the look in the old face was one of commiseration, not of hate or malice or fear. She looked at Rosemary in a sad and friendly way too. Then she reached up, putting one withered hand to the side of her skull, the other under her jaw, fitting them carefully, sighed, and pulled her head off. The first and second quickly followed suit. From their sagging old necks rose, like gnarled and crooked arrows from grotesque quivers made from the bodies of trolls, the branches of trees, stripped of bark and white as bone, bare of leaves, and tossing in the wind. She was largely unmoved by this display of witchcraft. She recognized it as something out of a nightmare, but accepted it as yet one more grim aspect of a reality that, it was clear, had infinite powers of derangement and that she would never fully understand. Buds appeared on the branches and this seemed to be a sign of better times just around the corner. From the buds tiny leaves eased forth and grew. The old women nodded and swayed over her and the succulent green leaves grew larger and larger. Rosemary swooned with the majesty of it, and lay down. When we awoke she realized she was staring into the beady but strangely still and calm eyes of a squirrel. He was upside down, clinging to the trunk of the tree among the roots of which she lay, no more than a foot or two above her head. They began to converse about the pleasant weather and the indescribable pleasure of a nap in the afternoon on a day when there was wind in the trees. Then they were silent for a time. Rosemary asked the squirrel how it made ends meet, and the squirrel spoke of life in the tree, of ordinary successes and failures in the familiar places, stories of its vastness, trials and tragedies in its most remote reaches, of proper conduct and good government. The squirrel wanted Rosemary to understand that while they were free, the quality of that freedom depended utterly on circumstances. Rosemary tried to give the squirrel the impression that this was elementary reasoning, but the truth was that she could not grasp the meaning of it. Then the squirrel said, 'The tree remains the tree no matter what I think about it,' and Rosemary awoke. 'Stop pretending your mother is dead. It hurts her terribly. Be dutiful and loving toward her,' said the squirrel. And Rosemary awoke a second time."

White spaces, in the time and confines of the minds of the storyteller and story hearer, were made irregularly and infrequently.

"Our mill was not merely a legendary worker's paradise; in fact it was famous for its looms—or rather, more precisely, for an innovation in the design of the looms' flying shuttles: they had lead tips and were ten times as durable as the all-wood shuttles, whose tips cracked and splintered and fell to pieces under the stress of the new high speeds with unacceptable frequency. But before we could get to a loom, we would have to spend several years—'the best years of our lives,' I liked to say, making Rosemary laugh— on the drums, working the 'jumbo exotic carders,' as they were technically known. There were eleven drums of varying sizes connected by belts: the big central drum was called 'the swift' and ran clockwise; two drums about half the size of the swift, 'the doffer' and 'the fancy,' were high and low at the back of the swift, running counterclockwise. There was a little 'stripper' between the fancy and the doffer, and above and below the feeding tray, which was in front of course, where the cotton fibers entered the carder, at tit level, were two little drums called 'nippers,' with a little stripper on top of the top nipper. Going up over the swift were four medium-sized drums, two pairs of strippers and 'workers.' In the back, below the doffer, was the fly comb, tit level, where the cotton fibers left the carder, again at tit level. I stress this point of the description because we could never let our arms hang, they were always raised from the shoulder and spread. This was a job considered especially suitable, for an unknown or undeclared reason, for little girls, teamed, as often as possible, with their mothers. Rosemary's 'mother' was a devious and secretive harridan who hated Rosemary, and hated me too, again for an unknown or undeclared reason. Confronted with the truth, as she had been at the well by the witches, that harridan was Rosemary's actual, biological mother, Rosemary would hold up her hand and slowly shake her head: she was a distant relative who had hated Rosemary's parents because of their interest in unionism, and feared they had passed this interest on to a little girl who clearly had troublemaking on her mind anyway, and for whom she had an unpleasant but unavoidable responsibility. But whatever the cause of the hatred and the nature of the relationship, there was one constant in the acting out of it, and it required two actors and a long-forgotten understanding of who had started it. Rosemary, despite the fact that we were living out the best years of our lives in a worker's paradise, was deeply disturbed by the monotony and sensory assault of her job—it's hard for most people nowadays to imagine a child of six or eight or sixteen on the edge of nervous collapse, but not me."

"Nor me."

"Yes. The earthquake was hard on you."

"Easy to make light of it now. You can be callous when you're high."

"She would often fall to her knees in exhaustion and misery, or, if she had enough strength and will, would wander away from the drum. The mother would catch her by the arm and yank her to her feet, keeping one hand in her game at the other end of the carder, or, failing to the catch the arm, Rosemary's hair, sometimes yanking so hard she would snatch Rosemary off her feet entirely, stretching her out like a no-holds-barred wrestler and slamming her to the floor with a thud. But while the floor was not the rumbling, screeching, eternally rotating drum, it was no picnic down there, either. Its warped and clattering boards were coated thickly with oil and grease and mud, sawdust and cotton waste, tobacco juice and tubercular spittle, blood and pus and the dust of our very skins, but it was the only place where a little girl might powder her nose. Given the carefully regulated clockwork mechanisms of the mill's fundamental movements, we were encouraged to eliminate our waste prior to or after the bells. Company policy stated clearly that no employee would be, indeed could be, allowed to vacate a station for any reason whatsoever—not even to urinate. So Rosemary—and I, later, though not so regularly or with such blasé facility—learned to piss on the floor at her station. The mother would grab her arm as usual, but a sign from Rosemary that urination was underway would almost always result in a loosened grip and a general tolerance. 'You filthy little beast,' the mother would chuckle. 'You are ignorant of the world below,' piped Rosemary, drawing herself up like an opera star and delivering her lines with a recitative-like eloquence. She was annoyingly precocious and took a great deal of undisguised pleasure in unusual tropes and words dense with multifarious meaning—as did I. It was another one of the ways in which we in effect whistled while we worked. They had to shout to hear each other and really couldn't make out much of it even when they did, but understood each other well enough, reading lips, remembering, imagining. In spite of the hatred that underlay it, the nervous tension that harried it, and the deafening thunder of the looms above, the constant but irregular banging of the rows of drums and creaking spools and thudding engines, the ordinary remorseless cries of horses and men and clanging bells and piercing shrieks of steam that overwhelmed their conversations, Rosemary and her drum-mother had somehow come to agree that whether or not there was 'another world below them,' they could at least argue about it. Somewhat in the manner of a prisoner and guard, they exchanged warm and candid, if not altogether friendly and sympathetic, observations, fanciful hypotheses, hilarious syllogisms, and straw men. Rosemary posited a world no bigger than the mill sunk a mile or so into the earth at the end of something like a mineshaft. It was a utopia in which hard but calm and therefore satisfying work alternated with intellectual seductions and sensual pleasures of the simplest and deepest kind: wind in the trees, water rushing over rocks, hugging, kissing. The people refused to take advantage of each other, and governed themselves with quiet talks and broad deliberations. They grew old very slowly, and death was almost unknown among them, but—and what a big but, I always liked to say at that point—they depended utterly on a magical precipitate, a gentle rain that fell upon them like mercy from their tiny heaven, coursing down their tiny mountains and running swiftly past their tiny mills, an elixir derived solely from the germ-laden phlegm and urine-sodden dust as it percolated down the shaft from the big mill above the ground. When they coughed in their anomalous illnesses, their germs sprayed up at her in turn, in faint puffs, like little angels of mercy. The drum-mother dismissed all this as fairy-tale nonsense, suggesting that whatever they got from the big mill came upon them like plague and flood. It was very likely a flammable liquid as well, igniting infernos where it didn't drown or cause pustules and lesions to form in the lung, the face, and the genitals. 'And as for the utopia—!' 'You are as ignorant of the world below as you are of this world!' 'Dream on, you little nincompoop!' 'I shall, allow me to assure you!' 'Why would they behave any differently down there than they do up here?'

    "'Because they wish to!' 'I do not wish you to speak of it again. You must pay attention to your work or risk a break in your concentration. You might fall behind, your work will pile up, something might snarl or jam or catch, and you will place not only the steady functioning of the line but yourself and your fellows in terrible jeopardy. If the line is destroyed, so are our jobs and consequently our lives and our souls. Yes, it is a sin. God will wonder what is wrong with you. You don't want God wondering what's wrong with you, Rosemary, do you understand me? Do you understand me? I will not have you starve to death!'"

"You seem to know a lot about the Willimantic mill."

Vera looked at Charles when she answered him. It was the first time the dreamy look drifted away from her eyes.

"I do."

"You have never talked about the Muscatine mill this way."

"My job in Muscatine was much simpler. There were no machines involved. I was younger and if I worked there longer, it doesn't seem that way now. Too much happened in Willimantic."

"From buttons to thread."

"American Button to American Thread."

"Are you really from Muscatine? Is your name really Vera?"

Vera looked away and sighed. After a while, back in character, she continued her story.

"Because our drums were necessarily near the loading docks, we were privy to tantalizing portions of the conversations of the men who came and went there: the suggestive small talk and boasting and whispered rumors, the thick accents and humorous imitations, bits of news and gossip, jokes and the tag ends of strange lines of dialogue, oratory and performance of anecdotes to pass the time—and of course, observation, analysis, commentary, complaint, and passionately voiced frustration, which became, with what seemed like the passage of the years of our young womanhood, slow-boiling anger and isolated bursts of terrifying outrage. It was, in the absence of real family and friends, with these men that we learned to speak—first to ourselves, but after not too long, publicly and socially as well. Rosemary became a favorite of some of these men. She was pretty, I was not."

"Don't be absurd! You are fantastically beautiful!"

"You *are* sweet, but it's not true."

"Oh, Vera . . . ."

"They sought her out and kidded her while the drums turned and we pushed the dirty lumpy cotton along the feeding tray. She kidded them back, telling them of her merciful, nutrient-rich urine and the deep little people who prayed for it. The men found her inventions startlingly witty in one so young. It's not too much to say they found her fascinating, which attention in turn encouraged her to act more audaciously, to broaden the reach of her narratives, and to deepen their meaning. By the time we were fourteen, in the year 1910, she was the center of a devoted circle. The men (boys, really, not much older than she) would appear in the several proscenia of the open loading dock doors, lit and backdropped according to the weather, sometimes silhouettes against the bright sunlight, sometimes colorful heroes striding out of the ravages of a storm, conduct their business, tease her a little bit from a distance, making big obvious gestures and shouting, then drift nearer and nearer, refining remark and gesture as they came until at last they were speaking into each other's ears and there was fondling and wrestling and kissing and all our drum-mothers would scream abuse—early days, or, later, blow their whistle. It's not hard nowadays to imagine the extent to which the sexual play went, but we couldn't believe what was happening. Then, one day the next year, they stopped coming. We did not know why, but suspected that the drum-mothers had said something to someone, and someone perhaps had supplied them with the goddamned whistles, and now had taken even harsher steps to restrict the flow of communication into and out of the mill. Rosemary fell into a deep depression—I did not—and kept climbing up and tumbling down the sides of it. Her old nervous unease and disorder—the tics only she noticed, the fluttering feeling and the feeling that something other than blood was coursing flammably through her veins, and her heart, racing for no reason until she felt ready to faint, then hovering on the edge of unconsciousness until it passed—began to take hold of her again. Her head ached ceaselessly, her whole body ached and trembled, and she fell into nearly incoherent rages over nothing. It was either that or weep, almost undetectably but uncontrollably, while staying physically steady, pushing and spreading the cotton as the drums screeched in their eternal revolutions. She became fixated on the idea that there were little girls inside her drum, dead little girls playing games and singing, girls who could be our dearest friends but for the fact that they were trapped in the drum and forever tumbling. Noises would suddenly sharpen and penetrate her head, then fade out again, there were dark curtains around the familiar shapes of her station. She could make out distinct and interesting conversations inside the drum and outside it simultaneously. She might hear bells ringing, horses nickering and snorting, greasy smoking engines thudding away, then suddenly clear human speech."

"I think it was you who imagined these things."

"*It wasn't me, you dumb bunny.*"

"Why do I think it was?"

"If she looked up and saw her mother's mouth moving, she would sigh and stop listening; if a man's mouth and bushy moustache across the room were moving, she would listen as long as she could. On the worst days the noises would join and become unbearable, but then, as if under the control of a just and surprisingly merciful god, cease utterly. She might look up and see her mother's mouth working some terrible curse—she knew the patterns of lips and tongue and jaw by now—see that she was sobbing, but hear nothing. In that silence, when she knew perfectly well that something inside her had broken—or perhaps only relaxed?—she could hear the little girls, our friends, inside the slowly turning drum singing whispery mournful songs, simple little dirges in time with the drum's reemergent banging and creaking. Dazed by this silence and the warmth of the sad songs, she would slip to her knees and, sometimes, urinate. One day she did fully and completely faint. She was having trouble hearing anything at all—the sounds of the mill were muffled and she could only see the drum-mother's lips moving as she hectored and judged almost good-naturedly, and she made a motion as if to squat and pee. The drum-mother reached out with her habitual gesture almost of comfort but of restraint too, but Rosemary went unsteadily down. She began to urinate, then blacked out and went over backward. The drum-mother panicked. Fallen workers were to be left to their own devices and the assistance of floor managers, so she stepped over Rosemary, hurriedly pushed some cotton along the tray, then dashed to the back to the carder. Rosemary awoke a second or two later, having no idea what had happened or where she was. When it came to her—when she realized she was not in a strange white room but in the mill—she tried to get to her feet. Her mother reached out now without even looking at her and caught a hank of her long dark hair. She tipped over again but her mother wouldn't let go this time, bending awkwardly but keeping her fear-filled eyes and one hand on her work. Rosemary crawled toward her, grabbed her ankle, and bit hard into her calf. Her mother yelped inaudibly under the noise of the machines and let go of her hair. Rosemary stayed low, slapping and banging the filthy floor as she made her getaway. One man laughed at her, again inaudibly, a grotesque grimace of pain, it looked like, and another shook his leg at her like he would a dog. The kick caught her a glancing blow, altering her direction and ultimately bringing her to her feet. The sound of the mill and its workers was now deafening but she could hear every note of it. She looked over her shoulder at her drum-mother, who stared back at her in panic and horror, and at me, wide-eyed, frightened—then bolted. I swallowed hard and followed her. She ran as fast as she could up the aisle into the heart of the mill, shouting, 'STRIKE! STRIKE! STRIKE!' I suppose I hollered the same or similar. Our fellow workers did pause in their movements, some for only a second or two, some for longer, and confusion began to mount. Leaping up the stairs to the second floor, we struggled—still dizzy as well as being ordinarily weak from the poor food we ate—with the weights and pulleys of the big iron door that led to the looms, pulled it open just enough to squeeze through, then lost our way in terrified inner darkness for a crucial moment. The door caught us as it swung heavily back into place. We screamed and fought the door and slipped through: the looms clattered and hummed. It was a noise on a higher register than the noise below, but more penetrating. Rosemary took a breath, started shouting 'STRIKE! STRIKE! STRIKE!' again, and dashed into the center of the room. It was exactly at that point that one of the mill's famous lead-tipped shuttles shot from its loom. It was 'a convergence of the twain' worthy of Hardy. The shuttle traveled straight as an arrow, then, just as it began to lose momentum and descend, struck Rosemary in the temple. It was like the hand of God. That she should faint, then revive and race to a distant point only to intercept a missile streaking toward the very spot where she would be—and not simply be but be in an act of outright rebellion—seemed incontrovertibly theological in its parabolic progression. Because the danger posed by these powerfully ejected and effectively rifled shuttles, the room was laid out so that no one who was standing where he or she was supposed to be standing would be hurt when one of them fired itself out of a loom; the obvious corollary revolved around the ancient belief that if you weren't where you were supposed to be, even for an instant!—you deserved what was coming to you. And it would always come to you. And because company policy was company policy no matter what floor you worked on, she was left in a heap on the floor. What had been coming for her for millennia had arrived. She was nervously glanced at over shoulders and under arms, and there was a great deal of surreptitious talk, but she remained where she was and as she was. Her long black skirt (in which was sown the flat little package of family documentation) was spread out around her and hid most of her body so that from a certain angle she looked like she'd fallen in a hole filled with black water, with only her head and arms above water, weakly hanging on to the edge."

"After He smote her, God spoke to her. He spoke to her for a very long time, and when she awoke, she knew the Almighty to be a fraud and a coward. A handsome young man had her in his arms and was standing up. He was whispering to her that it would be all right, she was fine and everything would be all right, she should not worry. Rosemary was not to worry. The handsome young man repeated this injunction. No stranger to the protocols of the fairy tale, she immediately trusted the young man and found herself as incapable of worry as of suspicion. His princely, heroic beauty held no trace of treachery or even vulnerability to vice—and in fact his only fault seemed to lie in an apparent double standard: he was visibly worried, stricken, it was not too much to say, with anxiety. If he was outwardly reassuring, he was also clearly gripped by a fear of what might happen if he failed to get Rosemary off the filthy floor and into a warm bed in a clean room. He carried her across, it seemed, the whole of Willimantic, me bouncing along next to them, moaning and whispering and petting Rosemary's head, then through the door of a small house, up its main staircase, and into a room that was clean and warm but nearly empty. There was a bed in it, and he put her gently under its covers. I crawled in too, and he seemed not to think I was being presumptuous. He brought more blankets and more pillows. He brought some food, which we ate together, conversing with polite awkwardness about conditions at the mill, the weather, opera, and romantic poetry. There was evidence outside of a growing commotion, but we were able to ignore it. Rosemary was warm and happy and thoroughly amazed at the depth of the young man's knowledge of beautiful, truthful things—as was I, even though I saw very clearly that I was not the object of his tender little attentions, but merely an object. We were as well unspeakably grateful to him—so grateful and so admiring we found it impossible to find out who he was or even where we were. After a while, in which we must have dozed, the commotion outside became so loud and strange that we could ignore it no longer. We stood at the window, the young man holding the curtain back just enough so that we could see. It was a strike. 'They're saying you started it,' laughed the young man. 'Me?' asked Rosemary. 'Yes.' 'Who is saying that?' 'The men who saw you take the shuttle to your head.' 'Oh,' said Rosemary falteringly. 'Is that what happened . . . ?' 'Yes. They think you're dead. Some of them do, anyway. It was too much for them to bear. You're a legend in your own time.' 'I ought to join them.' 'Certainly, if you feel better. But do you in fact feel better?' Rosemary suddenly found herself sobbing. 'No,' she said. 'Then,' said the young man, 'you must stay.' 'Perhaps until the morning . . . ?' Admitting her weakness made her feel even worse, and she sobbed wretchedly. 'Certainly. But while you are resting, think about those men who know you are not dead.' 'There are men who believe I'm alive?'

'Of course there are, darling. But you're safe here. If you expose yourself, whether you feel better or not, you will be less safe. You may in fact find yourself in terrifying danger. You might get shot. You might go to prison for the rest of your life.' The young man stared out the window. 'I'd lie low for a while,' he said, not turning around. 'You too, of course,' he said to me, turning abruptly and putting his hand on my shoulder."

"Rosemary sat on the edge of the bed. Her feet were cold. It was hard to believe, but she thought she could eat some more, if more was available. The young man said he would find more if it was the last thing he did. His pose of ardency seemed even more authentic than it had been earlier, but what he actually did was give me some money and send me out. Earlier, prepossessingly resourceful, he had found a Victrola and a complete recording, forty sides, by La Voce del Padrone of *La Gioconda*. We listened to this long masterpiece in its entirety, and then I went out for bread and cheese. Rosemary and the young man listened to it again, in its entirety, playing over and over 'The Dance of the Hours,' because it took me, no surprise, quite a while to get the food. We listened to it yet again, mad for it, really, as who would not have been, given all that had happened, all that was happening? The next morning, the young man gone, we decided we were finished lying low. Rosemary was pregnant. Though of course we didn't know it at the time, she couldn't keep the news of the fuck to herself. The young man had disappeared. Had he fathered the presence she suddenly insisted she unmistakably felt within her? She did not know. She did not know. How was one to know? I did not know. She did not care. I cared but was helpless. Strangely, her skirt was missing too, the one—the only—in which she believed she'd sewn the family document. Since her undergarments, stockings, boots, blouse, and sweater were all still available to her, but strewn here and there about the room, the corridor, landing, and stairs, she concluded she was merely being hysterical and could not trust herself to look carefully and search thoroughly an environment in which so much had happened in so little time. 'I could be,' she said, 'looking right at it.' Wrapping herself in the bedsheet with snug ingenuity, she dressed herself and we went out into the crowded street. It was a cold day but not so cold that we shivered, and if the gray sky threatened snow, it was still dry. Rosemary liked to speak of herself, and perhaps to think of herself, as a fairy-tale innocent, but she was not naïve. She knew she hadn't caused the strike, but she felt in an obscure way responsible, even guilty. There is no explaining such guilt: it had something to do with a frivolous lightheartedness that informed or was at least present in or witness to her darkest deeds. There was no romance in a strike, and she knew it; it could only seem so in retrospect, in, as it were, a ballad. It took place in darkness and the light it shed was explosive. But it was not a darkness of evil, and that was the difference. It was a darkness of despair and fear, and a light of pain and anger, and so it was unreasoning and unrelenting. Good was not an inherent consequence. In fact no good could come of such a force, unless reason could be brought to bear upon it, unless people around whom the water was rising and swirling could be encouraged to somehow not mind the ominous roaring in the distance, could be encouraged to think and act calmly even in the face of . . . this is where Rosemary Thorndike eventually made her single historically documentable mark . . . brutal repression. And so we clung to the steps of the house while our people raged past us. If we had heard singing from the window earlier—it was possible but we viewed the possibility with suspicion, given what had been happening—no one was singing now. The flow of the crowd was so fast and turbid that it was impossible to stay in one place for longer than a few seconds. Some people we recognized who in turn recognized us, but nothing was made of these recognitions as nothing could be made of them in such uncertain circumstances: the mill had been struck and shut down and the street was a river in flood just as surely as if a dam had been dynamited. Men, women, and children would certainly drown, it was only a question of how many; and when their bodies finally fetched up in some psychological backwater, slowly rotating in the faint current, recognition would matter even less. We heard fragments of talk, asked a question here and there when we could, and, with what we already knew from the men on the docks and rumor, slowly fashioned a narrative, which went something like this: the Commonwealth of Massachusetts had begun to take measures that would raise the standard of living for millworkers and protect them generally from the zealotry of mill owners and other smaller-minded, meaner-spirited capitalists, but Connecticut was slow in following suit. There was a corresponding diminishment of patience for the scaling down of the sixty-hour workweek. Fifty-four was the goal, and fifty-eight would be acceptable as a first step, but both goal and step were rejected as mill owners testified to insurmountable disadvantages in the marketplace: it could simply not be done, no matter what Massachusetts may, in its folly, have set out to do. Fifty-eight was nevertheless mandated. In acceptance of the mandate, the owners reduced wages. This was seen as a more or less reasonable compromise, but the 3 percent cut was felt by the workers receiving it as salt in a wound. Rosemary felt wounded, so wounded, as I have said, that she was in a nearly perpetual state of hallucination and understood as well as was necessary, with a mind not at all at ease with numbers—with in fact a mind in which numbers elicited a kind of feverish loathing—that the weavers had been forced to work twelve looms at forty-nine cents a cut instead of seven looms at seventy-nine cents. This was probably why she ran upstairs when she regained consciousness on the floor before her drum. These men did in fact respond to her cry. They were ready to walk out, and when 'the little girl' ran screaming into their presence, it was nearly impossible not to act. Most workers, however, in other parts of the mill, stayed at their stations. It wasn't until the next morning, when she was feeling the first uneasiness of pregnancy, that pay envelopes were opened and the wage cuts made incontrovertibly manifest, and violence broke out. After a period of nervousness and actual embarrassment—Rosemary's word for the general sentiment that universal principles of right conduct had somehow been subverted—shouts of anger could be heard here and there, and before anyone could think of doing it, some gear works were smashed and some drive belts cut. One man, who seemed lost and who had obviously been crying—she could see the tracks in the grime on his face, and his eyes were puffy and red—told her that someone had been killed, a little girl had been shot down by soldiers. 'Soldiers?' she cried. 'Where did soldiers come from so quickly?' 'They shot her. I saw it,' said the man with sudden disturbing calm. 'No,' said Rosemary. 'No they didn't. There aren't any soldiers in this town.' 'A little girl was shot and killed,' insisted the man, now with a kind of indifference. 'NO SHE WASN'T!' shouted Rosemary. 'THAT WAS ME! I AM THE LITTLE GIRL AND I'M NOT DEAD!'"

"Ah," said Charles. "I think I understand now."

"Don't rush me! You don't know! Whatever you're thinking, it's quite wrong!"

"Rosemary *was* in fact shot by the soldiers."

"No."

"She is your martyr."

"She spun away and staggered back up the steps to the door of the house. I followed. When we looked back, the man was gone. Confused and alarmed, suddenly, and to the edge of panic, we went into the house and found its kitchen. There around a table were three Wobblies. We knew they were Wobblies because they were extremely dangerous looking and handsome. Despite the dashing good looks, however, Rosemary was instantly struck by their similarity to the women at the well. 'One Big Union,' said a big man, describing himself and his companions to her, telling her everything was going to be all right from now on. A woman told her that the young man who had saved her from her nearly fatal descent into unconsciousness was a friend of theirs. He was part of the One Big Union, but more specifically was from New Bedford. This she was told as if it meant something crucial to her understanding and well-being. 'He's not exactly local, but it's not like he's from some mining camp in Colorado!' she laughed. 'He grew up in a mill just like you two did. He writes songs for us. Did he play his guitar for you?' 'No,' said Rosemary, as if she was confident of her place not just in the conversation but in the greater scheme of things, in life itself. 'I'm afraid he didn't.' 'You really missed a treat!' the woman assured her with a kindly smile. They told her they would take us to Lawrence, Massachusetts, where an even bigger strike was taking place, if we wanted to go. They made it clear they wanted Rosemary to come with them, myself as well, nodding and smiling at me, and implied quite strongly that she would be considered highly valuable in a very short period of time, as the dreams of the One Big Union were beginning to be realized. So we went with them, Rosemary accepting a skirt from the woman and reconciling herself to the loss of her own, feeling a tremor of anxiety when she remembered what she was pretty sure she'd sewn into it. Someone had put the opera record back on upstairs, so that the last thing we ever heard in Willimantic, the door slamming shut on it, was 'The Dance of the Hours.'"

"The woman wore a tall red hat pinned to her hair, and Rosemary snuggled so close to her in the car that she could study with her diseased but powerfully concentrated imagination the whorls and folds of the little enamel rose at the head of the pin. She perceived it as a living thing. The woman seemed to know a lot about her, and Rosemary accepted this without worry or question. The woman said she understood that Rosemary had been very helpful in not just the triggering of the strike but the priming of it. The men she'd been briefed by had put it just that way, she said, narrowing her eyes and clearly implying that there was something wrong with what she'd just said. 'You will read Bakunin,' she said, 'like I did, and Nechaev in the cool shadows of your delirium and in the bright fever of it, and you will believe as I did, for only an hour perhaps, or a day, but no longer, and say to yourself, honored sister, there are three classes of women. The first consists of empty-headed, senseless, and heartless women who must be exploited and made the slaves of men. The second consists of those who are eager and devoted and capable but not fully committed, who must be pushed until they do, or, more likely, perish.' I knew instantly, Charles, fatally, that I was part of the second group."

"Balderdash."

"'In the third class,' the woman continued, 'are the women who are truly ours, our jewels, whose help is indispensable. I underscore this last phrase, and urge you, honored sisters, to compare your own knowledge of what you have done and what you will do to this corrupt and poisonous passage and believe it for as short a time as you possibly can.' 'Who is Nechaev?' asked Rosemary. The woman peered deeply into Rosemary's eyes as we jolted through Worcester and said, 'He was a murderous twerp with a lot of moxie. You will find men like him all over the place.' She sat back and pretended to fan herself, though it was quite cold in the car. 'Don't get me wrong, honey,' she said, 'I am terribly interested in Mr. Bakunin's cult of violence, deeply so, it gives me goose bumps, but come, pull yourself together, we could not possibly have left you in that shit hole, we'll all go to Lawrence together, where the woolen mills are bigger than ten Willimantics or wherever we were. The strike there has shut the whole town down. Can you speak any foreign languages? It will come in handy, believe me, in Lawrence. Oh, you poor little things, you poor little women. There is another look, isn't there, in the bloodshot eyes of men when they see the only solution is to destroy and kill and maim and burn and pant like dogs in the light of the dying flames? When they lie down with us and how does it go? Jet the stuff of a superior race?'"

"When we got to Lawrence, we were immediately put to work: we were to mind the children, the ones who were hungry, the ones who were cold, the ones who were lost, the ones whose mothers and fathers were off rioting. Rosemary hatched a plan and insisted money be raised specifically and solely for her plan. It was a fantasy she had nursed for as long as she could remember, she told me, and then the others: to get the children out of danger. Money was found, and Rosemary's job became one of getting the children, more than one hundred of them, on a train bound for Philadelphia, where sponsor families would care for them until the strike was over. Management spies got wind of the plan, and it was quickly publicized as one in which the children, following a pied piper, would be precipitated off cliffs. When the day of departure came, however, there was no need of a cliff. At the station, mounted policemen bore down on the children and their mothers like Cossacks, herding them at first then knocking them flat with deft little movements of their great horses. Guns were fired into the air over shrieking little heads and several policemen lost their heads: they began laying about themselves with light batons, clubbing people to the ground indiscriminately. Panic overtook the brigade and the flight of the children out of Lawrence seemed doomed. The police and their henchmen managed to create a no man's land of the platform, charging up and down the length of the train upon their steeds, while cops on foot waded into the swarming hysterical crowd with whistles and fists. Rosemary entered the no man's land. It was the greatest thing I have ever seen and will ever see anybody do. Three horsemen galloped toward her, fast as they could go. She was four feet tall and they were twelve feet tall—something like that. They were going thirty miles an hour, and Rosemary was standing still. Look at this."

Vera handed Charles an old newspaper clipping that she kept in a frame. The headline read: LITTLE GIRL DEFIES COSSACKS. A grainy, faded yellow, and torn photograph shows a train shape on the right, crowd shape on the left, a little girl half-standing, blurry with motion, a beached whale—the fallen horseman and his horse—in front of her, and two wide-eyed horsemen, still mounted, the whites of their eyes dominating their gray shapes, staring down at them.

"'I felt,' she once told me, 'like a chicken buried up to my neck in the ground, waiting for them to come pluck my 'iddle head off. They came, I stayed, they came, I stayed. I stayed and stayed and still they came. The station was shaking with the thunder of their hooves, a ton of horses and riders bearing down on me, and still I stayed. At the last second, they reined back. One of them wasn't paying close enough attention, I guess, and he went over the top of his mount. Landed at my feet. Actually rolled into me and knocked me down. That's when the picture was taken. Just as I was scrambling to my feet.'"

"For this show of fearlessness she was broadly denounced and publicly humiliated. Not only mill owners and conservative newspaper editors, but prominent socialists and leaders of mainstream unions—even some theorists within the dreaded IWW itself—had characterized 'the evacuation of the children' as a sensational stunt. 'It was a sordid piece of advertising. Parents were bullied and children all but abducted from their homes,' a House investigative committee in Washington, DC, was told. 'We are to the labor movement what the high diver is to the circus,' an old white-bearded Wobbly told us, in a stern but grandfatherly way. 'Our big mouths can bind an audience with spells of hellfire and brimstone as surely as any old wild-eyed Puritan scourge. We can foam at the mouth like mad dogs and wink at the same time, and the audience cries out for more, and more, and more, and finally gets bored with thrills and marvels and goes home and the workers remain unorganized. We are like drunkards: very amusing until we take a swing at somebody and pass out.' Nobody formally blamed Rosemary, and certainly there were many who all but canonized her on the spot, myself included, but because she was the girl in the photograph, she endured, as proxy or figurehead, a great deal of frustrated haranguing and oblique vituperation. She was only vaguely aware of it, but was being used in some way as a pawn between Wobblies based in Chicago, who were thought of by Wobblies based in Detroit as lawless boys playing at revolution, who in turn characterized the Wobblies based in Detroit as parlor-room socialists with sticks up their asses."

"Yes. These characterizations persist. My masters at the MCPS speak in those flights of rhetoric as well."

"One of the more dashing and devilishly handsome Italian men from Chicago befriended Rosemary in Lawrence, began to school her, and, after he'd secured an abortion for her, to sleep with her. By the time we arrived in Paterson, New Jersey, for a strike by silk workers that would last nearly half a year and include twenty-five thousand weavers, loomfixers, twisters, and warpers, she was again pregnant and again in charge, at least nominally and picturesquely, of 'the evacuation of the children.' Many years, a lifetime, and no time at all, seemed to have been passed—or rather, a moment was imperceptibly repeating. Rosemary found it nearly impossible to fix herself in a secure and ordinary sense of time and place, in the life of the community—on which fixing, of course, sanity, almost solely, depends. The irony of her situation was lost on no one, and the belief that her first child had been aborted not by a doctor but the fat Irish cop who fell off his horse and knocked her down, became common, and eventually legendary. Some versions even had her shoved off the platform and under the wheels of the train, which had just begun to move, or within days and not months of delivery, that she had given birth to a dead baby in the cloakroom of the station. She was also informally apprenticed to the editor of the *Passaic Weekly Issue*, a socialist who was shortly to write an editorial critical of Paterson policemen that would land him in prison for fifteen years. In the course of becoming something like the press secretary for the Chicago IWW, she found some purchase, entered into some valuable routine, and remained more or less sound."

"This sounds unmistakably like you. Your life."

"She learned to defend herself calmly and articulately: she had hurt and coerced no one, she had not even argued with people, she had simply stood there looking out for the children, who would tell you if you cared to speak to them of lives the stink of which would never leave their nostrils. And in this way she began to develop as well a persona and philosophy: 'If you cannot obey'—she wrote with the aid of the PW editor, who had also begun to fuck her—'you cannot command. I have found in my short life almost no one whom I wish to obey, and therefore must decline command. Obedience and commandment are the surest means of terror I know.' She was something like a pacifist-anarchist, and people who could not conceive of anarchism as anything other than deeply, inherently violent—that is to say, nearly everybody, found her paradoxical stance, in a word, fascinating. Lusty young men who liked to sing songs in bars about mining camp massacres and stage free-speech fights on street corners were particularly mesmerized by her, though it seemed to me she was growing less beautiful—more crazy-looking, sometimes even scarily so, with her huge bright

eyes and the dark exhausted flesh surrounding them, lank, unkempt hair
that not even the sturdiest hats could organize, the long, sharp nose, the extraordinary curves of her mouth, the big pigeon-toed feet and big-palmed,
long-fingered hands. She had a charismatic but self-effacing presence:
people liked, even longed, to be near her. One night at Mabel Dodge's fashionable Greenwich Village salon, the Broadway producer David Belasco
declared he would find a vehicle for her ascent to stardom. 'I can't act,'
said Rosemary. 'Even speaking in a room like this makes me nervous.' The
room was blindingly white, from a burning white porcelain chandelier to
a polar-bear-skin rug before a white marble fireplace, wherein pale birch
logs appeared to give off pure white flames. The furniture was delicate and
Florentine. Rosemary was a dark, quiet, untidy center of gravity.

'Ah, but we've all seen you act!' shouted Belasco, referring to her stand
against the mounted policemen. 'That's not acting,' said Rosemary. 'There's
acting,' said Belasco, 'and there's acting. Shakespeare said that all the world
is a stage.' 'Who,' asked Rosemary, 'is Shakespeare?'"

"Who is Shakespeare? Who is Vera! That's the question!"

"Tittering laughter failed to discourage Belasco. 'If there's an audience
and they applaud, you are acting.' 'And if they throw rotten vegetables?' 'You
are still acting, but less . . .' he searched for the right word, 'popularly.' '*Oh,
Mr. Belasco*,' said Rosemary coquettishly, 'you say that to all your little Joans
of Arc.' And the titters became whoops and guffaws. He'd made a nearly
identical sally at Elizabeth Gurley Flynn, whom the novelist Theodore Drei-
ser had called 'the Eastside Joan of Arc,' and who had brushed him famously
aside saying she preferred to 'speak her own piece.' Though we hadn't known
it until several weeks later, it was Gurley herself who had rescued us from
Willimantic. Belasco settled back in his chair and smiled good-naturedly,
undeterred. He was smitten not only with Rosemary's ungainly allure but
with what he called 'real realism, genuine objects—'"

"'Real realism!' Don't make me laugh!"

"—genuine objects on his stages and not props, walls that did not shake
when doors were slammed, an apple pie one could eat and not painted card-

board. If he was going to do a show about a poor little mill girl, he wanted a poor little mill girl to play the part, wearing her own authentic clothing, usufructuary rights to which he was willing to pay handsomely for. He had astonished beggars in this very way—"

"Yes, yes, I know the ridiculous story."

"—his assistants stripping the shirts off their backs as he peeled notes from a wad.

"The idea of a play about the Paterson silk workers did take hold that night. It would be a pageant, a series of more or less static tableau-like scenes depicting important episodes in the life of the strike, as vast and emotionally resonant as any ten productions in a cathedral by the great visionary of the theater Max Reinhardt, because it was real, with hundreds of workers onstage, playing themselves, moving from sorrow and desperation to triumph and glory via courage and principle. One of the wealthy intellectuals, John Reed, who had acceptable credentials as a daredevil journalist—he had ridden with the infamous bandido generale Pancho Villa, and had been in jail with scores of rank-and-filers in Paterson—made himself responsible for the mise-en-scène, both financial and artistic. A light-hearted lothario, he saw a lovely weird target painted on Rosemary's back, and endeavored to be the salient feature in a world that she was surely experiencing as more and more delightful by the second."

"'Although it may indeed happen,' I once read aloud to Rosemary, 'that when we believe the truth A, we escape as an incidental consequence from believing the falsehood B, it hardly ever happens that by merely disbelieving B we necessarily believe A. We may in escaping B fall into believing other falsehoods, C or D, just as bad as B; or we may escape B by not believing anything at all, not even A.'"

"You—*what's* that you're saying?"

"I have to stop and think about it for quite some time—"

"I can't believe I heard what I just heard."

"—and all the thinking I've done about in the past never seems available to me or applicable when once again I turn to it, but that sums up our feelings quite as fully as is humanly possible. At least for me. At least in that wonderful moment when I am able to return to it, to think it again. We did not want to be caught up in belief and disbelief—and yet at the same time we wanted to act, we wanted to live! And you can't live freely and fully, you can't act boldly and easily, if you don't properly believe in something. Conversing in this way, we—Rosemary, myself, and a friend of John Reed's—turned on Twenty-Third and walked up Madison to the Garden, its yellow bricks and terracotta fading in the twilight while at the top of the tower, thirty-two stories high, the Saint-Gaudens statue of Diana swiveled back and forth two or three degrees in the gusty spring wind and caught the last red light of the setting sun. We entered the ground-floor arcades and I said that I liked arches, liked looking at them and walking through them. As the baffled wind blew through those arches, following us, gently carrying us, Rosemary asked me why I felt that way, but I had no answer. It was no great secret, I suggested, that people were drawn to archways, but whatever it was that was at work in that kind of architecture, I felt it very strongly. 'It makes me feel soft and safe,' I said, an admission that would have astounded if not choked us—we were Wobblies!—in any other circumstances. John Reed's friend suggested—"

"Jules Beveridge."

"—suggested we visit Seville and Florence someday, see the loggias and porticos and so on. 'I'm not even sure what those things are or where those places are in the world,' Rosemary admitted with candor equal to my own, 'but I'd go there in a second. Anywhere in the world, I would.' She squeezed my hand. 'With you.'"

"Jules wondered if there was a lift to the top of the tower. Thirty-two stories seemed a great deal to ask, especially without authorization, but it turned out that we could get to the parapets and columns surrounding the little space, the lantern, it was called, beneath the many-tonned but mobile Diana, almost without moving a muscle. Thus was the horrible noise of the city swallowed up. It was another world altogether. The city was not real. All we could hear was a faint but steady grinding of stone on stone, and the wind, buffeting one ear and then, turning to consider another aspect of the island city, the other. The arm of the ancient goddess moved above us, in the upper corners, as it were, of our eyes. There were fewer and fewer people in the lantern lookout, night had swallowed up the city, there were only a few floating streams of light . . . . 'Or we could just stay up here,' murmured Rosemary. Jules had his arm around her. 'We could move to San Francisco.' 'Yes,' he said. 'We could just stay up here. We could move to San Francisco.' Diana groaned and creaked in the darkness and stone just above our heads. A week or two later, up in the lantern again, Rosemary had an idea, an image of something that might happen and somehow matter. We went down a flight of narrow stairs, painfully, then another and another until they came to a room that appeared to cater to unused utility: electricity! And based on what Jules thought he understood from his engineers he had come to know and to talk to about this and that, he thought it could easily be drawn from this room. A little old man, so quiet and still we hadn't known he was in the room, Rosemary and I at least, Jules giving a faint impression of prior meetings if not old acquaintance, began to speak from a tiny triangular desk in a dark corner. When Diana had been unveiled twenty years earlier, they had draped her legs and belly with ten thousand incandescent electric bulbs, so that her lovely breasts and forbidding face could be seen by anyone who cared to look up, all night long. Jules said we were associated with the Paterson Silk Strike Pageant, which would be performed in less than a week, surely the old man knew of this spectacle? Yes, yes, he thought he did. Well, we were wondering if Diana might be somehow relit, to help us advertise our show. The old man said that she would be lit now, lit eternally, if he had anything to say about it, but that the scandal of gigantic titties lighting up Manhattan, mesmerizing people and drawing them nearer and nearer her magnificent safety like a lighthouse—it had been too much for decent people to bear. Three hours later we were in the offices of the *Passaic Weekly*. Rosemary took care of a neglected duty—using a typewriter to make daily reports of news gathered shop by shop, job by job, everybody from the native-born, highly-skilled, and relatively well-paid ribbon workers and weavers, to the immigrant loomfixers and twisters and horizontal warpers—while Jules and I sought and found old light-bulb boards, electrical wire, flashers, and fuses. When he had everything he thought he needed, we hired a wagon, though it was nearly midnight now, and brought it all to the apartment in the Village he shared with John Reed, put as much as we could in three suitcases, and locked them in his bedroom. Then we had a late supper. It was the first time in our lives when we could count on all the food we wanted whenever we wanted it, and we never tired of eating. When we finished eating, we walked to the Garden and ascended the tower once more. It made all the sense in the world as we listened rapturously to the sound of the goddess atop her little six-pillared lantern, grinding from one minute of perspective to the next. *Here is what I see now. Here is what I see now. Here is what I see for a moment then never again.* The lantern was evidently something of an attraction and was filled with people even at that late hour, the lift going ceaselessly up and down, up and down, up and down, but Jules was quite sure there would be a slack period in the wee hours when they could rig their lights. Secreting the contents of the suitcases wherever we could, here and there in the tower's highest rooms, another three suitcases each day, we waited for opening night."

"An exhibition of the latest art was on display at the Armory. Jules, with whom, yes, as you have been suspecting, I had fallen hopelessly in love, he was so handsome and capable and so clearly desirous of the kind of life I had slowly been working up a description of with my friends, had seen many paintings and sculptures in his life, and been moved by a few, but Rosemary and I had not. But because the work in the Armory was new to everybody, Jules found no precedent for it in his imagination. He therefore thought he did not much care for most of what he saw, but as he and I and Rosemary walked—Jules and Rosemary hand in hand, me waiting patiently for the time when I knew someone would snatch Rosemary away and Jules would turn to me in astonished love, as if a storm had passed and I was the one who was still there—from one curtained gallery to the next, under the canopy of bright yellow streamers billowing up into the darkness of the somehow still military ceiling, amid the boughs and sprays of evergreens and baskets of flowers, I think he could not help but feel some of our amazement and excitement: the tumbling but suave sweep of geometric shapes in Duchamp's mockery of the 'cult of big women,' *Nude Descending a Staircase, No. 2*, the strange but vivid, too-vivid colors and objects in Matisse—I heard someone call it 'epileptic'—the hallucinated landscapes of van Gogh. . . . No, he could not deny what I was saying with such conviction: the affinity many of the paintings had with narcotic perception, or with narcotic thought, with what it was like to work in a mill. And so he was annoyed for our sake to hear people buzzing in every room about what former president Roosevelt—had he just been there, and if so, how had we missed him?—had said, suggesting Americans take the work no more seriously than they did P. T. Barnum's mermaids. Which was to say, somewhat seriously, as you could look far and wide and not find a more striking, beloved, archetypical example of an American than Barnum, but skeptically or at arm's length, with tongue in cheek, with an eye toward amusement and belly laughs rather than edification and sublimity. Certainly there was more repugnance than beauty in much of the work. One left a canvas too often irritated and confused, and there was even a sense of outright falseness in every one of the eighteen octagonal rooms, either the result of ineptitude and childishness, or the calculated deceit of a huckster. But Rosemary and I were thrilled with the recognition of something essential in our lives. She was holding my hand tightly now, and could say little more than *oh oh ohhhh*, as if she were having an orgasm—a sensation I could not help but feel drawn closer and closer to myself. We could only be responding, in our completely untutored, inexperienced way, to what we sensed was the life in the paintings. That too Jules could not deny: there was life and ecstasy in them, some of them. There was life somewhere. He could smell it. It stank but it was alive. I shivered. And then we came to Odilon Redon, whose first works were ridiculous and grotesque: the huge grinning spider, the hot-air balloon that looked like an eyeball, worms and deliquescent flowers, the puerile doodlings of a bored but gifted little boy. A sad, creepy Cyclops. Six lithographs inspired by Poe. Rosemary drifted away. When she came back, her face was clouded. She stood over us and we could see her eyes were wet and that tears had run down her cheeks. Then she smiled and it seemed the tears were of joy. She pulled us to our feet and told us he must come and see *The Druid Priestess*. She was in profile, and her head and neck and shoulder were clothed in a kind of silken fluid gold that became a reddish orange on her arm. Her jaw and cheek were darkened, and at first glance she would be taken for mannish, the dark staining an early growth of beard. But then it began to look more as if she were made of wood, the lower part of her face darkened with age or mold, or the nose and large dark eye and forehead bleached by the sun. The blue, green, and black background suggested a luminous forest at twilight, and there was a spattered yellowish moon in the upper left corner. Her golden hood appeared to be raining around her. Her eye grew deeper and darker, her sharp nose and thin lips more feminine. Hair flowed from under the golden rain, like a deeper, darker current. We were hypnotized. 'I think that's my grandmother,' said Rosemary. 'She is a strange but lovely woman,' said Jules. 'Grandmother,' I repeated reverently. We waited for a large group of murmuring people to pass into the next room, then swung around the burlap-covered partition wall and came face-to-face with the first of the horses. It was a dark, earth-brown and gold demonic Pegasus, embroiled in its own fury, writhing and contorted as it struggled to fly, or having flown, to not fall. Next was a silver and white Pegasus, rearing up on a black, blue, and silver mountaintop, majestic, magical, and beautiful—but alone. The winged horse and rider in *Roger and Angelica*, or *Perseus and Andromeda*, was purely golden, with very small wings. A kind of wormy serpent and mutant fish monster—possibly the Medusa but possibly not—

menaced them in the blue clouds. We decided these paintings were beautiful, but troubling, and admitted we had become distinctly uneasy. Finally
we came to *The Chariot of Apollo*. There was the blue sky again, now frighteningly blue—not dawn, not noon, not dusk, not midnight—and the white
horses in agony. Only a small smear of the sky was that shade of strange
bedlam blue; the clouds were brown and green, as if the world were upside
down, and the chariot, stolen from Apollo by the brash young reckless Phaeton . . . seemed to be falling. Phaeton's head appeared to be on fire, and the
chariot was falling."

"Though playgoers lined the sidewalk the length of the Garden, went around
the block and nearly the length of its other side, most of them, assevering
poverty or union brotherhood, would get in for pennies, or without charge, if
they were Paterson silk workers not appearing in the show. The pageant's
backers, Jules told us as we stood in the park across the street, had been depending, in the face of sky-high—we all looked up involuntarily at the statue
of Diana—Garden rental fees, on subscription and the selling out of the pric-
ier stalls to intellectual sympathizers with money. These sympathizers had not
been as forthcoming as had been hoped, and Jules said the backers reckoned
that they would probably not break even. Worse, it was looking like he was
being left holding, so to speak, the books: bills had been left unpaid, and while
some vendors and lenders would be happy to write their losses off in a good
cause, some would not. There wasn't much he could do, but it looked like he
would have to deal with the part that wasn't any fun. I said that that was because he was a good, kind, decent man who could not help but do such things
for the welfare of others. He sat down on a bench that was out of the lamplight
they'd been standing in, and Rosemary instinctively sat down next to him,
held his arm and snuggled close. She liked him, and that was all there was to
it. I think she knew I loved him, but she liked him, and when she liked people,
she showed it. For his part, Jules liked nearly everybody he met, but felt he
would, without thinking, risk his life, just like that, for Rosemary. How could

I discredit such a feeling? Why would I? And, again, without thinking or any sort of articulation, he was confident that the feeling was reciprocal. It was simply the kind of man he was. Was he a daredevil? Not in any way that you would notice. Was he handsome? Yes, but not incredibly so. Was he charismatic? No. But I loved him. His eyes were kind and intelligent and he was not afraid to suffer, not afraid to die. And here is where I began to see things, as it were, peripherally. Nothing bore in on me. I could see everything floating past me but focus on nothing. Even perfectly clear shapes very near did not startle or impinge on me. They moved at ordinary speed, but seemed to drift and were quietly making ordinary noises. I could see things very far away and it was soothing to have it all so far away. It was something like being high, but I wasn't, and I was glad I wasn't. All three of us had fallen silent, listening to the shouts across the street. Once most of the crowd was inside and the Pageant had begun—you could hear the first choral shouts even in the park—we made our way with a small hand truck from the shipping dock to the tower lift. From the hand truck to the lift we moved four big boards holding red-painted electric light bulbs, a roll of electrical cord, and a little leather satchel of tools. We appeared to be handling scenery and to be involved in ordinary stagecraft; the people milling about didn't give us a second look as we closed the iron-grill doors of the lift's little car and set off, rattling and banging our way upward. We passed up through many floors in the darkness of the elevator shaft, but came suddenly to the Parthenon-like summit of the tower's first twenty floors, and glimpsed, through the massive columns, the little streams of light flowing into the vast darkness beyond Central Park. Slowing and swaying and creaking, we went up another fifty feet into a once-again-closed dark space, that looked something like a miniature neoclassical bank or government building, the lift coming to a loud banging stop at its roof, which was the floor of the first of three, successively smaller balconied arcades, the last of which was the lantern, on top of which Diana rested and turned. We would have to climb narrow circular stairs now, with our awkwardly big and increasingly heavy light boards, each of the four six feet by three. Halfway with the first board, Rosemary, going first, said *oh no* sharply, and slipped. Though all she did was sit heavily, the board came down with a crack on the top of her skull, and I was jolted backward. I let go of the board with both hands to grab the handrails, and somehow managed to hold the board on the rack of my arms and shoulders while it pressed into my throat. It was as if I were standing before the carder with an immense weight choking me. Rosemary struggled to her feet and quickly pulled the board up so that I could breathe. Satisfied that we were all right, we made our way slowly and carefully up to the lantern. We propped the board against the balustrade, and waited for Jules, who was carrying the second by himself. Then we went down for the third board. Halfway up, the same thing happened again: the step was somehow irregular, or slick, and Rosemary, careful as she could be, slipped. She made the same sharp sound, and I, hearing something this time in the intake of breath just before the cry, was able to ready myself, hunching my shoulders to protect my throat. Up in the lantern we panted and waited for Jules and the last board. Rosemary then went down and came back up with the electrical cord, and Jules set about cutting, separating, and splicing it. Then without a word she went through one of the window arches onto the ledge, a good wide ledge of about two feet, running the perimeter of the lantern. She looked up and told us she could see the splendid swell of Diana's breasts above the folds of her toga. She was all alone at the top of the city, as calm as an angel, seeing everything. Jules, being a man, said she should come back in: he should be the one on the ledge. I slowly pushed my end of the first board out farther and farther through the opening into the darkness. At precisely the point where I thought I would lose control of it, Rosemary dropped it lightly and quickly to the ledge, and crawled back in. A single short piece of rope secured the board to a column. Again and again and again she went out onto the ledge while I slowly, slowly, slowly pushed the boards out at her, thinking with every breath that something terrible was going to happen and I would be responsible for her death. Again and again and again she dropped the boards into place and popped back into the lantern with us. We were, I suppose, in awe of her. Breathless all of us, silent, feeling we were living so fully we were nearly at the edge of it, that real things were seeming less and less real, and unreal things more and more real. Then we went back down the winding stairway, unspooling cord as we descended, until we were back in the confines of the bank-like structure. Here was the utility room. The little old man who presided over it was not to be found. Jules cut and spliced more cord, studied a fuse box, said *this ought to do it*, and flipped a switch. Up we went one last time to the lantern, to see if in fact the bulbs were lit, and Rosemary hopped out onto the ledge. We waited for her to say something, but she said nothing. I thought I heard a faint whistling, and I turned to Jules and said, or murmured to myself, or merely thought: *whistling while we work.* By the time we worked up the courage, or rather the saliva, to speak, to call out her name, we knew she had fallen, knew that she was gone. We said nothing to each other, thinking somehow that if we remained calm all would be well. Jules went out onto the ledge. I could hear his shoes scraping around me as he made the circuit. Then he came back in. He shook his head and I began to tremble. We went down to the lift, jammed its door open, and walked down thirty floors and out one of the loading dock doors. A cab took us to Penn Station, and three days later, we were in San Francisco, reading various accounts in five or six newspapers of the terrifying lights above Madison Square Garden: NO BOSS spelled out the board facing south. NO DOGMA shone to the east, NO GOD to the north, and finally, in the west, NO FEAR. The identity of the young woman who had evidently engineered the feat was eventually revealed. Her name was Rosemary Thorndike, a well known anarchist."

In Saint Paul, Charles took up a new project: understanding William James and Plato; James because he was such a genial and erudite companion, the explorer of the will to believe when there was 'nothing' to believe in, Plato because Plato defied understanding at every turn and yet seemed to have set out a model for government that no one could shake off. If Charles could bring James to Plato or Plato to James, maybe he could find 'something' to believe in strongly enough to efface his bone-deep feeling that it was an illusion that he was even alive—along with the honing of an ability to keep the world of objects and other people in close but not threatening proximity, while at the same time maintaining in perfect, nearly silent but faintly humming equipoise, the working of his own physical organs and processes, and the turbulent, sometimes frightening thoughts his mind bore and nurtured, in what seemed a universe parallel to, but completely separate from, the one in which his body took up space.

Vera and he spent a good deal of their time observing the proceedings of the Minnesota legislature, which was heating up and drawing consequently a wide variety of persons to its hearth to warm their hands. A delegation from the Chicago office came up to participate in hearings, and Vera found herself functioning as a kind of spokesperson, a secretary briefing reporters with regard to theory, practice, history, and current positions of the Industrial Workers of the World, moderate and radical socialists, and the dreaded anarchists. The sudden visibility of men and women perceived as shadowy figures inclined toward sabotage and murder (when they weren't singing songs and talking sedition on street corners hoping to be arrested and have a grand old free-speech trial) caused an uproar. The milling district, it was relentlessly rumored, was going to be blown up several times over; the city would be destroyed, and IWW participation in the hearings was decried as suicidal. An attorney working for a number of lumber companies grew so rabid and obscene in his denunciations that he was made, by legislators, to apologize before he would be allowed to continue.

They would meet him again, fatally, in the spring.

Vera's friends from Lawrence and Paterson, Joseph Ettor and Arturo Giovanniti notably, were hailed, astonishingly, as charming and intelligent citizens of the republic, as helpful as the legislators listening to them thought possible. Great strides were in fact made as the winter wore on. Crowds of many thousands formed to listen to antiwar speakers, and the socialist mayor of Minneapolis was seen everywhere beaming with satisfaction and delight. Despite Vera's philosophical devotion to the abolition of all states and all governments, she found herself caught up in the day-to-day pressures and pleasures of politics. And found herself caught up as well in a night-to-night fantasy that struck her in the mornings as even stranger than idle daydreams of sabotage: settling down and having children. Only in moments when she was taken, as it were, by surprise—by low spirits or low blood sugar, exhausted nerves, a bad head cold—did black thoughts of their murdered and maimed friends in San Francisco whisper at her, like the cold wind seeping under her doors, like the slowly leaking corpses of boys dying too quickly and in too great numbers to be buried in the war that now seemed would never end, like the girls playing with dolls in the revolving drum—only then did she acknowledge that all was not well and that she was a fool to think it was. Yes, the vision of the little girls in the drum was a very bad one indeed.

In February—a month in which not a single inch of snow fell, and temperatures climbed above freezing every day—the United States severed diplomatic ties with Germany. The Minnesota legislature concluded its overwhelmingly reformist session with a violent about-face in which were passed three profoundly repressive bills. In March, half the snow on the ground melted, only to be replaced by three more wet and heavy feet of it in a late blizzard. Charles spoke openly and ardently of his desire to take Vera to London, where they would wait to see in what way he would serve. There was no hope, he said, for America. He suddenly wanted to get out and stay out. The Gilded Age was giving way to the Age of Empire, and it would be founded on commercially viable xenophobically poisonous Christian fundamentalism. In April, the United States declared war on Germany.

In the lovely spring weather Vera walked two miles every morning, past the mansions on Summit Avenue, then down the hill and along the river downtown to Rice Park, the Hamm Theater, the Saint Paul Hotel, and the wonderful new neoclassical Federal-style library, where she stayed, enraptured, until it closed, and walked two miles back home. She had begun work on her autobiography, she told Charles, and felt fit, clean-handed and cool-headed. It was his idea that a writer ought to be clean-handed and cool-headed—he believed he'd gotten it from Flaubert or the Goncourts—but they were still fond of alcohol, of drinking alcohol by themselves and with Daisy Gluek and others until they all blacked out. Charles was waiting to hear how and where and when he would join the war, each day more concerned that something was wrong; and Vera was waiting for a spring speaking tour with Daisy to be organized and funded—and for the roads to dry, since they would not be traveling by horseback, as Vera had, through the long cold dark winter, daydreamed they might. Oh, they were like sisters, Vera Dark and Daisy Light, in their characters, not their looks, and they were deep in a giddy drunken confusion of newspapers and small talk of saturnalias and bomb-throwing one night—they vehemently agreed with each other, over and over, that *reckless* bomb-throwing was just another form of authoritarian coercion, but that the *careful* use of explosives was as American as apple pie—when a group of people they had met from the Saint Paul Peace League sat down at their end of a long warped table. Vera had thought, at some point, that there was someone, a man, sitting across from her, reading something she'd wanted him to read while she continued to scribble notes, but he had apparently departed without saying good-bye. She stopped scribbling in the middle of a sentence—"If no one cares I will . . ."—and welcomed the new group to her country. The women, two of them, seemed lost in their voluminous hats and interminable feather boas, mumbling what Vera made out to be bons mots, while the men, two also, smiled and bristled with great energy, saying very little while talking nonstop.

"It was Malatesta who shot King Umberto at Monza," said one of them.

Vera wasn't even sure if it was a male or female who'd spoken. They all, including Daisy, looked at her while she drank.

"What's your question?" she demanded at last.

"*Wasn't it?*" asked a second.

"No," Vera shook her head, "it wasn't."

"What did he do then?"

"Malatesta?"

"*Yes*, Malatesta."

"What did he *do*? You're asking me what Malatesta *did*? For God's sake, man, woman, he's only one of the—"

"She wants to know who he killed," said a woman. "Or rather, who killed King Umberto at Monza." This woman spoke as if she were listening to music. Vera looked at her notes, then at the group, then back at her notes. Daisy leaned conspiratorially over the table, causing everyone else to do so as well. Charles was sodden but beginning to glaze over. Then a troupe of musicians paraded past them, down the aisle to a little bandstand. Their instruments were shiny and exotic: an oboe, a flute, a bassoon, a clarinet, a French horn. The musicians and their instruments exerted a powerful attraction over most of the people in the saloon and seemed particularly to mesmerize the Peace Leaguers. A sixth man joined the musicians, conferring quietly with them for a moment, then walked down the aisle, winking at Daisy. He went through a little door, and closed it, only to emerge seconds later with a much bigger horn. Again he smiled at Daisy, who said, "Tuba, or not tuba. That is the question." It was not an especially funny thing to say, but Daisy was just generally amusing, and there was loud laughter up and down the long tables and from the bandstand, where the musicians grinned around their reeds and blowholes as they tuned up.

"Okay," said Vera slowly, "it goes like this. Say, you know what? Things really *jump*, don't they, in the Peace League? Am I missing something, because you don't seem all that peaceful to me . . . . Never mind. Malatesta is lecturing in West, I don't know, Hoboken, I think, West Hoboken. Guy name of, uh, Domenico Scarlatti or what was it, Scarlatti, yeah, I think that was it, Scarlatti pulls out a pistol and shoots Malatesta at the podium. Ooo, got me, right in the podium! Nobody knows why. Not then, not now. Main theory seems to center on the idea that the Italians, hey, they know how to *cook*. But Malatesta is seriously wounded by the gunshot. Scarlatti, no, wait, what am I thinking, the guy's name was Pazzaglia, Pete Pazzaglia, he looks like maybe he wants to finish the job, but this other guy, can't think of his name, either, jeez, Provenzale, Legrenzi . . . Leonardo Leonardi . . . ? Bresci!

Gaetano *Bresci*, he tackles him and subdues him. Malatesta refuses to press charges against Pazzo because he is a *brother anarchist*, and Bresci meanwhile is hailed as a man of peace and temperance and justice. A year later, he turns up at Monza, not infamous anarchist Malatesta, not trigger-happy Pazzo, but Bresci, and *he* guns down the good King Umberto."

"Maybe Bresci tackled the other guy *to get the gun*," said one of the men.

The women rose to go to the ladies' room. "What is it with you folks?" Vera asked.

"We've been taking drugs," said one earnestly.

"Well, yeah!" said Vera. "But which ones?"

The woman who had looked earnest changed her look to bland and turned to her friend, for corroboration, Vera thought, or maybe just to see if she was still there. "We came across a bit of cocaine, and the boys took that, they're so excited they're boring, and we have been experimenting with opium dreaming for some time now."

"I see," said Vera. "Why aren't you dreaming?"

"Do you want to try it? Or don't you approve?"

"Oh, I have tried it, I have certainly tried it!"

"Are you addicted?" asked the second woman, who was staring at herself in the dirty, spotted mirror.

"Well, I don't know, I suppose I was, still am, in a way, on some level. I started . . . very young. It was given to me as part of a plan to keep me quiet. If I was crying too much, they'd slip me some laudanum and lock me in a closet. I don't know if you ladies are familiar with Iowa button mills or Connecticut thread mills . . . ? They had discounts on bulk purchases in the company store—of laudanum, I mean. Folks would work their eighty hours, or sixty-eight if they'd just had a successful strike, limp home, and relax with ten or twenty drops of the stuff. Or they'd take it in the morning before work to relieve the tension *at* work. It was either that or run shrieking out of there. And if you dreamed, as you say, your way into a crushed limb or perforated organ, that was better than starving to death, which is what would happen if you shrieked and ran. Always better to dream yourself to death, we said around the dinner table. That's the title of a chapter, by the way, in my forth-coming autobiography, *I Don't Know Why I'm Surprised*. When I was little, when my parents were still alive, we lived in Willimantic. I mean Muscatine. Poppa had been employed for several years as a—oh, never mind—and he went to pieces. Of course, with the new laws, the new drug laws—LAWS LAWS LAWS. GOD, AREN'T YOU SICK TO FUCKING DEATH OF LAWS? Poor people now have to drink themselves to death. The opium was judged to be far too pleasant a way to die—*and* it cut into profitability. But I suppose I was high too, when Poppa went to pieces. I wandered about the town and eventually adopted a talking squirrel."

They walked back to the long table. "Returning to the new drug laws," said Vera. "The most recent figures indicate, um, say, what's wrong with your friend there?"

"She'll be all right," said the first woman. "You were saying."

"I was saying health and safety? Next person who talks to me about health and safety . . . ! It's control that matters! Control and productivity and predictability. Whatever the problem is, the solution will always be to clamp down on the pleasures of poor people. You got some vast burner putting up clouds of coal smoke, you can't go out for a ride in the carriage with-out choking half to death, why, you just pass a bill that outlaws candles in the home! Any poor person caught using a candle will be hustled into jail. Health and safety, my eye. I don't know why I'm surprised."

"Right . . . " said the first woman. Her friend giggled. "Carol Kennicott! Stop looking like that. Stop giggling! You're giving us the creeps!"

"Ditto that," said Vera.

"I'm sorry," giggled Carol. "It's just, you know, a speech like that, there in the ladies' room," and here her giggling changed key, "as if it were possible to change anything at this late date!" She seemed now on the verge of hysteria. "I am afraid if I move, my face will stay the way it was painted on the mir-ror." She clapped her hand to her mouth. "But my mouth is moving and I can feel it moving, so all must be well." She swiveled her eyes at her friend and Vera and Daisy, blinking at each in turn as if they were the mirror. "What we ought to do is get as much opium as we can and go to Belgium. Or are they just in France now? If we ever came back, we could . . . we could *speak with legitimacy of the end of time*. We could be the final witnesses. Like the Black Death. Wander across fields of corpses, trees blooming with severed heads, somnambulists and magicians, metallic chattering of guns, bombs instead of thunder, children staring at clouds of poison gas and saying they see a ducky or a kitten, homes with no doors or windows or roofs but you walk in anyway, right? As if there were?" Vera nodded in such a way that Carol was forced to pause and consider herself for a while in the mirror of Vera's face. "You walk in and there's someone sitting there in the dark staring at a pot of water, they don't even say hello, generals writing their memoirs, but they can't come up with the right word because they are actually as stupid as the day is long, and, and you're right, poor people being battered to death for lighting a candle. I keep seeing these children, can you see them . . . ? They're trying to play a game. They're standing in a circle, blood on the ground, smoke in the air, and they can't figure out what the rules are, or what the . . . what the . . . what the fuck the point is."

Vera's eyes had been locked with Carol's for the entire length of the speech. Now Carol turned away and it was as if lightning had indeed struck and transformed them where they stood.

"The game," said Vera at last, "is hide-and-seek."

They were, she thought, the counterweight to mystic speculators in the grain trade, weird people trying to call chemical clouds together in the hope that peace might rain down upon them, as lost to the world of protest, negotiation, and reconciliation as the speculators were to altruism, philanthropy, and food grown and cooked with their own tired hands.

It was seductive, but she wanted to stay in the trench. A friend of hers, she told the women, someone very close to her, was addicted to narcotics, and so she saw things in a little different light. Without warning, she collapsed in a chair, held her face in her hands, and began to cry.

"More prisons, more police, more mobs, more lynching," said Vera. They had returned to the table. The men looked like they'd been sobbing

too. The women sat down and ignored what the men were trying passionately to say. Vera lost her train of thought and the first woman, Louise, asked
her again if she felt she had been addicted to the opium she'd been given as
a child. Vera again began to cry. Louise had meant to introduce the topic as
a subject for group discussion, but now didn't know what to do. She raised
and lowered her palms several times. Vera stopped crying as quickly and
surely as if she'd been faking it.

"Certainly I was sick and crazy as a child, and I can say now just as
certainly that I felt something in me call out for it, daydream about it without saying its name, imagine circumstances, maybe other worlds, maybe
an ideal world, ominously enough, prophetically enough, in which I might
indulge myself in this nameless desire . . . but I tell you, my friends, what
makes me burst out in tears of grief and loneliness is the knowledge that I
have gone on for so long feeling free, acting as if I were free, only to find
out that I am not. Oh, it's a question I can't answer! I can tell you I resisted
it, that I resisted all gross pleasures and extreme pursuits. Alcohol and tobacco and firearms. Meat. I thought purity was called for. Purity of limb
and thought. It may have been an elaborate disguise for a fear that I was in
some way being controlled, but how can I think of something as artificial as
rectitude when the world is upside down? How can I be pure when I can see
with my own eyes that there is nothing pure, that there has been nothing
pure in the history of creation! And is not the seeking of purity, friends and
neighbors, just an elaborate disguise for terror? What do you miss when you
seek purity? Poetry from your life and passion from your politics? I mean
real passion, not the costumes and soliloquies and power. Oh, ladies and
gentlemen, I lived in New York once, for a very little while, and I knew the
bliss of art, the peace that it brings. So yes, I say, opium *yes*, and whiskey *yes*,
and cigarettes and pistols and Coleridge and Baudelaire and and and *Edgar
Allen Poe*! I am twenty-one years old and I lecture, mostly to myself now,
like some pompous magister-cum-tyrant in a gown, of freedom, but—" and
she began to cry again, because she was quoting someone who was dead,
more or less verbatim, "but the truth, ha ha, is that I am a slave to a world of

simple objects and superficial perception and mechanical thought and naïve ideals. If I'm not a terrorist it's because I'm a coward."

As if she'd not made her extraordinary speech, the man who had been so insistent about King Umberto said, "Don't give up your ideals. God, this cocaine is wearing off already!"

"Oh, the world is rich and strange and horrifying and mute and I have confined myself to newsprint in the tiniest of fonts," Vera continued to rave, as if the man who'd interrupted her had not spoken after all. "Doctrine and frankly bourgeois comforts. I want the revolution to be like the fall of Nineveh, the feast of Belshazzar, strong red wine in heavy golden goblets, clothes of scarlet silk, a spectral hand writing on the walls of the homes of these vicious assholes: GOD HATH NUMBERED THY KINGDOM AND FINISHED IT, THOU ART WEIGHED IN THE BALANCE AND FOUND WANTING, THY KINGDOM IS DIVIDED AND GIVEN TO THE IN-DUSTRIAL WORKERS OF THE WORLD!"

Everybody in the big back room of the Oregon House applauded and whistled and cheered. "I am either a block of lead, friends and neighbors and citizens, or a nervous bird and *I am tired of it.* I want to hear music in every waterfall. I want to see time going backward as well as forward: 'the dark backward and abysm of time,' I want that, I want that badly! I want the past, the present, the future! Life, as we have lived it, comrades, is meaning-less. It is a life that has been recommended to us, forced upon us when we balked, by people who do not care if we are happy or even alive, so long as there are others in line behind us. Therefore and in conclusion: opium, whiskey, pistols, and dynamite!"

It was not her last speech of the night.

Charles was braced in a cone of yellow light over a large relief map of Min-nesota, the Dakotas to the river, Wisconsin, and the Upper Peninsula of Michigan. Vera threw open the door and it came back at her, knocking her sideways a good distance. The doorway jumped to the left and jumped to the right, but she made her way in, only to have the spring-loaded floor fly up and slap her in the face. Later, he told her that she tried to speak, but I hadn't been able to make out the language. "You were slick and pale and but looked, somehow, contented and amused."

"I made great speeches at the Oregon House," she said blearily but proudly.

"And then you vomited."

"When was this?"

"Just a bit ago. I was there and then I came here."

Charles cleaned her up with looming movements and sounds and tucked her in bed. The next day he told her that because of the slapstick the-atrics of her entry, she probably hadn't noticed Daisy sleeping on the couch.

"No, no," said Vera. "I saw her."

"She says she has the job."

"Job?"

"Traveling. Speaking. It's planned and waiting to happen."

"Oh no . . . ."

"'Oh no'?"

"This is what everybody's been waiting for."

"As I said. Why 'oh no'?"

"Because I am unwell."

"Who is everybody?"

"What kind of question is that? I've got a headache. Leave me alone."

"Everybody must include me. What have I been waiting for?"

"Once again a terrific question that I cannot help you with."

"Vera, please, you are mistaking me for one of your pinheaded nihilists. Just because I don't think any of this is real doesn't mean I am indifferent to things everybody is waiting for. I am not apolitical or amoral. I am my fa-ther's son in more ways than I am not. I think I have demonstrated as much pretty persuasively in the last few months. Have I not? Vera? Have I not?"

"Charles, I love you. Don't you understand what that means?"

"No, not at all."

"I couldn't love, wouldn't love you, if I didn't know what was in your heart."

"What's in my heart?"

"Love."

"Whatever you call it, it's as illusory as everything else."

"If you say so."

"Well, how can I not and remain honest?"

"I don't know."

"I can't."

"If you say so."

"Well, you must. Please."

"I tell you my head hurts horribly and—"

"Head hurts horribly, hurry home."

"—and you insist on *metaphysics*."

"Daisy travels and speaks. The roads are now hard and dry enough for her to do so. Why is everyone waiting for these speeches? Are they new speeches?"

"Charles Minot asks me if a speech is new?"

"All right."

"All right is right."

"Let me see if I understand."

"You do understand."

Some dreary weeks later, two men, Wobblies Vera knew from a short visit to Los Angeles—one of the times Charles had been unable to find her—had come to visit her once in the machine shop where she'd briefly lived, in the Andersonville section of north Chicago, before coming to Charles and Saint Paul. They caught her in the middle of a very dark wood. It was a deep, black, fugal consideration of her life, not unlike ordinary narcoses, but very much more resigned to self-evident truths, and consequently, serene in a clear way not usually afforded by drugs. The questions, the rhetorical questions she posed herself, all received clear, peaceful, inarguable answers. Her life was over. She had failed to maintain the beautiful, the magnificent arc of her trajectory. It was possible that the godlike archer who had released her had done so imperfectly, but if that was so, it mattered not at all to the arrow. She had been struck by some harrier, some raptor, stripped of fletching and point, deflected, nearly stopped dead in midair, hairline cracks fissuring her length—and was tumbling back to earth. She would not finish her flight. The greatness of her daring, her willingness, her nonchalant ability to draw breathtakingly near death and flaunt her life—had come to nothing. There was no shame in this knowledge, no resentment—the thing had simply not ended as it had begun. So when the Wobblies wondered at her relations with Daisy Gluek, she said she felt nothing but affection and admiration for her. Daisy reminded her of Rosemary. Who seemed so far away and so close— she could hold her, as it were, in her heart, and let the gulf between them widen and widen until she too was dead. In no way did this sense of her-self, as spent and falling, failing, dying, interfere with her devotion to saintly Rosemary—and by unavoidable but faulty extension, Daisy—her love of her. The thought of the way she had made her way in the world pleased and sat-isfied Vera. The way she had learned, her method—it was a thing of beauty because she expected so little of it. Her rejection of power—or was it fear? It did not matter, because she was afraid in such a graceful way. She had been so from the beginning, long before they'd met. . . .

"We see each other once a week," Vera told the Wobblies. "I am helping her with certain aspects of her autobiography."

"We have entered into a kind of association with the Nonpartisan League," said one of the Wobblies. They were just coming into individual focus for Vera. The speaker, whose name she had already forgotten, had thick wavy gray hair, bushy gray eyebrows, spectacles, and a bristling gray moustache. He looked a little, she thought, like Mark Twain, but had a deep somnolent voice, occasionally garbled with phlegm. An old man, probably older than he looked, but fit. The second man was much younger, younger even than herself—and suddenly she remembered him. His name was Joe and he had ridden around Los Angeles with Jules when they'd been tailing scabs and scab organizers and detectives and councilmen to their homes.

"Joe!" she shouted and got unsteadily to her feet. "I knew I should know you—can you forgive me?"

"It's great to see you again, Vera," said Joe. His eyes had filled with tears. They embraced, and because Vera was weak and high, she began to weep unconstrainedly, causing the emotional, young, and politically sincere Joe to shudder with a sob or two as well. When they released each other, they were grinning and brusquely wiping away tears. The older man appeared unmoved. Once Joe and Vera were again seated, he resumed his brief. They wanted Vera to join the speaking tour with Daisy, who had already gone west from the Twin Cities to the Dakota border, north through mostly wheat-farming communities, and was about to angle southeast through Big Timber.

"Is Big Timber a town . . . ?" asked Vera, careful to seem to know nothing.

"We refer to the industry," said the older man.

"Two of our boys up there have disappeared," said Joe.

"'Disappeared,'" Vera repeated. This she genuinely did not know.

"Two weeks, no word," said Joe.

"And this is the tour Daisy has been, um, alluding to for . . . ? She's going on a speaking tour through . . . through . . ."

"Big Timber, yes," said the older man.

"Big Wheat *and* Big Timber," said Vera, not only getting the hang of things but beginning to feel heavy with fear. She could hear her heart in her throat and she felt as if she might have trouble breathing and speaking. "Oh, I am dead already," she thought, but apparently said aloud. "I was dead before this, but I am very, very dead if this is what I have come to. The delicate but virtuosic balance of immense forces was life, and awkward heaviness is death. Perhaps true death will be a condition of light and balance again, but dying is clumsy and sodden."

"What would you say to be acting," continued the older man, "as a kind of companion, and why not say it, *bodyguard*, for Miss Gluek."

"I am not violent in the least," said Vera.

"We understand that. No one who knows you could fail to feel sympathy for any aversion you might feel for . . . for violence. But perhaps you will do things other people are . . . afraid to do."

"Yes," said Joe. "That's the main thing we wanted to say to you."

"And if something should happen to Miss Gluek, you would be there . . . to take her place."

"Ah," said Vera. Did they know that that had been the plan, or were they suggesting it in all innocence?

"If something happens," said the older man.

"When something happens," said Joe.

"Something is going to happen." Technically it was a question, but she posed it so flatly as to render it a prophecy.

"Yes," said the older man. "When Miss Gluek says something about American women not being brood sows for war profiteers, she will be arrested."

"I am afraid on her behalf," said Vera, sounding oddly like an orator, "and I do not want to be arrested."

"We made a good deal of progress in the last legislative session up there," said the older man. "The eleventh-hour turnaround and the repressive bills were a blow we didn't see coming, but we made friends. We were very impressive and we made a number of important friends. They are the kind of friends who may be instrumental in keeping some of us, if not all of us, out of prison. We don't want to get our hopes up too high, as Justice is planning a very thorough sweep, but we have high hopes anyway, and see a clear opportunity *in this moment* to hurt some of the big people."

Vera felt a fiery acid pump through her veins and then she felt clean and serene again. She felt objects around her withdraw ever so slightly and hold steady, and the nearness of the human beings who were speaking so softly and articulately to her. What was it that they said the old Indians used to say?

"'Heaven is no place for a man,'" she said, again apparently out loud. "But something else . . . something else about dying . . . ."

"It's a good day to die," said Joe.

Vera stared at him with nearly overwhelming gratitude and love.

"Some of our new friends," said the older man, "have been demanding that the reactionary and repressive forces running the Minnesota Commission of Public Safety open themselves up to participation by other limbs of the body politic, limbs representing citizens with just as much patriotic desire to fight the good fight against the German tyrant as the next bunch."

"Who," interrupted Vera, "are our friends this time around, exactly?"

"Socialists are very strong across the river in Minneapolis. The mayor is a socialist. And in Saint Paul we have some daredevils in the streetcar union leadership."

"I interrupted you," said Vera.

"The MCPS has scoffed at such proposals heretofore, likening our friends to traitors in waiting, collaborators, spies, and of course cowards. But as I suggested a bit ago, we made some inroads. Our friends are going to front a candidate of our choosing for a very crucial job: shadowing whomever the MCPS sends to follow you and Daisy. Shadowing in the British sense: the opposite number, not in the sense of a spy. No doubt there will be other shadows—at least one if not several, but our man will be what the MCPS will call 'a friendly face.' Someone to prevent violence, not to foment it. Our man will make himself available to the NPL speaker and anyone else in her company—the NPL is nearly bankrupt and we expect the party to be very small—"

"You and Daisy," said Joe.

"—as a kind of liaison, more or less a neutral observer and cooling influence if anything gets out of hand or flares up. Our man will have to be interviewed by one of the MCPS's tough guys, and he will have to be able to pass himself off as someone with Pinkerton-like capacity for deceit and violence but be something considerably more able intellectually than a thug. In the end, the idea is to keep the young ladies out not just of jail, but harm's way. Any kind of harm that might crop up. To intervene and maybe get them the hell out of Dodge. Or at the very least to see that they are treated with ordinary legal safeguards. We want the IWW to look, for lack of a better word, electable. We want to show the MCPS up as thugs, not the other way around."

And Charles, upon hearing Vera's recapitulation of the conversation, thought: *WRETCH! Dost thou ask what thou hast done? Look back upon a dreadful misspent life, and ask thyself what thou hast not done!* It was something out of Defoe, he thought, *Robinson Crusoe* most likely. He was being given a great gift. He could not quite sort it all out, but neither could Vera. He doubted anyone could, or would even care to. The thing was to be there and to act. He would do one last brave thing. And he could do it for Vera!

"I have been on services," said Rejean Houle, "where I have been compelled to shoot, and I am chain lightning with a pistol. I do not intend or wish to pose as a killer, sir, but I think you realize that before this mess is over—"

"What mess?" asked Charles.

"The one you're in?"

"Okay, go ahead, I'm sorry I interrupted you."

"A fast and experienced gunman will be a valuable asset to your organization. I am, I know all too well, unprepossessing and often in need of a bath, but I have been told too many times for me to ignore it that I am unusually intelligent. You may have heard how it is, sir: if enough people tell you that you are drunk, you ought to consider lying down. I have no wish to read books or learn a profession, but I am gifted with brains. I have skill in persuading unwilling witnesses to testify in court, and for finding witnesses willing to testify in court. For mixing, generally speaking, with the lower classes, I am first-rate."

"I like to close interviews on a note of class superiority."

They shook hands warmly. Rejean Houle had a big black moustache and was wearing a suit and tie and a bowler hat.

"Ray-zhan Oool-uh," said Charles. "I think we'll call you Ray John Howell, if that's all right with you."

"Certainly it is, sir," said Rejean. "Call me what you will."

"By the way, Ray."

"Yes sir."

"Does the name Charles Minot mean anything to you?"

"No sir."

"Ever been in San Francisco?"

"No sir. Never west of zuh Mississippi."

"And are you, let's see, a narcotics addict yourself?"

"No sir. Never west of the Mississippi."

"Never west," the man muttered as he scribbled on a pad, "of zuh—" and now spelled it out in a kind children's sing-song, "*Mis . . . sis . . . si . . . pp . . . i.* That used to be so hard to spell it used to be make me cry, but since I studied spelling . . . it's . . . just . . . like . . . puuuumpkin piiieee." He dotted the several i's with dramatic taps of the pen on the pad, looked up, and said it was terrific. He told Ray he didn't have a political bone in his entire goddamned body and hoped Ray felt the same.

"Welcome aboard, Ray, welcome aboard."

Or rather, he thought, welcome overboard, into oozy eel slime of indistinguishable and effectively invisible plot and counterplot. Ray's job would be the simplest of all, save Charles's own, unless somebody decided to pay him more money—though such a sum was hard to imagine coming into easy being: make sure that no one killed Vera. Was there a real chance of this? On the surface, of course there was not; but just below the surface, of course there was. Charles believed he now had only a single role, an omnipart, if such a thing could be said to logically exist: to keep Vera safe and happy. That he would dash into burning buildings went without saying. He would plunge into icy rivers, as well. He would throw himself upon a suitcase bomb. He would die for her, and he would kill for her. His thinking was very clear up to that point: everything in the world could be easily and swiftly replaced—except Vera. Beyond that point it was not clear, but beyond that point he no longer had any interest.

On the first truly warm day that spring, a day objectively not all that warm but which seemed so compared to the months they had spent below zero, the great white mountains appeared to subside in geological time, an orogeny, leaving only gentle brown hills of matted grass and streams flowing everywhere with melted snow. The skeletons of what had seemed permanently dead trees—skeleton was the wrong word: more pencil tracings of exploded and frozen nervous systems, of brains—had green buds popping out of softening, moistening gray wood. The gray of the windblown clouds was bright and rich, partaking as much of their sunlit white regions and the sweet blue of the dome as of the darkness of the gentle, warm rains they held and promised.

It was on this day as well, a Tuesday, the last in April, that Andrew Minot arrived in Saint Paul with Gus and Tony. They were on their way to New York, a first visit for the younger brothers. The next day, Amelia and Pastor Tom arrived, on their way to Washington, DC. There was a good chance they would move there.

Amelia was wearing some kind of Swiss village costume: a long red skirt tied with cloth belt embroidered with red, yellow, and blue flowers and ended with tassels, a long black velvet apron, a kind of heavy cloth breastplate with a medallion of the Appaloosa Society in the center, a dark blue ruffle around her neck, and her long hair piled up under a fez-like toque embroidered with very small flowers of every color you could quickly think of.

Given the trim gray suits, starched white collars, and quiet ties that her brothers and husband were wearing, she stood out in a way that was not simply colorful and different, but faintly alarming.

They were all staying at the Saint Paul Hotel, top floor, with a lovely view of the stark and muddy Rice Park, a view that appeared to change before their eyes, as if a pointillist were touching the scene with his smallest brush dabbed in a tender green. To the left was the great white library, to the right a pink granite castle with turrets and gables and towers and a red-tile roof, the Richardsonian Romanesque home of a fairy monster that housed the post office and courthouse; directly across the park was the Hamm Theater, a colossal structure that could hold five thousand opera-going prairie oligarchs.

Lunching in the hotel's restaurant, waiting for Charles, who was conducting some business, to join them, Amelia remarked that it was a very pleasant little city, an ideal place for a person, like Charles, who needed a real spring and fine weather and calm business to restore a sense of rightness in the world.

"I would like to know what's wrong with the world," said Gus.

"I," retorted Tony, "would like to know what 'rightness' is."

Because the table was occupied solely by immediate members of their family—Pastor Tom was an uncle by marriage but seemed very much more like one of the older brothers—but in a public place, Gus and Tony were exploring manners. When Charles arrived, they were planning to shake his hand and say, "Good of you to come, old man," and, "Good to see you," and go around the table shaking everybody's hand, having received this myth of a behavior Charles had long abandoned, and perhaps never truly possessed.

"The Canaanite festivals," began Pastor Tom, "regeneration, redemption, Jesus Christ."

Charles could now be seen entering the restaurant with the woman from his cast.

"I don't remember her name," said Amelia.

"Vera?" said Pastor Tom.

"Ye-e-s," said Tony, musingly.

"Vera," said Gus celebratorily, almost as if he were making a toast.

"I rather enjoyed being backstage," Tony continued, still musing.

"Buddy boys," said Andrew quietly. "I don't think we'll be wanting to talk about that, all right?"

"Right you are, Brother Andrew!" sang Gus.

"Thanks awfully for the tip, setting us straight, old chap," drawled Tony.

"Your friends died," said Amelia, "and you are laughing."

The boys were not at all abashed, and in fact wished now to perform a bit for Vera.

They appeared to prepare, to in a way rehearse, as Charles and Vera drew up to the table.

"Friends come," Gus began.

"And friends go," finished Tony.

They stood and moved around the table, shook Charles's hand, embraced Vera, and returned to their places.

"I'm sorry we're late," said Charles.

"He is late," said Gus, "and he is sorry."

"We are just so glad you're here," said Tony.

"I think we all know each other," said Charles, ignoring his younger brothers, "but in case you've forgotten, this is my wife, Vera."

"That's splendid!" shouted Tony.

"We hadn't forgotten, old chap," said Gus.

"You are not married," said Amelia flatly, but smiling.

"We are not married," said Vera even more flatly, as if in a sort of riposte, smiling only after she had gotten Amelia's eye.

"I think," said Charles, "that the Obscure Jude put it best when he said—"

"Old Mr. Hardy!" cried Tony.

"Dear Tom," sighed Gus.

"Boys," said Amelia, "you are behaving badly. Will you stop now?"

"Certainly," said Tony.

"We have offended?" asked Gus.

"You know you have," said Amelia.

"That we are smiling," said Pastor Tom, "is no indication of the depth of our disappointment."

"We do apologize," said Tony.

"What are your smiles indications of, if we may be so bold as to inquire?" asked Gus.

"*Of what* are your smiles indications," corrected Tony.

"The lads," said Andrew, "have taken to their education like ducks to water. And while I have got a word in edgewise, I'd like to say, spare us the Thomas Hardy. I want to know at what point a novel becomes so 'good' that we can forgive it for causing us such pain."

"Pain," said Charles.

"If you care in the least for the characters he has created, you cannot help but feel the most lacerating, the deepest sort of pain imaginable."

"I'm glad to hear that you give the imagined world so much credence," said Charles. "I've taken a great deal of ridicule from this family over my advocacy of the priority of the imagined reality."

"I would just like to say," said Pastor Tom, "that I quite understand his—"

"'O you most potent gods,'" said Charles. "'Why do you make us love your goodly creatures and snatch them straight away?'"

"—his, Mr. Hardy's, so-called atheism, as expressed in his poem 'God's Funeral.'"

"Vera," said Charles, "is, as you all know, a godless anarchist."

"Vera!" Andrew faked dismay and hurt. "Tell us it isn't so!"

"Only too true," said Vera, joining his act with a sad pouting face.

"Andrew," said Charles, "let us see the real dismay."

"Once again," said Amelia, "I'm not sure this is something we want to joke about."

"Not joking," said Charles.

"Was that Shakespeare, Charles?" asked Pastor Tom.

"Yes," Charles admitted.

"A strong line, no surprise, but I don't quite see the connection . . . ?"

"I think you do," said Charles, "or will, shortly."

"Something along the lines of . . . ?"

"Yes, you've got it."

"I don't think I have but thank you for the encouragement!"

"You do, Tom, I know you do."

"There's very little," said Gus, "that Chick doesn't know!"

"It's a little bit frightening, Gus, don't you think?" asked Tony.

"Indeed."

"One's brother knows all."

"Indeed."

"Gus? Tony? I've had just about enough out of you," said Amelia.

"Good of you to say so," said Gus.

"Thanks for the tip," said Tony.

"Gentlemen," said Andrew. "You need to button up now."

"Right you are."

"Very good."

"Something along the lines of . . . the deepest pain imaginable."

"Yes."

"And the certainty that that pain is, in fact, only imagined?"

"Yes."

"But no less painful for being illusory?"

"Yes."

"I am afraid," said Amelia, "that I do not quite understand who or what are these goodly creatures of God that have been snatched away so straightly from you that you feel you must question the nature of reality. And not just your own philosophical reality, which would be fine if you kept it to yourself, but everyone else's too. People whose reality suits them just fine, most of the time. But which you feel you must meddle and tamper with, judge and rule over."

"Sometimes," said Pastor Tom, "we need to keep in mind the very things we want most to forget, the very things that sometimes seem to place our minds in actual peril. In this case of course I mean the public horrors that have hurt us all. The—"

"Yes, of course," murmured Amelia, abashed and blushing. "I'm so sorry."

"Not at all. Amelia is quite right," said Charles, addressing the table grandly, "to make distinction between those we love and those who happen simply to be acting with us on the same stage, so to speak."

"By all means, distinguish," said Pastor Tom, "but not at the expense of—"

"I understand, Amelia," interrupted Charles, "that you are being protective of your husband. He doesn't need it, though. I'm sure you know that, and am sure you are being protective simply out of the powerful love you bear him. He has one of the gentlest and strongest and most open and capacious minds I know. I admire it and place it next to Vera's."

Vera and Pastor Tom exchanged good-natured rollings of the eyes that demonstrated how willing and how able they were to simultaneously keep in mind and dismiss from mind the public horrors.

"My own mind is strong but violent," continued Charles. "It is open only via a conduit to a distant and strange place. I rule only upon the tiny stage I find there, which I also happen to believe is illusory, and therefore make only the most tentative of judgments."

"You take the words right out of my mouth. I don't know why I'm surprised."

"How are Mother and Father, Andy?"

"They're fine, fine. I've been speaking to Father a lot these days."

"What about?"

"Oh, you know, this and that. Lots of things."

"'God's Funeral'?" asked Pastor Tom.

"Mmm," nodded Andrew. "In our way, I suppose we do. That might be one end of the spectrum, and Charles's work here might be the other."

"I do have a thought or two I'd like to share with you all," said Pastor Tom, "seeing that I have you here like a congregation before me and have never been able to resist such an environment."

"Hear! Hear!" said Gus.

"We are all ears!" said Tony.

"Incorrigible little rakes," said Amelia, not unkindly.

"Rah-ther," said Gus.

"If anyone sees a waiter," said Tony, "I'd like a glass of wine."

"You may not have wine," said Amelia.

"Pray, why ever not?" asked Tony, agog.

"It is an extraordinary thing to say, Amelia," said Gus, gently.

"I believe," said Tony, "that I will have a glass of wine."

"I second that. Motion carries," said Gus, beaming.

"I'm laughing," said Amelia. But she was not.

"I too am amused," said Pastor Tom, and he appeared genuinely to be so.

"That doesn't mean I approve," continued Amelia.

"What does it mean, Amelia?" asked Tony.

"Laughing, he means," said Gus helpfully. "Not just yours, but laughing, anybody's laughing, at you or with you. What's it all about, Amelia?"

There was a significantly long and table-wide pause both of speech and of movement. After this pause, it seemed everyone was looking at Amelia, whose head was still slightly bowed.

"I don't know," she said simply.

"Now," said Andrew somewhat wanly, "if we could just get Chick to admit he doesn't know something, we'd really be in business."

Pastor Tom cleared his throat. It was hard to say if he was trying for comedy or truly needed, in the wake of rising and falling emotion, to clear his throat.

"*In re* Thomas Hardy, 'God's Funeral,' godless anarchism . . . ."

"Do go on," said Tony.

"Shut the fuck up, Tony," said Charles.

Another significant silence ensued.

"Well!" exclaimed Amelia. "Charles is at least at a loss for words!"

"'Shut the fuck up, Tony.'"

"Gus is only repeating what he thinks he heard because he honestly can't believe what he thinks he heard," said Tony.

"'Shut the fuck up, Tony,'" Gus repeated.

Pastor Tom sighed with pointedly rueful recognition of the ungovernable nature of the boys' hilarity.

"You know what?" asked Charles. "I still don't have a sense of humor so your routines are lost on me."

This reproof seemed to actually dampen their spirits. There was, however, a subtle but unmistakable suggestion of two vaudevillians failing to impress an agent. It was most visible in the looks Gus and Tony shot everybody, craning their necks left and right, up and down the table, including the neutrally masked Charles. No one looked the least willing to play along, but only Andrew's disapproval—*apparent disapproval*, they encouraged themselves—truly troubled them: he had after all been their master in these intrafamilial coups de theatre.

"Vera," said Pastor Tom, "perhaps you will help me understand this."

"Of course, I'm more than willing," said Vera. "Able is another question."

"It seems to me that it is only an image of God that has died. A conception of a practical God, if you will."

"I will."

"A sort of everyday, working God."

"I understand you, but I'm not sure I agree with you."

"Very few of the people who are mourning God believe we are bereft in an absolutely materialist universe. Do they?"

"I'm sure I don't know. My guess, however, is that very few do *not*."

"I see."

"Perhaps we are overreacting."

"Throwing the baby out with the bathwater?"

"Tom!" laughed Amelia, incredulous but amused.

Gus, Tony, and Andrew laughed. Vera let a snicker escape.

"The God that is being mourned in the poem," Pastor Tom continued, smiling, "is an image we have thrown up, as with a magic lantern—"

"Or movie projector," said Gus.

"Zoopraxiscope," offered Tony.

"—lantern, yes, thank you, gentlemen, like a movie projector on a big white screen of our human fears and desires. It is purely human. It is not God at all."

"What then is God?"

"The manlike shape that is dead is as Mr. Hardy so beautifully says, 'the junk and treasure of an ancient creed.'"

"Beautifully said indeed. But what then is God if not the junk and treasure of an ancient creed, and, moreover, the cause of endless hatred and war?"

"The spirit of loving-kindness that both constitutes and animates the universe, that makes the music of the spheres so achingly beautiful."

"Perhaps. But religion, its time is up. I'm quoting an anarchist. Misquoting."

"Religion? Or politics wearing religious robes."

"Hard to tell the difference between a politician wearing priestly robes and a priest wearing a suit and tie."

"Only if you are looking at their clothes and not listening to what they say, watching what they do."

"No god, no dogma. That is my ancient creed."

"You anticipate me: your ancient creed denying the existence of God and abjuring the consequently baseless dogma of belief in that God sounds . . . religiously dogmatic. Surely you see that . . . ?"

"Hmmm, yes. But it's a slogan, rather, a rallying cry, not dogma. And my belief, if that's what it is, and I'm not admitting it is, is not religious in nature. It's practical."

"Ah, but there's nothing more essentially practical than the religious urge!"

"Hmmm, yes, I'm afraid I don't see it. It seems essentially impractical, rather?"

"What could be more practical than finding a path, a method, an idea, that takes you away from existential misery and toward peace that passes all understanding?"

"Well, that's just it, isn't it? That's what 'we' both want. And yet I see your way as essentially impractical and you see mine as . . . essentially superficial?"

"Not at all."

"How do you see my way?"

"If your way is toward social justice, I see it, for starters, as wholly admirable."

"Thank you, I appreciate your open-mindedness."

"My way is toward social justice as well."

"Perhaps you can describe that way . . . ?"

"It is a Christian way. It is the Christian way. I most emphatically do not say that the Christian way is the only way toward social justice, or that only the Christian possesses the desire and tools for work along that way, but I do say it is essentially Christian to work for social justice. I profess a social gospel. You may have heard of our movement."

"Yes, I believe I have."

"Have you spent any time exploring it?"

"Frankly, no. I don't trust it. I trust you, Pastor Ruggles!"

"Please call me Tom."

"I trust you, Tom! But I'm not sure I—"

"Let me put it to you this way, if I may?"

"Tom! Are you asking an anarchist for permission?"

Vera and Tom laughed. Amelia frowned.

"It's not so much a question, Miss . . . I don't know your last name, pardon me—"

"Vera. Call me Vera, please."

"First-name basis with an anarchist! What a world!"

"Think nothing of it."

"Oh, but I can't help it!"

"In a world where no one rules, first names are—"

"One can only imagine: one big happy family! The observation I'd like to make—if I may?"

Everybody but Charles laughed. Because she very often failed in her attempts to make people laugh—failed so often and so completely that most people never suspected attempts had been made—Amelia was more than pleased that everybody around the table was laughing. She noted Charles's abstention, which troubled but did not tumble her, and smiled and chuckled as she finished what she had set out to say.

"However we may wish to define anarchism—"

"We're going to stop laughing now, Amelia," said Gus.

"Good show, old girl," said Tony.

Amelia continued to smile and faintly snicker.

"However we may wish to define anarchism, it has already been rather thoroughly defined in at least the popular mind—and effectively so in the governmental mind: murderous criminals. A friend of our father's was shot but by the grace of God not killed: the former president of the United States, Theodore Roosevelt."

"Oh, for goodness' sake, Schrank was insane, not an anarchist."

"And because attempts have been made on the life of our father, as well, by lawless criminals who were not *nominally* anarchists either, we, who may know better, often decline to make the proper distinction. It strikes us that murder is wrong no matter what the circumstances, no matter how strongly and persuasively they may seem to mitigate against outright and final condemnation."

"You are opposed to the death penalty and to war, then, as I am, as we anarchists are."

"I shouldn't speak for Tom, but I am both opposed to the death penalty and to war, and reconciled to their existence in this life of nearly ceaseless suffering."

"For what it's worth, I am opposed to murder. There is nothing at all in anarchism that calls for it—precisely the opposite. Anyone who claims murder is a necessary means to an end is a very sad, mad, bad person, in my estimation. As for reconciliation with various forms of sanctioned murder, to the suffering you rightly characterize as ceaseless, I am less able, or perhaps less willing, than you are, to do so. That goes, interestingly, for Charles, as well: his theory of theater called out for what I saw as a truly bizarre kind of reconciliation with what he saw as a profound illusion."

"Fascinating," said Charles, "and repellant, yes. I don't see the reconciliation as bizarre—the illusion, rather—but that's . . . well, that's quibbling."

"Quibble on, old chap!" cried Gus.

"By all means. Don't let us stop you!" cheered Tony.

"Speaking of fascinating and repellant!" said Andrew. "I've got new nicknames for you village idiots!"

"Oh dear," said Gus. "Which one of us is repellant?"

"We are a one-two punch, old brother of mine, and you are usually the lead, which means you repel, while I finish them off in dazed confusion."

"Charles is going to tell us to shut the fuck up again."

"Well, he had better not."

Charles said nothing and refused to smile.

"The naughty words are really not funny," said Pastor Tom.

"Tom sits on the president's Ecumenical Council," said Amelia.

"I'm not sure," said Pastor Tom, "that that means anything to anybody, much less to Vera."

"It means a great deal," said Vera.

"Thank you," said Amelia.

"Not at all," said Gus.

"I'm glad Uncle Tom doesn't have to squat."

"Please forgive me if I say this as plainly as I can."

"Nothing would please me more than plain speech."

"It is astonishing to think that my husband can advise the president on spiritual matters one day and speak to you the next."

"Ah now, Amelia," said Pastor Tom.

"Don't you agree, Vera?"

"I do agree. It is astonishing."

"It's because he sees—because we see, and that is a very inclusive we—that there is in fact a good deal of common ground between some of what is talked about in radical political circles and some of what is preached from pulpits."

"I have no trouble believing that is so."

Pastor Tom leaned in and spoke over folded hands.

"Vera, I'm going to continue speaking plainly, in the great tradition my wife has laid down here today. We don't think people like you should be tarred and feathered."

"What do you say to that, Miss Vera?" asked Gus.

"Can't say fairer than that, can you, Miss Vera," said Tony.

"Boys, I am bowled over, I tell you. Bowled over."

"Not run out of town on a rail, not hunted down and arrested and deported because of your political affiliations. This is a free country. You can peaceably assemble every which way. You don't have to come down the aisle and be born again in Christ. But those beliefs that are essential to Christian practice—or rather ought to be—can make this country better, stronger, and more beautiful in exactly the same ways that those beliefs that are essential to anarchist practice do. I dare say—"

"That Jesus Christ was an anarchist, yes, I do see that."

"You're going to imply that we are being naïve and unsophisticated," said Amelia, "in our idealism. Aren't you, my dear?"

"Yes, my dear," said Vera, "I am."

"But you are forgetting that my husband has the ear of the president."

"My dear ear," said Gus.

"Your ear, dear?" asked Tony.

"I'm not forgetting that. Whether he does or does not is not the point. Whether he does or does not makes no difference."

"I am sorry to hear you say so."

"I'm sorry to say so, but really!"

"I think you are caught in some kind of current or tide that is sweeping you toward apathy and nihilism."

Charles laughed. Everyone stopped and looked at him.

"I'll let Gus and Tony speak for me," he said.

But neither Gus nor Tony were up to it, falling abruptly back into the stupid little rich boys they were afraid they truly were.

"I believe in acting," said Vera.

"Propaganda of the deed?" asked Andrew.

"I don't see how propaganda is necessarily related to deeds. I have no control over how my deeds are heard and seen. Any intention I have is very likely to be the first to be destroyed in the maelstrom of consequence."

"My husband does not act? My father does not act? The president does not act?"

"I have no faith in their action."

"Oh, I see! Only in your own?"

"Not even in my own. I have no expectation whatsoever that acts will be anything but show and tell. That was what drew me to your brother and what kept me near him when his babble threatened to drive me away."

"Show. And tell," repeated Amelia. "Have I got that right? Life is show and tell?"

"Yes. If you want to live, you show and you tell. That is what living is all about."

"I never put it that way," said Charles, "because I never saw it that way, but that is exactly right."

"Your Jesus Christ was fully alive, as I define life: he showed and told what it occurred to him to show and tell, freely and with commitment. In that way he was indeed an anarchist, but I can't see the comparison going much further. He suffered to the extent that he had expectations, and that, too, now that I mention it, is something he shares with anarchists and nearly everybody on the planet. The social gospel you espouse and that you say he espoused—"

"Are you capitalizing that 'H' in your mind, Vera?" asked Gus.

"Do you see letters in your mind, Vera, when you talk?" asked Tony.

"—has no relation whatsoever to . . . how shall I say, Gus, Tony? To the timeless exigencies of the finding and the keeping of political power."

"Took the—" said Gus.

"—words right out of my mouth," said Tony.

"Our words."

"Our mouths."

"Political power is also on my mind," said Andrew.

The table once more fell silent.

"If you have no expectations of change, and we must assume 'change for the better,' why act? And if you do act, how do you handle the consequences?" asked Andrew.

"The charge of apathy, again," said Vera. "Soon to be followed as if perforce by charges of nihilism."

"I see," said Andrew, "that you have an alternative, and that would be a kind of serenity that we are learning to associate with oriental . . . wisdom."

"Don't stick out your front teeth, boys, please," said Pastor Tom.

"And please don't try out your comic Chinese accents," said Amelia.

"Father does all the time," said Gus.

"He really does enter into the spirit of it," said Tony.

"Niggers and Jews too," said Gus.

"All in good fun," said Tony.

The table once again observed a moment of silence. In it, genuine uncertainty could be seen in the eyes of Gus and Tony. It was as if Tony had asked a question instead of making a declaration. For everyone but Vera, it was an unparalleled, perhaps precedent-setting moment in their growth.

"Is there solace in your serenity?" asked Andrew. "I wonder if you have replaced the solace of the warm, flawed, human God with a cold inhuman serenity?"

"There's nothing inhuman about it," said Charles.

"I couldn't replace a solace I never knew, could I?" asked Vera.

"I need a replacement!" said Andrew, abruptly and loudly. "I need a replacement for God and I need a replacement for the religion of progressive politics! My life is neither godless nor anarchic but I am in very deep despair."

Charles was caught off guard: "Despair?"

"Everything I worked for—everything we've worked for, Al, Father, me, Teddy, Hi, even you, here, I suppose, if I understood the setup—it's all a lie. Big, fat lie. I'm an idiot for having played along. And quite an asshole as I did. You have to be an asshole if you're in politics, but you don't have to be an idiot. I chose to be an idiot. An idiot and an asshole in the service of a Big, Fat Lie."

"Andrew," said Pastor Tom. "No, now, come on."

"I don't know what made me say that."

"We never know what makes us say things," said Charles, "if you stop and think about it."

"Come again?" asked Andrew.

"We can point to provocations and causes but we never truly know what our next thought or speech will be until it's over. Even when we have a script. I mean a 'real life script.' Examine it for yourself. Don't take my word for it."

"That is utterly beside the point," snapped Amelia. "Are you actually trying to suggest that when a bomb explodes we don't know what to *think*?"

"Yes. But I am only suggesting it. A bomb is a good example, the perfect example, of how reality may have holes ripped in it, exposing a truer, deeper reality: you don't see it coming, you don't plan on it, it makes your little dreams of control seem childish, and in its wake your thoughts and shouts *seem* as unpremeditated as they in fact *are*."

"Well," said Andrew, "I don't know about any of that. Chick may be right, he may be whistling in the dark, he may be wrong, he may be perversely wrong, he may be dead wrong. I don't know."

"Your brain is too busy protecting its Little Andrew in the eternal present that it can only make decisions after the fact. The apprehension of cause and effect exists only in the past. President Brain can only *register* the changes as they occur—slightly *after* they occur. It's an illusion of the brain to think it can *make* changes."

"Again I must say, reacting helplessly to your thrust, that I just don't know."

"I don't know either, Andy. I say only that I think about the possibility."

"But why," asked Pastor Tom, "have you turned so suddenly and decisively away from your ideals? From the shared ideals of millions of people? People from all walks of—from anarchists to Christians, from peasants to presidents! Whatever they don't have in common, they at least have progressivism!"

"No," said Vera, "I have to interrupt: anarchists and Christians do not have shared goals, nor do peasants and presidents."

"Not even in theory," said Charles, "not even at an ideal source."

"You are surrounded by the best minds, and most effective leaders, in the Progressive and Social Gospel Movements! I mean, what caused it?"

Dejection was suddenly and dramatically upon him. He began to answer, but stopped, shook his head. Then:

"I don't know who I am, much less what I am to do."

Charles and Vera exchanged a glance.

"They're the same thing," said Vera.

"That's the only lesson of the little stage set that came apart at the seams."

"To be is to do," said Gus.

"To do is to be," said Tony.

"Do be a do-bee, and don't be a don't-bee."

"Doo-be doo-be doooo."

"A do-bee and a don't-bee," said Amelia. "Every once in a while I am reminded of how young you boys actually are."

"Look here, Chick," said Andrew.

"I'm looking, Andy."

"You're working for the governor here, right? Burnquist sits on the MCPS, right?"

"Yes. I think of him as the 'Affable Man.' There is a 'Triangular Man' and a 'Silver Man of Wrath' as well."

"McGee and the AG, right? Hilton?"

"You know them, I see."

"Of course I do. I was helping Father."

"You've remarked their names."

"Of course I have."

"More than I have done. They are characters without names. Some day, if their legend lives on, their characteristics will give rise to new, truer names, in some language related to ours but indecipherable. Nonsense sounds with meaning forced willy-nilly upon them."

"Yes. Let me clear my throat and try to move on to a thought, an actual train of thought that I see coming around the bend."

"You didn't know you were going to put it so colorfully until the words came tumbling out."

"Woo-woo!" shouted Gus.

"Chugga-chugga-chugga-chugga," said Tony.

"Again," said Charles. "Who could have predicted the arabesques and rim shots of our wee brothers?"

"Two incidents," said Andrew. "One in the south of the state, in Rock County, Luverne is the town, I believe. Another in the north, Duluth, the port on Lake Superior. Wheat growing and wheat shipping. Nonpartisan League and railroads connecting the two, with stops along the way for the Equity League, two quarreling factions of the IWW, the Minnesota Socialist Party—"

"Featuring the mayor of Minneapolis," said Charles.

"Featuring the mayor of Minneapolis," agreed Andrew. "The Minnesota Farmer-Labour camp, and our substantial progressive presence. And God knows who else."

"Or possibly Vera."

Pregnant pause.

"I do not know," said Vera.

"Everybody take a deep breath and relax," said Charles.

"What Vera knows—" Andrew began.

"I say that to all my actors," interrupted Charles.

"I don't know who's more annoying here: you or Gus and Tony."

"What happened in Luverne?"

"Elderly farmer with ties to the NPL was escorted out of the state—Rock County borders Iowa, very near—"

"I know where it is," said Charles. "I've been there."

"—very near South Dakota as well. Ruffians drove him to Iowa and left him in a field. He came back to help his sons with planting and was tarred and feathered."

"And in Duluth . . . ?"

"An immigrant from Finland felt that, because he wasn't yet a citizen, he was exempt from the draft. He was tarred and feathered. Then hanged."

"The old man in Luverne survived?"

"Yes."

"I don't know what's worse: being tarred and feathered or un-tarred and un-feathered. Some fellows who've been tarred and feathered might prefer to be hanged."

Andrew smiled. "You sound very much like Father when you talk like that."

"Speaking of Father talking, what does he have to say about Luverne and Duluth? I take it he knows . . . ?"

"I'm not sure that he does."

"I missed the connection," sighed Amelia, "between Luverne and Duluth and, well, say Father, for starters, and . . . all your 'characters,' Charles. And the . . . what's the word, *organizations* that, um . . . *Vera* . . . is . . . how shall I say . . . *associated with* . . . ?"

"Try that one more time without the hesitation, the lack of confidence, the implicit burden of the heavy, dense veil you choose to wear over your hostility, and I'll see if I can make a little more sense of it."

"What's the connection between Father, mob violence, and terrorists?"

"Jesus Christ?" asked Gus.

Charles, at long last, exploded with laughter.

"Well, hush my mouth," said Tony.

"By Jove, I think he's got it!" Charles chuckled and sputtered. A few more high-pitched yelps shot out of his mouth, followed by descending ha-ha-has, and finishing up with low, round ho-ho-hoes, each phase of his laughter exploring a new facet of his delight.

"Father's progressivism is a sham. It always has been, and the best example right now is this Burnquist knucklehead, a pillar of Progressivism, who is sitting on the Minnesota Commission of Public Safety, an organization that is using thugs to incite hatred, fear, and riot, to beat and kill whoever happens to catch their eye, while the splintered Left is tearing itself apart in the shadow of the crackdown, roundup, imprisonment, and deportation of undesirables that the FBI and DOJ is commencing. 'Undesirables' of course being people who speak their mind about a given issue and are deemed criminally disloyal. That is to say: traitorous. For which they may be executed. Do you think I'm exaggerating? I ran the Bull Moose campaign in California!"

"The principles of Progressivism," said Charles, "are just one more badly written script, and the Progressives are just another cast of bad actors. Surely you saw what you were actually doing long before this."

"I did indeed! I was caught up in your wacky world of no cause and no effect, thinking, hoping against hope, that I saw causes anyway, and believing I could produce effects."

"What does Father say?"

"He says not a whole lot. He says—murmurs—that the jig was up when he saw a company he partly owned wasn't going to be able to deliver water to our burning little city."

"He also partly owned one of those French restaurants," said Amelia.

"The Poodle Dog, yes," said Andrew.

"And had affairs with several women there."

"And you've never forgiven him," asked Andrew, "is that right?"

"I have not. Why should I? He destroyed Mother's will to live."

"Sweetheart, you know very well why you should forgive him."

"*I forgive him.*"

"Good."

"How has the world changed? How has anything changed?"

"Oh, it's changed, all right," said Charles. "It's changing and it won't stop. Were you expecting applause or a paycheck for your act of forgiveness?"

"Of course I was!"

"Many actors do."

"He says a man," said Andrew, "who runs a newspaper called the *Minnesota Mascot*—"

"Björnsen," said Charles. "Speaks for ascending Scandinavian Lutheran farmer-businessmen at odds with the small-town elite."

"Sounds right. Father saw him as the kind of man he saw in Fremont Older and the other Regenerators in the newspaper business, in the Golden Age of Graft. You know what I mean: someone who wasn't afraid to say startling, painful truths out loud and damn the consequences."

"One quick note?"

"Go ahead."

"The consequences are quite different if you don't have someone like Father approving your truth-telling."

"Granted. And maybe that's what Father is seeing now."

"All right. Tell me more about what you see him seeing."

"How wonderful Mother has been nearly all the decades of his life?" asked Amelia.

"It's interesting, Amelia, how you can champion poor Mother who did little more than tell you to shut the fuck up all your life."

"Shut the fuck up, Charles."

"Well said, Amelia! Do you feel an exquisite relief?"

"Brava!" shouted Gus.

"Brava!" shouted Tony.

"No, I feel perfectly awful. I'm sorry, Tom."

"We live," said Pastor Tom, "around the table at which we have been seated!"

"Because Father thought he knew the sort of man who was in effect talking to him—I mean Björnsen—he was inclined to trust him, believe what he was saying, take it to heart, however you want to put it, and he thought he saw the hollowness of Progressivism, and by extension, the racism and xenophobia in populism, the hypocrisy of, of . . . of the Regenerators, of himself, the tyranny of power that runs under even the most admirable social and political ideas. On what flimsy pretexts that admiration is founded."

"Even the most admirable applications of Christian ethics?"

"Yes."

"Aha!" shouted Charles, looking at Amelia.

"Shut the fuck up, Charles," said Pastor Tom. But he was smiling.

Charles ceased to smile. "So it's an instance of, a variation on, say, the *Timon of Athens* transformation? Generous Christian Becomes Disillusioned Misanthrope?"

"Let me appear to ponder this," said Andrew. "No."

"No," said Charles quietly. "I don't suppose Father could ever become . . . misanthropic. The Old Poker Player probably saw that Progressivism was just a card for shrewd, energetic men to play but that the game was over because it had ceased somehow to be the great hand it had been only moments before."

"You see, Vera," said Andrew, addressing her singly and most earnestly—almost ardently, "he came to his principles naturally. As did Colonel Roosevelt."

Charles laughed shortly, mirthlessly.

"Who does not?" asked Vera.

"Yes, you're right. What I meant to say is, his political principles appeared, to him and to the people around him as he was developing them, to come directly and immediately from his goodwill and generous nature, from virtue, Christian virtue, I suppose, but virtue nevertheless."

"Why," asked Vera, "did it take him so long to see through that shimmering surface? Was he hypnotized? I apologize if I seem cold. Ungenerous. But I really do not understand. Evil and suffering are readily apparent. Ignore it? Sure. But fail to recognize it? I don't think so."

"I think he recognized it and wanted to believe that it was . . . nothing if not changeable."

"Excuse me: I misspoke. I meant the hypocrisy must have been—"

"Excuse me, Vera," said Amelia. "I'm sure the hypocrisy was as evident as the suffering and the evil. But when you are predisposed to see the good, you may be chagrined at instances of hypocrisy and worse but want more than anything else to shrug it off and—"

"He has sinned," said Andrew. "He sees at last that he has sinned. I am not making fun. I am dramatizing because that appears to be in the family blood along with everything else. Dramatizing genuine religious conviction being reborn. He has sinned. That is to say, he has missed the mark. He now repents. That is to say, he is thinking again."

"And," said Charles, even more quietly, "I imagine the physical experience of his life has vitiated his will to . . . think differently. I mean . . . he must be very tired."

Amelia's eyes filled with tears and she murmured indistinctly.

"Yes," said Pastor Tom, "we are all very tired. So tired, sometimes, that we wish for a sleep like death."

"A deathlike sleep," Charles murmured only slightly more distinctly than had Amelia. "A sleep-like death."

"Mother and Father have both aged quite a lot in the last year. Al looks very bad. And as selfish as it is for me to say so, I feel very bad. I have always looked to Father for guidance and support. I never had a problem doing that. Not looking to him for guidance and support would have been a problem. But that never happened. If I seemed too lighthearted sometimes for that sort of attitude, that sort of dependence, if I worked my mouth . . . *over-joyously* sometimes—like certain others here today, I won't name names, it's in the blood, I guess—it was because I felt free and easy and confident. I was happy to carry on what I always thought of as 'Father's work.' Maybe that was work of expiation for his part in the Spring Park Water disaster, maybe it was something else, I'm not sure. It certainly didn't start out that way, before the quake and the fires, it wasn't that way in Arizona, but it may have become that. I say again I'm not at all sure. Maybe when I say that Al looks bad and Mother and Father look old I'm completely wrong. Maybe Al looks great and Mother and Father have never been more perky, vigorous, healthy, wealthy, wise. Maybe I am only talking about myself. I'm not stupid. I know that could easily be the case. I'll even go so far as to say that's probably the case. No, tell you what: that *is* the case."

"Mother and Father," said Amelia, with the strange breeziness that had alarmed everybody who knew her all her life, "will be dead before the year is out."

"Excuse me. I must be rude and cold again. Inexcusably so, but I beg your pardon anyway. I don't know Mother or Father or any of you around this table except Charles. I will be even more frank and revealing and come, I hope, swiftly to my point. I don't want to know any of you. I know and love Charles almost against my will. Maybe that's the nature of that kind of love. I don't know. But you can't have been awake while you were manipulating the kind of power you have, or had—and very likely will have in the future if you are honest with yourselves!—and not seen at first hand everywhere you looked the sacrifice of public good for personal power or wealth! You may very well have lied to yourselves about your determination to change things, but all the while you were cultivating power, were you not? Because to change things you must have power, must you not?"

"But Vera," said Pastor Tom, "surely you are guilty to some degree of the very charges you level against us?"

"Not at all. I have no expectation—"

"Isn't everyone guilty?" asked Amelia.

"—*no expectation* of anything remotely like success or change or gain—certainly not increased power. I merely act. I despise power. I love to act."

"You love to act but have no regard for consequence?" asked Andrew.

"You're being naïve or foolish or selfish," said Amelia.

"I don't care if I live or die."

"Nonsense," said Amelia.

"I'm not here to convince you of a thing."

"Well, neither am I, I guess," said Andrew. "So allow me to be frank and revealing and come swiftly to my point as well."

"Please do. I'm sorry I am so rude and cold."

"There have always been, in my world, in Father's world, people who were outright villains. And if not exactly, actionably so, at least detestable and 'worse people' than we were. I think primarily of the railroaders. The engineers and builders were men of science—"

"And slave drivers too," said Vera. "Racist slave-driving profiteers."

"You can no longer apologize for being rude and cold," said Amelia.

"I no longer wish to."

"Perhaps because we were so focused on the railroad men, we failed to take notice of all the other . . . characters entering the stage. There were suddenly so many factions, and agents within factions whose motives were never clear, that we became confused. We became confused because we wished to continue to think well of ourselves, and not throw in with anybody who we thought might be worse than we were. We wished, for example, to continue to think of men of science as the clear-thinking, politically neutral allies of the progressive spirit of reform—which was itself a kind of clear-thinking political science. But for every one of those, there were—suddenly, it seemed—ninety-nine of the other. Worse, for every good man and every bad man there were ninety-eight people milling around, haplessly, irrevocably human—and maybe that's why we found our Christianity, our social gospel, our progressivism to be such a . . . a fortress. It accommodated good and evil and everybody just bobbing along in the river of whatever this is. God wasn't dead, but if you will allow me to use a popular catchphrase, we were beyond good and evil, beyond bliss of heaven and the torture of hell. Beyond spirit and matter—which is I think what Chick's been talking about all this time."

Charles said nothing and chose not to alter his gaze, even though the last line of Andrew's speech had been a clear and sincere appeal to not just brotherhood, but an understanding that had grown directly from obsessions officially ignored by the family: of a great moment, in other words, and probably unprecedented, but embarrassing, as if any application of the "reality versus illusion of reality" paradox to what most people insisted on thinking of as "reality" must always be somehow embarrassing—as theater must always be somehow embarrassing.

Andrew drooped. No one else was willing or able to say what he had wanted to say, what he had hinted at.

"Get beyond power and glory," said Charles at last, "let me know."

"I no longer have much faith in the goodness of those ninety-eight other people."

"Ah," said Pastor Tom.

"Faith comes and faith goes," said Amelia. "I speak from personal experience. The important thing is to be seeking it."

"Well that's just it, isn't it? I no longer have the slightest interest in seeking it."

"Ah," said Pastor Tom.

"The meek will inherit the earth by taking tips from tyrants."

Pastor Tom waited a beat, then said "ah" again, with a kind of finality and rigorous sadness.

"Now is precisely the time to stand up and shake off despair, Andy," said Amelia. "There is really no other time to do it."

"A despairing person, Amelia, doesn't give a hoot for standing up. And shaking it off doesn't even enter the question."

"But it does, Andy, truly it does."

"Now is when it counts," said Pastor Tom. "Now is when it matters."

Amelia, Pastor Tom, and Andrew all now had tears visibly filling their eyes.

"Father is coming here," said Andrew. "He wants to talk to you generally about political marketing practices, and specifically about who you may be aligned with."

"We know who we are aligned with."

"Well then maybe you can just tell Father that."

"I can't tell him not to come, I suppose."

"I believe he's already on his way."

"And Mother?"

"Mother's on her way to Rome. Unless you make a trip there yourself, I doubt you will ever see her again."

"What about Al?"

"Al is busy trying to make the case to whoever will listen that innocent men are in prison and that the bombers—people he thinks, believes with all his heart, were trying first and foremost to kill his little brother—are walking around looking for the next opportunity. You can imagine how long he will remain viable in Sacramento."

Vera began to weep loudly.

Charles paled frighteningly.

Father did not make his train. He had died while anxiously—everyone re-marked the oddity of it—supervising the packing. Charles chose not to go to the funeral, which, because it was immediate and small and simple, he stood a good chance of missing anyway, even if he dropped everything and raced across the country. The show, he felt, must go on. He cabled Mother and told her that the show would go on willy-nilly. Nothing had been lost that could not be easily and swiftly replaced. He thought he finally understood how such a motto could be perceived as something other than cold and brutal.

He was, in other words, sorry that Father was dead, but was determined to not go to pieces over it.

They went north by northwest. As the train swayed and night fell past it and down—the darkness appearing to be wind-borne—a condition of dreamy contentment swept gently over Charles, almost returning him to an un-spoiled San Francisco, a moment of twilight from very early in his childhood.

It assuaged the featureless dread that slept in every moment, and the homesickness for that lost family, and the guilt, the mute guilt that would not describe to him what he was doing wrong. He had a list, but could get no answer, the guilt staring hotly at the drowsing dread, either fearful of its awakening, or impotently desirous of it.

But in that swoon he became quietly determined, as one can only be-come in sleep or near sleep, to banish the old soul and find a new one. What could be finer than to become a new person overnight? To stay fixed in a role too long was a kind of mental illness, was it not? It was likely now that he would enlist. The country was going to hell. He certainly wasn't going to lead men to certain death on its behalf, certainly would not die for it—no, not for *it*, not die *for* anything, but simply confront the Great Illusion in what had always been known as the Theater of War.

The dreaminess was interrupted—he thought the cause was some un-toward motion of the rocking hurtling train that he could not immediately pinpoint—by swellings of unease, dread's eyes heavy-lidded but open, in which he was forced to wonder a little anxiously who he was, if no longer himself. Deep drifts of black-needled trees clustered blurrily, enveloped his view like a storm cloud, then burned off like fog, like a dream shredding itself into streamers of the real and the unreal, revealing what at first, in dark but overexposed flashes, seemed a flat and empty ocean of tallgrass. Towns were advanced upon like islands, mounds of earth humped up out of marshes and built upon strangely, with an air of tidal forces having been ab-rogated only for a short time . . . and stranger still, within that vast sea, lakes, the inverse of the mounded villages, benthic settlements as if the land of the towns had been quarried and the pits filled with water. On the map, un-folded carefully so as not to disturb the slowly spreading concentric circles waving out from his brain, and glimpsed in the flare and slow blackening of a long wooden match, were plotted these thousands of lakes, in shapes that could be repeated nowhere in nature and with names that could not have been suggested by their shapes, only by private and unreadable histories. In the no-man's-land of the train at night, he recollected murmurs of science, lectures he'd audited at Berkeley, discussions between fiercely committed but quiet, articulate, idealistic men. What had they said? That these northern lakes, lying shallowly like mirrors on the face of the plain, had been formed when great blocks of ice, remnants of glaciers buried in outwashed alluvial dirt, had at long last melted? So that these lakes actually rose up from below, welled up rather than gathered?

And was this the old soul or the new soul whispering to him? He couldn't say, of course, and didn't really care as he drifted in and out of sleep. Great minds, great men: Father had endeavored mightily for him. Ah, it was somehow comforting to think in this way, of wise men and sound thinking, and a bountiful, loving father . . . but as he did he found himself wishing only that he might continue north in the dark and splendid smoking train until such a destination might be reached whereat it would be clear he was now safely beyond the world of actors, in an eternal north of the mind and infinite abode of nameless heroes. Yes, that was it, a place where the poor and the weak could smash, in stunning miracles of justice, heavenly light blazing all around them, angels attending horns blasting tribute, the wealthy and the powerful—then vanish into thin air, as evanescent as the power they thought to seize. Oligarchs and their dead-eyed spies. That's all it was, all it ever had been. Father was a fool, a powerful, kind, smart, loving fool, and so too were Alexander and Andrew bloody blinkered fools. So was Teddy "The Great Charlatan" Roosevelt, for that matter. At least Father and his brothers, and yes, sure, Roosevelt too had been, were still, kind and loving. Oligarchs and would-be oligarchs, kind and loving or not. Spies and traitors and those who had not yet had a good chance to betray or murder, kindly and lovingly or not. *Oh, I am forgetting my lines! Can't wake up, can't fall asleep, everyone expects me to know exactly what to do and when to do it, but I am lazy or cowardly or . . . or something has happened that prevents me from learning my lines, and now, now they will know, there will be terrible consequences because the lines are of Absolute*

Importance no matter what you might think about the world or illusion of world you're living in. I'll stand there and the light will fall on me and I won't know what to say, I won't be able to fake it, and that's all I've ever done. I'll have to admit that I do not know what to do. My God, the wrath . . . they will hate me so terrifyingly. All these long, long lines of people whom I know I must know but do not, everything is on fire, metal is shrieking and bricks are bellowing and we have no past, no future—and yet here they are, demanding that I speak the speech, that I confess. They have drawn together again in the darkness, waited and waited and waited until they could find a seat and now all the seats are filled: I could have saved them. SAVED YOU FROM WHAT? I shout like an actor, a politician. But they remain silent and unmoving in the plush red seats. Their wrath makes them mute, just as their fear had in the old days . . . the little boy, Joe in the beginning but I never even knew the name of the second one, the Son of the Plumber Who Runs the Gas, opens the box of the limelight . . . we hear the sound approaching before it hits us, like a wave, sends us rolling and slowly, slowly tumbling, dancing silently upside down, and carries us out to sea.

The station was shuttered and damp looking. He stared at it through the greasy window, monochrome in the first light of day. The window smelled of hair tonic. Fellow travelers arose about him, webbed of orifice, petrified of tendon, organs sagging and leaking, tissues matted and discolored, cheeks ballooning with weariness, eyes red from fitful sleep—and prepared themselves for the day. Vera remained deeply asleep next to him.

He felt somehow that the train's motion through space had sucked him clean. He did indeed feel devoid of personality, of feature, and as he watched the gray lines of the platform seeming to assemble itself as if from out of a fog, he imagined himself a tiny hallucinating demon-naif. The wood of the platform, the flesh of his body—he could see right through it, chemicals pooling, drifting, breaking down. Vera had murmured in her sleep, as if they had been sharing a dream, the dream, and wanted to know who she was, who she was becoming, and what she was to do. But it wasn't clear if she meant herself or some other woman entirely, and there was no peace in knowing that anyway, in knowing one's self, no peace in living according to principles . . . it was all just holding something at bay, and now he wondered if he hadn't given way, sometime in the infinite night, hadn't slipped free like a suffering anchorite, a Hindu, a Chinese sage.

He continued to stare at the platform and for a moment was convinced that he had slipped away, that he was dead.

Father was not dead. *He* was dead.

Then, like the flick of an electrical switch or a chemical reaction that had just passed into the realm of his perceptions, he saw his thoughts and his freedom as a prison and a nightmare, a slow, droning, uneasy, insanely peaceful purgatory, a limbo from which he was now being roughly shaken loose.

A young but weathered-looking man walked heavily past. He saw only his hands, knotty blocks of sun-darkened muscle, and took him to be a farmer. Charles turned away from him as the young farmer made his way to the front of the car, back to the smeared smoky window, and saw a young woman walk past on the platform. She carried a sack of what he guessed were potatoes over her near shoulder, obscuring her face.

Vera rose but could not quite straighten up. She put her hands to the small of her back and massaged herself. Charles got off the train and saw Vera walking past a window, only the top of her head visible until she turned to him, but apparently did not see him. He hobbled achily up and down the platform.

The air outside seemed composed in strata, dry upon moist upon dry, channels of cool air cutting through the warm, a confluence of sluggish gray rivers. The angles in the lightening sky seemed wrong. A curtain hung in pleats in the east, fabric worn to translucence, ragged across the horizon, black lines like dangling threads to the earth. Charles stood still, facing north, and watched the sky moving east. Turning south, his face clammy, his hands cool, it looked to be moving to the west. He rubbed his eyes and opened them on the woman with the heavy sack. She was crossing the street on the other side of the station. Her clothes were suddenly bright against the dark sooty orange brick of the nearest building.

He followed her across the street and saw her enter an alley. Vera had silently joined him, and they walked to the mouth of the alley: it appeared to lead to a kind of inner court, as the immediate passage was dark, while the farther parts of it were lit up with the mineral colors of the sky. They waited a moment, then walked the length of the alley, the end of which was indeed a small courtyard. They glanced about for the woman—why, Charles didn't yet exactly know, still the demon-naif though his role as an agent of the MCPS was beginning to fizz in his hands and feet like returning blood—even called out a greeting, as if to an old friend, but saw nothing, heard nothing. Liquor in crates was stacked ten feet high around them, lining the walls, three or four crates deep. It was a lot of liquor, he thought, for a small town, but there was evidently no place else to get it: a wet town in a dry county surround- ed by other dry counties. Local temperance gangs had complained—these rag-ends of thoughts dragged through his foggy memory—of the violence and despair the place attracted, its twenty-four-hour-a-day operation, the tremendous volume of its off-sale business, and its reputation as a gather- ing place for foreign radicals. The MCPS—but not Charles—had swung into action then, getting the court to limit the saloon's commerce to liquor con- sumed on the premises between nine in the morning and five in the evening. The proprietors had suggested that they lived and worked in the land of the free and the home of the brave, and would therefore conduct their business as if it were indeed their own. *If we leave the place unguarded,* they argued, *some goddamn teetotaler will burn it down.* They openly defied the ruling.

Charles became entangled in the phrase: *some goddamn teetotaler will burn it down,* and Vera remarked the vacancy of his face by snapping her fingers in front of it. He mumbled what he'd been thinking, and that he had never been able to sleep on trains, and that travel was deranging even in the best circumstances, then finished the thought: The sheriff, decried in the only state-approved newspaper in town—there had been two others but they had been shut down by a senator, or rather by his friends on the MCPS, after editors of the newspapers under scrutiny had refused to stop running stories critical of the senator—as a "half-breed Finn," said he would close the saloon only if he was absolutely forced to do so. The MCPS had decided to withhold judgment until they had taken sufficient counsel, heard from everybody, deliberated carefully and thoroughly, and allowed the saloon-keepers to dig themselves more deeply into their already dark and spacious graves. *We will let them fall asleep in this bed they have made for themselves up there,* Triangle McGee had informed him. *It's always much more effective to beat down a bedroom door, so to speak, and haul someone squealing out of dreamland and that nice quilted comforter their grandma made for 'em.*

That was where things stood, or at least had stood. Things, it was assumed, were different now that there was an NPL speaker in town.

The saloon's back door was slightly ajar. Vera and Charles stood for a moment before it, heard voices inside, and walked in. It was quite dark. A single light hung low over a long table, and another over the bar, illuminating a man with his foot on the rail and a woman behind the bar with her arms folded. Rejean Houle stood in the darkness between the two cones of light. The two Wobblies who had come to Saint Paul to talk to Vera, Joe, and the older man whose name she had never learned sat at a table in darkness so deep they were nearly invisible.

"Morning!" Vera called out, over-brightly. The man and the woman looked over. "Are you open?"

They smiled, both man and woman, at the same time, and Vera took it as an encouragement. She walked toward them, smiling, Charles following.

"Just what I was wondering," he said pleasantly.

"Who you all are," said the man, "is the question."

Charles set his bags down. "Charles Minot."

"Pair in the front door, pair in the back. Must be a raid."

"Ray John Howell," said Rejean Houle.

"All right for starters," said the man. "What do you do, Charles?"

"Friends call me Chick."

"What do you do, Chick?"

"I have done many things."

"You sound like an Indian, but you don't look like one."

"Long train ride," said Charles, alarmingly in the manner of a vaudeville Indian. He could act and lie as recklessly as he wished. The stage was
wide open. There was absolutely nothing at stake beyond the preservation of
Vera's well-being, if and when Daisy was arrested for her speech, and if and
when Vera took her place. "Thirsty. We not ourselves yet."

The woman sniffed a kind of laugh and the man smiled what appeared
to all concerned to be an acknowledgement—one not lost on Charles, who
heard it as applause.

"One of the many episodes of great interest and excitement in my life
has been the racing of motorcycles. I was associated with a shop in San
Francisco, Beveridge's, which is where I . . . hail from."

"The racing of motorcycles? You don't say. What's that like?"

"It get old, like everything," said Jules.

Vera was concerned at the continuing attempt at comedy, so concerned
she turned fully around and stared at him.

"What bring you here, chief?" asked the man, adopting the tone.

Charles, glancing at Vera, stepped sideways into the light. "We are inspecting
the weights that the millers and the elevator people and the railroads are using."

The woman sighed and Charles looked closely at her. Her face was more
clearly lit now and his eyes had adjusted: it was the woman with the sack and
she looked like Vera.

"You're not a Kolessina, are you?" he asked, coming closer. "Family down
around Muscatine, Iowa?"

"No," said the woman incredulously. "Why?"

"You look like my associate here, don't you agree?"

Charles tugged gently on Vera's arm, and she came into the cone of light.

"I don't see it," said the woman.

"Nor do I," said Vera.

Charles chose that moment to try a character. "We're subcontracting
with Pinkerton's."

The woman looked at him as if to say, *I do not look like you or your associate, and you know I do not.* But this was not necessarily a hostile or even a guarded look—rather a recognition that a gamble had been taken the stakes of which would not be completely and immediately reckoned, much less lost.

"Miss Kolessina is a Russian," said Charles. "Allow me to pause provocatively here, and then put quote marks around that 'Russian,' for even more emphasis. She's a RUSSIAN," he shouted, "*and* she works for Pinkerton's! What do you think about *that*?"

"Darkness," said the woman, "is on the face of the waters."

Because he was an actor, and only because he was an actor, Charles did not flinch, or in any way betray the salience of her phrase. "What," he asked, "have you got something against Pinkerton subcontractors?"

"What," countered the woman, "you got something *for* 'em?"

"Last time I checked," drawled Charles, "they were tracking down the godless animals who are throwing bombs into crowds of innocent people."

The woman laughed derisively.

"Into crowds of innocent people I happened to know!" Charles was all but laughing back at the woman—or rather, with her.

"I suppose it never occurred to you that the Pinkerton gang was doing the actual throwing . . . ?"

Now Charles laughed out loud. "Oh, it occurred to me, all right!"

He and the woman engaged in what seemed to be genuine mirth.

The man cleared his throat and returned to the subject of weights. "Better get rid of 'em all. They're all bad, Charles."

"Call me Chick."

"Take my word for it, Chick. Save yourself a lot of time and money and effort and I know all about time and money and effort going down the drain. Just go down to the foundry and say, 'Hey, I need new accurate weights for every elevator in the state of Minnesota! It's either that or every farmer in the whole goddamned Midwest dries up and blows away!'"

"Well, sir, that's the way we heard it too," said Charles.

"Only way there is *to* hear it."

"Can I get a drink? Big glass of water and a shot, and for—"

"Fraid not. As a representative of the state government, you ought to know better than to ask."

"I hear you. But if I could convince you that there's more to me than meets the eye, and that the part of me you can't see is 100 percent in favor of your running your business twenty-four hours a day and seven days a week or however it is you feel like running it, what would you say then?"

"I would say no soap, stranger. But in the friendliest way possible."

"Not even a glass of water and—"

The woman poured four glasses of water from a bucket and set two of them on the bar. Charles and Vera drank thirstily, even noisily. The woman took the other two into the darkness for the Wobblies. Passing Ray, she asked if he wanted one too. He said he did, and thanked her. When everybody was done, the woman filled their glasses again, spilling water from each glass onto the bar, laughing and saying "ooops" each time, picking the glass up, mopping the bar, setting the glass back down.

"Good water up here," said Charles.

"We don't have any trouble with it," said the man.

"Can you direct me," Charles continued briskly, "to the sheriff's office and to a doctor?"

"The sheriff's office and a doctor," repeated the man. "That kinda sounds like trouble, if you don't mind my saying so."

"I've got a prescription for the latter and some questions for the former," Charles said. "I must, as per the outline of my duties, visit the sheriff, and I want, more than anything else, to find morphine for Vera here, who is in a great deal of pain from a recent bombing. I fear she will go to pieces on us, and we need her rather desperately to stay together."

The woman laughed, as if anticipating something the man was about to say. "No, the prescription should be for our poor old sheriff and it would read, 'Get out of town before they tar and feather you,' and the question would be for the good doctor: 'Doc, how much you charge to set the broken bones I aim to come to you with when I suggest those darned old weights aren't quite what they seem to be—or I should say, there's more to 'em than meets the eye!'"

The man and the woman laughed privately and lengthily.

"Not exactly sure what you're saying," Charles said with a polite smile, "but I guess it won't take long, is that right? For me to get it?"

"BIG DOINGS IN TOWN!" shouted the man.

Charles clapped his hands, feeling altogether upstaged, and said, "HOT DAMN!"

"You're not the first guy," said the man, shooting an amused look at Vera but speaking to Charles, "that I've ever seen before to come in here wanting a drink to start the day out right. How do I know you're a Pinkerton? How do you know I'm not? How do I know you're not from the NPL pretending to be a Pinkerton for God knows what nasty-ass reason—to decoy another goon from the Justice Department who's actually a militant prohibitionist striking a deal with the Chicago Wobblies to thwart the, uh, the, uh . . ."

"Detroit," said the woman.

"Detroit Wobblies. How do I know that's true or not true? How do you know that? And while we're at it, who are these other men here? Do you know? Do I know?"

"We're Chicago Wobblies," said the older man at the table.

"How 'bout you, buddy?" The man at the bar lifted his face to Ray.

"My name is Rejean Houle. I am a hired gun."

This was inspired stagecraft and Charles brightened.

"Who hired you?"

"Mr. Minot."

Charles applauded.

"YOU'RE UNDER ARREST!" the woman hollered at the top of her lungs. Then she and the man collapsed in laughter. It was now clear that they were both quite drunk. Charles stepped down the bar to an open bottle of whiskey, picked it up and saluted the two of them with it, then took a long drink.

"Jesus Christ," said Vera. "Mr. Minot? You're gonna make yourself sick." He took another long drink. "Charles? Chick?" Vera tried. "You look hypnotized. Come on, let's go. Yes, these people are comrades and they are charming, but let's go."

"Yes indeedy-do!" said the woman. "Mr. Minot, aka Charles, aka Chick, wants to find that darn doctor and the sheriff before he tips over, which will be in a second or two, because whatever I don't know, I do know who can't hold liquor!"

"Good luck to ya!" the man sputtered.

Charles had begun to make his way to the door, following Vera, but came back to shake the hands of the man and the woman, as he was evidently not going to stop swilling whiskey. Vera let him tug him a step, still drinking, then stopped with a jerk that threw him a little off balance. He reached out and slammed the bottle down on the bar and to the saloonkeepers said, "The blonde is with the NPL, and was with the Wobblies in Paterson and Lawrence. It's possible she met the old man and the young man at the table over there in Paterson, or possibly had a hand in some goings-on in Los Angeles and later in San Francisco, where we all met. I am an heir to one of that city's biggest fortunes. Family owned a theater and it was bombed—by somebody trying to look like somebody else. Then there was this parade. We all left when it got bombed. Some of our friends have been framed for the bombing and some of our friends have been killed in the course of the frame-up. Because I have connections in DC, I'm working way up high, the high wire, don't you know, with the MCPS. And yes, you heard right: I'm a Minot. That's my little town they got out there somewhere in the Dakotas. We're riding along together up here in the dynamic northland, kind of on a little picnic, because we were in the right place at the right time. I don't know why we weren't put in the same all-purpose frame in San Francisco, and I don't know if anybody here knows exactly who we are, if we're on a tether or just the lucky recipients of high-speed bureaucratic incompetence, or if nobody really gives a shit. My father is—was, sorry, just died, hasn't sunk in—an important enough man for the railroad folks in San Francisco to have tried to kill him. In court! So maybe I'm just a pawn. Maybe I'm a target. Maybe I am being used. Maybe I am being used up. I don't know, and I don't care."

The man and the woman ceased their nearly hysterical laughter and watched neutrally as Charles made his speech. Vera looked thoroughly disoriented. The old Wobbly took her by the hand and started to lead her out the door. The man behind the bar repeated his wish for generalized good luck, this time without the irony and snickering. The woman looked at Charles, because he had picked the bottle up again and was drinking from it as if it were a teacup, pinky extended. He told her she was right, he wasn't finished, that the main thing for an actor to do was *be clear in his action*. The audience had to know why he was doing what he was doing.

He said, "It's really true that I am a rich young man from San Francisco who is doing special work for the government because it seems like that's what a guy whose Father once thought he might be president someday ought to be doing—until a proper outfit is located for me . . . *over there*."

He sang the last words and repeated them. "And it's also true that Ray John works with me, for a group you know very well, the Minnesota Commission of Public Safety. It's true that Daisy, who isn't here, is on a speaking tour on behalf of the Nonpartisan League, and that Vera, over there—where'd she go, is she gone . . . ?—is going along with her because it appears the NPL was just going to, you know, let Daisy do her thing and hope for the best. And it's true that the IWW is aiding and abetting her because she's kinda like the only card they got to play right now, up in this game anyway, if I understand correctly—and please understand that I myself am not a Wobbly. No ma'am. No sir. My brother is chief of staff for the governor of California, and my other brother ran the goddamn Bull Moose campaign in that state. My father was nicknamed "The Regenerator" when he and some likeminded fellows tried to clean up the graft in San Francisco. He ran afoul, as we all do eventually, of the railroad people—And here now is where it gets complicated because I can no longer speak of things I know to be true, only things I suspect to be true: I think the MCPS gang knows that I have been living with Vera. I'm not sure if they think it's because I'm in love with her or because I'm in league with her. I can tell you folks it because I'm in love with her," he whispered. "I also think they know that Ray John here is an old specialist in dirty work who has come out of his narcotics-addicted retirement in Chicago at the behest of old friends in the IWW, the Chicago Wobblies now, not the Detroit Wobblies. At their behest because they know he is a tried-and-true daredevil who will gladly sacrifice his life to keep Vera safe. They thought they were slipping me into the MCPS via the usual kind of ridiculous deal-making that goes on all the time, the Socialist mayor of Minneapolis demanding that the MCPS, you know, open itself up and be a real governmental operation, not a secret one. But the MCPS boys didn't believe that for a second. They suddenly, and without really planning such a thing or even dreaming of it, had me and Vera riding in the same train together, regrouping after the San Francisco Preparedness Day Parade and Minot Theater bombings, knowing there would be fireworks and hoping, thinking on their feet, that they could do a very great favor for some real friends of theirs, railroad men out west. Fellow by the name of Durwood Keogh: My father caused his uncle—to whom he was devotedly close! Never were uncle and nephew so spiritually matched!—to flee the country. My father was so hated by the United Railroad men that they tried to kill him in court. And yet here in what they persist in calling the Great Northwest but which they're going to have to start calling the Great Midwest a Minot is a railroad man! I'm repeating myself, I'm so excited. The Western railroad men hired some idiot to waltz into court with a six-gun and fire a few rounds! And they so loathe and detest the spirit of progressive reform, of Christian soldiers, of honest devotion to the commonwealth, of temperate and wise men of business—of the principles of an enlightened and democratic—excuse me, a Platonic republic, of higher good, of common good, of decency, of compassion—that the idea of a Minot running not just a railroad but the country drives them to murder. Relentless, remorseless murder. Smart thing for me to do would be to take my beloved Vera and get the hell out of Dodge, wait for things to blow over, and then be a decent chap and citizen, or say to hell with it all and move to Alexandria. Not the one here! The one in Egypt! But I'm not smart. I'm a daredevil. I'm an anarchist. Not like you hear about in the news, but like this: if no one is ruling, all are ruling. I can't obey and I can't command. I see things as they are, too clearly, for any of that."

Once they got Charles outside, he wrenched himself free of Joe the Young Wobbly's grip and said, "Forgot to pay." He went back inside and slammed a dollar on the bar, took the bottle, and stalked out.

A letter from Alexander was waiting for him at the Detroit Lakes Hotel.

"Dearest brother, this is the saddest moment of my life. I am sobbing my eyes out every time I try to write another word. I was able to speak by telephone to Andrew and Amelia and Tom and Gus and Tony. Or rather, spoke to Andrew, who spoke to the others, as I was unable to speak once I told him what had happened. The telephone is such a strange machine: I spoke calmly and coolly, like the diplomat I truly am, not believing it was Andrew on the other end, not believing, somehow, that *anyone* was really there, that it was some kind of trick. But when he started to talk, I could hear his confusion and anguish, I could hear my brother, and I broke down. Couldn't go on. Mother does not know, as everyone agrees that a telegram will not do in these wretched circumstances."

Mother, thought Charles, *most certainly knows. What in the world is Al going on about?*

"Everywhere I go," Alexander's letter continued, "everything I do, I think of him. I see him. I don't mean I see a ghost. I see with something other than my eyes. But I see. It's not memory, and it's not imagination, and it's not a ghost. I don't understand, dear brother, I just *do not understand*. I have lived a good life. I am a strong, capable, intelligent, resourceful, sympathetic man. And I became that man largely because that was the kind of man Father was. I never lose my temper but everyone knows that the metaphorical revolvers I wear strapped to my hips are loaded and if I draw them I shoot them and if I shoot them I hit what I'm aiming at. I learned that from Father—and there! I managed that highly ironic statement not with tears but with laughter! Ha! I feel nearly as hysterical as Amelia! And let me tell you, Chick, I understand all that so-called hysteria that we heaped at poor Amelia's feet. She just saw all this sooner than we did. In your way too: you saw this coming. I spent a lot of time being angry at you and embarrassed by Amelia because you, I don't know, you didn't seem to think we had any right to be who we were, as a family, as people, as a particularly powerful and interesting group of people and as solid individuals. We are—we were—cool-headed and clean-handed people. We loved beauty and we understood the ugliness of politics. We loved God and worked to make the world a better place! We were Ideal Citizens! Why do I feel so ashamed when I write those words now? Why couldn't we take some pride in how handsome we looked in the trappings of wealth and power that God gave us and of which we were, merely and happily and always, the modest stewards? Why did we have to renounce ordinary human friendships—all of us, even you! Surely we had the right to the consciousness of our gifts, our capacities, our skills, our wills? You will forgive me, Chick old man, for going on like this, because this is something like the conversation Father and I were having the day before he was to get on the train to come to you—the night, rather. It was a conversation that went deep into the night, long after men like he and I should have been in bed, sleeping soundly. He was uncharacteristically ironic about his role as a Regenerator: *I shoveled Chinatown into the bay because the Chinese were nothing but garbage to me. I put a Jew in prison because Jews aren't Christians. When TR was shot in Michigan I gave not a thought to murder and the insanity that drives people to it but condemned labor unions instead. I imagined that if he'd been in California, Andrew would have been standing next to him and might have taken the bullet for him and I am the basest of hypocrites not simply because I blamed labor unions for this danger but because I knew, I have known all along, that Andrew could not have been easily and swiftly replaced. And if I make it to Minnesota I am going to beg Charles to do anything but go to the front because a war is no place for a Christian and I want him to live a long and happy life.*"

It was Wisconsin, thought Charles, *not Michigan. Milwaukee.* Noting that he had neither initiated the thought nor welcomed it, and did not approve of its appearance in his mind once it had endured sufficiently to make a kind of stamp, a mere nitpicking correction in the middle of what was clearly the cry of a rent heart, he wondered if one's thoughts were ever truly one's own. If not, who's were they? What were they? And of what possible use to him when one fine day a thought might not just be tracer fire of action passed and action to come, but somehow truly matter?

"I of course," continued Alexander's letter, "asked him why he said 'if I make it to Minnesota,' and he said he was not feeling well. We had only one lamp burning in the little room so it was hard to see his face. He spoke of the Spring Park disaster and I couldn't see his face. He sounded as if that burden was lying very heavily on him—and of course you know that he never felt a burden to be heavy. Never. But I couldn't see his face. The lamplight was so weak and flickering that the shadows played tricks with me. He was uncharacteristically cold as well, all wrapped up in his chair with a blanket. He began to go on and uncharacteristically *on* about how guilty and wretched he felt about his 'profligacy' during the hey-day of the Poodle Dog. He laughed loudly and bitterly about how he had thought that a man of power actually deserved that kind of pleasure, that kind of relief. After a while, a long while, he seemed to have emptied himself out. He sounded calm, maybe resigned to something he didn't like, but calm, empty in a good way. I said I would go get some fresh air. I wanted a very big drink, which I had, and went for a walk to the park. When I came back he was still sitting in his chair in the darkness but I could smell the gun smoke. I don't understand how it could have happened, in that place at that time. I left him very much himself, if exhausted, and returned to . . . nothing. He was gone. It doesn't seem real. His absence doesn't seem real. The world doesn't seem real without him. I disbelieve the world that doesn't have him in it. Even if I accept the facts—even if I hear Father saying what he always said and which I had no trouble 'believing' or using as a creed—I don't believe it, I don't profess it. I don't know how I could ever have been so deluded as that."

Charles paused over the breakdown of the grammar and noted too the breakdown of the handwriting: it had become sloppier but pressed deeper into the paper, and strokes that should have been graceful were jagged. He could feel his own hand cramping. There were smears and spills of ink now too, on this last page. He thought helplessly of something Strindberg had written, probably in his Paris diary, or his chemistry notes, or *Inferno*, or the *Occult Diary* . . . ? Hands burned by chemicals, wounds into which was spilled salt, or rather coke dust. "He testified this solemn truth, by frenzy desolated, Nor man nor nature satisfies whom only God created." That was not Strindberg, was it? No, that was somebody else. Who had nothing to do with Strindberg? Probably not. The blackened and cracked hands, burned and deformed, crusted over as if by a process of smelting with black dead blood . . . they will never be clean, *my apparatus is insufficient, I need money!* Oh, Father, I wanted to introduce you to Strindberg. I wanted you to put him next to Teddy so I could say, here is a man who lived a strenuous life that wasn't handed to him on a silver platter, and here is a man who grieved what was lost, who saw that it could not be replaced, who believed in your God but who saw that life was an illusion.

I have neither a cool head nor clean hands, Father. I wish you could forgive me. I never saw the need.

"I sometimes find myself thinking he had to have been murdered," Alexander continued. "But the terrible truth is that an old Stoic would certainly think twice but not shy away from taking the matter in his own hands. Clean hands. Cool head. The end."

Charles secured a bottle of morphine pills without much trouble, and when he and Vera had taken a dose, he told her about his father's suicide. She said nothing, and they remained silent for several hours, thinking, in a deep, ceaselessly absorbing twilight that never changed, of the peace that passed all understanding: death.

Mastering an urge toward immediate and pointless violence, or not so much mastering it as feeling it ebb back whence it had flowed, Charles watched an old couple approach Vera and Daisy.

"Daisy!" the man shouted. "Daisy! Over here!" the woman shouted.

Charles watched the three embrace, three small plain people holding each other by the shoulders, patting each other's backs, and thought he saw in it a dignity of purpose he wanted for himself. Daisy seemed to know where she was going and what she was doing and why she was doing it, and it was fascinating to watch. It was the simplest or rather most ordinary of acts, but she was committed and persuasive and pulling it off so well he was sure she must have some sense of how porous her molecular structure was with all the other structures around her. Her act would seem to be false or superficial otherwise—accepted of course, as all such acts were, but accepted with that yawning indifference that marked all mediocre acting. He was quite sure he lacked—now that the change had come—this dignity—despite a hope, a wish to believe, to tell, and to act the story that he was becoming a good man—that everything beguiling and forceful in his character was there now only to hide that lack, and he found his face hot with embarrassment.

There was something in her gaze; in his own—admitting that he perceived it from the other side of consciousness—nothing, just a lot of darting back and forth, reconnaissance of the audience and deep studies of the sky. And with that thought he looked up, saw that Daisy and her friends had gone, that the background of the picture had darkened perceptibly, as if it were a very old oil painting, but that the colors had become somehow richer for it. He wondered how much longer he would be able, be allowed, to play the fool—and recognized instantly what most identified him as a fool: this belief that he could choose a role, that he could pick and choose as it were amongst the great parts of history. Almost a year now had gone by and yet it seemed that a fraction of a second, the flash of a thought, could undo it all, could unwind the clock, could make these people milling about this train station in the middle of nowhere disappear in a cloud of smoke. He had been pretending to be someone else, but he didn't know whom. *I have not been convincing. I have been an object of derision. My duplicity has been effortless and yet I am very tired. I am too tired to sleep. Every room I enter becomes not merely a stage—that would be unremarkable—but the same stage I just tried to exit, which is impossible.*

Hillsboro was a town of a thousand people on the Goose River in North Dakota, ten miles from the Red River of the North and the Minnesota border. Its town hall was a brilliant, almost translucent white, with startling black doors, upon one of which was tacked a large white poster with large black lettering announcing an informative speech by a representative of the Nonpartisan League. Next to the hall was a three-story red-brick hotel, called the Wheat Growers. Vera too had watched Daisy as she was met by an old farmer and his wife, gaunt, dark-eyed, windburned people whose hands looked fantastically, almost grotesquely powerful. The man's legs seemed like tree trunks and the woman's dress seemed as if draped over iron. Signaling their recognition with sudden white grins that made their dark eyes flash blue, they greeted Daisy. The man shook her hand and the woman embraced her. They moved slowly but surely, their gestures strong and fluid, as if of a heavy viscosity.

Vera looked away and the white hall was now pale red, the hotel orange. Between the setting sun and these few buildings stood nothing. Charles touched the small of her back. A man who had been lounging on the steps of the hall took a step toward them, getting their attention, staring openly at them. Then he furrowed his brow and lit a cigarette. Puffing, he nodded at them and moved off.

"Another secret agent," Charles said in a stage whisper. "Let him make the first move. Remember who you are?"

"No, who am I?"

"My wife. And you don't believe in free love."

"Oh yes," said Vera. "I am pretending to be delighted, but thinking, no, no, I can't be two people at once. I get too confused. Something bad will happen."

"No: you do *not* have to be two people."

"Something bad will happen anyway."

"It's impossible to be more than one person."

"Something bad will happen anyway."

"I fear that is merely your growing dependency on narcotics talking."

"Something bad will happen and the cause is irrelevant."

"When you're high, the assumption that something bad will happen is intact and clear but you don't care."

"That is a terribly dispiriting and counterproductive thing to say."

"When I first met you, you had a very different view of things that happened and why."

"Yes! It's remarkable, isn't it? I was very much in line with the aphorisms of your old buddy the Colonel!"

"Roosevelt? How so."

"'Get action. Do something. Be sane. Be somebody. Get action.'"

"The action gets you. Something does you. It's impossible *not* to be somebody. It's insane to think otherwise."

Vera said nothing. Charles snorted.

"'Be sane.' Jesus fucking Christ on a flatcar. The assassin Schrank was only doing what Teddy advised."

"Teddy's voice was at least one of the voices he heard."

"Schrank was getting action and being somebody in the only way he could."

"I sometimes think that was why, at least part of why, the former president was apparently so unmoved by the bullet in his bone and the blood all over the place."

"I think you're right. I don't think he held grudges. He was moving too fast. I will give him that. I will give him more than that. But I won't say he hasn't got it bass-ackward where the self and the act are concerned."

"He's not the thinker you are, Chick."

"I don't know if you're being sarcastic or not."

"I don't know, either."

"My father too," said Charles, "was a very forgiving man."

"Not at the end, he wasn't."

Vera spoke so softly Charles wasn't sure what she'd said, or even if she'd said anything. Maybe it had just been a sigh that wanted to be words.

"I can't forgive the bombers," he said.

"No," said Vera.

The sun shone across the flat wind-surging windless-falling land as if it were a simple world of clear light, black dirt, and green plants, of wheat growers and wheat and a little hotel where they could rest when they could not get home.

"I have been—*I am*—scared to death," Vera said, completing her thought.

Charles began to suspect the presence of a force, a new kind of gravity, that had begun to draw things unto itself.

Daisy spoke and Vera studied her critically, thinking her altogether wrong for the part. She was too funny for this dry routine. The subject was the "double profits" the millers were enjoying as they shipped grain to Liverpool and war-hungry England. She had a chart that showed the price spread between Duluth and Liverpool, the handling, insurance, ocean freight, and elevator costs, and the amount of the second cut of profit—and Vera, the true performer, thought she was reading her text. It was possible she was simply trying to appear calm and rational, but it was flat, nobody was being moved. Carefully Daisy began to suggest that the war was not a good war, that it was not the war that was being advertised at all. She made reference to a newspaper report that had German women being required by their government to bear children. And then she said that she believed American women would never let themselves be used as "brood sows for future wars."

Everybody in the hall felt the drop in pressure. Daisy was applauded bravely by a few people in the crowd, but Vera and Charles could see the needle of the barometer moving counterclockwise around the dial. And yet nothing happened.

Charles's question: Why had nothing happened? He didn't mean "a dramatic arrest"—he meant "nothing." The pressure dropped and that was that. Was somebody waiting for somebody else to do something else, something more? Did certain somebodies know less about who all the players were than Charles thought they did? Not likely, but possible. Another slim chance: even dead, Father's power wasn't entirely illusory, and he—and by guesswork extension, Daisy—was being handled with kid gloves. And re Father: Why had he not moved to have Charles removed? Was it possible he too had been biding his time—until suddenly he decided his time was up? Did he think Charles might do something politically, actionably, profitably heroic? Or had he—where had he been before he came to rest finally in San Francisco? In New York or London or . . . ?—letting power slip through his fingers like sand? A genuinely good man cannot withstand the vicissitudes that come of power wielded—not forever, he can't. Hadn't Father been a genuinely good man? Charles found himself thinking that he had been, whatever that thought might be "worth."

Perhaps Charles's removal was underway.

The expected explosion—he paused over the word as it appeared and faded in his brain—over Daisy's key phrases had failed to occur: was this like an actor forgetting his lines? Or was there a greater script than the actors realized. The force, the gravity, was similar if not identical to the force he felt onstage in ideal circumstances—or even less-than-ideal circumstances. The force he believed he felt. Perhaps in any but the most amateurish circumstances, when the force, if it was present at all, was reversed, repelling all the people and things in the space.

Had he just equated bad acting with detonation, a supersonic exothermic front driving a shock wave through a medium that cannot withstand it?

He had: there was a weird beauty and justice in it, somewhere, somehow . . . that nevertheless failed to address his certainty that some other kind—or simply degree?—of power was coming into being.

He had felt the supersonic exothermic front driving the shock wave only as one feels the wave of ocean water after it has crashed on the beach, when it is all but spent and about to recede, back into that from which it had come, a tremendous but dying energy—lapsing, paradoxically, not into quiescence or something "lesser," but into a greater energy. He had felt it twice, the waves each time strong enough to knock him down, but only because another body had taken more of the blow before it reached him, and he was quite sure he understood how it ripped a hole in one kind of reality, exposing another kind of less stable reality; and he had witnessed a far greater force, perhaps the greatest force in the universe, visible, apprehensible, for only as long as it took to cause everything he had before that point assumed to be the only reality to disappear; and he had seen in its wake an apparently equally relentless force recreate, rebuild, make visible once more what had disappeared. He had felt the impalpable, incomprehensible, so-called psychological gravity of two actors acting selflessly on a stage and drawing thereby the concentration of a hundred or two hundred "observers." But what was happening here, now, was different.

The next stops were Fargo and Moorhead, where nothing—it was preposterous now—other than angry shouting and angry applause in a cold wind under a low, dark, swiftly but barely perceptibly moving sky, like a dark turbulent river, also happened. Small groups of rough-looking men glowered and spat threateningly and told them to get out of town, as if they were in a play. Charles, imagining himself to be a person who could no longer be "troubled" in the ordinary sense, did not think he could be more troubled in the ordinary sense—which was even more troubling in the extraordinary sense he had reserved for himself and Vera. The bomb had exploded on his stage in San Francisco. Now, here, where gunfire was expected to erupt, where he had planned on it, according to a very real sort of script that he had not actually seen but which he believed with all his heart existed, where the explosion of a bomb had to be considered a strong possibility, seeing that improvised violence was the modus operandi everybody had tacitly agreed to, here there was only a group of bad actors in the shadows, representing "consequences" in a way that seemed only sordid, cowardly, contemptible.

Get out of town?

They did. They cut across the state, out of the wheat and into the woods, into Big Timber, to the headwaters of the Mississippi River, where Wobbly strikes had been failing for a decade—failed very much in the way a man might enter a wood, walk strongly and confidently for a while, only to find at the first moment of doubt that he was lost.

The two Wobblies who had in fact gone missing more than a month earlier were still missing.

Several people had told them that Bemidji would be the big stop, that there would be trouble, and someone in Chicago had even gone so far as to counsel against Bemidji, against even getting off the train to stretch their legs. The question was: Who was the someone in Chicago—nominally from the IWW, but did they know that with working certainty?—and was he speaking out of genuine concern for their welfare, or was there worry that the NPL would have some kind of "success" in Bemidji? If so, who did not want NPL success in Bemidji. The MCPS certainly—but how, in this hypothetical scenario, had the MCPS managed to influence the Chicago Wobblies? The Chicago Wobblies were as pure a current as could be, even in the most turbulent stream.

Were they not?

Three telegrams awaited Charles at the Paul Bunyan Hotel.

The first: DISAVOW ANY CONNECTION WITH IWW.

The second: DISAVOW ANY CONNECTION WITH TROUBLE-MAKERS CLAIMING ASSOCIATION WITH US.

The third: YOU ARE OPERATING WITHOUT USUAL SANCTION. PLEASE EXPLAIN.

The news that certain "watchdogs of loyalty" had become "junkyard dogs of loyalty" and were embarrassing and compromising the MCPS was of course not news. Disavowal of a relation between the MCPS and the IWW was something else that went without saying, making the saying, of course, profoundly suspicious. And while the whereabouts of the two missing Wobblies remained unknown, "a drifter" had been found dead. His identity and the circumstances of his end were not known. As for the lack of usual sanction: he had it. He had it in writing, in his briefcase, as was usual with sanction. If whoever had telegraphed him was under an impression to the contrary, it could mean one of two things: sanction had been reconsidered and made to disappear, perhaps like the Wobblies but with the additional pretense of "never having existed in the first place," or the divided house that the MCPS always had been, perforce—how could so many powerful men agree on any notion of safety, public or otherwise?—had become dangerously destabilized.

The women wore dresses with flower prints, anticipating by days or perhaps weeks the actual blooming of spring, the men clean overalls, some with a tie and some without. Charles overheard one man defend his tie by stating the business here was every bit as solemn as the business of a Sunday morning and he would show it a like respect. Some men and women looked about themselves, eager to share their outrage, while some laughed and conversed. A few smoldered, moving awkwardly about with hatred and fear constricting their limbs and faces—lungs, hearts, stomachs too. The same man who'd defended his tie said, "I agree that times are bad, but I don't care to be told how to do a thing, neither by the railroads nor by the socialists." A line of men stood at the back of the hall, and Charles could not say if they were embarrassed to be there or had a darker purpose in mind. To his left he felt Vera stiffen; he turned and saw the man he'd seen at the Hillsboro town hall.

"Excuse me," said the man, his face suddenly, without Charles having noticed the movement, very close to his own, smiling. "Are you one of Winter's people?" He looked and acted like an overzealous salesman.

"You betcha," said Charles. "I am a man for all seasons."

The man cocked his head stupidly, and Charles crossed himself for no apparent reason. Then he nodded as if with unction. The man stepped back and looked at Charles, as if not terribly amused but willing to play along. Charles crossed himself again, with a hint of truculence, and nodded. Then he said he knew John Winter. He knew him better than the man knew his own daddy.

"All right," said the man. "Stay here and listen to what she says and then—"

"Don't tell me how to do my job, bud," Charles interrupted him.

"Where's your notebook, sport?" the man demanded in an angry whisper that caused spittle to form. "I'm going to get the sheriff. I've already got some folks lined up to press charges."

Charles had his little black notebook out and was flapping its cardboard covers at the man's face like a yapping mouth. "You do that."

When the man went out the door, Daisy came in. She looked long and hard at Charles and Vera as she walked past them. She made her way to the front of the hall, mounted the platform, and moved behind the podium. After a moment, the quack and whine of voices settled, and she began her speech. She got through the "double profits" section and started in on the war. She mentioned the newspaper report dealing with the forced impregnation of German women, then repeated her belief that American women would never let themselves be used as brood sows for future wars, at which point three men and three women left their seats and departed the hall. The men at the back began to boo and heckle her. She continued to speak without seeming to notice, as the action seemed rather perfunctory, rehearsed as things are rehearsed in the early days of rehearsal—not menacing or even intrusive. When she was done and the audience was making for the doors, the sheriff and several deputies walked in, bowling people out of the way until they got to Daisy, who paled and stepped back. People still in the hall stopped in their tracks, and a few outside came back to crowd the doorway.

"What is the charge?" asked Daisy weakly.

"Sedition, you stupid cunt," said the sheriff irritatedly. "Get with the program."

He tugged on her arm so violently that she lost her balance and would have fallen to the floor had the sheriff not been holding on to her, carrying her along like one would a stumbling toddler.

Marched past Charles and Vera, she appeared to pull herself together and again looked straight and meaningfully—or was it imploringly?—at them.

Charles's knees and bladder immediately weakened. His face began to burn and his vision to blacken around the edges. Had he gotten himself into something, mainly because he could? *I am an anarchist. I am a daredevil. You see? Excellent. Where is everybody going? I haven't even—*

Then it got worse. He felt as if something long and sharp had punctured his stomach and was being driven upward through his lungs to his heart, which was about to explode. He felt as if this great incorporeal spear were hoisting him off his feet. Dancing a strange little dance to keep his balance, he felt absolutely certain that his new role was to draw a weapon and rescue Daisy, to warn the servants of evil back back back, and then to run off into the night and never be seen or heard from again.

It was the heroic act that would link the lost past and the uncertain future, a great surge of blood in a flash of light that would reveal the great world, the good world, but which could only last seconds.

And indeed by the time he reached the door, Daisy and her captors could no longer be seen, and he was blinking and swallowing in confusion and darkness—feeling not shame but something more absurd, like regret.

"We should get the hell out of here," said Charles.

"Yes," said Vera. "No."

"We should let what's his name bail her out."

"Who?"

"Whoever runs the NPL."

"Townley."

"Townley. Where is Townley."

"Good question."

"Why have I never met Townley."

"He probably knows more about you than you know about yourself and decided he doesn't want to meet you. I mean, in person, rather than in his head."

"We should let this son of a bitch Townley get Daisy out of jail and we should go to the south of France. Or we could go to a Greek island, one of the Cyclades. Or Skyros, rather, one of the Sporades, north Aegean. We could go to the Levant, to Alexandria, the real one, in Egypt. I think you'd like Alexandria, Vera. You speak five languages in the course of a short conversation on a street corner. Money and words feverishly exchanged night and day. Easier access to better drugs. Beirut, Smyrna. Or we could go to Japan, as Father counseled in the wake of the Russo-Japanese War. Would you like to go to Japan, my darling? Study Zen and the Tao?"

"But we have . . ."

"We have what?"

"Don't we . . . ?"

"Don't we what?"

"Have a duty to stay here and see this through?"

"DUTY!"

"Yes. Don't we?"

"Did you say 'duty'?"

"Yes."

"No. We have no duty whatsoever."

"We do."

"Yes, all right: we do, but we won't know what it was until after it's over and done."

"We have a duty to see that the show goes on."

"The script may very well call for our exit stage left. It could call for that as easily and surely as anything else."

"No, because . . . because here . . ."

"Here what."

"Here is where we are."

"We do not have to stay here."

"This is the stage. We can go offstage but offstage is still the stage."

But then Winter's man had come back, and Charles had him by the arm and wouldn't let go, no matter how hard the man shook and how loud he yelled. Charles was speaking, but he could not make himself out. He was simply bellowing incoherently, as if in pain.

Vera separated them. "Something," Charles said breathlessly, "is a little fucked up here. Wires get crossed or something?"

"What the fuck are you talking about?" the man panted and fumed.

"Somebody, ummm, tell you *expressly* to have her *arrested*?"

The man laughed brutally. "Yeah, that's right, somebody did!"

Charles appeared to become angry. Strangely, he wasn't. "Well, somebody told *me* expressly *not to.*"

"TALK TO WINTER!"

"I TALK TO MCGEE!"

"YOU DON'T TALK TO MCGEE!"

"I SURE AS HELL DO!"

"IF YOU TALKED TO MCGEE YOU'D KNOW TO BE TALKING TO WINTER AND NOT MCGEE!"

"I TALK TO MCGEE AND I KNOW NOT TO BE TALKING TO WINTER!"

The man kept smiling and shook his head, a combination of gestures Charles had always found, for some reason, irritating and provocative. He could no longer say if he was angry or not: things were changing too quickly. He stepped forward too quickly, brought his head in too close to the other man's, and actually tapped his forehead with his own.

"There is a *plot*," Charles cried, "she *is* part of a plot to *do something*, we don't know *what* yet, throw a bomb or shoot someone, as part of, as part of a *plot*, I mean a *demonstration* connected to the streetcar strike in Minneapolis and Saint Paul."

There was a flare of wild hatred in the man's eyes. "Don't ever do that to me again," he said, foaming.

Charles bugged his own eyes out and darted his head forward, coming perilously close again to the man's forehead. "WATCH HOW YOU FUCKING LOOK AT ME THEN!" He felt entirely committed to the role: as if he had jumped off a cliff.

"What are you *talking* about? I didn't look at you! What, are you *crazy?* 'Don't fucking look at me'—what the fuck are you talking about? I'll fucking look at you however and whenever I feel like looking at you! And you know what else, you stupid fuck? THERE AIN'T ANY STREETCAR STRIKE!"

"Fuck you," said Vera, intervening. "Wise up." She stepped back, smiled broadly, and shook her head in exaggerated swings. "*Fuck* you. You are an *idiot.* We will take care of this ourselves. *Fuck* you and good-*bye.*" She too had committed to a role. It took Charles completely by surprise but as a dedicated *improvisateur*, he was thrilled.

"Fuck you too! What's your fucking name anyway?"

"Didn't you hear me? I said *fuck you.*"

"Fuck You? I thought so! Well, so long, Fuck You! Good luck, Fuck You!"

The man continued his loud calls of farewell even though he was walking right next to Charles and Vera, matching pace and length of step like a clown. At the steps of the sheriff's office, he stopped and slapped his head. "Oh wait, I get it. I get it, you're *fucking her.*" He looked at Charles. He looked at Vera. "Both of you maybe?" The man looked again at Charles, who maintained his newfound unpredictability by knocking him flat.

The other man went him one better, however, by leaping to his feet and disappearing inside the sheriff's office. Charles waited a moment, looking with plaintive exasperation at Vera, then followed him in. At the desk, he shouldered aside the man he'd knocked down, clearly having a physical advantage now, and asked the deputy if he knew who Mr. Winter was.

The man sputtered and the deputy nodded.

"That's good," said Charles, "how about Mr. Minot and Mr. Roosevelt?"

The deputy again nodded, now appearing somewhat nervous, as if he in fact did not know.

Charles asked if Daisy Gluek was in a cell close enough to overhear a telephone conversation, and the deputy shook his head uncertainly. Charles then asked to use the phone. The candlestick was pushed across the desk, the deputy now seeming perhaps half-witted. Charles had a long list of emergency numbers, at each of which he learned that nobody of consequence was available. Finally he tried Winter's White Bear Lake residence, where he spoke to the secretary or butler or spy and explained the situation to him.

The secretary or butler or spy said, "There is no streetcar strike. I am told you should talk to Commissioner McGee if you are concerned."

"You're right, there's no streetcar strike *right now,*" Charles said patiently, but looking up to see the other man, who had finally recovered a sense of himself, feigning a chuckle and waggling his eyebrows at the deputy, who returned this merriment blankly, "but, you see, *there will be.* And it will be a more interesting strike than any you've seen yet. Pickets, speeches, the wearing of blue buttons and yellow buttons and the spitting upon of nickels? Forget about it! The Wobblies know we're coming down on them and they want to go out, listen to me, this is what I'm out here in the middle of fucking nowhere doing, they want to go out literally with a bang, do you follow? I'm telling you I am actually learning something important out here, I'm not just winding up feebleminded vigilantes and watching them strut here and there until their fucking *keys run down.*"

"There is nothing," the secretary or butler or spy said some two hundred miles to the southeast, "to be done right now. Your position, Mr. Minot, is that Gluek should be allowed to continue her tour? In the hope that . . . ?"

"That's right," Charles said as if to a child, "yes, and can you tell me please why, if you wanted her arrested, nobody told me? Told us?"

"I can't answer that."

"Well, okay, but that's the kind of thing that really, you know, mitigates a guy's effectiveness."

"I think you mean 'vitiates.'"

"Sorry, can't hear you, Mr. Vi-shitty-ates."

"I'm sure there's a good reason for it."

"Like what, for instance, for Christ's sake."

"I'm sure there's a good reason for it."

"I'd like to hear it when you know what it is!"

The secretary or butler or spy changed the tone of his voice. "Whole thing sounds fishy, Minot. Are you fucking this Gluek or something?"

The sun was out but the wind was cold. Shadows of clouds shot across the land like high-speed whales. The smell of cattle and cattle shit came flying across the town as well, straight at the hotel. Charles came out onto the wide porch and immediately made a face, though there was no one near to appreciate it. He was in his shirtsleeves and the wind felt as if it were coming directly from the North Pole. He took another lungful of the pungent icy air and went back inside. Vera sat in an armchair with her head in her hands. When she heard Charles approach, she raised her head, but kept her hands on her face, so that only her eyes were visible: and they were red. She was not going to pieces, but had become very irritable. Charles sat in another chair, put his hands in his lap, and a look of chagrin on his face that seemed slightly lopsided, one eye larger than the other, lips compressed to a single pale red line that angled down from the larger-eyed side of his face.

"Will you do me a favor?" Jules asked me from behind his hands.

"Yes."

"Get me the fuck out of here."

"A two-bit spring, for sure."

She looked terribly tired, so tired and irritable that Charles could not help but feel uncomfortably superior to her. And yet it was quite true he was overexcited, out of control—still falling from the edge of the cliff. He was certain that his improvised deceptions, which he now saw as infantile, had run their course, were no longer necessary or useful. He was one step away from condemning himself wholly for what he was afraid was merely frivolous trifling with forces that were properly the domain of pure, ruthless, power-mad fools. Perhaps this was what had finally convinced Father further life was a ridiculous proposition. It could not have been the melodramatic seeing of the light that Al had apparently witnessed, the falling of the wool from Father's eyes after a series of soul-searching conversations while logs crackled in the fireplace. Either Father had been a pure, ruthless, power-mad fool whose will had weakened unexpectedly, possibly because he spent so much energy maintaining a disguise as well as simple physical vigor, or he had indeed been "the good man" he had appeared to be all along, and could no longer tolerate what must, therefore, have been a life of tremendous defeat.

There is an evil, he daydreamed, in our land, growing day by day, that will soon be as great an evil as the one over there, in the land of the other people, that we will fight.

Perhaps greater. Over there: decay and aggression, falling and rising lines on a graph matching each other perfectly in their descent and ascent off the chart. Here: infantile greed and tyranny dressed up as the Straight Talkers of Main Street.

Charles sat back in his chair. He flexed his fingers around the arms of the chair and his gaze softened. "I admire what we have done," he said to Vera. His tone was rather flat and seemed to be undercutting what he was saying, but he went on. "It was bold and thrilling. I say to you, we are the greatest of lovers. Our minds and hearts are one in these Deeds of Propaganda in the Cause of Nothing."

"We are not acting in the Cause of Nothing."

"You can see it however you want to."

"The cause is 'Life As It Is.'"

"Could not have said it better myself!"

"The cause is remaining calm as we stare horror in the face. But I am now compromised. I am crippled. I now prefer this easy way of acceptance that we get from the perfect pills in the little bottle that was slipped to us while we were distracted by the shouts, whistles, whispers of the bazaar. It is increasingly difficult to be calm without it. Soon it will be impossible. We will be neck and neck with death no matter how fast we run, no matter how sharply and suddenly we turn. And when we stop, panting, hysterical, it will still be there. We won't be dead, we will be staring at its face and it will be staring back. Death will be calm! But we won't be."

"Old behaviors do not fit new experiences. The play is always new, always fresh. The actors are blown into the wings by supersonic exothermic fronts driving shock waves through media that cannot withstand them."

"Are we going to bail Daisy out or not?"

"But the wisest course when you don't know exactly who you are or what you're actually doing, actually trying to accomplish, when you don't know who knows, if anybody does, who you are, really, well, the thing is to lie low and keep a watch. Make notes. You're improvising, you're acting via reflex, and if I can't help but smile in appreciation and, you know, fond remembrance of the good old days, I nevertheless have to point out that you are not in control. You are out of control. You have been out of control for six months and if you don't calm down *without the morphine* you're just going to be a spectator watching more of your friends die."

"Well, aren't you the fine one to be talking!"

"We will become merely intellectual anarchists for whom daring deeds of propaganda are perfectly precluded by the poetry of the poppy."

"Are we going to bail Daisy out or abandon her?"

"Maybe it's just yourself, maybe what you're aiming for is just a closeness to it, a constancy. I shouldn't say 'you,' when I clearly mean 'we.' Capitulation to the dream drugs, the sleep-givers—that would teach us a fucking lesson for sure. Are we ready for that, Vera? We're pretending, we're acting as if we're in control, when what we really want is to be in control and *then* act."

He'd not altered his monotone until the penultimate word, which he snapped angrily.

"I'm just thinking out loud," he caught himself, feigning a chuckle.

Vera sighed. It was almost a gasp. She was shaking.

"It is true," said Vera. "I can see that it is, but it's pretty much going in one ear and out the other.

Charles stood up and struck a fencing pose. He looked at Vera and he looked at the clerk at his desk. "Yes?" he asked and nodded when they did not. "He thrust and I parried. I turned his thrust and my parry into a thrust of my own. One fluid motion. Yes, I was acting reflexively. No, I was not out of control."

"Do you remember," asked Vera, "that newspaper photograph of John outside the motordrome in Detroit?"

"I'm not sure that I do."

"No, no, it was an advertisement for Oilzum maybe . . . ? Daredevil Derkum? Paul Derkum? You never met him? NECK AND NECK WITH DEATH? These daredevils use Oilzum brand lubricants? And John had put a white cross over everybody's head but his own?"

Surprising himself, Charles stormed out of the lobby and headed for the Western Union office. Vera followed him, hugging herself as she crossed the street, making a face and blinking several times as the stench of the stockyard assailed her. She found Charles writing out a telegram. His billfold was next to him on the counter, and she picked it up, thinking he might have miniature pictures of his famous family in it. She asked if he did, but Charles, lost in thought, pen in mouth, didn't answer. Then she found one. It was a reproduced painting, cut from a book, a portrait of a man in a white periwig. The man was a soldier; in whose army she could not say. When she looked up in inquiry, Charles was staring at her. She asked who the man was, and he dropped his gaze. Not sure that he'd heard her, she repeated herself. He held out his hand for the picture.

"The older brother of my great-great-great grandmother," he said, putting it back in the billfold.

"So this is circa . . . ?"

"He was born in the Savoy in 1763."

"And what army is he—"

"Piedmontese. The King of Sardinia. In 1790 he was arrested for dueling. Sentenced to forty-two days confinement in his house. He wrote a long poem that was very popular in royalist circles."

"Royalist."

"That's right."

"He was opposed to the—"

"The French Revolution, that's right."

Vera held out her hand. "May I see it again?" Charles hesitated, but produced it. "He looks like you, you think . . . ?"

"Yes," he said. "Put a wig on me and it's quite striking. He emigrated to Russia with the Russian general Suvorov, the man who forced the French to leave Turin. Fought Napoleon at Waterloo, served in Finland for a while, then gave up the military for a literary life, in Petersburg. Had a salon, actually. He once said, 'I could no more have written that poem in my uniform than I could have fought a battle in my bathrobe.'"

He ceased the speech abruptly, exhausted by it, and returned his attention to the telegram, tapping the point of the pen against the pad. "I don't know why it's taking the NPL so long to bail her out. Maybe they don't have the money. Maybe that's why she's traveling alone. But I don't care what the reason is. I'll do it myself. What do you think of that, Vee?"

He looked up from the note, angry, but suddenly, strangely, full of love.

"I think," she said, responding to the first concern, "that their finances are certainly disorganized. They likely cannot lay their hands on that kind of money, you know, just like that." She snapped her fingers. "May be tied up elsewhere."

"Well, I can, and that's exactly what I'm—"

"What do you want from her in exchange?"

"—I'm going to, what? Nothing. I don't want a thing from her. What a strange thing to ask me!"

"I am only saying she is currency. Legal tender. She has been set up. The formal act of exchange is the arrest. I suspect the NPL sold her, probably with her knowledge and cooperation—she has one script and they have another and only the beginning and the end are the same, which is that select members of the NPL will escape the Justice Department's, the FBI's, Pinkerton's big old roundup, whenever that happens. Which I'm sure Mr. Townley thinks, and Daisy probably thinks as well, is a good thing because it means they will be free to pursue their goals when the war ends. Their goal being the enlargement of the small businessman we know as the Jeffersonian yeoman farmer, our ideal citizen, drenched in the vivid neoclassical colors of democratic, agrarian virtue, the bedrock of our country and of civilization, as painted by, say, David or Greuze. Sculpted heroically by Canova. Enlargement, I say, at the cost of a few farmers along the way, because they can't all be titans, can they."

"So I should or should not bail her out."

"Again I ask you: What do you want from her in exchange?"

"What do you want from her?"

"Me? What do I have to do with it?"

"Oh, Vera. I only want to do what you want to do. I don't care about any of this anymore."

"Well, you spoiled little brat, you! I want you to care about this! We're in danger of being flushed down the toilet by the dream-givers!"

"Don't get hysterical."

Faster than lightning, she slapped him.

Charles began to speak, but stopped himself, actually putting his hand to his mouth.

"I want to do what is right," said Vera, breathing heavily but speaking softly.

"'It's never wrong to do right.' Pastor Tom said that once. Amelia corrected him: 'Unless someone disagrees with you about what is right.' And let us not forget Heraclitus in our mad rush to do what is right: 'They vainly purify themselves with blood when they are defiled with blood, as though one who had stepped into mud were to wash with mud. He would seem mad if anyone saw him doing this.'"

"I don't want to run from consequences, Charles. That is not the kind of acting I signed up for."

"I don't understand you."

"I have been associated for nearly ten years, since I was thirteen, in Willimantic, with men and women who are not going to escape the big old roundup of 'seditious shitsuckers' bright and early next year. You will make it possible for me to escape these consequences, to run away from the traitorous doings I have had a hand in for half of my life—and all you want in exchange is life-long devotion. You want me to run away with you to the other side of the world and leave the men and women I love all alone, to rot and die for my sins. You'll what, publish my memoirs and hire expensive lawyers for me, first-class passage the minute it looks like I'm going to be railroaded, and all I have to do is pretend to be in love with you?"

Charles laughed. "'Pretend.'"

"That's right, pretend!"

"What, do you think I can't tell the difference?"

"If you think that I—"

"You are pretending not to be in love with me, Vera."

"Oh wait, I get it," said Vera, as if comforting Charles. He ripped his message from the pad and moved to the window, a small arched opening from which slid a pair of hands. He bent slightly and saw the operator's distant meshed face. "I get it," repeated Vera. "What could be more daring, right? To thumb our nose at the government of the United States of America? At your father's government?" She grabbed his arm and angrily shook it. "Right? *Right*?"

Charles said nothing, waiting for the telegraph clerk to return.

"I feel so sick," said Vera. "You might as well know: I am afraid I am pregnant."

Where had she gone wrong? She had to have turned away, lost the path, because everything was wrong, day after day, just wrong enough for her to notice, for her not to be able to ignore it: nothing looked familiar. Charles had become like some strange pagan statue, a totem pole, and she had stared at him, couldn't take her eyes off him, honestly, while landscapes and skies and crowds swirled around them, out of focus, smeared with rich colors. She had appealed to him and he had responded in his strange pagan way. And now there was this.

They went outside. It was warmer now, and the wind had shifted enough to take the stockyard stink out of it. They walked toward the jailhouse.

"The cat," Charles said, "is out of the bag now."

"Well, no, not quite," said Vera.

Charles couldn't help but laugh.

"Not a laughing matter," said Vera, smiling in spite of herself.

"Oh, but it is!" shouted Charles. "We have been given one of the biggest and greatest cues the world's stage can offer!"

Vera suddenly stopped smiling but said nothing.

"What do you think is going to happen?" she asked Charles.

"No idea! I'm just an actor! Do you know what's going to happen?"

Vera said nothing and remained neither smiling nor frowning, finding a neutrality naturally easy to come by and hold lightly.

"I don't think you can honestly say you do," said Charles. "Neither of us knows a damn thing. Nobody does. I'm very excited, though, in spite of myself."

"I think your mother will come after me if she finds out. Your brothers and sister too. Maybe they've gotten used to the idea that you can't be trusted to live in the center of things."

"I don't know what that means."

"Neither do I."

"I really don't. Not a clue."

"NEITHER DO I!"

"'At the center of things'?"

"I'm sorry."

"At any rate, the cat and the bag I was talking about are Daisy and the slammer. I am pretty sure if I bail her now, I will mess things up for more than one party, and our . . . how shall I say . . . our 'effectiveness' will be compromised to the point of—"

"We never had anything remotely like effectiveness. The only question is, do we let her sit here in *this* jail *now*?"

"We are assuming that she does not want to sit here in this jail now."

Vera began to speak but stopped herself.

"And are we assuming, as we use those specific terms, that you will seek an abortion?"

Again Vera began to speak but stopped herself.

Outside the jail, she stopped and said she wouldn't go in. When Charles insisted, citing Daisy's almost certain despair—no matter what her intentions might be over the long haul toward a promised end—she thumped him repeatedly on his arms and chest and cried *no no no no no*. Because he'd been hit, twice now, violently, he looked, he supposed, like a little boy and she apologized, going through exaggerated motions of calming herself that in some way calmed her, minimally. She tried to describe what had happened to her when she'd visited Daisy earlier, the suspicion that she was slipping away from herself, that she had always been in danger of slipping away, and the fear that if she were to take Daisy's place and be arrested and jailed just as Daisy had been, incarceration would rip every joint from its socket. "I wouldn't be insane, but I would be alone. I wouldn't have any arms or legs."

"I am familiar with the condition," Charles said.

"Of course you are," she sighed. "What are you not familiar with?"

And he gestured at the jailhouse, the hotel, the land empty of everything but the stunted trunks of second-growth popple, to the horizon, to the sky.

They bailed a silent Daisy, for whom a car was waiting at the curb.

Vera peered in and confirmed that it was Townley.

"Odd couple indeed," said Charles. "Their ways are strange to me."

And so they got high and traveled deeper into what had been the southernmost reaches of a white pine forest that had circled the globe, the aboriginal inhabitants of which had believed their doctors could fly over mountains and trees, to heaven and to hell: the three-tiered world. Charles, thinking that he might soon die, maybe in the next town, or the next time he got on a train, along the way somewhere, middle of nowhere, that his soul might drift out like smoke from the ponderous rocking car—which, he fantasized, would seem to be going only just fast enough to make possible the drift of smoke out an open window, as if the night, the darkness, were viscous. Vera snored lightly next to him, her face half muffled by a pillow. His eyes were closed but he was wide-awake. They had been musing, talking of the farmers they had seen, coming and going in their wagons, standing next to fences or in front of stores, talking so quietly you had to strain to hear them. He had wanted to align himself, somehow, with them, but as he rehearsed these scenes in anxious dopey idleness, he realized he could do no such thing. They had spent long years working with their hands, with black dirt and animals, with rotting vegetables and stinking guts and blue skies and howling blizzards. An even more stark difference: they were businessmen. The second they could be done with the guts and the dirt and the bad weather, they would be. He, on the other hand, was some kind of sliding entity, no fixed residence, no fixed character even, or so he mused, blaming himself obscurely for some psychological crime he could not grasp, but which had become some kind of gigantic thinking, moving thing in the wake of Father's death. Perhaps one or two of the farmers secretly believed themselves to be that way too, some kind of double agent, an odd mingling of forces that could only, as to their nature and origin, be guessed at, the man only nominally "himself," the person others took him to be, the source of wildest heartbreak and unbearable sorrow if one day he should become what he was afraid he was. If he and the giant were to become one. It was also possible he did not know himself and did not want to know himself, satisfied with the binding of his responsibilities and the way they shaped and filled him in. He had nothing like that, and he suspected it was what Vera wanted most from him. He had struggled free of them, his responsibilities, every one of them, in an eye-rolling panic he only just barely managed to conceal from the people around him, to find himself now able only to manufacture facsimiles, each one less and less convincing, arriving at last at the feeble conclusion that it was his duty to strike a blow for cheated working people, with some hideous spectacular act of violence. Oh yes, there were tyrants everywhere, left and right, and he was sick of them all. He returned again and again to the image of the Marble Man, Swanson, in San Francisco. There was a man he could kill. The only thing that had kept him from becoming a tyrant himself was the wheel of pain and relief, pain and morphine, that he found himself on. *If I were strong,* he told himself, *I would surely be a monster.* Vera, he thought. She had worked. She had spent her childhood negotiating a terrifying responsibility, nerve-wracked, a little more exhausted each day, a little more sick each day, a little more blind and deaf and dumb, and of course it had made her mad, of course it had made her crazy. What was she to do with her intelligence, her dreams, her heart, her mind? She'd had no recourse, she lived in a prison, and when she saw how she might be free, she let her mind go. The bitter but bracing wind of the present moment snatched it like a bonnet and it shot away over the trees. She looked up, first in dismay, then in delight, and raced after it. He loved her dearly. He leaned over to her and whispered that he wished never to leave her. *I'll teach you French and we will have a child together: surely you are free to go now, wherever you want to go, even if I cannot.*

On an island pedestal in the middle of the main road, surrounded by an oval of white picket, directly across from the station, stood two wooden statues, one ten feet high, of the famous lumberjack Paul Bunyan, and the other ten feet long, of Paul's familiar, Babe the Blue Ox. The carvings were rude, rough, childlike, and they were painted garishly. Paul's face was brilliant white, his eyes simple black dots in the middle of black rings, his mouth a thick red line in the shape of a sausage, inside which were blocky white teeth with straight black gaps between them. His beard was shoe-polish black and could not be distinguished from his hair. The squares of his red and black plaid shirt were in fact square. Babe was a rich bright sky blue, and had a sign hung around his massive neck: WELCOME TO BRAINARD. Vera thought that the legendary lumberjack looked like a confused and alarmed transvestite. Whoever or whatever he was, he presided over the town, which was more than big enough to warrant an IWW hall, but that hall had never managed to remain operational for longer than a month. The violence that attended its opening and closings had become routine, but "the new laws" and the sanction of the MCPS, it was being said, were reinvigorating the form, perhaps even transforming it. They found the building where the last hall had been located, on a short street just off Main, of single-story storefronts: it was not merely closed, but ransacked, nearly demolished; a part of it had evidently been burned. The door was missing, and that seemed, to Vera, the most profound evidence of disaster, more troubling even than the charred back room. The windows too were gone, shards like spikes in the sashes and muntins. IWW MEANS I WON'T WORK, a standard call when heckling a Wobbly speaker, was painted across a wall. But where they expected to see files and papers and books ripped up and strewn about and defecated upon, they found only the hardening residue of numerous defecations. The filing cabinets and desk drawers were empty, upended, and broken apart, but somebody had collected documents in a very thorough manner; certainly the collector had been a representative of the United States Department of Justice. Muddy boot prints were everywhere on the floor, two neatly and illustratively placed before one pile of shit, the biggest by far, prints slightly splayed in evidence of the man's struggle for balance, a cigarette butt between them, as if the agent had been casually smoking, and very likely reading, while he symbolically moved his actual bowels. Probably written into the procedural manual, Charles thought: always defecate upon conclusion of search. Flies droned and worked carefully upon the shit. He turned to see Vera in a silent tableau with a tall, skinny man whose feet and hands extended many inches beyond cuffs, and who wore a bowler, Townley, he guessed, and Daisy.

"You have to get out of town," said Daisy. "This is a town where they will murder you if you confuse them."

They departed swiftly in silence, as was their wont.

Only to be replaced minutes later, as if they were on a schedule, by a tall heavy man made in the image of Paul Bunyan. He was standing on the threshold, and Vera knew then why the absence of the door had troubled her so: they were meant precisely to shield the occupants of a room from visions such as this.

"What's your name?" Charles demanded, a wealthy, privileged, influential young man, quick on the draw.

The man looked surprised and spat an unintelligible answer.

"Well, buddy, what the hell are you doing here?" Charles asked, perhaps friendly now, perhaps not.

The man started several answers, but discarded them all. Charles had clearly struck the appropriate tone with this coward: authority. Vera walked up to him, close enough so that she had to tilt her head back to look him in the eye. "Keep coming back to the salt lick, little deer," she said sweetly, "some mean hunter-man gonna blow your ass off for sure!"

The man spat and babbled again, wanting, it became clear after a while, to know what Vera meant.

"We mean," she said, "that the work is done here."

"I t'ought you vuss anudder Vobbly," said the man.

"No," Charles said. He was actually a little taller than the big man, leaner and harder against the man's questionable bulk, "Vee are not." He replaced Vera in the man's face, appearing, Vera thought, perhaps a little too truculent.

"Kind of overdid it here," said Charles, stepping in very close, like a fencer who has dropped his sword in arrogant disdain and come in to taunt. "Don't you think, Slim?"

He remembered the harmless fun of swordplay when the reins of rehearsal lay slack on the necks of the actors. His actors. His dead actors.

The man made no reply. He was visibly confused, a look not lost on either Charles or Vera.

"You the artiste?" Charles pointed at the shit and graffito. The man again chose not to reply.

Charles took it as a provocation and sad, too loudly, "Hit the road." When the man was out the door, he added, "You sonofabitch."

"You know what?" asked Vera. "I think we should get out of here."

"You don't want to give the speech?" asked Charles. "I've been reading this NPL stuff until I can't see straight, so I can ask the right questions during the informative Q and A afterward.

"This isn't wheat farming and railroads," said Vera.

"I know that."

"This is lumber." Vera came up to him and touched his face. "And you need to settle down."

"Fucking *castrate* that shithead."

Vera laughed dismissively, shortly, bitterly.

"Have you see Rejean?"

"No, I have not, but that doesn't surprise or trouble me. He'll be here when we, you know, least expect but most need him. He's a hero. Climactic scene. Nick of time."

"How can you think you know him so well?"

"I'm an actor and so is he."

They walked up the street to the intersection with the street that would take them to Main. There they saw an NPL poster that was, inexplicably, not torn down. Someone had written CANCELLED across it. Vera had another poster rolled up under her arm, and she now unrolled it, holding it in place while Jules worked the old tack free and banged it back on the new poster with a rock. Then they stepped back and looked at it from a distance, as if curious about it and deciding whether or not to attend. There was some car traffic ahead of them, crossing Main, there and gone between the corner stores, there and gone, and a couple of horses hitched to wagons across the street at a dry goods store, but almost no one on the street. They looked for a diner and found one. Vera bobbed her head, looking for a menu in the window, which amused Charles. When they entered, she strode about as if she owned the place, which appeared to not amuse either the customers or the proprietor. Charles hung back while Vera appraised the ambience, gave the waitress a more or less friendly once-over, and examined the specials board, walking up quite close and squinting at it, while two or three customers stared openly at her. They sat down at a table by the window and ordered.

"I am *starving*," laughed Rosemary.

"How are you otherwise?" asked Charles.

"I'm starved," she repeated. "That's all I can tell you." She stopped smiling in the sudden way that always alarmed him, but which also never failed to make him smile.

"I'm sorry," he said, as if participating in a different conversation, turning from the window, and back to their abiding concern. "I don't know what I'm doing anymore. Every once in a while I think I get it, but I no sooner get it than I lose it."

Vera looked at her hands in her lap, folded prayerfully.

"Maybe I am just a growing boy."

When the food came, Vera tried to smile at the waitress, but it went unreturned. "A sullen bunch. Sullen's not the word, though. What do I mean?" she asked Charles, who shrugged. "There's been a good deal of roughhousing going on around here, you can feel it in the air. Smell it. People seem jumpy or fed up or I don't know what."

"Scared," said Charles. "It's really simple. I smell fear out there," he waved, "and I smell my own fear."

"Oh, I don't know," mused Vera. "Maybe not so much scared as bored and nervous."

"You have always been the more talented actor between us."

"Well, we know there's been some violence. We know a number of deputies have been active. We know—"

"Did you listen in on that guy's telephone call? When we were waiting for Daisy to come out? The one who had her arrested? He kept referring to that guy from the NPL I talked to in Minneapolis. Not Townley, the slap-stick vaudeville star and wily financier. The other guy. I couldn't make anything else out. Blah-blah-blah the guy's name, blah-blah-blah the guy's name, over and over like that. I don't know what it means. But where is everybody? Where *are* the NPLers? Townely was talking like he would have the Brainard paper—what's it called? *The Daily Pecking Order?*—in his pocket like he did half a dozen others. Where are your fellow Wobblies? Have they all gone missing? Murdered in the depths of the forest where if no one hears it, it didn't happen? What does it mean?"

Vera shrugged with goofy emphasis.

"Means," Charles said, "what everything else we know means: not much in the long run."

"I do want to give this little speech, you handsome man."

"You're suddenly quite perky."

"I want to give a speech."

"Yes, I'm sure you do, and I'm sure it would confuse lots of people whom we have been warned can't bear confusion, but I'm tired of this. I'm really very tired." Charles fixed Vera with a careful but intense look, then closed his eyes. "If you only knew how tired I am. But only God knows how tired I am."

"Okay," said Vera, now suddenly cross again, "what are you tired of? I'm tired of you being tired. I'm feeling . . . *playful* now and I want to *play*."

Yes, thought Charles. There will come a time when all this will have been just . . . play.

"A little food, even the thought of a little food, makes me feel so strong!"

He turned with a show of polite interest toward her and made his answer.

"Tired. Me. Of working so hard to be sure what we're doing is good and not evil. If not good at least not evil. All that murk. Depending on the sketchy idea that honest play is all that is required of us, but never quite knowing what is honest. Because that is the nature of the stage. It changes everything. We think and we know but when we play, when we act, it changes. I am tired of fighting somebody else's fight because I hate the people they are fighting or because I feel I understand particularly the lines they are reciting and consequently respond warmly, energetically, convincingly—being at that crucial remove from the genuine, just remote enough to see too much of the picture. Spending my whole life resisting something that would have cost me nothing to subscribe to. If it was good I wanted to do, I could have done more good staying where I belonged." He reached across the table and took both Vera's hands in his own. He held her gaze but did not contest it. "Once you light a fuse and put a bomb under a PG&E tower, you've committed yourself to a lifetime of lighting fuses. I mean, where do you stop? Warren knew what he was doing. Tom knew what he was doing. Jules knew what he was doing. Where do you say, there,

I've made my point, now I can go on. As soon as you think that, someone lights a bomb under your ass and kills all your friends."

"*You* can say you don't care if you feel sure you've made your point," said Vera, "anytime, and go on anytime. To France or Egypt or Lebanon or Japan or wherever."

Charles shook his head. It continued to tremble when he thought he was done with it. "If you think it's good to blow up one tower or one newsroom, then why not all towers and all newsrooms? Why not the people who build the towers? And once you've made sure there aren't going to be any more towers built, what's next? Is it electricity you've got to stamp out? I just don't see where it ends. Thus am I made weary."

"I don't know where to begin," said Vera. "That is one of the most ridiculous speeches I have ever heard."

"Don't care," said Charles. "Too tired to care."

"You don't decide where it starts and stops. You are not the master of these things. No one is. And why are you all of a sudden talking about bombs as if you had one."

"I don't know. I just wish I did have one. So I could use it for the climax."

Two immense men, jingling and thudding, appeared at their table. Vera looked up; Charles emphatically did not. The lesser of the two men stared at the greater, who in turn stared at Vera.

"I give up," he said. "Who are you?"

"I am," Charles said loudly, "an inspector of weights and measures. Who *the fuck* are you?"

"My, my, my," said the man. "Miss? Oh, Miss . . . ?" Vera had looked away and would now not look up. "Can I have your attention here, please? All right, you don't want to look at me anymore, I understand, your conscience is full of guilt and confusion and won't allow it, so just listen then as I tell you that you won't be giving your speech tonight, even with Young Master Weights and Measures. Don't even squeak. At minimum you'll be arrested. If you start acting the least little bit confusingly, you're done."

"What do you mean 'at minimum,' asshole?" Charles asked. "Do you want me to call the Rough Riders in? I'll do it, so help me God, I will."

The man stared calmly at him. "I simply must get to the bottom of who you are, Weights and Measures." He spoke with the faintest of lisps and wore a big cowboy hat, which he touched in farewell, bowling his deputy out of the way as they departed.

"We can just walk out of town and hope for a ride, or go sit it out at the station, take the next one that comes in, wherever it's going. What do you think?" Charles looked at Vera, who wouldn't answer, wouldn't look up.

When she finally did she looked surprised. "Your face is dark red!"

"I can hardly see," Charles gasped.

"Calm down, calm down."

"I want to kill them," he whispered, choking.

"No, you can't do that, you can't even want that, calm down now."

They sat there breathing and after a while the food came. It seemed like a miracle and they ate greedily.

"All I'm saying is that just because you once thought something was a good idea doesn't mean you always have to think it's a good idea."

Vera now chose to laugh. "You *are* getting old."

Charles got up and came around the table to her. "Maybe you ought to think about growing up. Listen to me. Did you not hear what I just said? My head is going to blow off my neck and I want to kill one or more of these assholes before it's too late. Warren and Tom stink of dynamite, *but so do I, Vera.* And so do you, and so does anybody else who's near enough, because *dynamite stinks.* It gets into your blood and your blood stinks and all you want to do is explode, and if you're around later, pray to the sleep-givers."

"All right, all right, just . . . calm down, Charles, please."

Neither spoke for some minutes. Then Charles said that they should leave now but come back with money and men. Somehow the mention of "men" made them realize, just as the mention of "murder" made them realize that they could be murdered, that "men," from the NPL or the IWW or the MCPS or wherever, a crack squad of socialist commandoes from the office of the mayor of Minneapolis, were long overdue. The mention of "missing men" and the echo of the mention of "murder" made them think that there had in fact been some killing already, perhaps a lot of it.

Now was the time to see Rejean Houle and find out whose side he'd chosen for the day.

They chose the train station, and that was where the big man found them. "No one seems to know who you are. I've spoken to a number of organizations, both fair and foul, and nobody claims you. So you either got someone big pulling for you, or someone big pulling against you. Or possibly someone big not giving a shit about you, if they ever did. I guess I should say that you've got both, which is why you are standing so still and nervous-like in my town. So I'm going to treat you like I treat all strangers, and tell you plainly you better get the hell out of here, and I mean now."

"I have documents, asshole," Charles said.

"Is that French for asshole documents? That would be wiping paper?"

"I have documents from Teddy fucking Roosevelt. I—"

"No, no, no, I don't care who you are now. I just want you—"

"Don't show him the documents, honey," said Vera. "He doesn't deserve them. They'll just confuse him. Let McGee and the MCPS deal with him later." She laughed artificially but persuasively, and Charles helplessly admired it.

"Okay," chuckled the big man. "Show me 'the documents.'"

"No," said Charles, "second thought, I don't have to prove who I am to you, whoever you are, you big fat fucking asshole, or to anybody else. This is the United States of America, you goddamn thug. We've got plenty of money, we're not vagrants. You can't kill us. Even if you are confused."

Charles supposed that was when it became clear that he could.

"And look," said Vera, "look around you, you simpleton. Are we not at the train station?"

"My, my, my," said the big man. "Guess I'll see you later." He started to walk away, then stopped. "When are you people going to realize that we are making do here. We are facing up to the mysteries of life and the hard obstacles of making a living and we have nice little village here that you are interfering with. You are not making things better, see? You are making things worse."

When he was gone, Vera said she would wait to see if anyone from the NPL or, long shot, the IWW, showed up. If they did, she would try to give the speech; if they did not, she would not. Charles silently acquiesced, making a strong simple gesture with his head.

Night fell. A man whose name Vera did not recognize, but who seemed not merely authoritative in his argument but concerned for her well-being too, had reached them via telephone at the hotel, to which they had returned as if in a traveling spotlight. He'd made it clear the NPL would have nothing to do with her as a stand-in for Daisy, who had been quickly rearrested and remained in jail as a flight risk, no bail allowed. They would in fact disavow her; and, as there was evidently no longer an IWW presence in the town, she would find herself in a pickle. He wanted to know what the hell the IWW was thinking of anyway. "If they are around somewhere, are they just looking for a fight? Like in the good old days? Because this isn't the good old days anymore."

"I'm doing this on my own," Vera said, mouthing her words exaggeratedly into the little megaphone atop the candlestick, the awkward artificiality of the act making her feel even more secretive, even deceitful, causing her to make exaggerated faces and use her hands more than she would have were she face to face with the man.

"I don't understand," said the tiny squawky voice in its boiling ocean of static.

"Nobody does," said Vera. "That's okay." She smiled at the megaphone and hung the speaker in its cradle. It was hard to imagine herself as tiny and squawky in an ocean of boiling static, but she knew that it must have been so from the caller's perspective.

The men from the IWW hall, five of them, quietly appeared at the door of their hotel room. From a distance they passed for calm, serious men, but this illusion was quickly dispelled: they were in the late stages of crippling panic, either groggy with it as one would be when saturated by any chemical, dull and dopily indifferent to any kind of stimulation—a smile and a kind word as well as a threat or a loud noise—or bound by it so tightly they might have been in straitjackets, able to move only their eyes. Only one of them seemed able, or willing, to follow one thought with another, and he was dumbfounded: he could not understand the false affiliation with the MCPS—"It's not false," Charles said, "I am merely using it under false pretenses"—the purpose it served, nor their unwillingness to appeal to that organization immediately.

"That would remove us from danger, possibly," Charles said.

"Well, why the hell don't you do that?"

"We sorta came up here to be in danger."

"Nobody here gives a damn about that!" the man shouted too loudly. "We're already dead!"

"Ditto that," said Vera, who had been staring out a window at the tracks.

"This is not our home!" cried one of the silent Wobblies. "The world is not our home, you can understand that when you're left alone for a while. These, these people here . . . they've banded together so they can feel like this is their home. They're not afraid."

"Oh, they're afraid," Charles said.

"Not like we are."

"We aren't afraid," said the first Wobbly to talk. "We're dead. Nothing to be afraid of when you're dead. I've learned that."

"If there has been a little doubt sown in the minds of the big men around here, then maybe they won't act so recklessly," Charles said. "They won't act like such nasty bullies when all people are trying to do is feel at home for a while. Of course the happy functioning of the little village is in jeopardy. People they don't even know are suffering so they can have a happy little village. I could excuse them if they didn't act like they'd earned the right to their happy village. Of course I'm intruding. Intrusion is just as much a part of their happy little world as ignorance is. Doesn't matter what they *prefer*."

Nevertheless he went downstairs and persuaded the clerk to let him place a call, slapping coins down as hard on the desk as he had done at the saloon some days in the distant past. He spoke for a very long time to someone he did not know, who could not or would not connect him to anybody he knew. He was told that his concern for his personal safety was noted with emphasis, that steps would be taken, and that he was not to worry. He could leave if he wanted to, or he could hang in there and see what happened next. He was working, wasn't he, for the Minnesota Commission of Public Safety, and had something of a duty, did he not?

Charles trudged up the steps to his room. Did he in fact want to be safe? Wasn't it closer to the truth to say he wanted "revenge"? Against the greedy unprincipled arrogant assholes who had killed Father and all those poor players who were blown to pieces mid-strut, mid-fret, a beautiful, moving speech about what it meant to be human just beginning to flow in its strange and awful way from the brain to the vocal cords, the palate, the tongue, the teeth, the lips—most of all the oxygen-rich lungs? Which would soon be shredded and bubbling on the floor of the stage?

"They're going to have a parade tomorrow," said the Wobbly who was most able to speak.

"Oh dear," said Vera.

"I hate fucking parades," said Charles. He looked up. "I mean, I always have. Regardless of any bombing."

"They're going to kill us at the end of the parade," said a man who hadn't yet spoken.

"Nobody's going to kill anybody," Charles said. "I work for the Minnesota Commission of Public Safety."

"We're going to go back to the hall," said Vera, "and make it comfortable again, and we're going to watch the parade go by. That's all we have to do. Sit back and say, "There goes a parade." If we can see it's just a parade, then all we have to do is watch it. We don't have to fight them, we don't have to hate them, we don't have to fear them." Then perhaps she betrayed the coil of panic that had just begun to turn in her stomach, along with the swiftly growing, metamorphosing foetus. "Not one fucking little bit do we have to be afraid of these shit-sucking bullies." She caught herself and pulled herself back. "There's nothing they can take away from us. We give it all gladly because we are not afraid of anything."

Which of course was the moment they realized they were very afraid. The serene and undivided self was divided again. It took so little: some angry talk, some shoving and pushing, jail cells, phone calls that made both speaker and spoken-to feel as if the attenuation they felt was about to become terrifying, thoughts of killing and being killed . . . of course they felt they'd forced their way into a dangerous place thinking like the fools they truly were that a dangerous place was where they could best bring their serene and undivided self to bear. Images of the carnage in San Francisco played in loops in their imagination.

Then, strangely, during the course of this communal, unspoken confession, the daredevils found themselves feeling serene and undivided again. Perhaps something truly good might after all be accomplished. By the fearless ones, the ones who refused the Devil admittance.

They walked together to the hall and cleaned it up to the extent that they could. A fire was started in the Franklin stove that heated the two rooms, and bread and cheese were eaten around the stove. The town, counter to expectations, grew livelier. Someone came by and asked them what they were doing. Charles said he worked for the Minnesota Commission of Public Safety, which had come to the conclusion that a functioning IWW office was temporarily necessary. Wobblies, he said, had changed their minds and were all in favor of war now, so everybody had to work together. In this bubble he felt free and happy with these odd little lies. Gas lamps came on, a number of saloons did ominously brisk trade. A man with piercing blue eyes and a red puffy face sat down on a broken chair on the sidewalk outside the hall. Its one good leg wobbled, then snapped. The man held his quart bottle of whiskey high as he fell. Pushing the chair out of his way, he slid his back up against the storefront wall so that his head was visible at the bottom of the window. He sighed with pleasure, then began checking his pockets for something he did not find. Lurching to his feet, he dashed off, leaving the bottle on the sidewalk. Charles went outside, wiped the mouth of the bottle with his sleeve, and drank a long drink. Then he came in with the bottle and everyone drank from it. After a while, Vera got up with some difficulty and excused herself, saying she was tired. Charles's happiness became bolder in its expression as he contemplated the cause of his true love's fatigue, his sense of freedom more able to withstand attack. So much so that he welcomed it. He became quickly so bold and fierce in the defense of his bold serene freedom that he failed to note it when he slipped away from it again, when he realized that what he wanted was to stomp the shit out of the big man and his little men.

Just like that is it lost. The small good act, the idea of it, the serene contentment and true freedom inhering in it, is lost in the roar of the fire. The brain becomes white hot. The servant of the brain can no longer see around the flames in his eyes. The inferno's fuel is mistakenly assumed to be bravery when it is in fact fear. The Devil stands there as if he had been there all along. Vera pushed a bench against the wall in the back room and lay down on it.

"'I'm tired of you being tired,'" said Charles quietly. He was fixing himself. He continued to drink until the bottle was empty, the others quickly succumbing to the effect of alcohol on their shredded nerves. They assumed foetal positions in corners and were asleep instantly, in the way that people do whose nerves had taken more than they could stand.

Charles stood at the big window.

He went outside.

It might have been a carnival scene he entered. Men women children, couples, young lovers, families strolled and gawked at the ordinary street life of their snug town after dark. For every drunk there was a child eating ice cream. Groups of children darted and toddled about. Gangs of boys huddled, some of them perhaps nearly as old as himself, but seeming freckled and stupid even as they took on the air of important men discussing investment opportunities—only to dissolve in loud sneering honks of laughter. It was hard to say what was going on; sometimes people would look at him with menacing hostility and sometimes they would not. He even thought he saw a few guilelessly friendly winks and smiles and waves. What he thought was a firecracker went off not too far away. Then another and another. Then as if in a dream a horse stepped heavily against him and he fell to his knees. He looked up in the garish darkness but saw only the great head of the horse dropping swiftly toward him, and he rolled away. He must have taken a blow to the head as well because he was dopey. Where was Amelia? he wondered. Why could she not control her horse? He got to his feet awkwardly and wondered for the length of time it takes lightning to strike what his sister—now that he knew she was not there—was doing at that moment. He ached for her, because surely she was lost. He felt very heavy, as if knowledge had been dropped like a millstone around his neck: the firecrackers he knew now were guns, and the parade had begun, in torchlight.

He could see one of the Wobblies standing at the window, but now with a Winchester deer rifle, and he scrambled back into the hall, heart slamming in his throat.

"People will kill you," he told the man conversationally, "if you upset the kind of fear they're used to with another, no matter how persuasively you speak of its guaranteed safety features."

All of the men had weapons; only Vera had disdained arming. The Wobbly at the window set the rifle down on a chair and went to whisper something to Vera. Charles took up the rifle, a .30-30 lever action exactly like one he'd grown up with on the ranch. They were easy to use and he was

good at it, like he was good in all things. "Scholar," he said, "soldier, statesman, musician, belletrist. And say, that's funny: I say 'musician,' and I realize how badly I've let my musicianship lapse. I think I'll begin to compose.
Vera, do you remember, did you ever know, about those five strange notes
I heard in the park that day before the earthquake? They were a question."

The shouting from the street was astonishingly loud, he thought, nearly
deafening, and then he heard a clear sharp crack and turned to see one of
the Wobblies in the midst of a comic walk across a kind of stage, then fall
hilariously over.

"We are not going to shoot anyone," Vera was saying over and over and
then she was screaming it through the open door and smashed windows.
Bullets smashed glass and cracked through the walls.

Rejean Houle walked in through the front door, backing Vera up step
by step as he did so.

He was aiming his revolver at her.

He said, "My orders are first her, then you," but when he fired, it was
with a smaller pistol in the other hand and his target was one of the four
remaining Wobblies, the one who had made the first and biggest mistake
and stepped toward him.

When Houle saw that he'd shot the Wobbly dead, he paused, as if irked.
This was the second mistake: pausing as if he wanted to explain things to
Charles and Vera. One of the three remaining Wobblies shot him. A man
nobody knew came in through the front door, shot the Wobbly who'd just
shot Houle, then backed out the door and disappeared.

"I'll go out there and surrender," said one of the two remaining Wobblies, the one who'd done the talking in the hotel room, and out he went.
As soon as he'd firmly placed his feet and raised his arms over his head, he
was shot dead.

It had happened that quickly. Charles found himself wishing, vividly
and explicitly and with a kind of calm, that he could see the big man, the
slightly less big man, and the man who looked like Paul Bunyan, because he
felt he knew these men somehow, having seen them before, and therefore

had relationships with them, accounts, so to speak, that he might now draw upon. But three different men standing in front of him turned as one, almost like dancehall girls, and set themselves upon him. He cried out that they had it all wrong, they had it all wrong, "No, no, no!" he wailed like an ordinary coward, but they got him down and beat him until he was quite thoroughly listless, incapable of reflexive violence, not to speak of philosophy, at which point they carried him—or rather supported him as if he were a fallen comrade who could walk but who didn't care in the least where he was headed— to a railway car on an old siding around which weeds were growing. Inside the stinking black hole were five other men: three merchants with ties to the NPL who had only just been deposited there; and two Wobblies too weak and miserable to speak: they had been there for something like a month, so near and yet so far, when their friends had thought them flown or dead. Then Charles and the lone remaining Wobbly were rolled into the car, followed by a bruised and bleeding Vera. They lay there through the night and half of the next day. Reeling and nauseous in the glare and heat of noon, they were taken back to the intersection of the town's main streets, where a gauntlet had been formed and a public spectacle was in progress. They were all tied with hands behind backs and led by leashes through the gauntlet, in which they were struck, mainly with leather knouts and canes, by otherwise thoroughly decent people, people, some of them, unused to beating so that their slaps were awkward and didn't hurt us as much as they probably did them. They were called "niggers" and "Jews." At the worst it was a whipping and a flaying rather than a clubbing. At the end of the gauntlet they came to an American flag and a table on which an open Bible fluttered its pages. This town was prepared for war.

The flag billowed and collapsed, billowed and collapsed in the mild breeze. Charles could smell the mothballs in which it had been stored. The cover of the topmost Bible lifted slightly and fell closed again. "The goddamned Jew merchants" who had called "this plague of foreigners and radicals" down upon the town, were forced to kiss the flag, recite the Pledge of Allegiance, and then—he could not believe his weak squinting eyes, it was as if he were suddenly watching a touring company melodrama—kiss the hand of the big man and beg him—and through him, they were assured, the town—for mercy. When this was done, they were told that they had made atonement and that the town was pleased. They were asked to consider conversion to Christianity, given cheap little Bibles, then set free. The crowd began to move back to the railroad car, hounding the Jews back to their establishments along the way. Go on, go on, business as usual tomorrow, they were told laughingly. Charles wanted Father to catch a bit of this show sometime. At the railroad car, the two Wobblies were, in a surprise move, shot in the head. Those heads were then hacked off and placed on poles on either side of Paul Bunyan. As if they were giving a mighty god credit, he thought in the quiet little space he had found for himself in his mind, far from the organs of sight and sound and speech, the progenitors of action, the casus belli he half-felt he could never again trust, as if they were decorations for an important holiday. Which in effect they were.

Then the big man said, "Now we come to the mysterious ones. The young man from a proud and prosperous family, who won't defend his country, who merely pretends to be a person we all depend on in a time of war, is merely a coward. He shall therefore be tarred and feathered. The man, who insists on an identity we know to be false, who wishes to breed mystery and so confound and poison the minds of our citizens, he shall be castrated so as to make the fulfillment of his wish impossible. The woman, who was sworn she will not bear the children of fighting men and patriots, will nevertheless find herself full of their seed."

But someone was whispering in the big man's ear and the big man was smiling, smiling, then frowning, then smiling, then waving off the rape and torture.

Vera awoke on a couch in a gazebo. She had fallen into the kind of thick and troubling sleep that afternoons sometimes provide. Her head lay in Charles's lap. He was reading Plato. Some tall red pines stood around the gazebo, and a two-track path led from the door past a stable and assorted red and white outbuildings. She rolled away and stood unsteadily, then pushed through the light screen door of the gazebo. Charles got up and followed her along the path until it came to a fence and a stile, near a large rock that bore a copper plaque eulogizing a beloved dog who had once romped happily there. Beyond the fence lay a meadow of foxtail barley and hawkweed, the reddish orange flowers like a great dusty glaze on the grass, nearly as far as they could see, to a distant woods arcing along the horizon, a tuft of dark-green but arid-looking trees. The light was harsh beyond the stand of pines, and they regretted leaving the shady cool gazebo. Remote from all tyrannies, Vera thought again, then said aloud, not particularly to Charles. It was somehow the phrase she had dragged up from sleep. "But not so remote that I . . . that I what? All solutions, she thought, as if reciting something she had dreamt, taken too far, become tyrannies. Good becomes evil, and not a necessary, therefore better, evil, but one as evil as the evil one set out to vanquish . . . clothed in suits of principle. Chain-principle," she said giddily, as they made their way back to the gazebo, pulling the screen door open and hearing it bang behind them, hearing flies hit the screen and bounce away and hit it again, droning. "Conclusion? One must remain remote from all solutions as well." Oh yes, yes, they had indeed suffered the horrors that had been threatened, but it had all been theater, the horror was the threat, a bit of melodrama to scare and edify good citizens of Rome, Vera kept thinking, *of Rome, good citizens of Rome,* to promote right thinking by demonstrating the consequences of wrong thinking, and because realism was all the rage, Charles had only appeared to have had his balls cut off and burned with tar, Vera had only appeared to have been repeatedly raped—and those boys had authentically, Belasco-style, only appeared to have been shot in their heads. No one believed that the boys with bullets in their heads would repent—Charles had thumbed through Montaigne and come up with a lovely quotation—they were shot in their heads because it was the only way to make the rest of the act seem real. But Vera was confused: it did not seem real. Not at all. Decidedly unreal. And if the point was to scare and correct

. . . there too she was confused, because she no longer had a good working understanding of what it meant to be frightened, or more to the point, how one acted when one was reasonably frightened. The obvious responses, to run away or to lash out, were all well and good, but how was one to choose? Was it supposed to be instinctive? Vera begged to differ: it was not. Where was home? And what was one to do if one had no home?

It was not until his meeting with the silvery, vain, and wrathful Mr. Winter and the jovially triangular Mr. McGee that Charles was forced to accept and reconcile the kinds and degrees of various realities and realisms and acts and deceptions. Going into Winter's sumptuous, dark private office in the Grain Exchange, he had assumed a number of fundamental premises: number one was that Winter and McGee but not the governor had known who Rejean Houle/Ray John Howell was long before Charles had known; and therefore, number two, knew that Charles's association with such a man spoke not only of a scandalous lack of common sense in a rich young play-boy whose father had—had had, once but no longer had, no longer could have, especially given the spectacular collapse of his family—big political plans, but a possible infirmity, a serious one, in his actual private, personal politics—if they could put it that way? They thought they could. It would have been hard for Winter not to see this as an immense opportunity, once his suspicions had been aroused, and the only way his suspicions would not have been aroused was if he had been too busy to do anything but accept at face value the candidate being pushed toward him: an immense oppor-tunity to bring together railroading friends from the West with railroad-ing friends from the Midwest. The third fundamental assumption was that while Winter knew a great deal, he could not be completely sure of what he knew, or rather, what to do with it, practically speaking: it was possible that he was sufficiently impressed by the presence, admittedly in the deep background of the now deceased, of William Minot (which perhaps im-plied vast forces of Roosevelt loyalists as well), to not want Charles and his

Bolshevik whore seriously hurt, no matter the nature of their indiscretions and adventures; it was also possible, on the other end of the spectrum, that Winter had sworn allegiance to people who liked William Minot not one little bit—that it wasn't just a matter of bringing friends together after all—and who—he made this fourth assumption and saw that it was in fact the primary assumption, the fundament of fundaments—would not blanch at the murders of innocent people to advance their cause. They had already done so! What he did not quite understand, and which Winter might also therefore be confused about, was what Charles really had to do with it, with anything. Was he simply a rogue element that had forced its way into play, because he was a rich boy, an idiot courtier, a gambling gentleman who felt he was entitled to interfere in any sort of life he happened across? Or had he been marked early on as the means by which a man who hated his father might hurt and hurt and hurt him? In the middle was a kind of no-man's-land, or poker table, over which Winter and perforce McGee—whose hatred were political and not at all personal—would simply play out for Charles a good deal of rope. Charles was suddenly sure Winter had made some kind of deal with the URR men, but he had no idea what sort of deal, no understanding of its cost, no sense of how many rounds of consequence might be expected, and, finally, had seen no sign from Winter that he was committed to the deal. Maybe he had his own little plan. And what of Mighty McGee? Maybe McGee thought he could use Charles to gain advantage over the URR men, for some obscure but ruthlessly pure reason of his own. Charles had no idea. Really none at all. He was right to think that *not wanting anything* was a key to freedom, but very wrong to think he could walk through the Valley of Death and fear no evil *just because he didn't want anything.* The power of other people's desires could pick him up like a leaf in a tornado. Worse, most foolishly, most fatally, he had assumed he could trust himself to remain serenely indifferent. He had bought this idea from himself hook, line, and sinker. What he had wanted all along was an excuse to act violently, to punish people . . . to punish them for wanting things and being willing to . . . act violently to get them.

To punish the people who kept from them what they wanted. Whatever kind of sad little trinket of self-delusion it might be.

He remembered reading the article in Hearst's ridiculous newspaper, about the cleverness of anarchists and the need for precise amounts of rope, pretending to not be able to read very well, making his brothers laugh, if not Father.

McGee, for the moment a gregarious blustering small-town booster to Charles's pensive aristocrat, settled matters and set the tone very quickly. He admitted that there had been serious miscommunication, but wanted, in return, for Charles to admit that he had been behaving a little oddly in Fargo or Moorhead or wherever the hell it was, when he interfered—"Perhaps correctly!" Winter shouted generously—with the arrest of Daisy Gluek. He then went a little further and said that the patriots in Bemidji were indeed out of hand, that was in the nature of patriots, but insisted that no real harm had been done, and that in fact a real service might have been provided Charles.

"How's that?" Charles asked, smiling. He started to take off his clothes so he could show Winter his burn scars. Because all three men were suffering some kind of breakdown, Charles ended up naked, McGee talking on obliviously, Winter turned away in musical comedy disgust.

"You're not going to be the kind of leader who lets other people do all the dirty work, are you? You're not going to be that kind of fucking playboy progressive, are you? Your brother-in-law is a notable man of God: Are things going to be very prim and proper in the Minot White House? When you or your people finally get your ass in the war where it belongs, will that ass be lounging about on mounds of Louis XV bullshit, pouring tea for generals? Or will it be getting itself shot off in the trenches with the little people you apparently care so deeply for."

"My God," said Charles. "You are one glib mound of bullshit yourself."

McGee roared at the insult with apparently genuine amusement.

But Charles had opened the sluice a bit too fully. "You're what, a kind of good-old-boy American version of a middle-ranking pea-brained Hapsburg bureaucrat? Abusing the little people—shooting them in their fucking HEADS AND LICKING YOUR BOSS'S BOOTS?"

McGee took a long time to stop laughing, and did so by degrees. He then became briskly sincere. It was no doubt a calculated sincerity, but it worked, as Charles sat back in his chair and realized that not only was he ashamed of himself, not only was he hotheaded and losing focus—losing *everything*, losing everything again and again and again when he could see it, see peace and freedom so clearly—he was naked. Whoever had gotten shot in the head, for whatever reason, had simply vanished, as he knew all illusions eventually must, revealing only the deepest, most beautiful truth. Winter finally smiled at him, in a lovingly avuncular way. He said he understood that a place in the war was being prepared for him, and that Charles would be leaving soon. Whatever the nature of his duties might turn out to be, Winter was confident that they would be important duties, and that he would perform them in a way that would make all Americans proud. He even went so far as to say he hoped Charles would stay in touch, suggesting that the MCPS would be only too happy to make use of his patriotic valiance as they explained to members of Congress and so on, and yes, sure, *publicized*, one had to nowadays, in order to justify budgets and so on, their work on the home front.

"Do put your clothes back on, though, will you, please?"

McGee then cleared his throat and spoke much more quietly, with much more gravity. There was one last job Charles could do here, in the time he had left in the land of ten thousand lakes, a job that was actually quite dangerous, something only a daredevil political operative could take on, and certainly one that would be forbidden him as he rose to greater and greater power. It would be, McGee said candidly, his only real chance to indulge himself in the kind of hard, necessary work that most men—not just the lazy cheats who tried to ride other men's backs into cushy situations, but good, honest, practical men, scholars, soldiers, leaders!—tried assiduously to steer clear of, but which one of TR's boys would seek avidly. One needed clean hands and a cool head and an *unresentful* acceptance of the world for what it was. One needed a kind of indifference.

Charles looked up at this word, frightened, and Winter looked at him as if he had been reading Charles's mind all along and knew everything. Yes: one smart daredevil was called for, and a young man who was going to be president of the United States someday soon could not hope for even once chance to be a *real* daredevil. He would have to content himself, if that was how he wanted voters to see him, to merely act the part as his responsibilities grew exponentially every day he remained alive, as more and more people came to depend on his presence, as America became the mightiest nation on Earth.

He would also be able pluck his trollop from the net, and whatever fate might await her once she was entangled.

The opportunity Charles was presented with was clearly to hang himself: he was to organize and manage the planting and blowing of a small bomb at a rally of striking streetcar operators, similar in nature and scope to the Preparedness Day Parade bomb, in the lost city of San Francisco, but hopefully without any loss of life. It was the simplest kind of frame-up, maybe even one people were getting tired of—thus the wish to keep the bloodshed at minimum—in which the streetcar union would look like the usual bunch of mad foreign nihilists, and the owners of the line straightforwardly the good American businessmen they in fact were. But because it involved railroads in some way, and therefore the loathsome idiot Durwood Keogh—the Midwestern "railroad" Minots might as well have been Martian Minots for all they appeared to care, which was perhaps a snub to the high-living Western dandies—and because his troubling but profoundly real love of his late father was finding a kind of expression in the desire to harm "railroad people," he thought he might turn, as it were, the bomb around. He knew that in any case he had to play along for a while longer, if only because he didn't understand everything that was at stake, everything that might be at stake. What he knew incontrovertibly to be at stake was the health and welfare of Vera and the foetus she was still somehow carrying.

Charles told Vera that he had taken his clothes off, and that while he was standing there naked, he smoked a cigarette that Winter had offered him. As the three men smoked they had conversed as if sincerely about Charles being the president of the United States. He told Vera that though he remembered it clearly, vividly, the way he had just described it, he did not think he could believe it. Vera, however, had no trouble believing that it had happened, and happened just like Charles said it had. She said she had to wonder at Charles's confusion and disbelief: Did he think he was in a play where there were rules and regulations about how people appeared and acted in reality? He readily admitted that he did not, but was nevertheless surprised that Winter and McGee did not, either.

"They don't care if you're naked or flayed or covered in tar and feathers or dressed up like Pierrot for a fancy ball!"

"And they sounded so bloody sincere about me being president! I had to wonder myself, if such a thing was possible! That they could create me and work me like that! When I know good and well that for all TR's faults, he would lead a revolution before he allowed something like that to happen! Those men are mad, aren't they, Vera? I have to ask. I mean, truly, clinically mad? As in, they ought to be in straitjackets in a hospital?"

"Yes, they are mad. Yes, they create reality."

"Why did Rejean tell us he was going to shoot us, and then not do it?"

"I don't know."

"Did Rejean perhaps actually shoot us?"

Vera stared at Charles with a kind of languid fear that brought goose bumps out on him and made the hair on the back of his neck stand up.

"Was his intention to shoot us, and he changed his mind at the last second?"

Vera said nothing, but looked away.

"Maybe he was talking to someone else but looking at us?"

"Maybe," said Vera, "we'll never know."

They were in a rented house on the other side of White Bear Lake from Commissioner Winter's monstrous folly, and walked from the white- and gold-painted gazebo with fluttering flags of every other color to the shore. The two-bit spring had become lush and humid, balmy and four different shades of green: dark, earthy soil green; airy green that almost passed for blue; a saturated, dripping green; a startling fiery lime. The lake was still cold and a warm breeze was moving over it. There were clouds in the sky, just enough to soften the glittering of the water.

And yet it was not soft. The air was clammy and the light was sharp, like pinpricks into her sweaty eyes. To say she was tired was euphemistic to the point of falsity. She felt weak, so weak it was unpleasant to move at all, and stupid, so stupid she hated herself. These were unprecedented feelings and she would have found them frightening in their dreadful unfamiliarity had she had the strength and consequent desire to examine them. The thing, she believed, was still alive inside her, but once again she found she had no desire to contemplate it. She felt nothing. She did not want to talk to Charles. He was trying to compare life and death as he imagined it was being experienced on the Somme, for instance, with life and death as they were experiencing it. The death was methodical, he opined, and continuous and unremarkable to everyone observing the action, even the actors, whereas here the method was only just being discovered and explored, death happened unexpectedly, in clots that trailed off in streams and drips into the past. It was remarkable only insofar as it was largely unpredictable. He was remarkably tiresome and, even though she had no interest in being right, remarkably wrong: wrong to taxonomize it. She had always known how to act. She had always known how to be alive in that wholly mysterious "moment" between the past and the future, and all those things Charles had maundered on about—pretentiously or mock-pretentiously, she still did not know—in rehearsals she actually found corresponded with her truth, with her understanding of what it meant to be alive, what it had meant to be alive in *every* moment that she could remember having, a reality both transcendent and immanent that had been there before her birth and would be there after her death, a manifestation of which she was both the greatest instance and the greatest illusion. Death had existed only and as exactly as life had.

But then she had become weak. How had that happened? She had become weak and stupid and the deaths she had witnessed had been far more real in their screaming violence than anything she could have imagined possible, far more hideous, far more terrifying. Life was everything now, and death was now torture, a torture that would deprive a person only of the means by which to live. It was eternal horror. Death had been there in the friendliest and most natural way, making life possible, continuously and eternally possible—then had suddenly become what the poor human brain, with its insistence on paired contradictions, had always suspected it was: the opposite of life, nemesis, terrifying end of life and beginning of torture, unimaginable horror becoming relentlessly imaginable, and cosmic anomie. Death had become life. When she closed her eyes all she could see were scenes of violence and degradation; and when she opened them she could see nothing except a screen on which images were projected, the shadows on the wall of the cave . . . shadows in the shape of people, who were pointing at her and gesturing like they had on rehearsal, demonstrating and wishing to evoke laughter, derisive, bitter, mocking, hysterical, terrifying laughter. Death had destroyed the illusion of life.

It was the vision with which Charles had been vouchsafed in 1906, when his city had vanished.

She knew nothing of this vision, and he did not think to speak of it in direct terms.

Death was everywhere and everything. How could she not capitulate to it?

It was a kind of backyard grenade, a condensed milk can with a wooden handle extending from the top. The can was filled halfway with trinitrotoluene, into which a little blasting cap of mercury fulminate was set, trailing a five- or six-second length of fuse. Five or six seconds.

One.

Two.

Three.

Four.

Five.

Six—maybe, maybe not.

Seven? Eight? Nine? Ten? Who knew? Bombs could play dead. He had seen one do so. Only to leap onstage in a blaze of light and a blare of sound! TA-DA! *You gotta let me sing!* On top of the TNT was poured iron scraps, all the way to the top of the can. A hole was drilled in the top for the fuse, then soldered to the can. He put it in a lunchbox and waited, in Winter's—Winter's, not McGee's, the vain and arrogant man, not the ruthless mechanic— in Winter's disturbingly empty office, waited for a man to appear. When night had fallen and passed and dawn was breaking again, he telephoned the White Bear Lake house.

Winter apparently found it effortlessly easy to accept Charles's pose as workable: that he was a spoiled brat of a rich boy who wanted to cause trouble, be notorious and of consequence—that he was amoral and only interested in controlling powerful things. He also guessed that Winter was finding, apart from whatever he might gain by aiding and abetting the enemies of the California Progressives, the simple generic, schematic possibilities put into play irresistible: scion of wealthy do-gooder politico, secretly in the employ of nefarious foreign anarchist puppet masters, or not, double-crossing them by working for the state, or not, actually putting this playboy simpleton's hands on a bomb in the course of an insurrection and then calling in armed troops . . . ! What could be more fun for a man who hated people and was afraid of life? And in any case, he could get no clear word from the rest of the MCPS or the Pinkertons or the Department of Justice. There was going to be a big roundup of Wobblies and anarchists and assorted other radicals, there would be long prison terms, there would be deportment—but what to do in the meantime? That was the question. Did one sit back and let the war take over for the duration? Or did one extend and expand one's efforts under cover of the war. Did one become less ruthless for the time being—or did one become even more ruthless? It all depended on what one hoped to get out of it.

"We'll get you a nice little bomb," Winter had said, trying to sound like the gruff-but-jovial McGee, "to play with."

"Already got it," Charles had said.

"Well, goodness gracious!"

"I said I already got it."

"Yes, I heard you the first time." He was finding it difficult to maintain another man's tone.

"Well then. What do you want me to do with it?"

"Be careful with it! Don't move. I mean: Do you have it here now?"

"I do."

Charles patted his suitcase. The little dramas were still effective.

Suddenly May disappeared. It was as if winter had returned with Winter's rise in the psychosphere. The temperature was in the high forties but dropped quickly all day as an immense front moved in from Canada. Charles and Vera contemplated a sky of scratched tin that became darker and heavier, as if it were undergoing a kind of geological metamorphosis. The horizon was black, and when they could see trees, the trees were like soft charcoal lines and puffs of cloud more and more obscure against the deepening blackness of the sky. Rice Park in downtown Saint Paul was full of tough-looking men by misty murky noon. They came and went as the light failed and the temperature dropped, circulating in pairs, conversing loudly in groups, smoking, hunching their shoulders, sneering and leering, cupping their hands for lights, looking uneasily or contemptuously for signs of activity, progress, peace, violence, anything moving. The light failed faster than anyone expected, and both electric and gaslights came on in the unnatural dusk, more lights than anyone had seen before in the little park. The courthouse, a quasi-gothic building on one side of the square, was lit up like a fairy castle; all its windows were ablaze and Charles, of course, imagined all kinds of dramas being enacted inside: stricken gaping misery, capricious judgment, happy endings, love, death. Opposite the courthouse, the new glistening white library was so well lit they could make out the stacks in-side. On a third side, the Saint Paul Hotel, in which they had lunched with his family what seemed like years before, was warm and luxurious looking, the patrons of that excellent restaurant peering at the strikers through great walls of glass. Charles thought it was like they were eating dinner in a glass cage, their faces orange in the candlelight. Along the last side of the park, the Hamm Theater's doormen opened the way to people who were visibly eager to see—he could not believe his eyes when they first fell on the mar-quee—*The American.*

They sat at the edge of the park's central fountain and looked at the stone Indian boy poised like winged Mercury. Possessing such a weapon as he did, he thought, did indeed alter reality. There was no question but that he was in a different realm. He thought of Vera's notion of bombs ripping holes in reality, that whatever it was one saw in that hole, it wasn't real, and tried to reconcile it with his own belief that the earthquake and fire that had destroyed San Francisco had only destroyed illusion. Nothing, of course, made "sense" anymore, and he could not affect that reconcilia-tion, but felt nevertheless that he understood something in a way he hadn't been able to before. He had failed miserably to be the kind of hero he'd set out to be, when he lifted pen from notebook at Berkeley, and thought he would do civilization a favor. But now that he had squared with himself again—or, ha ha, did he mean *rounded on himself?*—admitted that he was not a hero but simply an agent of primitive unreasoning rage and fear, that all he wanted now was to kill someone he hated—because he was being honest again with himself, he felt something very like the undividedness he had earlier felt and found so calming and so invigorating—to kill an enemy and take Vera and their child to a safe place somewhere in the nar-cotic Levant. It was a mistaken feeling, to be sure, but he was convinced he felt it. He was in a realm that gave him magical powers, immense inhuman powers, but offered it in a place where there were no signs, no paths, no people wise enough or fearless enough to speak. No one ruled. There was no one to rule. Everybody had gone away, had died or fled. He was alone.

No calculation is necessary when you are alone. You don't have to play people against each other. You simply allow the hatred you feel to take you through an act. And then it's over.

Vera, who had wandered off, rejoined him.

Their little bubble of anomic wrath burst.

"I wanted to run away with you and live a quiet life."

"We can."

"Do you want to go? Now?"

"What are you going to do with the bomb?"

"I don't know."

"We can't go until you know."

"I will pick an appropriate representative of our corrupt government and hurl it at him."

"That's fine."

"It is?"

"Yes, but I won't go with you under those circumstances."

"You won't?"

"No. Absolutely not."

"Why not?"

"I don't know."

"In what circumstances—"

"I DON'T KNOW, CHARLES!"

The people they were actually rubbing shoulders with were as remote as elves, just as Vera's fabled friend Rosemary had believed so many years before, when she was a child and they had suffered a different kind of destruction. Provoked in this way, Charles and Vera looked across the park at the restaurant and were filled with grief at the thought of not being able to sit there, a little candlelit table between them.

"I want that," Charles said. "I can't help but want it. It's my childhood."

"I want it too. I want it so much I'm . . . I'm afraid of it."

Snow began to appear in the air, single flakes dancing past hooded, expectant eyes. Men slapped their hands together, some gloved now, some still bare and chapped and cold, and agreed that here it was coming, at long last, everybody's favorite weather event, a blizzard in May.

"Did you ever see a Christmas that wasn't white?" a man asked me.

"Christmas!" Charles exclaimed. "That's months away!"

"This is the beginning, the first snowfall. It will snow all summer. But did you ever—?"

"See a Christmas that wasn't white?"

"That's right."

"Sure have," Charles said.

"Where the hell was that?"

"Right here in River City."

"Bullshit! Never happened!"

"I'm kidding. It was in San Francisco, where I'm from."

"Oh man, San Francisco doesn't count!"

A little later, they walked through the park, happy and content-seeming with their baby bomb, or pretending to be, acting almost as if it were a baby, and found a space on the marble steps of the library. Charles opened the lunchbox. On top of the grenade were several ham sandwiches, made by Winter's cook, who'd said to save one for him, and a thermos of strong coffee. These things were temporarily and insanely delightful and they set it all out beside them on the cold stone. McGee was actually scheduled to offer a short exciting speech, then leave town to take up a new position in Washington, DC.

The bomb was not going to be exploded. Everyone knew that without speaking. They had been given a gift, a way to return to peace: dismantle the bomb. Speaking softly of dismantling the slumbering foetus, Charles said he wasn't exactly sure how far he had gone when taking off his clothes the other day, for McGee and Winter. He said everything ran together if he let it, thought and action, beginning and end.

"You very likely did not strip naked," said Vera. "I mean, *really*, Charles!"

A man near them glanced at them and Charles glanced back in a friendly, noncommittal way. The man glanced again and stepped over.

"Some coffee?" Vera asked, indicating the thermos.

"You one of Winter's people?" the man asked.

Charles stopped smiling and looked toward the park. "Yes. I am." Mother's love of baroque music came to the fore: "I am the Cold Genius. 'What power art thou, who from below, hast made me rise unwillingly and slow, from beds of everlasting snow? See'st thou not how stiff and wondrous old, far unfit to bear the bitter cold, I can scarcely move or draw my breath? Let me, let me freeze again, to death.'"

"I'll take a sip, if you don't mind," said the man, giving Charles a look. "You all set?" He appeared to relax. When both Charles and Vera nodded subtly, knowingly, the man shifted his gaze and looked at Vera over his steaming cup. "Don't hide your lights under a bushel basket, sister."

He was much older than he had first looked, and certainly not a ruffian. Vera didn't mind being called "sister" by such a man as she now thought she was looking at: a rough-and-ready veteran of labor wars. And Charles thought of Father, even though the man looked nothing like him. He was quite sure that Father, who after all had been as ruthless as any ten ordinary men, would understand what he was about to do, and why.

Charles smiled. Vera caught it and smiled too.

"*I mean*," said the man, "don't just find a secluded cozy little nook and blow it there. We don't want to hurt a lot of people, but the word is, and this is final, we don't want anybody to, you know, to *miss it.*"

"Grandfather," Vera said, "don't you worry about us."

And just like that, she was afraid again. She was afraid they were about to take the bomb away from her and that people would be killed after all. She felt panic twisting her stomach. Should she simply run, run away right now, run fast? Throw it in the river? She saw it drifting toward a little toy boat full of children slapping at the water with toy oars. She remained where she was, her arm locked in Charles's arm, from which dangled the big unwieldy lunchbox. He was not shivering: he was shaking.

The man shook his head in a kindly way and left, setting the cap back on the thermos and screwing it down firmly, patting it when he was done.

The temperature had dropped enough to make them feel quite remarkably colder. A wind had risen too, a hard and steady wind that made their eyes tear and the men around them turn their backs to it. The snow thickened in the air and dustings of it appeared on caps and shoulders and on the grass but not on the sidewalks.

Two trucks arrived simultaneously, one on the hotel side to their right and one on the theater side to their left. From these trucks came sections of speaker platforms and podia. Crowds began to form near the platforms as they were assembled, and the general feeling seemed to be that the weather was calling for some speeches that would be frank and revealing and come swiftly to their points. The carmen seemed more cold now than indignant, and the rally looked like it might in fact fizzle.

It was at this point, Charles learned later, that the Ramsey County Sheriff was getting himself in trouble by refusing the streetcar company's request for substantially more policemen, to protect themselves and to ensure the continued operation of streetcars in the vicinity. Outraged, the company appealed to the governor, who dispatched Home Guard units. The civilian auxiliary was also apprised of the company's need, and this paramilitary force converged on the park as well. When the strikers saw men with Krag-Jørgensen rifles held at the ready across their chests ringing the park, they began to shout and curse. The light was now almost impenetrably murky, nearly full dark, and torches were being lit, and then several fires burning in barrels could be seen as well. With the flames angling this way, then that way, snapping and flaring in the moaning wind, with the men shouting articulate words near them, and simply roaring farther off, with the snow accumulating and the temperature continuing its swift and steady plunge, the park became a frightening place, as if it were a zoo where the cages had been suddenly sprung, with hunters strung out around the perimeter. Speakers on both sides of the park began to speak and Charles asked Vera if she remembered the marchers in San Francisco marching in opposite directions and playing rival tunes. Had that been before her time there? He could hardly speak he was shaking so hard. He said, "No, no, don't worry, just a little cold. I want to compose music. I'm going to start as soon as I leave this terrible place. There will be American music, hymns and folk songs and marches and so on, and then underneath there will be something else, and then above it there will be something else, all of it verging on silence. My God! What has sound got to do with music? Think for a moment of Reverend Emerson's 'The Sphinx': 'The perception of identity unites all things and explains one by another . . . and the most rare and strange is equally facile as the most common. But if the mind live only in particulars, and see only differences (wanting the power to see the whole—all in each) then the world addresses to this mind a question it cannot answer, and each new fact tears it to pieces, and it is vanquished by the distracting variety.' And Reverend Thoreau: 'The falling dew seemed to strain and purify the air and I was soothed with an infinite stillness . . . . Vast hollows of silence stretched away in every side, and my being expanded in proportion, and filled them. Then first I could appreciate sound, and find it musical.'"

The first speakers at the company podium were three highly respected and actually irreproachable men who comprised an investigatory committee: the president of a fine local college, an attorney from Minneapolis, and a businessman from Saint Paul. All of them happened to own stock in the Twin Cities Rapid Transit Company, but that was not at issue. What was at issue was the trouble that the yellow union buttons were causing. Fights were breaking out in cars and at stops, rider rates were slipping, and the consensus was that the yellow buttons had to go bye-bye. The committee was going to issue recommendations, they said, that went something like this: the buttons come off immediately, and in return, the company will reinstate those who have lost their jobs *because* of the button. Did the good people of Minnesota follow them so far? Recommendation was the key word. The committee recommended, and the company and the union agreed: no buttons, no union solicitation for the duration of the war. Right now the understanding was that the union was going along with it, and they had put it to a vote, to make it look all right with the membership, who were very attached, as anyone could plainly see, despite the heavy snowfall, to their buttons.

A union speaker on the other side of the little park, however, shouted that on the twenty-sixth of the month, the company, which had already posted signs *ordering* the removal of the buttons and the ceasing of union organizing efforts—implying, citizens, implying a legal binding they actually lacked—on the day before it went to the vote, the company went around and immediately booted every bastard with a yellow button. The committee and the commission will back up the company, saying that the union has failed to bargain in good faith by allowing their men to keep on wearing their buttons when they were asked not to. It's flimsy as hell, as we are sure you can see, but they don't need much!

Charles and Vera watched from the library steps through curtains of snow. Unable to make out features, they saw arms raised, hands waving and shaking, a little white face turned their way, then a black back as the speaker turned toward another part of his audience. There was a steady flow of torches from one side of the park to the other, great brilliant masses of them now, like bonfires, before the platforms, and dark masses of men floating like islands in a polar sea. A number of men had materialized around them. They stood with their hands shoved deep in their pockets, their faces tucked into collars like nesting birds.

"What a lot of shit this is."

"Filthy cowards."

"Lying, cheating, stealing, murdering sonsabitches. I guess they'll murder us too, if they feel like it."

The steps were slippery with snow. They held the lunchbox closed and made their way across the park to the company platform. Speakers and company officials sat huddled around coal braziers while speaker after speaker said things like, "Now, you men, you listen to me because you know

I'm talking sense. This country is at war and we're asking you to set aside your grievances for the duration and pitch in like the good goddamn men we know you to be."

And there was McGee, in the middle of one of the semicircles. His face looked dark and raw and red, bulging out from a fur cap, the flaps of which covered his ears and were tied under his chin, so that his side-whiskers curled out girlishly. But for the dark hatred on his chapped face, he might have been some strange overgrown baby girl. He was standing with the Ramsey County Sheriff. Charles and Vera drew near: "Do not buckle under!" McGee was shouting. "We do not want the extra policemen here!"

Charles had no idea if this was a good thing or a bad thing. Was McGee trying to defuse a disaster? Or was he trying to make a bigger one.

Better to be a good man than to darken the hills with your ponies, he thought. That was what Crazy Horse's father had said, or was said to have said—according to Father, who revered the wisdom almost as much as he did Montaigne's. Well, Charles thought, but what was a good man? How did one describe him, what did he do? Truth excludes the use of violence because man is not capable of knowing the absolute truth and is therefore not competent to punish in its name. Someone else had said that. According to Father. *I am all wrong, wrong wrong wrong, I am a dangerous fool, I have no idea what I am doing but I am flying into it like I am walking onto a stage. OH YES! I WAS BORN TO ACT! But no: If I attempt to punish McGee, then, as a proxy for other bad men, I will have to consider myself a bad man. Can I live with such a consideration? Very likely I can; many men evidently do. It was perhaps a basic human condition, badness. But more practically, could I withstand the counter-punishment of the state?* Did it not make more sense, as some revolutionaries held, to do the deed and then escape, to "lie close and keep yourself for another go"? To surrender when there was no other way out, claim the act and pay the price? Violence was innate to human nature: ACT! One could see it in the daily lives of the calmest, most reasonable people. One could see it in the happiest and most secure children. It came from having one part or feature or function of a person, character, mind, opposed to another part or feature or function. It was there and that was all there was to it. It was the source of drama; the only question was one of expression, of art. The undivided self was the illusion! The undivided self—was shouting this aloud now? Vera was looking at him like she was listening and growing afraid of what she was hearing—the undivided self is the Pure Form, the Pure Idea, a Platonic Ideal, which is the source of our desire for it. We can only look back to it, worship it, and hold fast to our current stage of degeneration lest we degenerate further. It came from God and is steadily degenerating: soon we will no longer be able to recognize ourselves as human, and the world will end. These things go in cycles! Charles shouted to Vera. This isn't reality! This world! Our bodies! That's what Plato took from Pythagoras! You see? And from Parmenides he understood that REALITY, REAL REALITY, IS ETERNAL! ALL THE LITTLE CHANGES WE IGNITE AND ENDURE: PURE ILLUSION! STRONGER AND STRONGER ILLUSION THE LONGER WE SURVIVE! AND THEN THERE'S HERACLITUS! CAN YOU GUESS? THE SENSES ARE NOT TO BE TRUSTED! INTELLECT, DIVINE EDUCATION, ALONE CAN KEEP US SAFE FROM OUR ENEMIES AND WELL FED!

Some of the carmen were hooting in derision and throwing snowballs at the company speakers.

"Next," Charles said, ceasing abruptly to philosophize, "they will build little igloo forts."

A man came very close to them and whispered fiercely that they were to go to the other goddamn side of the park. They went straight across the park to the union platform, where they recognized men from the NPL, the IWW, and an attorney for the Equity Cooperative Exchange—all of whom would be arrested, that night or the next day—and the mayor of Minneapolis. "We are all patriotic men," one of them was saying. "We love our country as we love our families, and that is precisely why the demand for a union is a good one, an honest one, a reasonable one, one that cannot be denied by men of equal conscience and patriotism."

And as if a signal had been given (they supposed that one had), fist-fights began to break out here and there. They did not last long: blows were tentatively exchanged, and shoves and taunts, and then torches would arrive, the circle would be lit, and one combatant would disengage and disappear into the crowd. Then a streetcar stopped, its scab operator tossed from it and beaten. Carmen rallied around the car, and squads went off to stop other cars, beat other scabs. An order went round the perimeter for the soldiers to discharge two or three rounds into the air.

The crackling, rippling explosions went round the park like distant thunder, muffled by what was quickly becoming a blizzard. People could now be seen running up and down the streets radiating from the park, but the dark churning clots within the park only seemed to have grown in size and multiplied in number. It was Vera's vision of death made manifest! The fistfights had ceased to be punch-and-run; they were bloody now, melees instead of boxing rounds. Bricks and stones and clubs were being hurled at both platforms. Pieces of wood were lifted from the platforms and used as shields. Then thugs appeared on the union platform and all the speakers fled. One thug looked straight at Charles and Vera, hauled the podium above his head, and sent it crashing at their feet. Miraculously they did not move a muscle.

Charles thought that he could kill *that* man if he wished to and it made him implausibly immoveable and somber. *Oh, here is my lovely illusion of undividedness come to save me!*

Vera had disappeared. Sidestepping fighters, ducking flying objects, and even like a halfback fending off men who tried to tackle him, Charles followed the man who'd thrown the podium at them across the park again to the company platform. There was Vera staring up at another man, who looked like a horrible statue. It was the San Francisco detective, the railroad specialist Rudy Swanson, and one of his soldiers, a red-haired man she was sure she had seen repeatedly in the Beveridge motorcycle shop, boasting that he was, what, that he was going to fix a big Ford headlight to his Excelsior . . . ? And thereby make it easier to ride at night . . . ? And eclipse Iron

Man's record run from San Diego to Yuma . . . ? Yes, she could hear him speaking those words, see it all so clearly. She decided this was the man who had actually killed Lucy and John and Amado. As if conversing in a warm parlor, she said as much to Charles.

Charles snapped his fingers and shouted, "IT WAS YOU, WASN'T IT, YOU GREASY STUPID LITTLE SHITSUCKER?"

Because they were so clearly spiritually bound, tied more surely and lovingly than blood or money could have made them, he was not surprised to see McGee and Swanson together. Rather, he was relieved. Still: he had to admit he didn't know what was going on, who was arguing for what, what sort of consequence might ensue, what sorts of rewards might accrue.

Swanson's mouth was drawn down in a kind of pout, and he was blinking spasmodically, as if he were struggling not to cry. He looked anything but crazy or angry, but he snarled at them, at Vera and at Charles, out of that nearly impassive but blink-blink-blinking terrifying statue face that he was "going to start picking them off." And he laughed. "Fucking cold out here, eh Minot?"

Charles climbed calmly but quickly up the front of the platform and came at Swanson, so casually that his intent was perceived as perfectly ambiguous. McGee stood where he was but Swanson backed up a step, then held his ground. When they were face to face, Swanson said, "Hey, you better light that fuse, mister." Both Swanson and the red-haired man had guns in hands, dangling at their sides.

Charles jumped off the platform. Slipping in the snow, he went to his knees, clutching the lunchbox to his belly, inside his coat. Still on his knees, he craned just in time to see a brick flush against Swanson's face, as if an invisible hand were holding it there—and then Swanson was flat on his back and rolling from side to side. McGee had fled. Charles got to his feet. The red-haired man shot him once in his left thigh, and once more in the right, blowing the kneecap apart. He jumped off the platform, evidently ready to light the fuse and let Charles be the casualty.

Three other men appeared around them, one of them holding Vera lightly by the arm, as if he was going to help her up onto the platform.

"BLOW THAT THING NOW!" one bellowed. "LIGHT IT AND THROW IT IN THERE!" And he pointed into the dark raging park, at the swirling snow and the fires and the bloody faces looming into view and disappearing again. "WE ARE SUPPOSED TO GET OUT OF HERE NOW! THEY'RE GOING TO OPEN FIRE!" Another bomb went off and everybody went to their knees. It had been planted under the union platform, which had already been deserted. Now there was screaming and the park was emptying fast. Swanson and the red-haired man were gone. Charles tried to hold the bomb under his coat with hands that no longer felt like his own. His legs were off in some other Pythagorean place. His coat was ripped open and while one man held Vera in a bear hug, the other two held him down. One got hold of the lunchbox and opened it. Then he lit the fuse and all three men ran slipping and falling away. Charles croaked at Vera to run. He felt quiet and undivided and happy and free again, but she appeared unable, perhaps unwilling to do so, to leave him, it was very hard to see. Then, because it was not real, after all, he thought that was what she said, she took it from him and ran several steps as fast as she could away from him, then fell on top of it.

She might have been shot, he was never sure. There was a great soundless flash of brilliant glorious light that shot along the horizon and billowed upward to zenith carrying her everywhere at once. It blinded him for a moment and when he could see the dark shapes of the trees against the white snow and the fairy buildings soaring up into the night sky again, she was gone.

ACKNOWLEDGEMENTS

A long section early in Part Two was first published as "We Whistled While We Worked," in *The Massachusetts Review*, and I would like to thank Michael Thurston, Jim Hicks, Ata Moharreri, and Emily Cook for that. The "Prologue" was first published in *Spolia*, thanks to Jessa Crispin.